grace

PRAISE FOR *grace*

—— OF GOOSE LODGE WRITING ——

grace takes such a unique and refreshing perspective on a familiar story and familiar characters, creating something completely new.

———————

Delaney Parker is able to give depth and realness to characters. So few times in life are people entirely good or entirely evil. Delaney Parker allows us to see a glimmer of goodness in her worst characters and gives attention to those characters normally written off as one dimensional.

grace

novel by

DELANEY PARKER

BOOK DESIGN BY The Troy Book Makers

Printed in the United States of America

The Troy Book Makers • Troy, New York • thetroybookmakers.com

To order additional copies of this title, contact your favorite local bookstore or visit www.shoptbmbooks.com

ISBN: 978-1-61468-659-0

acknowledgments

To my husband, Matt and my kids, Evan and Elia, I love you guys so dang much. Mama doesn't give up. My kids are my reason for tangling with MS and taking no guff. Thank you for believing in me even when I was unable to myself.

Thank you to Mom for telling me to write. I always wind up doing what you say. I admire your ability to read hundreds of pages in one sitting. Including, all the versions of mine. I love you.

Lori and Joe, thank you for being great stunt parents and loving my goblins. Lori, my best girl since you looked out for me in kindergarten. Helping me cover my ass ever since. From five to ninety-five....we are family. After that, on your own.

To the coven, thank you for all the love, laughs and patience to get *grace* moving.

Chris H., You are a gentleman and a scholar. Thank you for reading the scenes and the back and forth.

Ralph and Sam, you two always kept me smiling. Thank you for all of it.

Intessa, Over, Under and Through.

James Hytner of Goose Lodge Writing, you are an amazing editor. I have learned an enormous amount from you. I can never thank you enough for helping to bring *grace* to fruition. Also, thank you for accepting underbreast as a word.

Meradith of The Troy Book Makers. First and foremost thank you for your patience. Also, thank you for all of your work in bringing *grace* to print.

Mike M, I am grateful to you for reading my first draft and being brutally honest. I started the rewrite as soon as we hung up.

Lastly, Stephen King. Thank you.

dedication

I dedicate this book to the black sheep,
underdogs and loners. It doesn't matter who
else doesn't believe in you. Yes you can.

ONE

WHEN NATE AND MARGARET first started dating, she had hustle. Now, four years in with her Multiple sclerosis diagnosis and forty eyeballing her from around the corner, she was keenly aware of her aged eggs. If she had a baby, the kid would be born with an AARP card. Their son James, was five. Or as James put it, "A whole hand, Mama!" Nate was frustrated with Margaret. Much as he admired his strong minded wife; he was the one who had to carry them. Her lackluster disability checks didn't come within a country mile of putting a dent in their expenses. The co-pays, medications and supplements for Margaret made sure of it. They were still living in an apartment and owning a house seemed a dream, at best. Money wasn't the only reason. Not even the biggest. Everyday with Multiple Sclerosis was different yet none of them were easy. The couple had been over this a million times for the last year-and-a-half and Nate's reasons made sense. What didn't make sense to Margaret was how those reasons were good enough not to try.

Margaret ran a yellow onion back and forth over a cheese grater. Their boy, James, didn't eat "bits" of food in his sauce. Bits were anything he could feel no matter how minuscule. Margaret couldn't live with no flavor so it was a compromise. Even shaking in dried Basil was done with caution. "It's time, Nate. Believe me, I'm scared of doing this again. Frankly, if I could knock your ass up instead, I would." Every time she got the chance to cradle a baby, her eggs could be heard pinballing down her fallopian tubes. MS had already stolen too many of her plans. It was not going to take away one more thing. "I want a baby more than I'm afraid of what I will go through. I may as well use this body while I have it. What am I saving it for?" Margaret tossed the spice jar in the cabinet and slammed it shut.

"What are you saving it for?" Nate raked his fingers through his near black hair as he came closer to Margaret. He didn't want James to hear. "How about saving it for those of us who are already here, like James and me? The ones who watch over and take care of you?" Nate's anger was heard even in his whisper. "It's not easy, but we have made the best of it. We have a great little family; you, me, and James. The idea of something happening to you..." his voice losing its venom. "It scares the hell out of me. You never had symptoms until you had James. What if it happens again?" Nate sounded so full of fear and doubt. He looked as if imploring her to listen to reason.

His fears and doubt echoed in her heart. She knew she hadn't one hundred percent recovered after the flare up. It was like this film over her everyone pretended not to notice. The lasting limp and her mouth's inability to say certain words correctly. Mixed in with fatigue and pain she could never catch up on. Margaret's shame and fear dressed in anger launched itself at

Nate. "Weren't those some horribly tough days for you? I can only imagine how difficult it must be to watch." The way Nate treated Margaret when she was first sick had absolutely and irrevocably altered things between them both. Yet Margaret kept her disappointment and broken hearted feelings to herself, mostly. This was not one of those times and Margaret was pissed. Planting herself squarely in front of Nate, filling his view. "According to research, women go into remission when they're pregnant. Nine months of symptom-free living. I know I could use a break." She folded her arms across her chest and gave a snide laugh "Well apparently you could use a break." Then she stepped back and let loose, "Yes, and what happened when I first got sick and knew something was wrong? I was in a flare-up and everyone denied me and wouldn't listen? It was more than a tough time, Nate. As hard as it was for you to watch, I was the one in it. Falling all over the place, smashing into walls, and slurring like a drunk. Everyone thought I was losing my damned mind. Even you! No one else had to believe me, but fuck, Nate, I knew something was wrong and you treated me like I was crazy. You're my husband and you just went along with crazy? Was it easier to think of me as crazy rather than sick? You know if it was you, I would have believed you and gotten you help. God! I was the one waking up with no use of my legs and hitting my head on the bedside table. You told me I was thinking myself sick." It was a lot easier to be mad than sad. "Except I wasn't crazy. I was right and I'm right now. I want to have another baby." She looked at him and said, "Are you saying I wouldn't be able to take care of another baby?" Her stare dared him to open his mouth. Nate was trying to be patient.

"No, I am not saying you wouldn't be able to take care of a baby. Of course you could, Margaret." He was running out of steam. "But, you have to admit things are very different now. You and I have changed. I don't want to fight about this."

"You don't want to fight?! Then by all means," Margaret set her jaw and arched her eyebrow. Whether or not Nate wanted a fight, he got one. "Even then, when I was so close to breaking, I took great care of James and you. Even when the doctor told me I was bipolar and filled me with Seroquel— which actually did make me crazy. Build a fallout shelter, kind of crazy. End is nigh shit. I was afraid my heart would stop in my sleep and wouldn't close my eyes. There was no sleep for days and still no one would listen to me. Not even you, because again, me being crazy was more believable than me being sick. Every single day, I mommed my ass off. When the symptoms started to settle, you all thought the medication had finally 'fixed' me." Margaret could hear her volume go. Briefly, she covered her mouth to quiet herself to keep James from hearing them. "No, it was because the exacerbation was ending after weeks of hell. For a year, I was a team of one. I had to fight for the MRI which you all thought was a waste of time. So much so, I was told I was a hypochondriac and they were only helping me to be done with my 'fodder'. Fodder my ass, the results were, Oh look! M.S." Margaret angrily wiped tears from her flushed cheeks. She looked away from Nate, done talking. Down the hallway, James called for Margaret. Instantly, she felt terrible for what he may have heard. Giving Nate a final ugly stare, she went to James's room.

Nate had grown accustomed to Margaret's guilt trips and for the most part, he could let her bark without getting too bothered. Yet, here now alone with himself, he knew he had messed up when Margaret got sick. He could have and should have handled it better. Instead, he threw himself into work and made friends with the idea that it was all in Margaret's head. It was easier to not see what he could not process. When they met, she was always on her way to or from something. Working, the gym, writing, Margaret had plans for her bright future and Nate inserted himself into them and made it their future. The idea that his girl was breakable was not conceivable. Nate thought of the devastation of their well thought out future plans. He buckled at the notion of all he would have to sacrifice. So, the resentment for the destruction of their future began building, a fortress of negative feelings he could never say out loud.

Nate found Margaret down the hall outside of James's room. Closing the space between them, "Come here." Nate wrapped his arms tightly around her and kissed her cheek. Although Margaret tried to hold on to her bad mood, his kisses and the assault of raspberries on her neck made it impossible. Despite herself, Margaret laughed as she wiped her neck. She never could stay mad for very long. "I'm sorry. I love you," Nate said, between raspberries.

"I love you too, jerk," she answered through her laughter.

James had been read three stories, given fresh water, and ten more hugs. "G'night, buddy. I love you." As soon as Nate pulled James's bedroom door closed, freedom rang in their parenting hearts as they made a run for the couch. Loaded up with snacks and the remote, they settled in to clear some room on the DVR. While Margaret rifled through the Doritos looking for the perfect cheesy triangle, Nate came out with, "Babe, I love you. If this is what you want, we should go ahead with it."

Margaret stopped mid chip. "What?"

"We should do it. Let's try for this baby." Not easily convinced, Margaret gave him a doubtful look. "I am serious. You're right. You're getting old and you should probably get on it."

Margaret gave him a punch to his arm. "I am going to kick your ass, you call me old one more time." Nate laughed at her.

"I can tell you love me by how sweet you talk to me. Come on. Let's give this whole baby thing another go."

Margaret smiled then put her cheesy fingertips on his face and kissed him.

"Are you sure? Like, sure sure? Don't mess with me, Nate."

"Yes, I am sure sure." Nate gave Margaret a smile with powdered cheese on his cheeks.

"Really? Really?" Margaret's eyes lit up. She smooched her husband on his nacho cheese tasting cheek and uncurled herself as she stood up to do a happy dance. "Oh, Nate, this is going to be great. I love you so much, thank you. James is going to flip. He wants to be a big brother.

She was already calling her girl Marie's number.

"Wait, now you love me, not before? So, what about up till now?" Pretend pain across his face.

"Nope. Nada. You were being a jerk up until this very moment," Margaret vollied back.

"All of this just to have your way with me." Nate was trying to appear wounded.

Margaret rolled her copper colored eyes.

"Yes, I was using you this whole time. Totally."

"Yesssss." Nate's phone sang out a message alert. Checking it, Nate put his phone on silent and back in his pocket. Although he was worried how a new baby would upset an already shaky apple cart, he just kept his mouth shut about it and went about his usual business.

"I'm going to run out for more snacks. I have a craving for candy. Do you want anything?" He already had the door open to leave.

"No, I'm good. Wait, let me think." Margaret took a moment. Nate checked his phone as it vibrated. "Mmmm nah, nothing. Well, maybe just chocolate. Nothing crazy though. Something like..." Margaret could not make up her mind. "You know what I like. Find something."

"Sure thing, sweets. Be right back." Nate closed the front door and dialed his phone before he got in the car. It rang twice and the call connected.

"Hello, handsome. Do you miss me?" Nate closed the car door and put his key in the ignition.

"Of course I do. Are you close? I don't have much time."

"Already parked and waiting for you, my love." She giggled. "Oh, and I can't find my panties."

Nate's smile turned to awe as the picture popped onto his screen. He dropped his phone and stepped on the gas.

TWO

VERY FOCUSED ON GETTING pregnant, sex to Margaret was all about the double line in the window. Basal temperature, ovulation charts, and buying pee sticks in bulk may seem hot, but surprisingly, they were not effective kindling for pants fires. Margaret knew she had to do something before they sank into a pit of timed missionary style despair. Nate was due back from a business trip to Chicago, so Margaret took advantage of the time to set up a romantic night for the two of them. Their friends, Marie and William, had just come to pick up James and they even took the dog. Lola had a doggy playdate with their new dog, Wes. The two pooches were basking in all the love from the boys.

Nate's seven p.m. flight landed twenty minutes late. Every minute added to Margaret's need to check and obsess over her face. She flipped the lighted visor down for her last makeup check. The smokey eye was at its optimal smoulder and her provocative lips were done in a glossy burgundy bow. Margaret caught sight of him walking up to the car in the rearview mirror. His strong chest showed through his business casual button down. His muscled forearms flexed as he carried his bags. Margaret had a weakness for the clenched jaw and focus of Nate's serious face. Her goal was to crack it into a smile..

Nate slid his messenger bag in the back seat and saw Margaret's thigh between the slit of a seductive merlot-colored dress. Her dark hair straight down her back. "Hello and whoa— you look hot. Are you wearing the dress from the hotel?" Nate grinned at the memory of them being scolded by hotel security for their volume. Security had insisted on seeing Margaret to make sure her screams were not cause for alarm.

"Hell yeah it is." Margaret gave him a wink. "Get in here and kiss me. I've missed you. Reservations at Karavalli are for eight o'clock. Chicken Korma and paneer naan are waiting."

"No problem, Sweetheart." Nate slid into the passenger seat. *Damn, she is sexy.* Her perfume threw fuel on the fire. His smile grew. "I've missed you." Nate leaned over, parted her cranberry lips with his tongue and kissed her deeply, his hand went to the slit of her dress and weaved his way between her thighs.

"Mmmmmm." Margaret's purr was low. "We have the house to ourselves. Don't you want to wait until we get home?" She knew better.

"Drive." Nate leveled his onyx eyes on his wife. He savored teasing Margaret while she drove. It had been a while since they'd taken a ride like this. "Drive," Nate whispered in her ear, biting her neck. Margaret shifted the car into drive. "Make sure to put on your signal. Wouldn't want you to get pulled over." Her left hand went to her lap, where Nate was already working on her. Margaret could feel herself getting swollen. Her toes curled and pressed down on the brake pedal. "Oh, you feel so damn good. Don't stop."

"I am not going to." She felt his words in her ear. Margaret watched Nate as he put two fingers into his mouth. His night eyes on her, his hand went under her dress between her thighs, parted her lips with his slick fingers and pushed them into her. Nate smiled at her gasp. "You still have to drive." His whispered voice created a dangerous heat and consumed Margaret, filling her body with a wave of desire. It was all she could do to signal and maintain speed as she got into traffic.

Pawing at each other the whole ride home had made the trip seem too long. Nate's hand was deep in the wet between her thighs. Margaret pulled into a park-and-ride and barely had the car in park before she had Nate out of his pants and in her mouth. Sucking him fully and slowly, moving up and down with her tongue swirling around the head.

Nate's head fell back against the seat. "Oh babe, you are unfucking real right now." Nate was rock hard and he didn't want to lose it without getting inside her. "Sit on my lap. Get over here and slide down me, I need to be inside of you now." Margaret sat up, wiped her mouth and gave a smile. straddled him. "Go slow. I want to feel all of you." Slowly, Margaret slid down him. Nate went deeper inside her. "Fuuuuuck." He moaned.

Margaret leaned in. "Fuck me like you paid for it," she whispered and nibbled his ear. Nate brought his hands to her tiny waist and pulled her all the way down on him. Margaret let out a sound of indulgent satisfaction. "Yesssssss." Nate started fucking Margaret hard, making her take every inch. They breathed deep and grunted like animals. "Mmm...mmm...mmm." The car had become so hot that condensation fogged the windows and they were both covered in sweat. Margaret started to peel her dress off when Nate stopped her.

grace

"No, wait." Nate took the spaghetti straps and yanked the top of her dress down. Her tits came free and Nate sucked a nipple with impatient urgency. He coaxed it with licks. He squeezed the other nipple hard enough for Margaret to let out a whimper of pain. He stopped then opened the car door. "Get out." Margaret nodded and slipped her straps back up her shoulders only for Nate to stop her. "Leave them down." She did what she was told.

Without a word, Margaret maneuvered herself off of Nate and out of the car. Nate pressed her against the passenger side of their car. His hungry mouth was biting and licking her salty skin. Nate flipped her around and pushed her belly against the car. He kicked his wife's legs apart and slid his hand in between them and fingered her while he bit her ear.

"Mmmmm, fffffuuu-" Margaret was pushed up onto her toes with every thrust of his hand. "Uh, uh, uh, uh." She opened her legs wider and pushed back against his hand harder and harder. She was on fire and wanted to burn. There they were, at a park-and-ride at dusk. Nate got to his knees and gave his wife a long, slow lick. He penetrated her with his tongue to taste how sweet he knew she would be. Margaret kept her hands on the side of the car and leaned back so she could ride Nate's face. From behind, Nate's hands came up and grasped her tits. Standing up, Nate turned her to face him and took her tits in his hands again and licked her nipples in between his fingers. She spit in her hand, reached down, and wrapped her hand around his hard cock. "I want you in me— now." She knew what she was in for. Margaret took all of Nate into her and Nate went at Margaret with no mercy. Grunting and fucking her, he brought her legs up around him and pulled her agsinst him and he fucked her harder and harder, listening to her yipes of pain and pleasure. He fucked her even harder until she came screaming. Her pussy flexed around him and almost pushed him out. Eager to get pregnant, she stayed wrapped around him. Nate kept fucking his wife until he couldn't hold off any longer. "Yessss, uuuuugh!" Nate got as deep as he could into Margaret and left all of himself inside her.

Margaret and Nate straightened themselves out. He tucked in a shirt, she pulled the straps back up, and they realized it was not as dark out as they had thought and people must have seen them. The thought made Nate and Margaret laugh and high-five as they got back in their car and drove off to make their dinner reservation.

THREE

THEY SPENT THE END of spring and the beginning of summer mixing it up between basal temperature taking boring, charted sex and fun, spontaneous dirty banging. This was the part of getting pregnant that had Nate's full support. By the middle of summer, Nate came home to see Margaret waving around a positive pregnancy test. "We did it, Babe! Oh I'm so happy," her eyes widened, "Okay and a bit terrified." She laughed, "But totally jazzed. Nate, I love you so much. I am beyond excited and this is going to be amazing." James popped out from behind his mom's legs,wearing his favorite red shirt with a T-Rex on it. He smiled with his whole body,almost vibrating with the news. "Dad, we're gonna get a baby!" He clapped his hands excitedly.

Nate lifted Margaret up off the ground, hugged her and planted a kiss on her face. Then, he put his arms out for James to jump into and lifted him up. "You are going to be the best big brother and it will be your job to show the baby the ropes. You know, the ins and outs of being a kid." Nate leaned in and whispered behind his hand, "The secret stuff Mom and I don't know about." Nate gave James a wink and a thumbs up. James gave him a thumbs up in return and did his best to wink, but instead blinked hard with both eyes. Then a sudden look of concern crossed his face.

"How much room will the baby need? Do I have to share my Legos?" His dark eyes were doing math on this baby business.

"Bud, you won't have to share Legos for a while. I wouldn't worry about it." James however, was not convinced. Turning his attention back to Margaret, "Hon you're right, this will be amazing and I'm looking forward to meeting our baby. I'm really proud of you."

"Proud?" Margaret asked, smiling. "Thank you. I am a great lay...there." They both laughed then Nate said,

"I do seem to remember you doing a bit more than just lay there." He gave her a wink and she playfully slapped his shoulder.

"You shush it." Margaret blushed and pointed at James. Nate pulled her close and kissed her deeply.

"I love you, Margaret." The familiar jingle of a dog collar and a whine, brought them back to the day at hand.

"Lola girl." Nate knelt down to say hello with a scratch behind the ears. She started to wiggle, excited for the upcoming outing. "Let's go, little La." He hooked her to the retractable leash and went out the door. At the stop sign, Nate liberated his phone from his pocket and hit the green circle. When the call connected, Nate did not bother with a greeting. "I need you to listen, and please don't scream." There was a sigh on the other end. Nate continued, "I know I told you about Margaret wanting another baby." The sigh became deep breathing on the other end. "Well, as it turns out, she's pregnant." Nate braced himself.

"You told me you wouldn't have another baby with her and that you two barely have sex. You told me you were making plans to leave her. You said you wanted to be with me and I believed you." There was no screaming, but anger punctuated her words.

"Listen, I do want you and I am making plans." Nate spoke carefully. The girls from the past were one-offs— no repeats— so to speak, which was what this was supposed to be. Even when it had become more than a one-off, it was supposed to be casual and fun. Not all this talk of future plans and love. Nate did not feel like he was having fun.

"Nate." Her voice sounded faint and sad. "Is there ever going to be you and me? Do you love me?" His silence answered her question. "You have no plans of leaving her, do you?" Again, Nate stayed quiet. "Oh my God, Nate. Can't you even answer me at all?" Chelsea had been in this type of situation before, but she thought this time was different. Like a sucker, she had fallen for it again.

"I do want to leave her. It just can't happen now. No one has to leave anyone. The only thing this changes at home is how much longer I have to stay. But it doesn't have to change what we have between us. I would miss you too much if you go. Say you'll stay."

"I will say no such thing." She was hurt and did not want to give in, although she knew she ultimately would. "Let's meet at our place so you can convince me."

Nate looked at the time. Soon, James would need to get washed up and put to bed. He needed to get home with the dog from what had become a thirty minute walk.

"I can't now. I need you to give me a couple of hours. After James goes to bed, I will be there." There was a sigh and pause but Nate waited out her hesitation.

"I will text the number if you promise me you'll come?"

"I promise." Nate ended the call without waiting for her response. "Okay, Lola, back home."

FOUR

THE FIRST TRIMESTER WAS, put simply, complete crap. There was no glowing, but more shining with sweat. Margaret was nauseous every waking minute of her baby growing life. Margaret's fatigue was no longer sporadic but an every day deal. Afraid Nate would regret agreeing to another baby, she did her best to carry through on her heavier symptom days by taking a minute for herself. These minutes were naps she took in her truck while James was at nursery school. In between errands, Margaret would park among the other moms and retirees at the grocery store. With the warm day breathing into her open window and Annie Lennox on the radio, the seat tipped all the way back with her phone alarm set, she slept. Most days, it was the best part of the day. However, there were the occasional concerned faces doing walk-byes in her driver's side window. One time an ancient old man with a pelt of furrowed eyebrow hair suspiciously eyed her. Margaret's worst fear was of being stumbled upon savagely snoring by one of the other moms from the preschool coven.

One especially stomach-turning day, Margaret and James were invited to a party that boasted a Bouncy Castle. She was bound by best friend's obligation to show up. Margaret's very best girl, Marie, was having a fifth birthday party for her son, Greyson. Margaret would not subject herself to this petri dish of a party for anyone else in the world. The place was covered wall-to-wall with sugared-up, sticky kids. On the plus side though, James got to go nuts for a bit and was out of her hair. It was a little fun to break up the monotony of dry heaving the day away.

Margaret prepared herself with an ice cold soda and a sleeve of crackers she always kept in her purse. James was already jumping up and down in anticipation of his bouncetastic time. Margaret spotted Marie and her husband, William, waged in a bitter battle, indeed. They were dueling with crazy colored balloon swords and matching balloon crowns. Greyson squealed with delight as he cheered them both on. Catching sight of James, Greyson barreled towards him and almost took James off his light-up sneakers. Both of the boys got to work, liberating James's feet. As soon as the second sneaker popped off, the boys ran to play. Margaret plopped into the nearest hard plastic seat. William gave a tip of his balloon crown and went in the direction of the boys. Marie's burnished hair weaved in a fishtail down her back. A white t-shirt complimented her caramel skin and her indigo jeans emphasized all the squats she had done. Marie wore her balloon speculator with pride as she sashayed Margaret's way. Watching her friend move with ease and without nausea made her sigh a bloated, jealous, and pregnant sigh.

Marie watched Margaret fan her puffy, sweaty self with a paper birthday plate. She pulled on the neck of her top and wafted some air down, hoping to stop her underbreasts from sweating. Marie didn't want to kick a pregnant lady when she was down, so she did not tell Margaret that there were already crescents of sweat on her shirt from her ridiculously large boobs. Marie took the seat next to her pasty friend and almost felt bad for the poor creature.

"So, you look good. Are you a model?" There was a sly smile on Marie's face. She tucked a lock of shiny hair behind Margaret's ear. Her mom bun was coming loose.

"Why yes. Yes, I am. I model for Moist Moms Monthly," Margaret vollied back. She rested her sweaty forehead on the red formica table and sucked down frosty cola in hopes of making the feisty fetus in her fundus less pissed.

"First of all, you are a disgusting animal. You know that word is not to be said."

"What word? Moist?" Margaret winked at her friend. Marie was sickened. "Secondly, I can see you're classing it up with those giant beige granny underwear riding up in the back."

"Yeah, well I am obviously going for a sexy look."

Marie giggled at her friend. "Seriously though, are you okay? How many weeks are you? Twelve? Do you need anything? Want something to eat?" Margaret rolled her head back and forth on the formica.

"No food." She sucked down more Pepsi. The ice cubes avalanched down the cup. Margaret handed the cup to Marie for a refill. From somewhere underneath the floppy bun and sweat came a hearty soda burp. Margaret raised her head only two inches off of the table, not even looking up.

"Yes. I am twelve very long ass dragging weeks pregnant. I am pretty sure I threw up a taco from 1982." Margaret put her hand on her puffy stomach, which was not yet an official bump. "You had better be really cute. You hear me in there? I am talking super cute. The kind I can exploit." Margaret stood abruptly, nausea circling back for the millionth time. She quickly stepped to the bathroom with a hand over her mouth. This is the magic she fought so hard for. Tada.

FIVE

Margaret could not stand the crinkling of the waxy exam table paper and so she chose to sit on the plastic chair instead. She had been called to the doctor's office about the results from her blood tests. She sat there and could hardly breathe, not ready to hear any bad news. Seriously, if it wasn't bad news, why was she here? Usually they send a form letter in the mail a week later, or even results over the phone. Instead, Natalee, the office manager, called two days after testing and asked her to come in that same day. She knew these were not some benign results. When Margaret got dressed for her appointment, her hands were shaking, and tried to use controlled breath techniques on the way over. She became light headed behind the wheel and knew she needed to reel it in. Then she remembered Natalee saying that Doctor Bunem needed to speak with her. The thought sent her back to over-oxygenating herself behind the wheel. When she got there, she was met right away and brought into an exam room to wait. Margaret stood up and walked around the square room snooping in drawers. She tried to sit still, but couldn't, so she stood again and paced some more.

grace

When the exam room door opened, not to a handsome, dark, British Doctor Bunem, but to a blondish young twenty-something nurse, Margaret became more anxious. The nurse let Margaret know Dr. Bunem would be right in. "We have a resident here today. Is it alright if they come in?" Margaret felt like a caged cat.

"No, not today. Just...no." Whatever this was, she didn't need an audience. The nurse nodded her understanding and quickly backed out, shutting the exam room door. Margaret was still pacing when her gynecologist softly knocked and entered.

"Afternoon, Mrs. Hall. How are you feeling?" The British accent she had always gotten such a kick out of, sounded all too serious. She momentarily stopped pacing to answer him.

"Hello, Dr. Bunem. Actually, I have been a puking pile of emotions since your office called. I know it's not great, so tell me, what did you need to see me for?" She resumed pacing back and forth.

"Alright I can understand you being nervous. You've also never been one for pleasantries so why don't we get down to it? Would you like to take a seat?"

Margaret stopped pacing and sat despite her insides, which were still in fourth gear. Dr. Bunem slipped his wire-framed glasses on and opened up her file to locate the results of the tests. Margaret's racing heart squeezed. "Remember before the testing when we discussed percentages and what the numbers mean as far as birth defects? We discussed how the possibility of these increases with age. You are thirty-eight and in fact, a geriatric pregnancy." Dr. Bunem took a beat then continued. "You are at high risk for trisomy 18. Your first-trimester screening came back with a one in fifty."

He quickly followed it with, "Mrs. Hall, this does not mean your baby will inde-"

"Stop," Margaret cut him off. This wasn't her first time at the rodeo and she was frustrated and scared. Margaret barked, "Tell me what it is. Just say it and let's go on from there." Dr. Bunem knew he needed to give her the information in black and white. So he did.

"Trisomy 18, also known as Edmond Syndrome, is a condition caused by an error in cell division. This can cause severe medical impairment. Only fifty percent of babies with Trisomy 18 are alive at birth. In this case, if the baby lives, he or she will need extensive neonatal care." Margaret dropped her head into her hands "Mrs. Hall, this does not mean it will definitely happen. There are tests if you want to be sure. We can start with a high-level ultrasound."

What if the baby needs more than I could possibly give? Nate was right. I have no business having a baby. I am selfish. Margaret's head was swimming in fear and not knowing and so, she looked to her doctor for the answer. She asked, "How can I possibly take care of a baby who needs so much?" The reality was right there and there was no more hiding in the happiness of pregnancy. Spry was not the first word to describe Margaret, and suddenly having another baby seemed so overwhelming. How could this broken woman take care of two kids? With the limitations Margaret had, how could she? The first trimester had come with an easing of her symptoms. It had lulled her into a false sense of ability, but this baby had a lemon for a mama.

A few hours later, Margaret was in her kitchen going through the motions of making dinner. Peeling, chopping, seasoning all with a heavy mind and heart.

grace

All the crying and twisting herself with the worst case scenarios resulted in a monster headache. Nate came up behind her, wrapped his hand around her, and rested his hand on her just starting bump. Margaret turned into Nate's arms. There was no need for music; they had their own rhythm. She and Nate held each other and swayed under the kitchen's soft light. Nate stroked her thick hair away from her face and kissed her forehead.

"I have to get CVS testing. Do you know what it is?" Margaret kept going, not waiting for an answer. "It's called Chorionic Villus Sampling. Some crazy test used to diagnose chromosomal abnormalities when it's too early for an amniocentesis. The doctor takes cells from my placenta and sends them to a lab for analysis. Guess how the doc does it, go ahead." Again, before Nate could even answer, Margaret demonstrated with her hands. "The needle is friggin' huge. Like, over a foot. I am crapping my elastic waistband pants."

"You know if I could, I would take the test for you." Margaret's eyes rolled like pool cue balls. Of course, he could say this knowing he would never have to. "I don't know what I'm supposed to say. I feel bad this is happening to you, but anything I say will sound stupid." Margaret was glad they agreed on something.

"This is a lot to take in and I am freaked out about all the things I've truly never thought about. It didn't even cross my mind that we could be here. Now I'm worried something is wrong— really wrong. You know me. Does anything about me seem lucky to you?" She rested her head against his chest.

"What? Nate looked shocked. He brought Margaret to arm's length, then let her go. "Look at me. Eh? Eh?" He turned in a slow circle. "You must certainly be lucky.

Look at the fantastic husband you have gone and roped yourself." Nate gave a dramatic bow after his slow spin and a wave of his hand.

Margaret laughed. "Yes, Nate. I was just counting my lucky stars." She looked up and counted out loud, "One, two. Two whole stars." she laughed. Yet again, Nate had pulled her from the ledge, tethering her heart to his. James ran up and hugged their knees. James wasn't a baby anymore and was even tall for his age, but he was only five and Margaret couldn't resist picking him up and kissing his sweet face. James buried his face in her neck. She rested her chin on his head and breathed in her boy's sweetness. His dark curls were soft on his little head. The three of them swayed together in a family hug she so desperately needed. At this moment, everything was okay. Margaret felt the vibration of Nate's phone through his pocket. He seemed startled as he quickly broke away from their hug to check his messages.

SIX

Dr. Bunem knew Margaret would become more anxious the longer she waited, so he did not simply pull strings, he yanked them harder than a rope during a tug o' war on field day. Two days later, Margaret and Nate were sitting in the neonatalogist's waiting room, playing Who's Our Doctor? Their fingers were crossed for the doctor with the full on pushbroom mustache. Their logic was that a man with such stellar mouth bangs had to have patience and precision.

"Mr. and Mrs. Hall, I'm Amanda. You can follow me, please." A young pretty girl in calm blue scrubs held open the door. The worried couple stood and weaved their fingers together and followed Amanda. The first stop before the procedure was with a genetic counselor. Nate introduced himself and Margaret to Ms. Kline, who was all of five feet and wore a taupe twin set with navy trouser style slacks. Ms. Kline gestured to the matching chairs on the other side of her tidy desk and everyone took their seats. Margaret's nervousness had a way of making her a smidge of a bitch.

"Good morning, Mr. and Mrs. Hall. How are you this morning?" A perfectly normal question, but emotions were already high.

"We are having a fantastic day." Margaret was hip deep in snark-infested waters and had no intention of stopping, but the "cut the crap" look Nate threw her way persuaded her to at least reign it in.

Mrs. Kline smoothed her blonde curl and set hair, "I know you have not had much time. However, did you both get a chance to fill out the questionnaire?"

To keep Margaret's salty mouth to herself, Nate fielded this one. "Yes, we did. As much as we could." With only mere hours to collect family histories, they had assaulted their loved ones, firing off questions in rapid succession. Neither Margaret's nor Nate's family had anything worrisome to report. With Margaret and Nate's grandparents gone, knowledge of family history was scant.

"Alright then, let's get started," Ms. Kline said with a flourish of official papers.

Although the information had its missing pieces, it still took quite some time to wade through. As Ms. Kline charted their histories, no red flags jumped up and signaled danger ahead.

Amanda, the same fresh-faced medical assistant, walked them to their ultrasound/examining room, where they would perform the Level ll Ultrasound. Those new details would help check their baby for birth defects, including Trisomy 18, the abnormality her baby had a one in fifty chance of having. One in fifty felt like disastrous odds and Margaret prayed for her baby to beat those odds. The ultrasound technician came into the room. "Hello there, folks. I'm Kelly. I'm going to be doing your ultrasound." The tech went about her business of clicking and measuring. Margaret's nerves felt more exposed with every click. The crown-rump measurement was taken. *Click Click.* The head circumference and femur length. *Click Click Click.* Karey took measurements of the nuchal fold. *Click Click Click.* This was an area of tissue at the back of the unborn baby's neck. *Click Click Click.* The tech recorded all of the measurements while Margaret searched her face, hoping to glean anything. Kelly's poker face was flawless and gave nothing away. Margaret knew the results would have to come from the doctor. Kelly excused herself to give the doctor the images from the ultrasound. Margaret and Nate waited and after a year and a day, the doctor came in and introduced himself.

"Hello and good morning. I am Dr. Kineke." Dr. Kineke was indeed the doctor with the luxurious mustache. Nate and Margaret discreetly pounded each other's fist. Now, it was the doctor's turn to examine the fetus. Mustache focused on specific parts of the baby. He looked at his or her brain, heart, and the other organs. He also double checked measurements taken during the ultrasound. The doctor seemed satisfied with the numbers. "Mrs. Hall, the measurements are right on for the age of the fetus." Margaret's clenched undercarriage loosened only slightly. She took what seemed like her first full breath in days. After all the necessary measurements were recorded, Mustache said, "According to all the measurements, the baby gives every indication of being healthy and normal. By all means, this is very good news and you don't have to do any further testing. However, if you want to be absolutely confident, we will perform the CVS procedure." Margaret was full of fear at the notion of the test. She had attempted to research (first two results on Google), images of the sword length needle halted any further research.

"Is the needle really big?" There was fear in Margaret's eyes. Could it be that she was remembering the needle bigger than it was? Her imagination playing with her? Margaret had high hopes Kelly would ease her mind.

"We will explain everything as we go and if you have any further questions or concerns, please ask. First, we will numb the area before we go into the placenta. Please try to be calm and not move during the procedure. The needle will feel uncomfortable, but not painful."

"So, this needle will go into my placenta and take pieces? It is going to go through my skin, fat, and muscle and through my uterine wall into my placenta?" Margaret's parts went back to clenched. As well read as she had become on the subject, it meant very little. Now, all she could see in her mind was a glistening super sharp three foot long (fear may have played a part in her measuring) needle. If Margaret needed to be numbed with one needle in preparation for the pain of the needle to follow, it was indeed a big ass needle. There was no friggin' way this was only going to be "uncomfortable."

"Yeah, this sounds completely painless. Absolute cake walk." Margaret feigned nonchalance. "I'm here—might as well do this now. I have been sweating this for days, only getting myself more flapped up over not knowing what is going on with this little one. I think I need to go ahead and get it done before I chicken out."

"You will also get to know if it is a boy or girl," Kelly said with a hopeful smile.

"Ah, it is the upside to the foot long needle to the gut." The technician ignored Margaret's mouth.

"Isn't my wife sweet? Delightful really." Nate said to Kelly while giving Margaret the hard eye. This was no time for Margaret's antics; she needed to listen and stay calm. Nate stood next to the exam table and held his wife's hand in both of his. Raising his hand to her lips she kissed the palm and put it on her cheek. He leaned in and said quietly, "You can do this," and for a moment she believed it.

Mustache chimed in, "I would like to take this time to explain the procedure to you before I begin. This test is similar to amniocentesis. However, you are only thirteen weeks and four days pregnant, which means we are going to perform a CVS, or Chorionic Villus Sampling procedure. This will be done transabdominally and will not take long. First, we will give you a local anesthetic to numb the area where the needle will be inserted. I will be looking at the ultrasound during the procedure and it will help guide a long thin needle through your abdomen to your placenta. I will draw a sample of tissue to be tested."

Margaret had to ask, "Can you please tell me how damned big this needle is?"

"The needle is approximately twelve inches long." Kelly added the visual of her hands entirely too far apart for Margaret. She mentally cursed Kelly for not telling her earlier. Mr. Mustache quickly became Dr. Kineke.

"Twelve? Twelve friggin' inches?" Margaret swallowed hard.

"Approximately," Kelly answered.

Nate gave an almost imperceptible shutter then said, "This is up to you Margaret. Believe me, I understand if you don't want to."

Margaret had looked to him for support in the decision. Nate thought shrugged shoulders and scared eyes were the answer. *A duh face and a shrug was what I got.* Apparently, this was something she would have to decide alone. Margaret's eyes narrowed in thought. Again, thinking of the impending harpoon had Margaret doing a giant perpetual kegel. Kelly the technician was back into view to help Margaret stay calm and shield the sight of the needle. It was time to prep Margaret for the procedure. Kelly pointed at the tiny beauty mark on the blue wing of the butterfly tattoo below Margaret's navel.

"The doctor is going to go in right about this area." Margaret chuckled when she looked at the once small butterfly tattoo spreading its wings and stretching out.

"Ah jeez, this thing is going to look like Mothra after the pregnancy. Maybe I should get Godzilla tattooed too and they can battle over my stretch marks." Kelly laughed and shook her head. "Listen, this seemed like a genius idea at the time. Admittedly, my twenties were not my best decision making years."

Kelly replied, "At least you don't have a tramp stamp."

Margaret laughed again. "Oh yes, I sure do." Margaret tilted to show her lower back tattoo of a rising sun. When I got this a thousand years ago, it wasn't called a tramp stamp. I was a trampy girl trying to impress someone with how badass I was."

"I have one on my back for the same reason." she smiled. "No judgement here. Okay, now we are going to begin the procedure. Are you ready?"

"No, but I won't be no matter how long I lay here sweating." She took a deep breath and exhaled. "Alright, let's do this."

On her back and out of smart comments. Margaret used the hand-sized brown stuffed bear on the desk on the other side of the exam room as her focal point. She stared at the heart holding bear. BE MINE, was stitched in red thread across the white heart. The local anesthesia was administered. Dr. Kineke moved the ultrasound machine for a closer view because he needed to see in order to guide the needle. The doctor turned his back to Margaret and he did his best to be discreet, the glimmer of the long silver needle caught Margaret's eye. Nate had been asked to step aside during set up for the procedure. Once everything was in its place, the technician waved Nate back over. The doctor took what seemed both forever and only a moment. Margaret stared at the little bear so hard that he became self-conscious. Although she was relieved the needle did not hurt, there was the oddest feeling of pressure that gave her a nauseating case of cold sweats. She could feel the doctor jiggling the needle as he collected a sample of the tissue from the placenta. Focused on the bear, Margaret willed the procedure to go as quickly as possible. Margaret was moments from yelling, "OK. OK. Enough!"

The amazing and efficient Dr. Kineke announced, "The needle is out, Mrs. Hall." Margaret had done it. The fear of the procedure had been tremendous and all of her nervousness about the pain had been unnecessary. Nate leaned in and gave Margaret a kiss on her cheek. "You did it. You are way tougher than me." Margaret smiled to herself. She was feeling pretty tough. As soon as all of the samples were sealed and labeled, Dr. Kineke peeled off his gloves.

"Please, take it easy the next couple of days. No lifting, vacuuming, or exercise."

"No worries there," Margaret said under her breath.

"Your stomach may feel sore for a bit. We will be able to get the preliminary results within two days."

"The doctor is going to monitor the baby's heart one more time," Kelly said. "We just want to double check the heart rate so we can make sure all is well." A recheck showed the little one's heart beating perfectly. "Alright, you two, get yourselves home and try to relax." Dr. Kineke gave a smile and a short wave as he and Kelly the technician headed off to go do this procedure to another future mother.

Their drive home from the appointment was much more relaxed. Behind the wheel, Nate hummed along with the radio with a smile on his face. Margaret couldn't help thinking, *Of course he's smiling, he had not been gored like a slow matador in a bullfight.*

"Well, you must be glad that's all done. It's crazy, isn't it? Can you believe we are going to find out what we are having? What do you think? Boy or girl?"

"I don't know, I just want to be sure the baby is healthy." Margaret had mentally distanced herself from her growing baby. Afraid to love and bond while simultaneously feeling guilty for the distance she had created in just days. What if the baby she'd seen in her dreams was not okay? The loss would be devastating.

"You're telling me you haven't given any thought to it? You won't jinx it by saying it out loud."

She whispered, "I want a girl and yes I am going to worry until we know for sure."

"Well, now we have passed the procedure and it will be smooth sailing from here on out. Now stop worrying." He took her hand and gave it a squeeze. Margaret was annoyed with Nate for telling her not to worry. She turned to talk to him. However Margaret could see in his mind, Nate was elsewhere.

SEVEN

DETERMINED TO CARRY EVERYTHING in one trip, Margaret loaded up her arms with grocery bags. She looked down at her belly, gave an aggravated sigh, stepped back, and kicked the cargo door shut before she made her way inside. Her cell phone rang from inside the bowels of her purse. She moved at a pregnant lady's pace, so by the time she was able to fish the phone out of her bag, the ringing had stopped. The screen alerted her to one missed call. "Damn it." Lola was full of tail wags and curiosity, running around Margaret's feet and sniffing the grocery bags. Margaret hit redial on the phone. After four rings, a recorded voice informed Margaret she had reached Neonatal Specialists. She waited on hold for what felt like forever. Finally, a real person picked up.

"Hello. Thank you for calling the Neonatal Specialists. My name is Amanda. How may I direct your call?" the young, bubbly girl from the office said.

"Hi, yes, my name is Margaret Hall. I am returning a call to your office."

"Alright, let me just verify some information. Please tell me your date of birth."

"April 27, 1979."

"OK, and just your address and we will get you started." Margaret verified her address and was put on hold again. With hold music crooning in her ear, Margaret began putting the groceries away while Lola sniffed the purchases. She was stacking Greek yogurts when Ms. Kline came on the line.

"Good afternoon, Mrs. Hall. How are you feeling today?"

"I am feeling alright, other than trying to be busy so I don't obsess. How are you today?"

"I'm just fine, dear. Well, we have the preliminary results of your tests. Would you like to hear them?" Margaret's heart was in her mouth. The very next thing out of this person's mouth could change everything. She couldn't possibly wait for Nate.

"I would very much like to hear the results."

"It would seem you are pregnant with a very healthy baby."

Margaret's heart instantly broke open. She hadn't even realized how much she had been trying to steel herself for bad news. "Oh, thank God! Thank God. Happy tears rolled down her smiling face. "Thank you, thank you. I gotta tell you, this was beyond scary."

"I do have one more bit of news for you, if you would you like to know the sex of your baby." The sex. In all of her worry and excitement, Margaret had forgotten about it.

"After all of this, heck yeah! I deserve it."

"You are having a girl." Margaret froze for an instant. Seeing the little girl from her dreams running toward her and jumping into her arms.

"Oh, a girl! This is fantastic! Thank you again, Ms. Kline." They spent a few more giddy moments on the phone in which Ms. Kline let her know the complete test will be finished within two weeks, but to rest assured that Margaret's baby was doing well.

As soon as Margaret ended her call with Ms. Kline, she dialed Nate. After a few rings, the call connected. "Hey Nate," Margaret said into the phone. There was a rustling sound and muffled voices in the mix, followed by the beep of the call disconnecting. Margaret pulled her phone from her ear and looked at the screen. "What the Hell?" She poked Nate's contact photo. The phone did not even ring, but went right to voicemail. Margaret ended the call without leaving a message. Instead, she figured to send him a text.

Margaret: Hey, I don't know what the deal is with your phone but call me when you can. I have news from the doctor.

Twenty minutes later, Nate called back.

"Hello, Sweetheart. I was finishing up at the gym. What's up?

"I just got off the phone with Mrs. Kline from the neonatologist's office." Margaret was trying to keep her voice even.

"Well, what did they have to say?" He cupped his hand near the speaker of the phone to keep the background noise from being heard.

"Everything is fine and the baby is perfect."

Nate's instant relief and happiness could be heard through the phone. "Yes! Thank God."

Margaret asked, "Do you want to know what we are having?"

"Of course I do! " Nate said.

"We are having a girl!" Margaret said, barely able to contain her joy.

"We are having a little girl? Nate hadn't anticipated how this would soften his heart with love. "This is terrific. I am going to have a daughter. I am really proud of you, Margaret. I love you."

"I love you, too. I'll see you when you get home." Nate ended the call just as Chelsea put her hand on his shoulder. Slowly turning to see her agitated face.

"What?" Nate was confused.

"Don't 'what' me. I heard you say, 'I love you' to her. How do you think it makes me feel?" Her hands went to her hips.

"You've got to be kidding me, right? She is my wife and she is pregnant. I don't need this from you right now. I'm going to go." Nate walked toward the door. Chelsea went after him, hoping to stop him.

"Please don't leave, Nate. You're right. I shouldn't be making things more difficult for you. I know you have to say it. I'm being too needy— please don't leave." As she put her hand on his arm, Nate pulled away and kept walking towards the door. Suddenly, Chelsea was afraid she had gone too far and now, it was too late. "Baby, please don't leave me." She tried again to keep him there by leaning against the door. Nate gave an annoyed sigh, moved Chelsea aside, then offered a, "night," and a curt wave in the air on his way out the door.

EIGHT

IN THE EVENING, MARGARET fell into what she called "a Bravhole" and binged episodes of *Housewives*. She heard the front door open when Nate walked in the house with his work out bag in hand.

"Well, well, well. Someone decided to come home." said Margaret, all dramatic and high pitched. She was smiling— in too good of a mood.

"You're crazy. I was working out. When I grabbed the phone, I hit END accidentally. I called as soon as I finished. Afterwards, there was a virtual meeting for work. I used my phone and took the meeting in the car." He planted a quick kiss on her cheek.

"I was only playing with you. Is everything going okay at work? You seem pretty tense these days." Margaret was hoping to celebrate the baby, but Nate didn't seem celebratory.

"What? No, I'm not tense. It's been a shit day and I'm tired. I'm going to jump in the shower." Nate dropped his workout bag and walked into the bathroom. When the shower kicked on, Margaret picked up her phone and dialed Marie.

"Eeeeeek! A little girl. This is perfect!" Marie squealed happily. Margaret said it didn't matter, but

Marie remembered the dreams of babies Margaret had and how deeply her friend wanted a girl. "This is big news. We will have someone to show our secrets to."

"Such as, saying we are going to the gym. Yet instead, we go on secret trips to the diner for a stack of pancakes?"

"Only on a cheat day and it counts as cardio. I know these things; I am a professional." The ladies both laughed.

Marie and Margaret made a list of baby things. With no patience between the two of them, they made plans to shop. "Good night to you and little mama."

"Night. I am about to go to town on another bowl of cereal." Margaret heard Marie gasp.

"It's late, you shouldn't be eating at—" Marie was cut off.

"Gotta go. Eating cereal… with those crunchy marshmallows. Bye." Margaret ended the call, chuckling to herself as she topped off her favorite cereal bowl.

NINE

SHOPPING FOR BABY GIRL gear revealed Margaret's lack of control. Marie was thoroughly amused by how corny pregnancy had made Margaret. She fawned over sweet sleepers and pink unicorn onesies. The coziness of baby clothes was addictive. Cottony, fuzzy, and addictive. The doll size candy-colored dresses with matching ruffled diaper covers. Margaret heard herself let out "awwws". Who had she become? After filling the cart, Marie slid her card across the counter.

"Get out of here. I don't expect you to pay." She tried to push the card in Marie's direction. Marie had no choice, so she whipped out another card and handed it to the cashier.

"Oh, for shit's sake, cut it out. This is my Goddaughter and I will spoil her if I want to."

"Wait, you *want* to be her Godmother?" Margaret was astonished. "You do realize, this will make you a moral compass for someone? The voice of reason. Help her make good choices?"

"I know what it means," Marie said, making a face. "Listen jackass, I love you and now I love Little Miss in there. So, now we are in this." She wagged her finger in the space between herself and Margaret's belly. You have to admit, I am a font of wisdom. I will be sharing all sorts of information because I will be her spiritual mentor," she said, laughing at herself.

"I see I have chosen wisely." Margaret shook her head.

"Promise me you will pick a cute Godfather. I don't want to be adjacent to some weirdo this kid's whole life."

Margaret smiled. "We want to ask Jeff and we're positive he will say yes. "

"Jeff is stellar Godfather material."

"Right? Nate and I think so, too. Well, now that we have the Godparent business situated, where can we feed Freshie?" Margaret rubbed her belly like a lamp, hoping for a genie. A taco genie.

"Feed Freshie? Is it Freshie who wants to hit the buffet at Panchos?"

"Uh, yeah it is." Margaret said in a matter of fact way. "I will eat tacos 'til I fall over. You can have one of those, Tito-ritas for me. You know, a margarita made with Tito's vodka instead of Tequila. No salty rim."

"Yeah, I know what it is. Speaking of salty, how is Nate these days? Is he getting excited about the baby?" Marie let the question hang in the air, waiting out the heaviness of Margaret's hesitation.

"Here is the thing," Margaret began. "Nate has been distracted and moody but he says it's because of work. And while I totally understand his job is stressful, it always has been. In the past, he didn't have a problem putting work away and being with me and James."

"Uh huh…." Marie wanted Margaret to keep talking.

"Well lately, he seems checked out. You know? Even when Nate is with us at home, he is not with us. His face is either in his phone or he is lost in thought."

"Okay, what do you think is up with St. Nate?"

"Stop it, Marie. Don't call him that. He really does try and he takes really good care of me and James." To which Marie snorted, at the ridiculousness of the statement. "He does Marie. I am a lot and It's definitely worse since I've decided to throw another baby in the mix."

"Okay, for one, you are exactly enough. And B--"

"You mean, second--" Marie cut her off.

"AND B! You did not throw anything at him. You talked about it and he agreed. He is a grown man, Margaret. He knows what life is, please stop coddling his self important attitude." Marie saw how sad Margaret's face was hearing about Nate and immediately regretted saying so much. It didn't matter if what Marie said was true, now was not the time for truth. "Margaret, I love you. Whatever you guys are going through, I'm sure you will work it through. I'm sorry I took out being hungry on you. It is nothing a chimichanga can't fix."

"I love you too. You're my best friend, you are just looking out for me. And yes, you are mean when you are hungry." Marie opened the door to the restaurant for Margaret. The pair traded the awkward conversation outside for insanely delicious tacos and chimmies inside.

TEN

MARGARET'S SECOND TRIMESTER was easier with the arrival of Autumn. The cooler temperatures were a welcome change. The end of intimate times spent wrapped around the toilet was worth celebrating. Margaret's energy was coming back and the need to be ready for Freshie had her nesting like a blue jay. Whole rooms of furniture needed to be resituated and moved again. Disinfecting and steaming every surface was a must. She organized everything in every bin and she retired broken action figures and toys with missing pieces. Margaret was whittling out the fray when a happy James came sauntering in with his hand jammed in a bag of Goldfish. "Mama, whatcha doing?"

"Well, James, your sister is going to be here soon. We will want some room for her toys too."

"Uh huh." James looked up at his mom. Big, suspicious, blinky brown eyes assessed her. Margaret could smell the tantrum in the air.

"Don't you want to make room for some new things?" Margaret held up an armless doll cowboy.

"No! I need him. None of my toys go. None!" He grabbed his wounded cowboy and clutched him to his chest. "I am not throwing my toys away. The baby can not touch these— or this," he said as he snatched up a three-wheeled truck. "She will have to live somewhere else." His little rat hands grabbed random toys. He was steadily headed to a epic level freak out. Margaret's phone rang.

"Thank sweet baby Jesus." Margaret slowly backed out of the room while hitting the green button. "Hello, and thank you for rescuing me."

"You're welcome and why?" Catherine whispered back as if she were right there.

"Mom, your grandson has lost his squash because I'm getting rid of broken toys and crap."

"Yes, but it is his stuff and to him it's not crap."

"Yes, Mom. I understand but we need to make more room."

"You know what you should do?"

"What, Ma?" Margaret couldn't wait to hear the gem her mother was going to throw.

"Have another kid." Margaret could hear her mother's snickering, proud of herself for zinging her daughter.

"Ohhh so funny, Catherine. Yeah, I used your name. Remember this when you're an old biddy. It's a state-run facility for you. Fish sticks and creamed corn all the livelong day." Catherine laughed

"Well, I happen to love fish sticks so, ha on you. Now, the reason I called was to check in and, based on your tone and overall sunshiney attitude, I am guessing you're fine."

James, the boy siren, had reached the apex of his tantrum. He yelled out for his treasures, too precious to be parted with. "My guys, my Play Dough, my stuff' animals…" He had heaped his stuff into an ever growing keep pile.

Catherine said, "Oooh he sounds really mad." Margaret could picture her mom smile.

"Right, Ma?! He is hot. I guess now is not the time to tell him that he's sharing a room with Freshie."

"Oh, Hun. Please tell me you are not going to do that to him. Not only will he lose his squash, but we may never find it again."

"No, Mom, I am not having them share a room. I am not crossing Toy Grabbing McGee." Margaret giggled. "We are converting our walk-in into a baby suite."

"What do you mean? In the closet? You can't put a baby in a closet, Sweety."

"You say it as if you're dealing with an idiot. When the baby is born, she will be with me anyway. Besides, the closet isn't exactly tiny. It's a walk-in with lights and a door. It's big enough to hold both her crib and dresser. All we need is some fun paint and we're done."

"When are you kids going to buy a house? Three bedrooms would be so nice."

"Yeah, wouldn't it? With a white kitchen," Margaret said wistfully. "Mom, believe me, I wish we had a three bedroom house. We crave all the trappings of the middle class. I ruined our plans when I got sick and had to stop working."

"Don't say such things, Margaret. It is most certainly not your fault. You seem to forget how hard you work at being a mom. I mean for Pete's sake, you actually listen to them. I'll be damned if I did when you were growing up." Catherine chuckled.

"Mom, I know this isn't the ideal situation, however it is indeed our current situation. Buying a house is our goal, but for right now, we're good here, in the apartment. We have plenty of room for everyone."

"Tell that to the town crier running around hollering his list."

Margaret laughed. "Seriously Ma? You're such a help."

"I am, aren't I? Well, I will let you get back to it. If you need anything, call. Love you, Pumpkin."

"Love you, Mom." Margaret ended the call, gave herself a five count, then headed back into battle.

ELEVEN

AUTUMN LEAVES AND temperatures fell. Jack o' lanterns and Flint corn were dressed in spider webs for Halloween. Margaret and Marie gathered their little costume-clad families and went to the mall for trick-or-treating indoors. Kids zigzagged from store to store for candy and raffle prizes. Margaret had ironed the word "pregnant" on a t-shirt with an arrow pointing to her belly. A black cape fluttered behind her. She was "Super Pregnant." While Marie's deep violet witch hat topped off her purple striped tights and tight black dress with bell sleeves. Greyson and James were wielding katanas while battling it out in matching Ninja Turtle costumes. Nate and William went as Nate and William. They were down to the last three stores and James and Greyson were already making plans for their first candy. Margaret felt a buzzing, so she reached for her phone in her back jeans pocket. It was not her phone. Her misfiring nerves caused the buzzing feeling and the stabbing hot needle pain going down her leg. Margaret felt it happen one more time before the end of trick or treating at the food court. However she didn't want to say anything and ruin the night. Instead she went along with their

46

plans to eat. They could not decide, so the group ordered a pizza and Chinese. James relentlessly badgered Margaret about getting into his candy. They all climbed in the car and Margaret made him promise to let her check the candy first. James did not keep his promise and dove into his trick-or-treat bag.

Nate had sequestered himself to his desk in the corner of their bedroom, otherwise known as his "office". He kept his phone notifications off so Margaret wouldn't be able to hear the constant ding of him messaging with Chelsea. They really needed more space if he hoped for even a modicum of privacy. When he clicked on all three work monitors, each opened to some fresh insurance nightmare. The workload was heavy with new auto insurance claims waiting to be queued up. Nate was inundated with calls and mouse clicks because he was the lead adjuster for all claims submitted.

When Nate began working for the company last year, he was looking forward to working from home because it seemed to be the perfect fit for the family. James was his number one silly and sweet guy, always chock-full of questions and declarations. However, James would randomly burst into the room excited to share these tidbits of news and sometimes, Nate was in a virtual meeting or on the phone. Once, James managed to pilfer Nate's cell phone and, using voice to text, started a text chain which was synced to Nate's work messenger. When Nate saw the live chat lighting up, he clicked to get in with the group. There on the screen was a text from Nate's phone, "I love Goldfish crackers." James had shared the news with hearts and a slew of goldfish emojis. Nate was too late and co-workers saw Nate's proclamation of love for Goldfish. For days, his team took turns sending him fish emojis. He needed his own space.

Then there was Margaret, who was constantly in and out, bringing in laundry or checking to see if he needed anything. When she would go, she'd leave the door open to the sounds of the house. He'd already come dangerously close to his being heard talking on his phone. Since then, Nate used taking the dog for walks as his cover. However, when being pulled by a small, fat dog and holding a stinking bag of poop, a bit of the fire goes out.

Although a lot of days were laced with happy squeals, bubbles, dog barks, and James dancing to his favorite shows, on some days, James would be a little goblin. An incorrectly cut peanut butter and jelly and a tired kid made for an apocalyptic kidsplosion that turned James into a yelling, crying, tantrum throwing little heathen. Now, Margaret was having their second baby. Thinking about it, Nate's heart constricted with anxiety. How could he possibly do this with two kids? This family would need more money, time, and soundproof rooms. Margaret was the mom who knew all the silly songs with the dances. She could draw a map of Sesame Street and give a guided tour. The woman could cut a grilled cheese in five equal slices and, that was after she gave them a double flip in the pan. No one else could touch her when it came to her momming skills. However, the damned MS changed things. MS gnawed on her brain and body, taking a little more of her with every bite. Even on the good days, she was battling fatigue, cognitive decline, pain, and numbness. At times, her skin being touched almost made her cry. Not being able to be touched hurt her soul more. During these horrible flare-ups, Margaret could be down for weeks with months of recovery. The physical impairment, the pain, and Margaret's guilt would throw her back and forth from angry to sad and back again. Nate did not do well with the emotional tennis and when he couldn't say the right thing, he often remained quiet. Margaret prickled at his silence because she felt lonely and unlovable, whiling away the hours in bed and watching the days fade outside her window. She was infused with steroids to battle the inflammation of a flare-up. Yet, the steroids seemed to inflame both her pain and temper. She would grow easily agitated with herself because she perceived her MS as weakness, not illness. At her worst times going through it, Margaret would tell him to leave her and to find a healthy wife. Someone who could be his equal, because she was certainly not. Nate spoke the words he knew she needed to hear. Nate told them to soothe her fears, but he felt differently. Things had indeed changed between them. With every twist and turn Margaret's course took, it seemed she lost some irretrievable nuance of her personality. Nate knew when she came out the other side, they would make it good again and Margaret would be mostly Margaret again. There was a glimmer of the warm happy excited woman he knew. However, the glimmer lost some light every time.

"DADDY!!" James screamed. "DADDY!!! Mama is on the floor!" Nate snapped out of his thinking and was up in a shot. He serpentined down the hallway to avoid the toys that littered his path. Margaret was lying on the kitchen tile in the fetal position with her hands wrapped protectively around her belly. As scared as the boy was, he was patting Margaret on her back. "It's okay, Mama. Daddy is here. He will fix you." *No pressure kid.*

"Are you alright? Can you sit up?" Lola was sitting in front of Margaret and resting her head on her belly, protecting Freshie.

"Yes, I can." She took a big breath and sat herself up. "Nate, it was crazy." She peeled her loose hair off of her sweaty forehead and tried to pull her hair back. Her shaking hands could only manage a sloppy sort of bun.

"Did you fall? Was something on the floor?" Nate looked her over for signs of injury.

Margaret was wild-eyed and almost panting. "None of those. I was washing dishes and this weird pain started on my left hip across my lower back. Almost like a phone buzzing. I even grabbed for my back pocket. All of a sudden, searing pain as white-hot as lightning came full force down my right leg and up to my waist. I... I couldn't talk. My legs buckled, so I went down. I twisted myself so I didn't land on Freshie. Margaret's breathing was slowing. Nate helped Margaret slowly stand up on shaky legs. Standing in place, she looked down at her feet. She was not optimistic .

"It's probably my sciatic nerve," Margaret offered. "The baby could be sitting funny in there."

"Okay, we'll take it easy tonight and we will call the doctor tomorrow." Margaret leaned into Nate's arms, the safest place she could think of. After navigating the hall together, Nate placed Lola in bed next to his wife. Wielding the television remote and the heating pad, she scanned the channels, stopping on reruns of *The Office*.

As soon as the bedroom door closed, Margaret covered her face. She had never felt pain so instant and ferocious. "Holy shit," she said out loud. Lola licked and nosed Margaret's hand. It had been a really panicky time for Lola and she was comforting her person. "You are such a good girl, La. Thank you for watching me." She pet Lola and gave her smooches. Lola cuddled up with Margaret as she picked up her phone and called Marie.

"I was just thinking about you," Marie said as she answered her phone.

"Was I naked?" Margaret asked.

"Yes, I have a thing for naked pregnant broads with ginormous jugs."

"I knew it!" declared Margaret. "Actually, I have to ruin this with some serious talk."

"Of course, Mama. Whatcha got? What happened? Am I punching someone?"

"Okay, first of all, I love how fired up you get. It's obvious you want me."

"Obviously. Other than that, what's going on?"

"I am not even sure what happened. Probably sciatica. It was the most intense pain in my life. Even my right ass cheek. Right to the hole!"

"Wait, you literally had a pain in your ass?" Marie couldn't help it. It was too good to pass up.

"Marie, between you and me. I have never been so scared. It was only a minute or so, but the pain made it feel like an eternity."

"I'm a little lost. Start from the beginning."

So, Margaret did. The retelling made what happened scarier. The pain felt much more real. "Nate was there. I didn't tell him about the butt pain. I would rather not share the story of my hole feeling like it was hit by lightning."

Marie tssked. "I can understand the edit, it's embarrassing. You can tell him though— he is your husband."

"Yeah, maybe I can. I am not going to though. I don't even fart in front of him. This is too much."

"Are you kidding me? Not even a silent creeper you can blame on the dog? I've seen you eat. There is no way you have survived a night of Mexican without so much as a tiny trumpet" Marie had a way of making Margaret smile when nothing else could.

"You really are completely disgusting. You are probably over there ripping ass like a barnyard animal. Does William wake up light-headed?"

Marie chuckled. "Sometimes."

"My Lord, you are foul."

"Okay, back to your asshole." Margaret sighed.

"Seriously, you are an asshole."

"Alright, back to the hopefully isolated situation. There is nothing to see. Nothing to worry about. Keep it moving," Marie offered optimistically.

"Exactly. We are going to ignore this little blip and keep it moving. Isolated incident." Margaret sighed. "Nate still wants me to go to the doctor tomorrow."

"Yeah, it is a good idea. I agree with Nate."

"I am going to go lay all over myself and watch TV with the dog. I will stalk you tomorrow."

Margaret hung up the phone, and pulled Lola to her. The little chihuahua curled into a brown ball next to Margaret's belly. Together, they watched Dwight talk about money beets.

A few hours later, unable to get comfortable, Margaret could not fall asleep. *Oh no,* thought Margaret. The weird feeling buzzed her left hip and across her back. Within three seconds, the lighting took over her right side. Her leg shot out and stiffened. Margaret pulled a pillow onto her face to muffle her scream of pain. The pain was more severe and had gone further up. She rocked her body and tried to keep breathing.

grace

Nate was woken up by what he thought was Lola whimpering. Still half asleep, he could feel Lola curled under the covers. Realizing it was not the dog who was whimpering, he whipped his head around to look at Margaret. His wife had her face smashed in her pillow, her body stiff with pain. Nate vaulted over her and was next to her side of the bed, his hand on her cheek. "Do you want to go to the hospital?" Her head went back and forth, unable to talk. In her head, she was counting. *How long would this last?* When Margaret got to 35, it started to abate. Her breaths became more regular and she lifted her head from the pillow.

"Nate, I am..." she hesitated. "This didn't happen with James."

"We can go to the hospital right now. I will grab James and we're out of here."

"It's the middle of the night, no, please don't wake him. I can see Dr. Bunem tomorrow." She was exhausted. The episode, or whatever it was, drained her. "I will call the doctor at eight a.m. They will see me."

"Okay, but what if there are no available appointments?"

"I'm high risk— they'll see me. Even if it's just to check on Freshie." Margaret rubbed her belly to soothe herself and the baby.

"Okay, then I'll take the day off so I'm available." Nate grabbed his phone to email work.

"No, you will not lose a day for this. If the doctor thinks I need to go, you know I will." Margaret's pride overrode her fear. She had argued about how she could do this and how he shouldn't worry, though now, it was all either of them could do.

"Seriously? Do you think it's a good idea to go alone?" Nate knew he should go to the appointment.

If he did though, he would miss his own appointment. "I am not a fan of you doing this alone." He had to play this carefully.

"Fan or not, I can and will handle this. I can go in between outbursts or whatever these are. The doctor is close and I am sure the appointment will be short."

"You are a tough woman. Let me know if you change your mind. I will go."

"Of course you would go, but really, I can do it on my own. It's time to get some sleep. James will be up at the crack." Margaret turned and closed her eyes, praying to sleep through the night without another one of these isolated incidents.

Spooned up behind her, Nate rested his hand on her belly. Soon, he could hear the familiar sound of Margaret's sleep breathing. He used her rhythm of breath to steady his own. Nate was truly worried. How could he not be? He needed to brace himself for what was to come. Nate wrapped himself around Margaret, squeezing her more snuggly to him. He breathed in the scent of her shampoo and face lotion. The worry rooted deeper by the second, vining it's way through Nate's mind. No matter what else he was thinking, it would soon get choked out to make more room for his growing concern and guilt. Sleep left him. All he could do was hold Margaret.

When morning finally decided to rise, a slim bit of sun was starting its journey across the bedroom carpet. Nate reached over and dismissed his alarm, not waiting for it to go off. Mercifully, Margaret had fallen asleep. He pulled his Matrix type moves to extricate himself from beside her, moving the bed as little as possible. He could get the coffee going and poke his head in on James. Hopefully, Margaret would keep sleeping for a bit.

Nate gingerly turned the knob until it released from the jam. He peaked in on James. Of course, James was already up and wearing Weebs as a cape. Weebs was James's blanket and constant companion. The boy's hair had been assaulted by his pillow. His big brown eyes blinked and there was a goofy grin on his face. "Morning, Daddy. I got myself breakfast."

"I see you did, Pal." Nate was going to let the pudding cup for breakfast go. It seemed like a good choice. The pudding cup had bite marks. "Did you need to bite it open?"

"Yes. See, like this." James picked up another pudding cup, opened his mouth, and pushed his top teeth through the foil. James looked at Nate with some leftover pudding on his face, beaming with pride. "I was going to ask, but you and Mama were sleeping. I did what I had to do, Dad."

Nate let out a laugh. *This kid.*

Margaret's eyes were squinty and only committed to opening halfway, as if fully waking up would somehow end this pain-free moment. Last night had been brutal on Margaret. She let out a deep sigh. "Time to deal with this." Then, she heaved her pregnant self into a sitting position. She picked up her phone from the end table and checked the time. Not even eight a.m. No need for the on-call doctor. She would call when the office was open. Margaret was on her way to the kitchen when it happened again. This time, the pain roared down her right side and sent her crashing into the wall, knocking a picture of James off the wall. Margaret crumpled to the floor, the corner of the wood and glass picture frame cut her back. With her hands balled up and her left leg under the pile of Margaret, the pain continued to ravage her right side. Her leg was sticking straight out, rigid and trembling. Through clenched teeth, Margaret growled in pain. Nate and James heard her fall.

"Mama!" James looked at his dad.

Nate fixed his face, bluffing calm. "Buddy, wait here. I will be right back."

"Okay, Dad." His little fists were wrapped in Weebs.

"Margaret, it's alright. I'm here." Nate took the picture off of his wife and checked her back. *Oh man.* The cut was bleeding, but it didn't look deep. *Thank God.* Nate sat on the floor with Margaret's head in his lap and he stroked the hair away from her face, doing what he could to make her any kind of comfortable.

"Nate." Tears filled her eyes. "This hurts so damn bad," Margaret said through gritted teeth. With all her concentration, she focused her breathing. *Inhale...exhale...inhale...exhale. In through the nose, out through the nose.* "11, 12, 13, 14...."

TWELVE

CHELSEA STRETCHED OUT like a cat. Sleep deprived and groggy, she reached for the ringing phone. It was Margaret. Chelsea smiled, knowing it would not be picked up. She rolled over to Nate. "Looks like your wife is calling."

Nate looked at the phone but let it ring. Margaret was calling about the doctor's appointment she went to, alone.

"Yes it was. I am going to have to call her back. It was a bad night. Listen, you have been great with the changes. I know it puts "us" off a little longer." Nate kissed her slowly as she moaned in his mouth. He was instantly hard. This "arrangement" was not supposed to turn into a relationship, but became more than either of them planned for. Originally, Nate had just wanted something for himself. To escape the overwhelming reality of his day-to-day. Somehow, this woman was under his skin and he was under her spell.

Yes, Nate had feelings. But he also had a pregnant and disabled wife and young son to think about. Margaret used to be fun and up for anything. Happy and optimistic about their future. With both of them working

57

and making good money, they were on track to a home and a secure financial future. Years of her chronic illness had extinguished the fire Margaret had in her soul. Nate couldn't help but see her differently. When a man goes from buying lingerie and high heels to heating pads and a TENS machine, things will inevitably change. Compartmentalizing worked for Nate so far. His feelings for Margaret: love, sadness, guilt, anger. They were kept in their own place. His son, the most precious of all, was in all the best places of his heart and soul. With Chelsea, he could be someone else with her and to her. He didn't have to be on the lookout for uneven flooring, or worry about core temperature and bowing out early because of fatigue. Chelsea's energy was astounding. She was how Margaret used to be. He did not want a life controlled by illness.

Nate traced the curve of her hip and asked "Everything is great how it is. Haven't these last couple of months been fun for you?" They had met at the gym during one of Nate's midday work out sessions. He decided to try yoga to stretch out his hamstrings. Now, Chelsea was his midday workout session.

"I agree, we've been having fun. I want more though, Nate. Don't you? Someone who can keep up with you." Chelsea kissed him slowly. Her hands slid down his back.

The mention of "more" tightened his chest. Nate audibly exhaled. Chelsea provoked a desire he didn't know he was capable of. Margaret was a solid wife. No matter how much pain she was in or how scared she was, Margaret remained his adoring wife. Nate would never actually leave Margaret. He didn't want to go out as the guy who left his handicapped wife and kids. However, when Chelsea touched his skin, Nate was willing to be any guy she needed.

"Hey, how about we let this go for now? You're naked. I'm naked." Chelsea pointed at herself. "Seems wasteful to spend all this skin on talking." Chelsea kissed Nate on the mouth. Her tongue licked his lips and she let her kiss linger. Their mouths were barely separated, sharing one another's breath. Nate slid his hand to the base of her skull, grabbed a fistful of her thick honey colored hair, and squeezed. Chelsea's head fell back with a smile. He put his open mouth on her neck and bit hard enough to feel Chelsea give. Her body went hot when Nate had her by her hair. Chelsea's will broke when he bit her on the neck. Nate put his lips to her ear and whispered, "Are you going to come for me?"

"Make me." Chelsea inhaled deeply, looked at him with fire in her eyes. "Make me." Nate wrapped one muscular arm around her waist. In an instant, Chelsea was on her back. He had quite the grip.

"So you can't get away." He dragged his lips down to her nipples. Chelsea let out a deep moan. Going back and forth between them, Nate sucked them both until her nipples were stiff. He slid his body up over her and whispered in her ear, "Are you ready?"

"Yessss." Her body arched. The heat in her body built up a magnetic sexual momentum— nothing could stop what was coming. Nate slid his hand down her flat stomach. Chelsea's hand met his halfway down, grabbed his, and buried two of his fingers inside her. "Oooooohhhh." His fingers stayed inside her. He pushed into her deep and slow. Nate went down and took her in his mouth and started sucking on her clit and fingering her in deep, steady thrusts. Chelsea clutched the sheets and yelled out. "Yesssss, go harder. Faster. Ohhhhhhh." She then wrapped her legs around Nate's head. "Keep eating me. Don't stop. Uuuuuuuhhh." Chelsea's body was Nate's to have. Her whole body was consumed by fire. She could feel Nate's fingers push deep inside her. Staying in and coaxing her with the last few breaths. Chelsea came hard, her arching back pushed her chest up into the air. "UUUUUUUUUUGH," she screamed as she came on Nate's face.

Nate smiled, wiped his hand around his mouth, then kissed her pussy slowly and licked her lips. Chelsea was beside herself. "You have to fuck me. I need it, Nate. Fuck me. "

Nate flipped her over and grabbed her hips. He pulled her up to her hands and knees. "I'm gonna fuck you slowly. I want you to come all over me again." He pushed himself into her. She yelped and grunted. She was completely full of him. It started out slow and she felt every inch. It was sweet torture. He turned her over, but stayed inside her. "I want to watch you come for me." He was on top of her. Then, he pulled back and thrusted hard.

"OOOOOOOHHHH!" Chelsea was on the ledge. As Nate slid out, her legs wrapped around his back and pulled him all the way back in. She held him there. She let him out and slammed him back into her in perfect rhythm with his thrusts. Chelsea screamed as an orgasm shook her. The feel of her pussy contracting pushed Nate off the edge. He came in her, all of his muscles stiffening. They fell into a tangle of sweaty arms and legs.

Later in the afternoon, Nate walked through the front door of their apartment. He let his gym bag slide off of his shoulder. It hit the tile with a loud smack. Other than the time of no thinking Nate got with Chelsea, his day was packed with work appointments, meetings, and deadlines. Margaret didn't pick up when he called her back, so he was sure the doctor appointment went well. He did have some guilt over aquessing about going to the doctor with her. Although he hoped to not be bombarded by an overexcited James and a Margaret full of questions. He was not ready to immerse himself in home. Luckily, Margaret and James were asleep in their beds. Nate made sure to stay quiet and not wake them. He hopped in the shower to clean his day off of him and got back into a husband's frame of mind. When Nate stepped out of the bathroom, Margaret was waiting for him.

"You were gone for a bit, huh?" Margaret made more of a statement than a question.

"Yeah, most of the time my coworkers are profile pictures attached to chat boxes. When we get the opportunity to get together, we can get pretty chatty." Nate gave her a smile and a kiss on the cheek. He sat on his side of the bed and started getting his sweats on. Margaret slid under the covers, "Where did you guy's go?" Margaret was hurt and disappointed in Nate. She would not have expected Nate not to go. However, he could have come home early. Or, maybe more than one attempt to call home. After the last couple of days, she had no energy to give for this.

"Sorry the night went so long. I did try to call you back but you didn't pick up. Do you want to tell me how the appointment went?" He put his hand on her shoulder. "Does he know why this is happening?"

"The baby is fine," then Margaret paused to take a deep breath. "It's me Nate. I am in what seems like the beginning of a flare up. Even though pregnancy can put Multiple Sclerosis in remission, for me it hasn't. I am so sorry to put us here again." Tears rolled down her face.

When Nate wrapped his arms around her, she broke down sobbing. She didn't need him to say anything. All Margaret needed was for Nate to be there.

Her coach bag was vibrating. Marie unzipped the top and fished out her phone. She saw it was Margaret. Instantly, she felt terrible. Her friend had called this morning. Not able to pick up then, Marie let her go to voicemail. Being so busy with clients, Marie had forgotten to call back. She hit the green button and started talking before the call could connect.

"Hey. Listen, before you say anything, I suck. I know it."

"Oh, you most certainly do suck. Yes, absolutely." Margaret didn't sound miffed. "The reason I called was because I had another one of those episodes."

"Is that what they are? Episodes?"

"Unless you have a better word for it. Anywho, I went to the doctor. Seems as if the pain I have is not sciatica related."

Marie got her serious tone. "Hmmmm. And?"

"And I am having a flare up. The pain is going up and down my whole right side. Sciatic nerve pain is in the lower extremities, butt, and back." Marie heard Margaret's long disappointed sigh.

"I thought MS went into remission when a person is pregnant. No?" asked Marie.

"Most times it does. It's not a guarantee. In my case, nope. It seems I am an exception to the rule."

"It will be okay. What did the doctor say you should do? Is there anything I can do? Please, let me know. This sucks. I love you, my friend. This will be alright."

Margaret despised when people said those words. However, no one could know the right thing to say. Margaret wasn't sure she knew the right thing to say either.

"I love your optimism. However, I want to punch things right now. There is not one part of me that has not been impacted. How I eat, sleep, walk, talk. How I have sex. Nate must be so done with me and I can't blame him. Damn it! I am tired of crying, worrying, always anticipating the next fall. Every single damn day, it finds a way to remind me of what I am not anymore. What I will never be again. I thought I could do this. Jesus, I am an idiot."

"I love you. You are amazing and you are doing a great job." Marie was stepping gently. "This is brave of you. I have no desire to throw down another baby right now. It looks too difficult. You still go to the gym and do yoga. When I was pregnant with Greyson, I ate and complained my way through it."

"Yeah, you really did." Margaret chuckled, wiping her tears.

"I was a majestic beast." Marie said in an uppity way. "Now, what are we going to do about all this?" Uppity, all gone.

"Nate spoke with the neurologist today, however, I don't know if there's anything I can do."

"Why? What do you mean?"

"There is no way I am doing a run of steroids. It is supposed to help with the inflammation. But, what about Freshie? I do not feel good about it. As it is, Dr. Bunem told me it was fine to take Hydrocodone. Which is a big NO for me."

"Wait, what? I don't even know what to say. How could that be okay for the baby?"

"I know, right? I was thinking the same thing. Those pills couldn't help me anyway. The pain doesn't just happen only when I am sitting, or standing, or something. It just happens spontaneously. My only warning is the two-second vibration I get across my hips. Within two seconds of the vibration, I am on the floor. The pain is more intense and further reaching every time." Margaret's fear was woven through her words. "Poor little James, too. Can you even imagine how scared this must be for him?"

"James is a lucky boy to have such a superhero for a mom. I bet the little man is more concerned with you. Try not to feel too bad, Mama. Life is messy. You're bound to get some on you."

"Nate tells me this will help James build character and grow up to be a strong person, which of course I want him to be. However, there are all sorts of ways a person can build their character. Why does it have to be this way for James? Building character from watching his mom falling apart?"

There was nothing Marie could say, so she said nothing. The friends kept each other company on the phone in silence. Neither of them were speaking or hanging up. They just listened to the other's breathing and felt better because the other was close.

THIRTEEN

NATE SAT ON THE ground beside his wife and watched her helplessly curled up on the floor again. It had been a couple of weeks since confirming the flare-up with Margaret's neurologist. All this time, the episodes grew in frequency, topping out at six or seven a day. The pain had become more disabling, dropping her to the floor. With no way of having control of *when* it would happen, Margaret did her best to handle *how* it would happen. No crying or yelling through the pain. The more keyed up she would get the tighter the grip of pain would be. She would try to keep calm while hissing the count between clenched teeth. "1, 2, 3...." This was where James came in.

James was very protective of his mama. During these character building moments, James was her bravest boy. He gently stroked his mom's head, encouraging her the whole way as he counted along with her, "1, 2, 3, 4... Mama, you're doing great." Then he would jump back into the count "...8, 9, 10..." When the pain subsided, James helped his mom rotate her ankles and move her feet and offered his official assessment of Margaret's sturdiness. After- ward, James and Nate would each take a hand. They gave her support while a dizzy Margaret slowly got to her feet.

The episodes became more aggressive. Margaret was always left with a vice grip of a headache. "Thank you, guys. I do not know what I would do without you." She was happy to have the answer to this question.

"You don't have to know. We will always be here," Nate assured her as he took her into his arms. Their heads bowed. Weaving themselves together, Nate's and Margaret's hearts beat in time with each other.

"I love you," Nate whispered.

"I love you too," Margaret said softly in Nate's ear.

"We love you too," James said, holding little Lola in his arms. He smooshed himself and Lola into his parents' legs.

Margaret refused to let pain or its severity dictate her days. However, she was certainly thankful that this Thanksgiving was a quiet one, just the three of them. In the morning, the Halls cuddled up on the couch to watch the parade on television. They waited until the very end when Santa made his debut and waved, marking the official start to the holiday season. The highlight of the day was when James wrestled an entire turkey, winning its leg as his prize. He looked like one of those kids at the Renaissance fairs, wielding his huge drumstick with grease dribbling down his arm and chin. There were a few times during the day when the pain reminded her it was still in control. Once, she almost dropped the carving knife on her foot. Thankful again— it missed her foot by an inch and stuck up from the linoleum.

November trudged into December and Margaret was still having numerous painful episodes. But James was having a holiday party at his school and what a mom brings to the holiday party can make or break her standing, as well as that of her son. When the party planning first began, a very ambitious, show-offy Margaret happily volunteered to make cookies for James's class. Gingerbread men with candy window pane middles. When it came to actually making them, Margaret became quite aware of her baking arrogance.

"Why didn't I just keep it to sugar cookies?" She said aloud. Margaret was attempting to raise an army of tasty cookie troops. Usually confident in the kitchen, these ginger jackass cookies bested Margaret. As she was shaping her dough into a flat disk, Nate walked into the kitchen.

"Wow, what happened? Did someone fill our flour with dynamite? There appears to have been an explosion." Nate's attempt at humor was not met with a smile from his wife.

"Nate, I am ready to pull my hair out. How could cookies be this difficult? The first batch of dough was a failure so it went right in the trash. I got the molasses all wrong. I used dark instead of light.

"Does the molasses make a big difference?" Nate couldn't imagine it would.

"The dark molasses isn't as sweet, but I didn't bother to taste it. Threw it out."

Margaret was tossing a plastic pile of people shapes in the trash. Whipping each one hand over feet. "I had to get new cutters too. These special safety BPA-free plastic cookie cutters suck ass and don't cut clean." Margaret punctuated her words with the chucking of cookie cutters.

"Screw those cookies, Margaret. These little rat-handed kids won't notice or care. I will run to the store and grab some store bought goodness, arrange it on one of our trays, and we can call it done." Nate's suggestion might as well have been a poorly timed fart. The look on Margaret's face spoke flatulence.

"What did you just say?" Her face still wrinkled as if she had smelled something bad. "I said, I would bring gingerbread men. They need to be real homemade ones and not some store bought bunk. As if the mom coven won't be judging everyone?"

Nate, who was leaning in the doorway, put up his hands in surrender. He was not about to cross Margaret in the kitchen. She finished wrapping the gingery disk and placed it in the fridge. "Now, only four hours and I will be on my way to complete insanity. I swear, if these don't come out right, I am going on a merry murdering spree."

"Can I help?"

"With my murdering spree? Kind of thought of it as a one man job," Margaret smiled, momentarily forgetting about the cookies.

"I meant the gingerbread army you're bringing to life. I am not saying you need my help. I just want to be around my sweet wife." Margaret raised an eyebrow in suspicion.

"Mmhmm, sweet huh?" She sized him up.

"The sweetest." Nate smiled and leaned over her small, round belly. Nate kissed his wife, who smelled of ginger and vanilla. "These will be the best cookies those kids have ever tasted. Besides, if anyone tries to show you up, I will crush their inferior cookies with my bare hands."

Margaret couldn't help laughing. "You would crush cookies in front of little children? At a class party?" She placed her hands on Nate's chest.

grace

"Pssssshhtt. Easy. I am not above making little kids cry. Their tears are my salve." Margaret gave Nate a light smack to his chest and kissed him.

"You are a diabolical man. Do I have to sleep with one eye open, Crusher?" Margaret winked.

"You'd better— never know when I am coming for you." He went in and bit her neck.

FOURTEEN

WITH TWO TRAYS OF gingerbread men with window pane middles, the Hall's made their way to James's classroom the next morning. When the commotion of arrival quieted down, the teachers motioned the parents to rows of way too small wooden school chairs. Grown-ups did some form of clumsy body origami to get their grown selves seated. The children went behind a curtain made from the story time quilt. The parents could hear giggles and the rustle of papers. Miss Jenny, the teacher, shushed them to quiet down— the show was about to begin.

The curtain opened to a goofy-faced, three-foot, cardboard snowman surrounded by equally goofy kids. *Frosty the Snowman* began to play. As the gaggle of little ones made a wiggly line across the stage, Margaret's heart squeezed. She was the class parent the day the kids had so much fun making their scarves. Their sweet little faces were proudly wearing the red felt scarves they decorated. Poms-poms were haphazardly glued on some, while others were weighed down by gold glitter, and a few used garland for real pizzazz. The glitter from James's scarf was in his hair and on his lashes; he was her little smiley disco ball.

grace

The parents sat on those tiny chairs not only through *Frosty* but, through two other equally spirited holiday diddies. With the entertainment portion ended, grown-ups unfolded themselves from those hobbit chairs. Nate and Margaret gave the cookie table a side-eyed once over and happened upon truly dreamy snowflake cookies. They were magically swirled in white icing and dusted in edible opalescent glitter. Nate motioned underneath the table as if he was about to flip it. "I swear, I will do it," He whispered in her ear. "Give me the go ahead." Margaret snickered, unable to cover her mouth before a spray of cookie crumbs whistled out. Nate laughed and Margaret quietly shook with laughter and a mouthful of cookie.

Miss Jenny smiled with pride during the tour of the new story corner while she showed off the new Suess corner. They were admiring the *Green Eggs and Ham*, pictures the kids had drawn when poker hot pain ripped down Margaret's side, and set her leg on fire with pain. Years of Margaret's MS had taught Nate to be ever watchful and always within reach. He quickly stepped back and behind Margaret and braced her against a fall. The giant plaid reading chair was a blessing, as it was both close and forgiving. Margaret plopped down into the cushy seat and all around her, people spoke. It was as if she could hear each voice individually and all at once. The laughter, squealing, and all the other everyday noises amplified in her ears. "Vroom vroom," from somewhere behind her. Margaret was frozen in pain with no signs of moving anytime soon. Nate stood in front to shield Margaret and give her space to recover. When he reached his right hand behind his back, Margaret took his hand, kissed it, and put it to her cheek. Margaret swayed back and forth, rocked herself while her eyes welled with tears, and silently counted. When Margaret got to thirty-three, the pain started to abate. The headache and dizziness always lingered. Margaret leaned into Nate, took a deep breath and cautiously pushed up to standing. After testing her feet, she smoothed her green maternity sweater. Both of them looked around to gauge whether or not anyone had seen.

"I don't think anyone saw anything. Look, James is off with his buddies and not one person is looking our way," Nate reassured a doubtful Margaret.

"Are you sure? I am not in the mood to try and explain this," Margaret said, making a circling gesture head-to-toe.

"Yeah, you're good. Lean on me and I've got you."

Margaret loved this man so much. "I love you, jerk." She let her husband support her.

"I love you too, jerk." Margaret rested her head on Nate's shoulder.

Margaret needed another minute. She and Nate stood together and took in the sight of the kids. The combination of sugar and upcoming school vacation turned the kids to rubber and had them bouncing off the walls. Clusters of little ones each engaged in some sort of shenanigans. James and his buddy, Bayley, were knee-deep in Thomas the Tank Engine. Wooden tracks and hills snaked around the play kitchen.

"Mama, Dad!" An excited James zipped over to them, a white wooden lighthouse in his grip. "Look at this!" The light inside turned on and a tiny foghorn bellowed. "Isn't it great? Can I ask Santa for one?" It was impossible not to get caught up in James's happy mood. Margaret gave his hair a little rustle.

"Sure, Sweetie. Is there anything else you want from Santa Claus?"

James stopped to look at his mom.

He put his hand on Margaret's and hoped his mama understood. James said, "Mama, Santa does not have claws. He has feet."

Several days later, Margaret was standing at her kitchen island. Dark roasted gloriousness filled her Mazel mug. Yes, Margaret knew about drinking caffeine while pregnant. One coffee couldn't cause harm. However, Margaret with no coffee could and would definitely cause harm.

Flipping through a baby furniture store flyer, it suddenly dawned on her: It was almost noon and she hadn't had an episode all morning. With a small smile on her lips, Margaret gave her hips a little sway back and forth. She took stock of herself. Margaret flexed each foot and made small circles with her ankle. She shifted her weight from left to right and did not feel dizzy.. Everything seemed okay. *Could it be? This pain was not here to stay?* Not wanting to be recklessly optimistic, Margaret kept it to herself. For the next week, the episodes still interrupted Margaret's life. However, they became shorter. Now, James couldn't even count up to thirty before Margaret would start to come around. The dizziness and nausea showed mercy as well. It was two days before Christmas and Margaret had not one episode the whole day.

Margaret gave a light knock on their bedroom doorway. "Hey, Babe. Are you busy?"

Nate popped his left ear from his headset, "No, why? What's up?"

"Your wife has not had an episode all day. The whole day. Since I woke up at six with James." Nate's smile spread across his whole face and she could see his relief.

"Get over here, woman. I'm gonna lay one on you." Margaret went to Nate's desk. He turned and placed a kiss on her belly. Then, he stood up and kissed his wife. "Now, do you think it's settling down? I was afraid you would be this way from here on out."

"You, were afraid? I was bargaining with the Lord."

"FYI, I was ready to make him a deal myself." Nate smiled his idiot smile.

"I don't doubt it. Hey, we had a good run." She returned his smile.

"We did, didn't we?" They high fived.

"Nate, MS has no rules. But, I am calling today a win."

"A definite win." The two high fived again. Margaret went to round up James for a bath. Nate resituated his headset and brought his screens back up. He had been working twelve hour days. The goal of saving up quickly became a goal of keeping up. A weary "Holy Christ" fell out of Nate's mouth. He rolled his desk chair closer to his desk and went back to work.

FIFTEEN

Soft music played in the dimly lit yoga studio. Chelsea was closing out the practice. "Please go from your seated pose into a savasana corpse pose. Please adapt the pose so you are comfortable in the pose. You may place your feet apart and drop your knees together. Or, if you would prefer, you may lay on your side." After a few minutes, Chelsea had the class slowly return to a simple seated position. "Inhale. Hands out to the side and above your head. Bring the hands together. Lower them into a prayer position. One more deep slow inhale. Then, exhale." She bowed her head to the class. "Namaste."

"Namaste" the class answered in unison, bowing their heads in return.

Margaret rolled up her mat and put it in its blue canvas bag. She was searching her purse for the car keys. "Hello there, yoga mama." Chelsea said, offering a hand to pull Margaret up to stand.

"Hey." Margaret said, taking Chelsea's hand. Margaret stood up. "Thanks for the hand. It is getting increasingly difficult." Margaret gave her belly an affectionate rub. Chelsea slid her shirt over her tank.

"You are doing great. Not many pregnant women are throwing down crow pose."

"Thanks, it's been a bit more complicated than I had anticipated. I'm still in it though."

Chelsea gave a small shake of her head.

"After this, I am doing a little more shopping for Christmas Eve dinner. What are you up to for the holidays?" Margaret asked as they both went outside into the chilly evening.

"Unfortunately, my plans fell through. I will be spending time until Christmas working at the salon." Chelsea only taught yoga part-time. Hair was her business. "Then, be lazy for the big day. Watch old black and white Christmas movies."

Margaret shook her head back and forth as if she could not stand for such an answer.

"Chelsea, you should come over to our place on Christmas Eve. It will only be a few of us. You know Marie from here." Chelsea and Marie worked together, but they were not friendly. For reasons Marie could not place, she didn't vibe with Chelsea. "And, Jeff will be there. My cute and single brother-in-law."

"Get out of here!" Chelsea laughed. "No set-ups. They're always so awkward."

"Okay, no pressure. You should come though. It will be a great time." Margaret smiled and raised her eyebrows, not yet giving up on the idea of Chelsea and Jeff.

"Alright. I'll come over. What should I bring?"

"Just bring yourself. I have everything else taken care of." Margaret left her with their address and phone number.

Chelsea was proud of herself. The gym had three locations and as of two months ago, Chelsea had not been scheduled to work at one the Halls used. A few subtle comments to the manager at the gym and she was in. Chelsea hoped the yoga classes two days a week would be enough to cross paths. And here she was with a freshly crossed path. Even better, this path would put her in Nate's path. Right in the middle of it for Christmas. She couldn't wait to see the smile on Nate's face.

"Helloooooo!" Chelsea sang out as she opened the door to the hotel room. She kicked off her sneakers then walked into the bathroom. Chelsea could hear the shower was running. Perfect timing. The glass shower doors were opaque with steam. The shower door clicked and Nate turned to see Chelsea standing naked with her legs apart. Her honey colored hair spilled down her back and across her face. He could still see her slate eyes and a mischievous smile. Nate stepped close and kissed her deep. He kept his eyes locked on Chelsea's gaze and went to his knees. He barely touched her with his tongue and licked Chelsea in soft strokes. Nate threw Chelsea's leg over his shoulder and put his mouth over her. He kissed her pussy as deep as he had kissed her mouth.

She moaned. Chelsea loved the way he ate her.

Nate reached up and squeezed her nipple between his fingers. She gasped and moaned.

"Say it to me. What do you want?" He was still on his knees. He licked and fingered her slowly. Chelsea went on her toes. Then, she sat down onto Nate's hand. Slowly, Chelsea slid Nate's fingers out. They were slick and warm. She brought his fingers to her mouth and licked them. Then, she put his hand on her throat.

"Fuck me." Chelsea's words came out in airy whispers. Nate stood up and shoved his tongue in Chelsea's mouth. He turned her around and pressed her wet body against the glass shower wall. Nate stepped back to admire her. She had the softest skin and her tanned body was lithe and strong from yoga. Chelsea stood there naked and waiting for Nate. He loved making her wait to get fucked. He tasted and licked her until he couldn't wait any longer himself. He licked and bit her neck and pulled her head back by her hair. Nate again reached around her throat and squeezed lightly. A satisfied hiss left Chelsea's mouth. With his other hand, Nate pushed up into Chelsea.

"Oooohhh. Harder."

"Mmm... mmm... mmm." Every thrust of Nate's hand went deep inside Chelsea. He knew she wanted more. "Let's get out of the shower. You need me to fuck you." They walked out of the bathroom, but Nate didn't let her get far. Chelsea had to grab the door frame. Nate's hot hands were already on her. From behind her, he squeezed her nipples. Nate's whispered in Chelsea's ear, "I'm going to fuck you so hard. This feels— mmmmmmhh." Nate pushed her down on the bed and climbed on top of her and made her his.

They were both so full of need. Nate drove himself into Chelsea and she immediately wrapped her legs around him. Chelsea pulled him in with every push Nate gave. One after the other their orgasms shook them. After they were both spent they clutched one another, letting the aftershocks pulse through their bodies and fizzle out.

Chelsea was curled up in the hotel's king sized bed wearing her Yankees t-shirt and relaxing on a pile of pillows. Nate walked over and gave her a coffee from the downstairs lobby.

"Well, this is perfect...." He looked at her t-shirt and shook his head. "A Yankees fan." His mouth scrunched into an annoyed frown. "You need a Sox shirt." With his own coffee in hand, he scooted around the other side of the bed and slipped under the blankets.

"How long do we have?" Chelsea needed more time with Nate.

"About half an hour," Nate responded. "I have to get home. With work and the holidays, things are crazy at home."

"What do you guys have planned for Christmas?" she asked as if she didn't already know. She smiled at the notion of Christmas with the man she wanted. She blurred Margaret out of her mental pictures.

"We're having our friends and my brother Jeff over for Christmas Eve." Nate saw a look flash across her face. "Is there something wrong?" Chelsea's expression almost betrayed her surprise for Nate. She would be there with his family. In his house with him, closer to him. She might get a Christmas kiss. She was briefly lost in thought when Nate said her name and placed a small velvet box in her hand.

"I got you something for Christmas. Yeah, yeah, we said no gifts." Nate wanted to reward her. She had brought out the primitive, testosterone-driven side of him.

"Nate, what did you do?" The silver bow on the box was waiting to be pulled. She gave the ribbon a tug and it fell to the floor. Chelsea opened the box and gasped.

A magnificent pair of emerald and diamond earrings were set on black velvet. The round white diamonds glittered all around the one carat emerald cut kelly green emeralds. "Oh, Nate, these are breathtaking. She freed them from the box and put the earrings on immediately. This makes me even more yours. I will always wear them so I have you with me." She leaned in and kissed him slowly. Nate could not resist her. Making out with Chelsea always led to more. Nate slipped her t-shirt over her head and twisted it to bind her hands. He licked her nipples and bit them playfully. Chelsea yelped at the bites, but loved the intense feeling. Suddenly, Nate stopped. Chelsea sat up. She pulled the shirt from around her wrists and tossed it off the bed. She looked at him for an answer.

"What?" she asked, frustrated with Nate for stopping.

"Oh shit. Damn it. I'm going to be late." He scrambled off of the bed and quickly got dressed, shoving clothes in his bag. He hastily put his button-up shirt on. "I've gotta go." Nate kissed Chelsea as he buttoned his shirt. "We have the room for the night. Leave whenever you're ready. I'm sorry to leave in such a rush. Text me later?" Chelsea rose to her knees and finished buttoning his shirt. She gave him another deep kiss.

"No worries— I can take care of it." The woman's kiss did him in. He checked his collar to make sure it was lying properly. "I love taking care of you. Yes, I will text you later. I will do what you tell me." She purred his ear. Hard as it was, Nate had to pry himself away from her. She spoiled him with her undivided attention. Chelsea was easy to be around. Being with her made him feel powerful; he felt more alive.

"Are you trying to kill me?" It was almost too much to resist. His phone rang and snapped him back to reality. "Okay. I am going." Chelsea followed him to the door.

"See you soon." Nate was already heading to the elevator. He didn't hear what she had said or see the very satisfied look on her face. Chelsea would be with

grace

Nate for Christmas. She would be with him at his house with his family. She would get to see their little boy, James. What could be more perfect? Perhaps if Margaret weren't there. However, Chelsea knew she would be close to Nate. Her eyes gleamed with excitement about how stunning she would be and outshining mousy Margaret .

SIXTEEN

"HAVE A HOLLY JOLLY Christmas...." Margaret half sang and hummed along to get in the holiday zone. She stood at the oak island Nate got her for her last birthday. She took stock of what was left to do for dinner and double checked her ingredients. Glass bowls of sliced shiitake mushrooms and diced shallots waited to be married to madeira wine and heavy cream. A head of roasted garlic was designated for mashed potatoes. Six perfect filets were wrapped in pink butcher paper. Two bottles of pinot noir, two cabernet, and a couple bottles of prosecco chilled in the fridge. Margaret spotted the clock on the back of the stove and noted people would be here soon enough. It was time for her to change out of her old Pink Floyd t-shirt and eight year old sweats and hop in the shower.

A couple hours later, Jeff spoke as he took a cocktail fork to the antipasto. "Wow, Maggs. This spread is unbelievable." He speared more marinated veggies and sharp provolone cubes and loaded his cheeks like a hamster. A charcuterie board of different cheeses with crackers, grapes, figs, and nuts held down the center of the table. Baked crab stuffed mushrooms, breaded and fried eggplant with marinara sauce. A buffet of marinated vegetables on a serving platter adjacent to a caprese salad.

"Yes, everything looks amazing. Thank you for having me. I would have spent the holiday brooding over my plans falling through." Chelsea had arrived soon after Jeff. She was a great girl. Margaret hoped Chelsea and Jeff would hit it off. "These mushrooms are ridiculous." Chelsea said, putting more on her hors d' vour plate.

"Yeah, Maggs is some kind of kitchen witch. Wait until dinner. This woman and beef? Lookout." Jeff said as he constructed another tower of food.

"There is more?" Chelsea asked.

"Oh, yes, there is more." Margaret had cleaned up nicely. She wore her shiny chestnut hair in a loose twist. Her Santa-red v-neck sweater was trimmed in white. "We are having a filet with mushrooms in a madeira wine sauce. Garlic mashed potatoes and sauteed spinach."

"Um, I went to the bakery and stood in line for like, ever. Then, I had the gruelling task of selecting desserts. Do you know how stressful it was? I damn near risked my life for those cannoli." Jeff's eyes were bright and he really got a kick out of himself. Nate walked in as Jeff finished. His dark red v-neck cable knit sweater matched the red of his wife's sweater. Margaret had to buy all of Nate's clothes for him. The payback came when she got to buy clothes for holidays and events. She always made sure they coordinated. He was just thankful that she didn't make them get Christmas photos in matching pajamas.

He walked up to Margaret and smooched her glossed lips. He noticed the wonderful display. "Wow, Margaret, you outdid yourself."

"Thanks, Nate. What looks good to you?" She thought he had meant the food. However, Nate had meant the display popping out of the v-neck of her red sweater. Margaret blushed a little. "You jerk. This is my friend, Chelsea, from the gym." Nate's stomach dropped. He turned around and came face-to-face with Chelsea. His mind could not gain purchase on what he was seeing. "Chelsea, this is my husband, Nate. You've probably seen him around the gym, too." There was a quick knock on the door. "I can tell by the knock— it's Marie."

Jeff walked out of James's room and met Margaret.

"Did she bring more food?" Jeff asked. "I will help." Jeff asked.

"You are a glutton." Margaret said on the way down the hall to get the door.

Nate followed Margaret and Jeff with his eyes to make sure they were out of sight then, he grabbed Chelsea's wrist.

"What the fuck are you doing here? Jesus, Chelsea." He was immediately on edge, but as bad as the situation seemed, he was more than a little turned on. What the hell was he supposed to do? Nate's heart was jackhammering in his chest when he noticed the earrings twinkling on Chelsea's lobes. An unspoken message just for him.

"Please don't be mad at me, Nate. I just wanted to see you at home. Baby, it's Christmas," Chelsea said, reaching out to touch his face.

Quickly, Nate moved away, worried about getting caught. Margaret, William, Marie, and Greyson sailed in, all smiles. Jeff was behind them with his arms full of coats and a disappointed expression. "No food, just coats." He shook his head at Marie. "Lame." Marie rolled her eyes.

William and Greyson wore matching forest green cable knit sweaters. Greyson was a mini version of William, right down to his smiley blue eyes. Marie loved when her husband and son matched. Marie was wearing a charcoal colored sweater dress with a thin metallic thread woven through the cashmere. There were intricate braids woven down the sides of her head and down her long shiny hair. "Merry Christmas Everyone." Marie said, "It smells fantastic in here, Margaret."

"Thank you and Merry Christmas to you, my friend." Margaret and Marie hugged. Then Margaret made the introductions. "Hey guys! Chelsea, you've met Marie. You two must have met each other at one of the gyms, right? Have you ever met Marie's husband?" Marie and Chelsea gave polite waves to one another as Margaret pointed to William. "This is her husband, William." William smiled and waved.

"Merry Christmas. Nice to meet you." William extended his hand and gave Chelsea a polite shake.

"Now, this sweet guy is Greyson." Margaret gave Greyson a hug and kiss.

"Greyson!" screamed a delighted James. The boy ran to meet his friend. His Lego Star Wars footie pajamas came shushing down the hall. "Come to my room. All my toys are set up so we can play."

"Yessss!" Greyson and James beat feet down the hall, almost mowing down Jeff on his way back from hanging up coats.

"Woah," Jeff quickly pressed his back to the wall. Then, he clapped his hands together, "Let's get festive, people."

The six of them moseyed into the kitchen to get themselves some Christmas spirit. Nate held Margaret's arm, keeping her back. Nate had to know how it came to be, Chelsea was here. "Margaret, what made you invite Chelsea?"

"I thought she would be good for your brother. He's single. She's single. They would be cute, don't you think?" Margaret whispered with a chuckle.

"I have no idea— you barely know her and I know her less than that."

"I took her class a few times, she seems perfectly nice to me." Margaret gave him a playful swat. "Oh don't be such a Christmas crab. It will be fun."

On the inside, Nate's stomach was flipping with anxiety thinking about Chelsea even being near his brother. This was some off the charts crazy. Nate was invigorated by the taboo of he and Chelsea being so close and having their secret.

The two walked into the group ready to be merry. The cork was pulled from the first bottle of wine and at the same time Margaret unscrewed the cap from a bottle of sparkling white grape juice. It was not nearly as full-bodied. The six of them cheered for the holiday and to having friends to celebrate with.

Chelsea wanted to know everything about Nate's life, which at the moment was painful. Jealousy burned in her belly as she watched Margaret, seething at her closeness to Nate. Poor Nate was always having to care for her. It was because Margaret leaned on him so much that Nate had no time or energy for himself. He was either working or at home. They didn't get near enough time together. Wives had impeded her before. It would not happen this time. She was determined to show Nate she would be the one who would love him better. He needed someone to take care of him for a change. But if loving Nate meant knowing Margaret, she could play along. "When are you due?"

"I feel like I am in my twelfth trimester. "We are having a girl. Freshie's due date is a day after my birthday. Margaret rested her head on Nate's shoulder. He kissed her head and placed a hand on her belly.

Chelsea smiled and said, "She will be beautiful just like her mom."

"Thank you, Chelsea. Hopefully she'll be a smartypants like her dad." Margaret smiled up at Nate. Nate smiled back at Margaret, keenly aware of Chelsea's gaze at the two of them.

"Aww, you two are the sweetest."

"Yeah, the sweetest." Marie could give a shit for their sweetness, she had questions. "Either one of you anywhere on a name? Or are we sticking my goddaughter with 'Freshie'?"

Margaret laughed at Marie and her need to know everything right now.

"You and Jeff will be her spiritual advisors— Obviously morals aren't really important to me. Why would giving her a name be."

"Oh, you are hilarious." Marie rolled her eyes. "So, any names?"

"We are keeping it simple. Jane. Jane Margaret Hall."

"Yay, we have a name. Freshie would have looked weird on the birth certificate." Jeff volunteered.

"So, you're telling me I waited around and listened to you read off like a zillion baby girl names and in the end, you have decided to go with Jane? Seriously? Should have expected as much from you." Marie looked at them with suspicion, then smiled. "You really are trying my patience. Jane it is."

"Cheers to sweet baby Jane," said William. They raised a glass to Jane and Margaret raised her fancy juice for a second toast. Chelsea clinked glasses with Nate last, smiling sweetly as she looked at him too long. For one hair of a second, Marie thought she noticed something between Chelsea and Nate, but then Chelsea turned her attention to Jeff. Marie didn't think she had imagined it, but the moment had passed.

"To Jeff and Marie," Margaret began. "Thank you both for being Jane's Godparents. We love you and couldn't have chosen better people. Also, feel free to save for her college."

William had caught his wife's long look at this Chelsea person. He kissed his wife behind her ear. "You are the most beautiful woman in every room," William whispered. Marie's eyes volleyed from Jeff to Chelsea. These two were certainly smiling at each other a lot. Now, she wasn't absolutely sure of what she saw. There was something about the girl Marie didn't like. Whenever they crossed paths at work, there were never any direct issues or awkwardness between them. She couldn't place it. Just some kind of something. Marie took a deep breath, turned to her husband, and kissed him fully on the lips.

Meanwhile, Jeff and Chelsea did indeed seem to hit it off. Nate kept them in his peripheral vision, which meant he had to watch Jeff and Chelsea flirt. He couldn't stand what he was seeing. All he wanted to do was grab her by the arm and drag her away. The thought of handling her made him hard.

Chelsea caught glimpses of Nate from the corner of her eye and loved every bit of his watching. All along she smiled sweetly at Jeff and twirled her blonde hair around her finger.

"So, what plans fell through? I mean, I am glad they did. Not to say I'm glad your plans got ruined... Umm...

If they are ruined…" Jeff was yammering like an idiot. In his head, he kicked his own ass.

"I was supposed to go tubing through this weekend. A bunch of us were going to head up for Christmas. You know, eating, drinking, tubing, merriment."

"Oh yeah?" Jeff's blue eyes lit up at the mention of tubing. "We went for my buddy's fortieth and it was a blast. We spent the day whipping down the hills."

"Right! I love it up there. Well, my friend's parents decided to surprise her. They showed up a few days ago. We didn't want to leave a soldier behind, so we'll go another time."

"If you do, let me know. I would love to go. Wait—not trying to invite myself. You go with uh… with who you want. I was just saying…" Jeff stopped talking. It was the best thing he could do. Every time he opened his mouth, stupid fell out. The drinks and his proximity to Chelsea made him dizzy. Margaret was right, Chelsea was quite beautiful. He thought she had the most mesmerizing blue eyes. Jeff could not pull his eyes away. A gold, off-the-shoulder sweater showed her tanned skin and she had an easy smile and full laugh. Jeff wished he was funnier just so he could hear her laugh. When he managed to pull together words in the form of conversation, Chelsea looked him right in the eye, holding his gaze prisoner and making him squirm as he spoke. The perfume she wore disarmed him. Everything about this woman disarmed him. He was caught up in the magic of Chelsea, happily distracted. He did not notice the numerous glances from his brother.

The next few hours were full of delicious food and conversation. Jeff was right. The desserts he'd chosen were amazing. The Christmas cookies were light and buttery. The cannoli were perfectly tipped in chocolate chips. Belts were undone and New Year's diet resolutions were formed. More coffee was made and with it, more cookies and cannoli disappeared.

"Well, we'd better get going." William said. "We have to go home and put together a bike. Apparently the lazy ass elves do not do assembly at the North Pole."

"Nothing worse than a lazy elf. Well, except the Elf on the Shelf. His only job is to narc on kids while squatting in everyone's house," Marie added. "So, Chelsea. What are you going to do with your Christmas? Meeting friends in town? Party 'til the partridge falls from the pear tree?" Marie watched the girl talk and to Marie, she seemed to be too much icing and not enough cake.

"Nah, no partying for me. I'm thinking I should save it for tubing. Which Jeff has invited himself to." Chelsea gave an open smile to Jeff and a nudge with her arm. Chelsea saw Nate's white knuckled grip on his coffee cup. She laughed to herself knowing she had affected him. "Actually, I think I am going to lay low. Drink some eggnog and listen to Christmas music. Throw down my mat and do some yoga."

"Sounds relaxing. Hope you don't get bored all by yourself," Marie ventured.

"Oh, I don't mind being alone. There is always something to do."

In Marie's head, she mocked Miss Namaste... *I don't mind being...pbbbbtttt.* Marie wanted so badly to raspberry the words coming out of Chelsea's mouth. It was official. This chick irked her bladder.

"We will be around, Chelsea," Margaret offered. "You are more than welcome to spend the holiday with us." Nate's body hadn't relaxed all night. The thought that Chelsea may come back damn near caused a rectal prolapse. "Well, it'll be us and Jeff. James needs Jeff or he will have no one to declare a Nerf battle on."

"And I will decimate the boy this year. No letting him win this time." Jeff threw down the first threat.

Nate laughed. "Didn't James make you yell 'mercy' just the other day during a test battle? Let me guess, you let him win? You went down in a firestorm of suction bullets. I even heard a high pitched scream and it wasn't from James."

"What you heard was my battle cry." Nate must have heard wrong.

"Oh a battle cry, was it? More like a baby's cry."

The ribbing went back and forth all the way to the door. Hats and gloves were fished from the sleeves of thick winter coats. Margaret had made sure to dole out rubbermaids of leftovers. James and Greyson begrudgingly said their goodbyes. When the door finally clicked shut, Margaret let out a sigh. She had crossed the dinner party finish line. Her back slumped as her hand went to her neck, which had been firing up since dinner.

Nate slid his hands around his wife. "I love you. You did a fantastic job tonight." He was relieved to get Chelsea out the door. He had looked forward to when he would be able to take a full breath again. If he was really lucky, his balls would make their way back down as well.

"Here is another bit of cheer. I have not had one episode since yesterday. I think we might be over the hump." She kissed him and wrapped her arms around his neck.

Nate gave his wife the sweetest smile. "I love you so much. I love our life together." He placed a kiss on his wife's cheek. His lips went to her ear and he whispered,

"So, you didn't give Jeff back the cookies from Bella Napoli, did you?"

"Are you crazy? Follow me." Nate followed Margaret like a puppy into the kitchen, where Margaret showed her husband the hidden stash of cookies. She had put them aside earlier. She knew he would be sniffing around.

"Oh, yes! You are the best," Nate said, already digging into the cookies. "Yessss, you saved me the sugar cookies with icing." With a cookie in each hand, Nate's goofy grin made Margaret laugh.

"It doesn't take much, huh?" She shook her head as she bit into a cookie. "Damn, these *are* good." She grabbed another cookie.

SEVENTEEN

CHRISTMAS DAY WAS COZY and wonderful. After making all the holiday phone calls to parents and friends, Nate, Margaret, and James spent the day playing with toys and stuffing their faces. Throughout the day, Nate got texts from Chelsea. At first, sweet Christmas wishes, but they soon evolved into pictures of her naked, wearing only a Santa hat and black boots. Here he was on Jesus's birthday eye banging dirty pictures, wondering if he could disappear into the bathroom to masturbate— again.

Jeff showed up for his holiday Nerf fight. Lines were drawn and sides of the living room claimed. Each man emptied their entire cache of ammunition in a melee where Jeff met his tragic end. Unbeknownst to him, Nate had sided with his enemy and when he least expected it, they pounced. It seemed the shooting would never end. Finally, out of bullets but full of laughs James pinned Jeff down. "Say Mercy Uncle Jeff!" Jeff lay there with his eyes closed. James got real close to Jeff's eyes. Jeff could smell the candy canes on his breath. "Are you dead, Uncle Jeff?" He leaned even closer.

Suddenly Jeff yelled out, "NEVER!!" and started tickling James. The boy collapsed into laughter powerless against his enemy.

After seeing to the wounds he gained in battle, Jeff wanted his holiday food package. While Margaret was getting the leftovers in a bag, Jeff's phone dinged. "It is a text from Chelsea," he said, going pink in the cheeks.

"Merry Christmas, little brother," Nate said. "She seems to like you." Jeff smiled, yet Nate was on fire inside. She had to know Jeff was here, which means they'd talked. If this was her way of trying to provoke him, the objective was achieved. He was good and provoked.

"I hope so," Jeff said as he left. Nate saw him texting on his way to his truck. It just shoveled more coal on the hate train heading Chelsea's way.

EIGHTEEN

THE DAY AFTER CHRISTMAS was an anticlimactic day which was made longer with the task of returning ill-fitting or poorly chosen gifts. Standing on lines that snaked around roped partitions, Margaret was so grateful to not be in a relapse anymore. Nate said he needed to do some work and stayed home.

In actuality, Nate had a fresh crop of nude shots from Chelsea to jerk off to. After sending her shots of him finishing, she said she wondered what Jeff would think of the pictures. She was trying to piss him off and it worked because there is nothing like having your dick in your hand when your brother's name is mentioned.

On New Year's Eve, the Halls stayed in and played Twister with James. What could be more fun than watching a pregnant woman play Twister? Afterwards, they ordered more Chinese take out than any three people should ever eat. Margaret emptied out egg rolls and filled them with chicken udon for Nate. James's favorite part was the fortune cookies. He loved reading the lucky numbers out loud. All three were asleep by the time the world welcomed the New Year. Nate woke in the middle of the night to a text on his phone. "Come outside and wish me Happy New Year. I'm waiting." From the time stamp, she seemed to have messaged an hour before. Nate backed out and then deleted the text. Outside, Chelsea sat in her car and watched Nate's front door. Chelsea saw when her message was read on her phone. Nate had read it and she'd already been waiting for over an hour. She thought he was finally coming outside. As time ticked away, so did Chelsea's patience. Nate heard the screech of car tires break the quiet of the night.

Margaret was happy her brother-in-law stopped by to break up the quiet of New year's day. Also, it was easier to interrogate him with home court advantage. "So..." Margaret let the word linger, waiting to see if Jeff would get the hint and start talking. He didn't get the hint. Margaret huffed. "Have you spoken to Chelsea? Other than text?"

"She seems like a real nice girl."

Another exasperated sigh left Margaret's mouth. "What the hell were you two texting about? Nowhere in the texting was there room to ask for a date? Jeez. You are a mess. Of course she's a nice girl. Idiot."

"Yup, you will get no argument. I am indeed an idiot."

"Do you even want to? I haven't seen you in a relationship for months. Trust issues?"

"No, my issues are fine, thank you. I'm not looking because work is busy. A state contract paying a lot of overtime in the winter. Being a foreman, I am always on call. It has snowed five times in the last week. Me and the guys are out for hours running the trucks." Jeff rubbed his scruffy face. He had been up since last night, to get ahead of the inevitable snow.

"Alright, alright, calm your snow pants." Margaret poured Jeff a cup of coffee. Taking a sip, Jeff winced at the bitterness.

"It's high octane, so don't be a baby. I need my coffee to vibrate my soul."

Jeff gulped more. Then, he pulled out the neck of his t-shirt and looked down.

Margaret had to know. "What are you doing?"

"Checking if the caffeine was growing more chest hair. Man, you were not kidding."

NINETEEN

Winters in Upstate New York are never ending. Windswept snow drifts rival rooftops for height. The frigid air digs into bones and makes them ache for the entire season. The needle on the thermometer fights to reach over zero degrees. Icy, gray day after icy, gray day with a promise of more snow on the way.

The best thing to do during those months is to hibernate, which was exactly what Jeff was thinking as he plowed Albany University's parking lots, again. Though he was thankful to be warm in the truck, it was five in the morning. He wished to be neck deep in his down comforter, on his fourth dream. His cell rang out a wicked guitar solo, the notification for Nate. Jeff watched his name light up the screen. This was the third time he had called this week. Jeff muted the ring, a bit tense until the phone's screen returned to its restful black mirror. Every time they spoke, Nate seemed distant and moody. Jeff tried to ask his brother how he was doing. Nate would brush it off as work stress then talk about more mundane things. Nate did, however, ask an awful lot about Chelsea. He wanted to know how it was moving along. Jeff liked her, but he was intimidated by her confidence and edge. He should have told her he was interested by now. God, he was an idiot. Chelsea made it clear she was interested, yet his dumb ass still remained polite. Jeff deeply inhaled, conjuring the smell of her perfume and feel of her skin. With a tight chest and a lump in his throat, Jeff kept plowing snow mountains in the corners of the parking lots. He knew college kids loved stealing their cafeteria's food trays and using them to sled, so he made sure the mountains had a little wall at the bottom. It usually helped keep kids from careening into a car across a parking lot.

When Jeff's phone rang again, it was a new tone. Trying to sound casual, he answered. "Hello, Jeff Hall here."

"Well, hello there, Jeff. How have you been?" Jeff's lump grew less lumpy.

"Hey, Chelsea. How are you doing?" He was still painfully aware of his rambling when they had hung out, so Jeff tried playing it cool. He had sweaty palms.

"How do I sound? Isn't this better than texting?"

"Uh, yes." Then nothing. Jeff opened and closed his wordless mouth. So much for being cool. Idiot.

"A bunch of us are going tubing this weekend and I remembered you had invited yourself."

"Yes, I did," he began. "It sounds neat." Neat? *Who says neat?* Jeff needed to stop talking.

"Well, we're going to West Mountain to go tubing from noon until whenever. If you want to go, you can carpool with me."

"Sure. Yes. Neat." Jeff wanted to punch himself in the face.

"Neat." Chelsea echoed Jeff's witty ways.

"Yes, I would like to go and yes, let's take the ride up together." I apologize for being off. It's early and I'm trying to get ahead of this falling snow. Which reminds me, why are you up?"

"Morning yoga. Getting my sun salutation going. I like early morning practice. It sets the tone for the day. Seeing as we're both morning people, feel free to call early. Now, remember this weekend. Me. Friends. Doing some neat tubing." Chelsea poked fun at Jeff.

"It will indeed be neat." Jeff laughed at himself. Back to plowing, he smiled along as he cleared the rest of the lots on his route. He even heard himself start to hum. *Dork*.

Laundry was Margaret's downfall. She found it mind numbing and hated it. However, she was focused on whittling the piles, in hopes of getting on Nate's good side. Lately, he had been very porcupiney. He threw barbs and was always so tense. Whatever was dominating his thoughts stayed close to the vest. Asking him what was on his mind didn't get her any answers. Nate would shake his head back and forth as if he was coming out of a dream. First, he would apologize for not listening and moments later he'd be lost again, his brow furrowed and his lips in a tight line on his face. So, Margaret waded through the clothes making piles. She had plucked Nate's gym bag up and reached in for his stale workout gear and pulled out a Yankees t-shirt wrapped up in Nate's gym clothes. It couldn't belong to anyone in this house. Nate would never stand for it. Nate was a Red Sox fan his whole life. His loyalty was undying. The curse of the Bambino just ended in 2004, and she would have no part in bringing bad mojo to his team. Margaret threw the cursed garment on the pile designated for charity, which always got bigger but was never dropped off. Then, she washed her hands, never one to take any chances with bad luck.

Marie was completely exhausted from the killer leg session she inflicted on her last client of the day. Leg press, deadlifts, three different types of squats, calves, and they still threw in thirty minutes of cardio. She could hear many of her parts creak. She'd been in the gym since seven a.m. and worked alongside six clients, and now Marie was focused on fighting her way out of sweaty gym gear. She dreamt of showering and collapsing into bed. Although Marie promised Margaret they would watch *Watch What Happens Live* together tonight. Being this tired, Marie wasn't sure she would make it. With spent legs and aching ass cheeks, Marie dropped herself into the driver's seat and her ab muscles clenched. She winced, clicked her seatbelt, and turned on the heated seats. Before putting the car in gear, she checked her phone. It was a message from Margaret about their date with Bravo. Marie made a mental note to call Margaret back after her shower. She threw the car into gear and arrived home cranky and sore.

"William? Helloooo?" Wes was dancing all around her feet. She set her bag on the upholstered chair in the two-story foyer. She loved up the terrier. "Who's a good boy? I missed you." She smooched his scruffy face.

"I missed you, too," William said, coming down the stairs to Marie. He was tall with silver hair and deep ocean eyes and his fit body was a welcome greeting on its own. "How was your day?"

"Hey there, Doc. My day was long and sweaty."

"Sounds a lot more fun than mine." He smiled.

"You ass." Marie laughed. "It was a long day and I am glad it's done. How about your day?" Marie's voice was muffled as she fought her way out of her hoodie.

"A regular day of pukey kids and overprotective parents. They gave me guff over the latest virus scaring the sense out of everyone. Half of them refused to listen to reason while waving an article they copied from the internet in my face. Did you have a lot of clients today? Hope you didn't break anyone down too badly." As William stepped off the last step, Marie rose to greet him, closing the thirteen inch difference in height to place a kiss on her husband's cheek.

"I had a few but I think I'm the one that broke down badly. How is Greyson? Did he have a good day at school? Is he still playing over at Kenny's house?"

"Yes, he's still there and everything is fine, but..." William's face grew very serious. "Earlier today, there were *words* between him and the Kenny kid." Her husband used air quotes.

"What? Why are two little kids 'having words' as you put it?" Marie mimicked the hand gesture. Marie hated air quotes.

"Oh, well, it was for a good reason. Kenny told Greyson that Superman is stupid."

Marie showed mock horror, understanding what caused them to have this fight.

"Uh, because Superman is NOT stupid. Kenny's parents are stupid."

"Marie." William fixed his stare on his wife and they both started laughing. When William smiled and laughed, he looked even more handsome. Marie loved how confident William was with her. The love between them was still deep and passionate. William was smart, strong, and fiercely protective of his wife, which was something Marie didn't even know she needed. She could not measure how precious and safe his deep love for her made her feel. Despite the sixteen-year age difference, they were very well matched in the bedroom. William was always hunting, hungry for another taste of her. Marie had always loved to be found and then eaten alive.

"I need to take a shower," Marie said, passing William on the stairs. "Are you coming with me?"

"In a bit. I really need to transcribe some notes. Wall-to-wall sick kids today with some virus going around."

"Please don't get lost in your office. I will be waiting." Marie gave her husband a wink. Then, she headed up the curved staircase slowly, knowing William was watching her the whole way.

Marie's scented candles filled her room with lemon and lavender. Standing at the end of her bed, she slowly peeled off her camo lycra leggings and unclasped the hooks on her matching sports bra and dropped it to the floor. Marie pulled the black hair tie from the end of her long, thick braid and shook out the twists in her hair. She breathed deep as she raised her toned arms above her head, reaching toward the ceiling. As her arms came forward and down, Marie bent at the waist and placed her hands flat to the floor. She relaxed into the stretch and her naked, athletic body folded easily in half. After a few deep, long cleansing breaths, Marie unfolded herself and fell back on the bed. She pressed her feet apart on the foot board. She looked up at the red light of the discreet camera and smiled for William. Marie licked her fingers then they gently skated down in search of the wet cleft between her thighs. "Mmmm," a small moan sang in her mouth. She stroked herself slowly with the tip of her middle finger. "Mmmmm." The heat between her legs was delicious and needed immediate attention. Marie flipped on to her stomach and inched up the bed. The drawer of the bedside table was pulled open and Marie grabbed her vibrator. She laid on her back and clicked the button on the purple bullet, sending it right to maximum. She bent her knees then fileted her legs. A moment before the vibrator kissed her clit, his voice came over the intercom:

"I want you on your belly with a pillow under you. I want to see everything." Without hesitation, Marie followed instructions and was face down, feeling the cool of the sheets on her cheek. The thick down pillows under her belly tilted her ass up, putting her on perfect display. "Now, put the vibrator on your clit and stroke your pussy. Get wet for me." William pushed back from his desk and undid the button and zipper on his pants. His hand around his cock, he squeezed and gave a gentle tug, feeling himself grow and stiffen. Grabbing it at the base, he stroked it and watched Marie press the vibrator to her clit and gyrate. "Whose pussy is this?" he asked through the intercom, spitting in his hand to rub the head of his cock. "Are you wet for me? I need you ready to be fucked. Now, whose pussy is it? Tell me." He felt himself hard in his hand.

"It's yours." Marie gasped the words while she pushed the vibrator harder against her clit, doing what she was told. Marie spread her lips open, showing the camera more of herself.

"Come on, you know what to say. Are you trying to get in trouble with me?" William's voice was low. Marie smiled and winked for him.

"Make me," Marie whispered. "Come, make me."

"Don't you fucking move." William's long strides and steps had him in their room in moments. Marie dared not move, but curved her lower back more, giving up all she had for the taking. William pushed open the door and asked, "Whose pussy is this?" Marie said nothing but smiled and winked at him again. His movement was lightning quick. He put his strong hands on her hips and shoved his tongue deep inside, fucking her with his mouth.

Marie gasped then breathlessly said, "Mmmmm, you feel so good. Please fuck me," she pleaded. William pulled her up to standing and spun her to face the bed.

"No, not yet." William stood behind Marie and shoved his fingers inside her to get them wet. He bent her over and wrapped his left arm underneath her.

He held on to her so she could not get away. She knew what was coming. He pushed his fingers into her ass while grinding his thumb into her clit. "No, No, No, ohhhhhh." Marie took it and loved it. She let out a mix of a hiss and whimper of pleasure and pain— a cocktail she more than needed. She craved it. When Marie began to buck and yell, William pulled her backward onto him. He fucked her while he fingered her ass.

"Whose pussy is this?" Her fire and fury got him harder. He loved the way Marie felt when she backed up into him again and again, furiously riding his cock and taking his two fingers deep in her ass. Marie screamed, "It's yours and I am yours." as she came but William did not stop or slow down. Again, Marie shook with another orgasm.

The two pulled themselves off the bed and made their way to the shower to finish.

"You are magnificent, my love," William said.

TWENTY

JEFF WENT OVER HIS list again. "Snow pants, check," he said and gave his legs a pat. He put his hands on his head. "Gloves. Goggles. Hat. Check, check, check." He slipped his arms into his puffy winter coat. "Coat, check." Jeff was wearing snow boots with two layers of insulated socks. He was ready and Chelsea was picking him up any minute. Any... minute. Jeff kept looking out his window every fifteen seconds. He was getting himself excited with daydreams of warming Chelsea by a fire after a long day out in the cold. The thoughts only made his GORE-TEX sauna even hotter. He was ready. Boiling inside, but ready. It was coincidentally Valentine's Day and tubing with Chelsea was a very good way to spend the day. When Jeff saw her car make the turn onto his street, he got jazzed. "Yessss," Jeff said aloud as he headed out the door. He greeted her with, "Hey, good morning." Jeff's words came out in puffs of breath on the cold day.

"Ready to get tubing?" Chelsea leaned out her driver's side. She was bright eyed and smiling. A thick white winter hat with rabbit fur flaps kept her blonde head warm. "Do you drink tea? I brought you some of a blend I put together."

"Uh, yeah, I drink tea. Love the stuff." Up until she asked, Jeff couldn't have given a rat's ass about tea.

"Great— get in so we can get this show on the road." Jeff went to the passenger side of her silver hybrid and got in.

"You definitely look ready." Chelsea gave Jeff's North Face a squeeze.

"I am so ready," he began. "Happy Valentine's Day, by the way." Jeff handed Chelsea a potted sunflower. It's yellow happy face bloomed with soft yellow petals.

"Oh, thank you, Jeff. Well, aren't you a sweetie?" Oh yeah, here you go. Happy Valentine's Day to you." Chelsea handed him the warm to-go cup of tea. "I wasn't sure if you were going to cancel. I completely spaced on Valentine's Day until this morning." Jeff sipped the tea. The tea was light and sweet. Jeff thought he tasted peach.

"No way. This is great. I had no other plans." Jeff volunteered, as if he wouldn't have canceled whatever plans he may have had for time with Chelsea.

"Oh. Do you have a girlfriend? Someone you are not with today, this most romantic day?" Chelsea's blue eyes were bright and curious.

Jeff realized he was staring and didn't hear the question. "Huh? Excuse me, I apologize. What was your question?"

With a laugh, Chelsea asked Jeff again, "Do you have a girlfriend? Someone to call your Valentine?"

"No, I..." Jeff could feel his face getting hot. *When was she putting this car in drive?* "No. I do not have someone to call my own."

Chelsea smiled as she backed out of his driveway and put the car in drive. "I don't have a Valentine either, in case you were wondering," she said with a grin and her eyes forward. She watched the road with a smile on her lips.

The drive out to West Mountain was less than an hour. Jeff and Chelsea got better acquainted on the drive. Jeff came to find that Chelsea had not been a yoga instructor for very long, although she'd practiced yoga for years. According to her, it was a great side hustle, but it was not her full-time job. Chelsea's nine-to-five gig was as a stylist at a salon. She got her license a few years back and now worked on the main strip in Saratoga. "I am blessed— both of my jobs help people feel good inside or out and sometimes both. Now there is the good stuff."

"Yeah, my job is a bit different. I work for the state plowing snow for the roads and parking lots in the winter. Then my crew and I do whatever other road work pops up during the other seasons." Jeff knew that his job was not a feel good kind of job. Hell, it wasn't even clean most days. He had never given much thought to whether or not he was making people happy. Jeff smiled thinking about the students having a blast sledding down the snowy mountains in the lots. He realized he did have a job that made people happy and this was turning into a sweet Valentine's Day.

When they arrived at West, Chelsea's friends were leaning on one of their cars, drinking out of thermoses. Standing next to Jeff, Chelsea made introductions to their fellow tubers, "This is Sadie, our color specialist." She was a short, thick woman with expertly overdone makeup and a huge white fur-trimmed hat. She smiled and adjusted her white goggles on her botoxed forehead. "Katie is my partner in crime. This girl is all around fantastic. She is magic." Katie offered a hello with a big smile. She was blonde and tall with killer green eyes. "Now this," Chelsea moved aside and gestured, "This is Bobby, my boss. He owns the salon and is obviously a real slave driver." Bobby held up his index finger while he finished inhaling on his vape pen. After holding it for a moment and exhaling, he extended his arm with a fist of salutation. Jeff gave him a pound. "Hey, you want a hit of this? It's the real deal. It'll put your head out." He held the button down again for another long drag. "I have a 'script. All legal."

Jeff put up his hand. "Thanks, I'm good for now." Although he didn't smoke, he didn't want to come across as judgy.

"Biddies, this is Jeff. The guy I've been telling you about." Chelsea smiled.

"Hi, Jeff" The three said in unison with big cheesy grins all across. Jeff didn't miss the part where Chelsea said she had been telling them about him. He gave a shy wave while he thought, *She has been talking about me.*

TWENTY-ONE

NATE HEARD YET ANOTHER text from Chelsea alert his phone. He had to make her wait, to punish her a bit for talking about tubing with Jeff on Valentine's Day. A few days prior, he stood in front of a naked Chelsea. He put his hands up on the wall behind her and he fucked her wet, velvet mouth and smiled when he felt her gag on him until he came and still, she sucked his spent cock until he was hard and came again. He then helped her to stand up and shoved his tongue in her dirty mouth. At the same time, he shoved his two fingers into her and stroked her inside. Her soft moans turned to feral grunting as she gyrated on his hand. When she came, she screamed Nate's name.

"Yes, you scream my name because I'm the one who fucks you." He went to his knees and licked Chelsea and felt her shudder at the feel of him sliding his tongue through her throbbing folds. Her second orgasm tasted sweet and Nate had Chelsea dripping off of his chin. While she lay exhausted on the rented bed, he got dressed and left.

So when Nate opened the text and saw a picture of Chelsea and her salon friends tubing, he quickly noticed his brother's familiar face in the picture. It did its job and pissed him off. "You've got to be fucking kidding me." Immediately, Nate deleted the picture. At the same moment, his phone chimed with a text from Jeff. It was the same picture Nate had gotten from Chelsea."I guess you aren't fucking kidding." Nate had to return Jeff's text.

Nate: Way to go little brother. Hope you are having a killer time.

Jeff: We are. She is great. Thank Maggs for me.

Nate: Will do.

Nate cleared the texts from Jeff, too. He knew that when the picture came from Chelsea, it was out of spite, but when Jeff texted, it was out of happiness. Nate would let him have it. He needed to go about his own Valentine's Day.

TWENTY-TWO

NATE GAZED UPON HIS napping wife, who was supported by a gajillion pillows with the hope of finding some comfort. The book she was reading was accordioned next to her pillow pile. Baby Jane was getting bigger by the minute and Margaret's ever expanding belly had her exhausted. She lay there with her mouth open and snoring. Nate smiled. In this moment, he was feeling a lot of love for his wife and all that she was going through. All his overtime helped him feel better about having the money he needed, and even a little extra. Nate figured Margaret deserved some of the extra. Although he happened upon a gift for her when he was out shopping for Chelsea, he was proud to have found something for his wife as well. Margaret's head fell back and the snoring got so loud that she woke herself up. Seeing Nate sitting there, she wiped her bottom lip and sat up.

"Hey there," she began. "I keep falling asleep all over myself." She rubbed her eyes and stretched.

"You're growing a person. I will allow—"

"Check this out." Margaret grabbed Nate's hand and put it on her belly. Little thumps tapped against his palm. A huge smile grew on his face and he laughed out loud.

"Well, hello there." He felt a couple of more little thumps. "You are a tough one, huh? Guess what, Jane? You get it from your mama." Margaret put her hand over Nate's. They floated in this sweetness together until Nate broke the silence with a question.

"Have you ever heard of the legend of the Red Thread of Fate?"

"No. Will you tell me what it is?" Margaret was still holding Nate's hand on her belly.

"It's from Chinese lore," Nate began.

"Ooooo, lore. I love some good lore." Margaret could not help herself. Nate shook his head and continued.

"Anywho, according to this lore, there is an invisible red thread connecting those who are destined for one another." He reached behind his back and picked up a small red box. "In a million different lifetimes and all the possible ways, I will always find you and make you mine. So no matter what happens in our lives, Margaret, you and I are meant to be." Nate was very impressed with himself as he placed the box on Margaret's pregnant belly.

"Nate! You are...what is this?" Margaret picked the box up from her belly and cranked back the top. Her hand clutched her chest and tears began to well in her eyes. It took her a second before she could even speak. "Oh, Nate, you have stolen my breath."

"Do you like it?" Nate asked as Margaret coaxed the ring from the box and prayed as she tried to put it on. The most satisfied look relaxed her face as her gift made its way down her pudgy pregnant finger. It was a polished white gold ring with two rows of illusion set diamonds. A delicate row of rubies gleamed in the middle.

"Mark this day. I am speechless." Margaret held her hand away to admire the jewelry. The sun streamed through the window and she held the ring in its rays. She marveled at the stones as the light reflected off them and danced along the walls. Nate had really surprised her.

"Every time you look at this ring, know how much I love you. How much I will always love you. Every good thing I have is good because of you. You are my sweet wife. Happy Valentine's Day." The two kissed. A rapid knock landed on their bedroom door and snapped Nate and Margaret out of their sweetness.

"Now, Dad?" A muffled James waited on the other side of the door.

"Yes, bud. Now." Nate raised his eyebrows at Margaret, stood up, and cleared his throat. "INTRODUCING the BEST dancer—"

"And singer, Dad! Don't forget singer," James corrected from the other side of the door.

"Sorry about that. Introducing, making his debut, the BEST singer AND dancer ...JAAAAAAAMES!" The bedroom door blasted open and James was wearing a red t-shirt with the saying "Ladies Man" across the front. He wore a pair of sunglasses to complete his get up. With his Little Virtuoso music player in hand, he set the player on the ground and pushed play.

James put his hand next to his mouth and loudly whispered, "Dad, don't forget you have to dance, too." Nate gave James a wink and thumbs up. James went to his starting point and waited for his cue. The boys danced and sang to a Valentine's dance song with Lola on back up, barking at the hijinx. Margaret was chock full of love and hooted and hollered encouragement. When the song finished, Margaret climbed off her pillow throne clapping and smiling.

"Wow! This is my best Valentine's Day ever!"

"Wait, Mama. There's more." James bounded out of the bedroom with Lola trailing behind. He was back in a flash, holding something behind his back. Lola sat on the ground and proceeded to lick herself like a classy girl. She didn't care about the surprise.

"Whatcha got there, little man?" Margaret could see the cellophane heart over his shoulder.

"You have to guess."

"Is it a Llama for your Mama?"

James giggled. "No. Guess again." James swayed around, unable to be still.

"Is it… peanut butter for your Mutter?" Margaret offered.

"MAMA!" James laughed, jumping up and down. "It's candy!" James shouted and held the heart above his head.

"Well, okay! Now we are absolutely having the best Valentine's Day."

James nominated himself host to the box of chocolates. The boy tore the top off and a long train of red cellophane streamed from the box. He studied the lid's map, showing the location of each coveted sweet.

"I know which ones are the best, Mama." He found the chocolate covered cherry and held it up for Margaret to see. "Look, Ma. It's your favorite."

"So it is." A delighted Margaret slipped the chocolate in her mouth. She squeezed the candy against the roof of her mouth with her tongue, and the chocolate burst open, filling Margret's mouth with liquid sweetness and maraschino cherries.

TWENTY-THREE

JEFF KICKED BACK IN his adirondack chair and watched the flames from the bonfire lick the night sky. The slopes were lit for the night skiers who zigzagged their way down the snowy mountains.

"Hey," Chelsea tapped Jeff on the arm. "Hey in there." She patted his arm to bring him back to reality. "Hello, nice to have you back." Chelsea smiled. "In a half hour or so the tube runs will be closed. You want to go down one more time?"

"Hell yes. I definitely do." Jeff shook off the effects of the toasty fire. Katie, Sadie, and Bobby were in a huddle nearby, taking hits from Bobby's vape pen. Jeff and Chelsea stepped up to the pack.

"Jeff and I are going to attack the run one more time. Anyone else in?"

Bobby took a long pull off of his pen and held the hit. Bobby offered the pen out to the group and, Jeff reached into the middle and plucked the pen from Bobby. Everyone raised their eyebrows and sat up in their chairs.

"So, I press this button?" Jeff's thumb floated over the little button.

"Yes, just press the button while you inhale. A ring around the button will glow red. When it flashes, stop holding the button down and stop inhaling."

"Sounds easy enough." Jeff put the pen to his lips and pulled. He inhaled until the flashing light signaled. When the flashing finished, Jeff took another hit. Again, the light flashed. Jeff passed the pen to Katie.

Chelsea was nervous. "Are you alright? Have you ever smoked before?"

"I smoked in high school. Only twenty short years ago. Is it like riding a bike?"

"Something like that." Bobby laughed.

"Well, let's get to it." They went to snatch up a tube and then the group got on the conveyor belt to slowly climb to the top. Jeff stepped off of the belt and was bumped by Bobby when his tube got away from him. The tube bounced around like an excited puppy on the end of its leash. They had ripped down this run all day, but now the trail seemed a lot higher.

"We should go down together. It will be a blast." Bobby took another drag from his pen. When he held it out this time, he gave it right to Jeff, who happily took a drag. It tasted lemony and light. Way better than the brown clown brick weed Jeff smoked back in high school.

When Jeff and Bobby's turn came up, Bobby quietly whispered to the line attendant to give them a good shove. Then, Bobby and Jeff sat in their tubes to wait for their push.

"You hold my leash and I'll hold yours," Bobby said, all excited and big-eyed. "This is going to be freakin' awesome."

"Are you boys ready?" asked the attendant. Jeff hit record on his body cam then gave a thumbs up. She yelled to the other attendant to come over and together the two gave Jeff and Bobby a serious shove. The tubes took off down the track going so fast that they whistled through the packed snow.

"WOOOOHOOOOO," Bobby sang as they whipped down the hill. Jeff faced the front on the way down, so he saw the fast approaching end of the track and the snow wall meant to stop them. They had achieved remarkable speed; the two and their tubes went up and over the wall and suspended in the air.

"AAAGH! Ohhhhh shit." Jeff's heart beat quickly.

As the guys slid back down the snow wall, their tubes slid into the neighboring lane. They looked up the run and saw a person gunning toward them. "AAAAAAGH," Bobby and Jeff both screamed. It could have been because they were high, but Jeff and Bobby seemed to be moving in slow motion. They flipped out of their tubes then clumsily crawled around and every time they would try to stand, the giddy loons lost their footing, falling all over each other, laughing in the snow. The girls were pointing at them, laughing uncontrollably.

"You guys." Chelsea was bent over, laughing too hard to speak. Sadie let out a snort. Katie made no sound as her body shook with laughter. Everyone on the conveyor belt had a first row seat, enjoying the show as Jeff and Bobby struggled to stand. When they finally gained their footing, they both thrust their fists in the air. The onlookers whistled and clapped as the guys did their stride of pride back to the fire.

Thawing in front of the fire, the girls were still laughing. They watched the video Jeff had recorded. He could hear them replaying the screams. It was hilarious.

Jeff's stomach hurt from laughing so hard. Bobby came and sat in the adirondack chair next to Jeff.

"Wooooo, back there was some funny stuff. You scream a lot."

"Me? I scream?" Jeff needed to be sure he heard correctly.

"Oh, yeah, like a preschooler. It was kind of embarrassing actually." Bobby laughed. "I only screamed so you weren't alone."

"Thank you for your sacrifice. You are a thoughtful man."

"Don't mention it." Bobby took a pull off of the pen and held it out to Jeff. Keeping the good vibes going, Jeff took the pen. He took two more long pulls and felt his head rush. He leaned back and relaxed in the warmth of the fire. It was the first Valentine's Day he had enjoyed in years.

TWENTY-FOUR

WILLIAM RESERVED A LUXURIOUS hotel suite for Valentine's Day. It had a living room done in rich fabrics and upholstery so thick, Marie could get lost in the sofa. The bathroom had two separate doors leading to private bathrooms which opened to shared space with dazzling white tile and chrome. The shower had four jets. White fluffy robes were on the bench next to it. The hot tub was warm and bubbly, ready for romance. The suite's bedroom was dressed in soft tones of blush and cream, with huge, fat, cream colored pillows luxuriating on the king bed to create a sumptuous welcome. The ivory down comforter was an airy dream. Marie flopped down into the heavenly feel of the bed. William deserved anything he wanted for booking this place.

There was a knock on the door. "You wait right here, lady," William said with a grin. He shut the bedroom door behind him. He was back moments later with the white fluffy robes from the bathroom. "We are going to need to wear these. Only these though."

"Uh huh. There's a knock on the door and now you want me to get naked? What kind of chick do you take me for?" Marie razzed him.

"I take you for the kind of chick who needs little provocation."

"You would be correct, sir." Marie began to undress.

Looking like terry cloth snowmen, William and Marie walked hand-in-hand into the living room. Two massage tables had been set up. The smell of lavender puffed from a diffuser. The massage therapists stood next to the tables with their lotion belts strapped on. "William, you have outdone yourself. This suite is fantastic. Now, a massage? Thank you, my love. You spoil me."

When the masseuse first laid her warm lotioned hands on Marie's back and began to massage, Marie realized how desperately her body needed it. For the next hour and a half every shred of tightness and tension dissolved away as Marie's muscles were softened to the tenderness of veal.

As soon as the tables had been folded, William walked the therapists out and put the "Do not Disturb" on the door before he locked it and went hunting. He found Marie naked and oiled up on the cream duvet. She had a sleepy bedroom smile on her face.

"Looks like you found me," she purred.

"Yes, I have." William dropped his white robe to the floor.

Marie loved looking at her husband. She was aching to have him inside her. She spread her legs and traced her fingers down her belly and between her legs.

William would not wait. He climbed in bed looking for a place to start. He kissed Marie's pussy like he would her mouth. He parted her lips, tasted her and moaned. "You taste so good."

Marie moaned. "William. Fuuu…" Marie's head fell back on the pillow.

William flipped Marie, gripping her hips. He raised her ass up and stuffed his face deep in her, licking her front to back.

"Ohhhhh, yesss," Marie hissed. She pushed herself into William's mouth. She was soaked.

William leaned down. "What do you need?" he whispered in her ear. His fingers searched inside her. She was warm and slick. Although William wanted to give Marie what she needed, she hadn't asked properly.

"Please, William, please fuck me. I need it," Marie whimpered.

William playfully tugged her lips and gave her pussy a light smack. "How bad do you need me to fuck you?"

"William, I need you in me. I am yours to take."

"Yes, you are mine." William pushed two fingers into Marie. With one arm around her waist, he fingered her hard and fast. Marie's legs were shaking. Just when she was about to come, William stopped. He went down on her and took one long, slow lick of her wet, swollen pussy. William moaned as he ate Marie. The heat and wetness of her made him harder. "I'm gonna fuck you however I want."

Marie's back arched. "I am yours." Marie was on all fours. They both needed each other. William wet his thumb and slid it into her ass while he fucked her. Marie pushed herself back into him and moaned. William loved the tight wet feel of Marie's ass and the heat of her pussy. William fucked her like a wild animal.

Marie wanted it too. "Give it to me, William. Harder. I need it."

William fucked Marie harder and faster still. He leaned over her, squeezing her tits.

"Fuck me, William."

William took her with a savage hunger. Letting her know she was his. He would fuck her how and when he wanted. Marie would take it every time, or he would take it for himself.

William pulled himself and his thumb out of his wife. Marie felt William enter her ass. His thumb was one thing, and William's cock was another. Marie's breath caught in her throat. She moaned with exquisite pain. William fucked Marie harder, pulling her onto him until she was almost sitting in his lap. Her pain made it better for both of them. William came inside his wife.

Marie moaned her satisfaction. "William. I love it."

"I'm not done with you. Lay down on your back. Now."

Marie flipped to her back.

"Spread your legs."

Marie of course, listened.

William knelt between her legs and caressed her wet lips. Slowly, he slid two fingers in her. He started out slow, getting faster as Marie got closer. She could feel herself teetering on the edge. Right then, William bit her nipple, pushing her off the edge into free fall.

Marie's orgasm was primal. She bucked and yelled in satisfaction.

As she lay there collapsed and exhausted, William said, "Now I'm done with you." He licked his fingers. Laying with her, William looked at his breathtaking wife. She had sleepy eyes with the long lashes that were always hiding some beautiful secret. He both wanted to own and revere this fierce, but delicate woman. Her strength and softness rivaled each other. "Happy Valentine's Day," William spoke softly to his wife.

TWENTY-FIVE

SITTING IN THE EXAM room, Margaret was lost in thought. She was happy and scared to be nearing the birth of Jane and her body was done with being pregnant. She was unable to get out of her own damn way and always felt like a sweaty round blob of emotions. She obsessively thought about how much longer it would be until Freshie would tear up and wreak havoc on her lady bits.

"Hello, Mrs. Hall. How are you feeling this morning?" Dr. Bunem was all smiles today.

"I am at maximum capacity. It feels like an episode of a baby ninja warrior. She is doing spin kicks in there." Margaret rubbed her belly.

"I have been looking over your chart. It is time to schedule your cesarean."

"Seriously? Can't I give birth naturally?"

"Because of your MS, I do not want to take chances with your body's ability. You have damaged nerves from past flare ups and I don't know of your ability to push. If we attempted to deliver naturally and you were unable to, it could become very serious."

"Of course, I understand." Margaret's understanding didn't keep her from being disappointed in herself.

This pregnancy had damn near broken her. At times, she barely had a fingertip grip on her sense of self.

"Taking your health into consideration, I don't want you going into labor." The doctor kept staring down at . his charts, not once looking up to notice the terrified pregnant woman in front of him. "I would like to schedule your cesarean for April thirteenth."

"Isn't the thirteenth too soon? It's two weeks before my due date." Margaret's crevices started sweating.

"The baby will be thirty-seven weeks which means fully gestated. She and you will do just fine." Dr. Bunem spoke so casually about the C-section. Margaret wondered how he would feel to be gut like a fish and have something yanked out. She was sure it would wipe off his toothy white smile. "I will have my medical assistant come in and give you all the information. You will have to come to the hospital the week before for your pre-op appointment and to fill out paperwork."

"Uhh, can I ask you a question?"

"Of course, Mrs. Hall."

"Are you good at C-sections? Like, are you fast?"

"I don't like my coffee to get cold." He never lost his winning smile.

"Okay. Good. Quick in, quick out?" Margaret was nervous and needed some good news. Why had she told Nate that he didn't need to go with her? With him there, Margaret would feel a lot better.

"Yes. However, I don't rush. If I need to take longer, I will. Please do not worry, Mrs. Hall. We are nearing the end. Soon you will meet your daughter," the doctor reassured Margaret. "Now, I will hand you over to my medical assistant. Again, please don't worry. I will take good care of you." There he went. Probably to drink coffee. Margaret prayed his coffee consumption didn't give him shaky hands.

After the appointment, Margaret arrived home and waddled from her car to the front door. She dropped her keys and couldn't bring herself to bend over for them. Instead, she popped off her ballet flat and plucked the keys off the ground using her doughy pregnant toes. She grabbed the keys from her monkey foot and put the key in to unlock the door.

"SURPRISE!"

"AAAAAAACK! Jesus Christmas!" Margaret's family and friends had their cameras ready. Surprising Margaret had always been impossible, however, not this time. Margaret grabbed her belly. Still only wearing one shoe, with her face somewhere between laughing and crying, Margaret began to relax. "You jerks! You almost scared the baby right out of me."

Marie walked up to her friend, hooked arms, and led her to a big white chair with pink and silver balloons tied to the back. Marie removed Margaret's other shoe. "You sit here, Queen Pregnant Pants. I cannot believe we surprised you."

"Me either. Surprising me isn't easy. I always seem to find out what's going on."

"Enjoy this day. We have all your favorite foods. Even your mom's eggplant parmesan."

Margaret craved eggplant parmesan during this pregnancy. Before this, it was a dish Margaret barely liked. Yet, it was all she wanted when she got pregnant. Catherine had actually been shipping eggplant parmesan with special urgent delivery for Margaret's craving to the house on a weekly basis.

"Of course my mom sent eggplant parm. I can't wait." Maragret rubbed her hands together.

"You could wait until it comes out of the oven." came from behind Margaret.

Margaret gasped. "Mom?"

Catherine came out of the kitchen doorway. Immediately, Margaret's tears started. "MOM! You're here. How?" Catherine lived four hours away, on Long Island. She had stopped driving long distances and was between husbands to chauffer her. Visits were rare.

"This one is how." Catherine pointed to Marie. "She sent a very nice car, with a driver. You should have seen the look on the old broad next door's face." Catherine cackled. A Hatfield and McCoy situation began years ago between Margaret's mother and the neighbor, who had once had the audacity to ask Catherine to move her garbage cans. Since then, their relationship consisted of stink-eye and disdain.

"Mom, I love you. I am so happy you're here. Thank you." Margaret hugged her mother and counted the minutes until she could eat eggplant parm.

"Oh look," Marie said. "Here comes Chelsea." There was a bit of something in Marie's voice when she said Chelsea's name.

"Hello, ladies. Margaret, you look beautiful. I got you a little something. A funny gift," Chelsea said, handing Margaret a soft pink decorative bag with sparkly tissue paper busting out of it.

Margaret dug in and pulled out a white t-shirt. Across the belly, written in pink, it said, "Namaste in here."

"Oh, this is adorable. Thank you. I will go put it on right now. Marie, can you help me? I'm getting too big. I need a spotter." Margaret took Marie's hand and walked to the bedroom.

Marie sat on the bed while Margaret rifled through her drawer of black leggings, looking for the *right* pair to go with her new shirt. Margaret did not need help getting dressed, but had to know, "Is there something going on with you and Chelsea?"

"Why would you ask me such a thing?" Marie asked with a caught look on her face.

"So, you don't deny it?" Margaret pushed.

"She just— I can't put my finger on it. It's--"

She's too much icing, not enough cake." Margaret finished the sentence. "I don't know what you have against her. Or why for that matter." Margaret's drawer looked like an exploding can of snakes.

"I don't feel any sort of way about Miss Bendy Busty McGee." Then, doing a breathy impersonation, Marie said, *"Oh, I got you a little something."* She *rolled* her eyes.

"Oh okay. You always get real mature when you're dealing with another woman."

"You get mature." Marie sounded like a petulant child.

"Wow." Margaret burst out laughing and so did Marie. Margaret separated a pair of leggings from the tangle. Victorious in her search, she did the cha cha into her pants. Wearing her gift and ready to eat, arm-in-arm, the best friends went straight to the buffet. The eggplant parmesan was calling to Margaret like a lover. She could only surrender. Two plates later, a near to bursting Margaret shoved one last saucy forkful into her mouth. It was time for gifts.

Margaret was tired and hot. Opening the gifts was an endless stream of girl things. Pink onesies. Purple unicorn fleece sleepers. A dozen pastel blankets. Pink fuzzy bears. Margaret was not trying to be ungrateful. She was just so full of baby and eggplant parm. The promise of cake kept Margaret smiling until the last pink pacifier was unwrapped.

Dolce had made a masterpiece. A light pink three-tiered cake with the most delicate white icing flowers cascading from the top, spilling down to the bottom. A fondant baby in a pink sleeper curled up in the bed of flowers. The wee one looked almost real, from the pink cheeks down to the perfect sweet baby toes.

"Thank you all for being here today. Nate and I are excited and this party was truly a surprise. Thank you again." Margaret wanted to get the "thank you" out of the way. Her eyelids were heavy. She was fading fast. Soon, people took an extra piece of cake and left. The apartment emptied out pretty quickly. Margaret's mom was putting leftovers in the fridge, making not so quiet comments about the cleanliness of the fridge the whole time. Margaret had beached herself on the couch. Marie sat with her and counted packages of diapers.

"You literally have twenty packages of diapers going all the way to size fours. I can't remember— do babies really crap enough to need a pallet of diapers to start with?"

"It's probably more." Margaret was running her hand over her forehead. "Damn, I am tired. Not for one second did I think this would be easy, I just didn't think it would be this damned hard. Believe me, I am so happy we are having Jane. We love her already and we're so excited to meet her. I would do it a million times for her."

"I know you would. Being pregnant is not for the weak, that's for sure." Marie put her hand on Margaret's.

Nate took his time coming home to avoid a run-in with Chelsea. It was beyond him how she could seamlessly enter his family. Since the picture on Valentine's day, he had not seen nor talked to her. It did not stop Chelsea from texting pictures of her and Jeff's conversations. Nate couldn't help the masochist in him from reading them. It was obvious Jeff really liked this girl. There was no way he was going to out himself to anyone, even Jeff. Did Chelsea have real feelings for Jeff? Or, was this some sick and twisted way to be around Nate? He shook his head at the thought. It was too crazy to think about. Yet, it wasn't crazy enough for him to back off.

When Nate came home, his mother-in-law was in the kitchen with a hot coffee beside her and a book in hand. Without looking up from her reading, she said, "James is in bed. Tweedle Dee and Tweedle Double D are in the living room." Marie and Margaret were asleep on the couch with their mouths open, cuddled together. Margaret had a bonnet made from the gift ribbons on her head. Marie was holding a tube of nipple cream. Watching the two sleeping all over each other, he smiled and took out his cell phone to snap a picture. He sent it to William with the caption: "classy broads."

TWENTY-SIX

MARGARET PACKED HER BAG for the hospital, her nerves were on DEFCON 1. Knowing the C-section was coming left her dripping in sweat. She tried to busy herself by unpacking the hospital bag, reconfiguring everything, and repacking it all. Breast pad placement was key. If she could get that right then everything would be fine. Who was she kidding? She was crapping her full-coverage, beige underpants. She was about to be wide awake while they cut her open. Once the baby was out, her empty uterus would be lying on top of her, waiting to be stitched closed and shoved back in. Organs should always be in— never out. The only thing that needed to be out was Margaret. Knocked out. Her underbreasts were sweating.

"Hi, Mama. Are you packing to get Janey?" James was leaning in the doorway. He was worried his Mom would miss him.

"Hi, bud. Yes, I'm getting ready."

James walked over to his mom and sat on her lap, or what little of it he could find past her belly. James carried his blanket, Weebs, everywhere. Today, he also had a little stuffed stingray in his chubby hands. Last summer, the three of them had visited Margaret's mom on Long Island. One of the days, the family went to the aquarium and James got the biggest kick out of the stingray pool. He couldn't get enough of petting the silky swimmers as they would glide by. The exit of the aquarium was through the gift shop, leaving no doubt that souvenirs would be purchased. James beelined over to the stuffed sea creatures and grabbed up a silvery stuffed stingray. Grandma made sure James got his stingray. James named him Steve.

"Mama, do you think Janey will like Steve?" He cuddled into Margaret.

"Bud, she is going to love Steve. Guess who else Janey will love."

"Who?" he asked curiously.

"Janey is going to love you, James. Being a big brother is very special. Only the best guys get to be one." Margaret had James wrapped in her arms. She kissed the top of his head. She closed her eyes and breathed her boy in. It had been Margaret and James for five years. All of her mom love was for him. Soon, it would no longer be just the two of them. James would have to share Margaret. Even tougher, Margaret would have to share Margaret. She hugged him closer.

"You can bring Steve to keep you and Janey company." James put Steve in the hospital bag. Margaret felt blessed. His heart was colossal.

"Sweetie, you are the best kid ever. I love you." She kissed his head again. "Are you hungry? How about grilled cheese?"

"Will you flip it two times?" His brown eyes blinked with excitement.

"You know it." Margaret would make James grilled cheeses until he was fifty.

"Can you cut it into five? Five is my favorite number."

"Yes, James. A cut in five double flip grilled cheese. On it." Margaret and James went to the kitchen. Together, they made grilled cheese sandwiches, cut into five. James was in charge of juice bags. Margaret grabbed a bag of pretzel Goldfish. They spent the afternoon munching snacks and watching Handy Manny. Margaret silently held firm to the opinion that Turner was a moody tool.

Nate finished work and suffered the long commute home, otherwise known as the hallway. He joined Margaret and James on the couch. Another round of grilled cheese sandwiches were flipped twice and served. It was a great night. James made Nate and Margaret laugh with his corny kid jokes.

"What did the mouse say to the mouse trying to steal his cheese?"

"I don't know, what did he say"? Nate asked.

"Hey, that's nacho cheese!" James cracked up. "Get it, Dad? Nacho cheese?"

Nate laughed at his son. "That is a good one. I got it." After the comedy routine, it was bedtime for James. Nate took James to brush his teeth and hop into his pajamas.

Once he had been tucked in and read two stories, James's eyes grew heavy. "Mama, would it be alright if I kept Steve with Weebs until you go to get the baby?"

Margaret pulled Steve out from behind her. She had a feeling the stingray would be missed. "Yes, James. Of course you can. Truthfully, I think Steve would miss you too much. It would really make me feel better if you kept him." James yawned. His long eyelashes fluttered. Margaret tucked Steve in next to James and gave them both a kiss goodnight. She turned to leave.

She stopped at the door to look at her boy. Oh, how she loved him. She crossed his room to place another kiss on his warm cheek. "I love you so much," Margaret whispered. "So much." She walked out of his room, leaving him to his dreams.

TWENTY-SEVEN

IT WAS THE DAY before they would meet Jane. Marie picked Margaret up to go out in the afternoon. Shopping and lunch would hopefully thwart some of the nervousness about the hospital.

"Have you figured out what your deal is with Chelsea? And don't give me your, "too much icing" crap. What's up?" Margaret poked at her salad, harpooning another cherry tomato.

"I don't *not* like her. It's..." Marie was trying to choose her words carefully. Chelsea and Jeff had been talking to one another. Marie didn't want her words to get to Jeff and make things awkward for the group. The girl seemed too choreographed in her ways, as if she was working an angle. Marie hadn't been able to figure out what it was—yet. "She and I are just very different. I have no desire to be *zen*. I'm built for speed. Chelsea is built for comfort." Marie shoved a forkful of spring mix into her mouth.

"Okay, I get that. I will allow you to carry on with this weirdness."

"Thank you so much for *allowing* me to carry on, ass. Let's talk about you." Marie needed to change the subject. Since the birth of their friendship, so many years ago, it was not their way to keep secrets from each other. From bad BMs to bad relationships, they had always been able to talk it through.

"Oh, Nate got a raise at work. All the overtime showed his dedication and it definitely impressed his boss. My mom, as much as I hate to admit it, is right. We need a bigger place. It sucks though. By this point in our lives, we should be in a house. Our house. My MS has definitely changed our financial situation. Disability doesn't even come close to what I would make if I were healthy. I get paid what works out to twenty dollars a day. I'm the dropped anchor keeping our ship stuck. Unable to cruise." For Margaret, not being able to work dulled her shine.

Marie felt for her friend. She wished Margaret could see herself for all that she was, not only her disability. "Stop it. You are doing a fantastic job. Besides, you are about to have a baby. You wouldn't be working anyway because you'll be too busy with your boobs out. No way you would go back to work with a tiny baby. Momming is what you do. Nate is lucky to have a wife like you. I'm talking about Margaret in front of me right now. You are more than your MS."

"Thanks, Marie. Yeah, I guess you're right. I just miss me, you know? The me before all of this. Remember, I worked four jobs while finishing college. Five hours of sleep a night was more than enough. My apartment was covered in books. I read two at a time. In my dreams, I can still run. Remember going for runs together?"

"Yeah, I do. We covered a lot of miles on those runs."

"Now, I'm shot by one o'clock in the afternoon."

"One o'clock is a great time for a nap. In all fairness, a number of those runs ended in pancakes at the diner." Marie laughed and gave Margaret a playful swat.

Margaret finally laughed too. "You said it counted as cardio." Margaret paused and added, "I'm just stuck in my own head. Fact is, this is going down. I won't know what to do until I'm in it. Once I'm in it, I will have no choice, right? Right?"

"Right."

"Thanks for staying over with James. Nate will keep you posted on any updates and he'll let you know when I'm settled in my room. Then, you and William can bring the boys to meet Jane."

"Yeah, of course. William is coming over in the morning with Greyson. The four of us will go eat breakfast at the diner. Afterward, we'll be back at your place. What time do you leave?" Marie had it under control. There was no need for Margaret to worry. Needless to say, Margaret worried anyway.

"We have to be at the hospital by 4:30 a.m. I'm going into surgery at 5:30. Why so damned early is beyond me. Bunem probably has plans for the weekend. I will have a doctor who already has his mind on Saturday. Great." Margaret was done chasing produce around her salad bowl. She pushed it away. The ladies got themselves and their handfuls of shopping bags rounded up and out the door. They went home to wait impatiently and succumb to their anxiety.

TWENTY-EIGHT

MARGARET CHECKED THE clock again. 12:36 a.m. With a frustrated sigh, she turned over. She looked at the clock a half an hour later. 12:42. Alright, it only felt like half an hour. This was how she spent the night— flipping and sighing. It was punctuated by time spent hovering between sleep and awake. Nate had been able to sleep, which was obviously something Margaret did not appreciate right now. It took all she had not to accidentally on purpose wake him up.

"I'm not sleeping either." Nate said. His eyes were closed. However, he could feel his wife's eyes on him. Nate opened his eyes. Margaret was sitting up in bed, scrolling through news on her laptop.

"Oh, you're awake." Margaret tried to sound surprised. "Did you know whale sharks have three *thousand* teeth? "

"No I did not. Thank you for that random fact. I will keep it in mind"

"Hey, you never know." She looked over at Nate. "I am so flapped up."

Nate sat up and took her hand. "I love you. Breathe. It really is going to be alright." As much as he tried to sound calm, Margaret could hear the tension in his voice. "By lunchtime, Jane will be here. We will get through this." Nate gave Margaret a hug. She rested her head on Nate's chest, listening to his heartbeat. She felt the thrum in his chest when he spoke. This was the best place to be. While Margaret got a bit of sleep, Nate held his wife. Between thoughts of Chelsea, Jeff, and how this could be happening to him, Nate was wound extra tight. He was glad Margaret could not tell.

The alarm didn't need to be set. Both Nate and Margaret had given up on catching any sleep by three a.m. Nate was drinking coffee in the kitchen, getting his head in the game. Marie came in, still wearing pajamas, and looked as if she had not slept either.

"Hello there. You look rested and relaxed," Marie started in.

"Fresh as a daisy. Yup, that's me." Nate took another swig of coffee.

Marie set herself up with a cup. She took out her phone to check her list for the plan of action. They went over the list and windows of time Nate would try to call or text. Margaret rolled up in the kitchen, already dressed to go.

"Okay, let's get to it. Let's get this done." Margaret was speaking in a calm and measured voice. Inside, the fear felt like hot lava.

It was still dark during the drive to the hospital. Check-in was swift and in no time at all, Margaret was in a wheelchair being wheeled into surgery. The nurse could see Margaret was pale, sweaty, and shaking. Even Margaret's teeth were chattering.

"Oh, sweetie, you're so nervous. My name is Sharon. I will be with you the whole time. You and I are together. I promise to take good care of you." Margaret instantly loved her. She needed someone steady to hold on to. She felt so alone. Nate was not allowed in until after the epidural.

In the operating room, the nurse helped Margaret up onto the table. "Curve your back into a C," the anesthesiologist said from behind her.

Sharon walked in close to Margaret. "You just put your arms around me and hug me. I will hold you."

"Do you have Scoliosis?" the anesthesiologist asked. Margaret's breath halted for a second.

"Really? Please don't tell me I have something else wrong." Margaret held onto Sharon even harder. It took a few tries to finally get the epidural administered. But there was one problem. Margaret wasn't going numb.

The anesthesiologist with the bedside manner pinched Margaret on her lower abdomen. "Do you feel this, Mrs. Hall?"

"Yes. I do. What is going on?" Margaret did not like this guy's tone.

"Are you sure? Do you just feel pressure?"

"No. I can feel you pinching me. On my left side. Why am I not going numb?" The table moved, scaring her more.

"We are just tipping the table a bit to help get the medicine moving. If we have to, you can take a little nap while we deliver your baby."

The petrified part of Margaret was all for being knocked the hell out, but the rational side knew women did not normally get knocked out for delivery. Which meant something may be wrong. Urgency hung over

grace

the operating room as everyone talked around Margaret. As a team they discussed their next plan to get Janey out. So many numbers and medical terms were charted and yet the table tilted Margaret one way then the other. "Someone please tell me what is going on? Is Janey doing alright?" The anesthesiologist looked at her.

"Did you feel something just then?"

"When I was talking? I don't think so, do it again." The anesthesiologist grazed her skin with vulsellum forceps then gave her another pinch. Margaret made no expression. "Did you do anything?"

"Yes the epidural has taken effect"

"Oh thank God. Thank you, God." Soon after, Nate was wheeled in. Margaret burst into tears when she saw him.

"Nate, what happened? Why are you in a wheelchair?" She couldn't wait for an answer. I'm so scared. I couldn't get numb." Tears were falling down the side of Margaret's face, landing in her ears. Nate rolled close to Margaret and kissed her wet face.

"Shhh Baby, they make all the dads sit in these. It's easier to move us when we faint." He gave her a wink. "We got this." The couple took it step by step. Nate talked her through it. Margaret cried when she could feel them tugging on her. "Baby is out. You are doing great." Nate was sweating and his face was full of worry. Then one of the nurses called out time and weight. When Margaret heard Jane was only five pounds and four ounces, she was concerned.

"Is she okay?"

An angry little lamb yell filled the O.R. Sharon was smiling and brought baby Jane to them. A teeny red-faced, angry Jane was here. Margaret wept and smiled.

"Hi, baby Jane. I'm the one who snores— I'm sure you know. I love you, little girl. Sharon took Jane to get cleaned up and recorded. Nate stayed close to Margaret.

Soon, Dr. Bunem finished his last stitch. After getting cleaned up, he came to see Margaret in recovery. He smiled at her and said, "Congratulations, Mrs. Hall, you did a wonderful job. You have a healthy, beautiful daughter."

"Thank you, Doctor. You did a wonderful job, too." The doctor and Margaret fist bumped. "Okay, back to my coffee." The doctor's eyes lit up with humor.

TWENTY-NINE

WHAT SEEMED LIKE FOREVER later, Margaret was wheeled to her room. She and Nate were reunited there. The three of them had a little time for themselves before family and friends crowded the place. Nate and Margaret sat cuddled up in the hospital bed, marveling at the sweet slice of cutie pie in their arms.

"She looks so much like James. I'm going to feel weird putting bows in her hair." Margaret touched Jane's tiny nose. The Hall nose. She was definitely Nate's daughter.

"She's got her Mama's olive skin." Nate held his daughter's doll-sized hand. "Look at my girls. You are both so beautiful." Nate teared up. These two ladies had been through a lot together. He was a very proud husband and father. "I love you, Margaret. Thank you. Janey is," he breathed in, "Absolutely precious."

"I love you too, Nate." Margaret and Nate kissed. Then, together, they cooed and smooched their sweet baby, Jane.

After a few days in the hospital, Margaret dressed Jane to go home. Five outfit choices for the car ride may have been a bit excessive. "Pink sleeper with monkeys, Jane." She spoke in parentese as she dressed Jane. "Oh look and your special hat." Margaret giggled as she put the knit hat on her daughter's head. It was a cream colored hat with a pinkish beige top. The very top of the hat had a pinkish beige nub in the center. The hat was crocheted to look like a boob. Margaret loved driving her mother crazy. This was the hat sure to do it. Catherine was from a very different generation. A generation of formula fed babies. Margaret was a formula baby, which her mother repeatedly told her. Margaret, however, was a breastfeeding mom. The boobie hat was not a show of her personal choice, but a real fun way to get Cathy flapped.

Nate and James arrived at the hospital. Nate carried the carseat. James carried a stuffed pink bunny. They were all excited to be together again. To start their life with baby Jane. "Hello, sweet Jane." Nate nuzzled her fuzzy little head. "How are you feeling today, Babe?" Nate gave Margaret a kiss.

"I am feeling ready to get home. We need to start being a family of four. Plus, I miss my guys too much to spend another day away."

"Look, a pink bunny for Jane." James held it up with pride. "I picked it out all by myself." James looked at his sister in her little hospital bassinet. "Hey, Janey. I got this for you. I named him Bill. You can change it if you want." The newborn did not protest the name choice. James was happy that Jane agreed. The family of four, and Bill, went home to start living.

Margaret was surprised and relieved when she saw her mom back at the apartment. "Mom. I thought you were coming just for this weekend?" Margaret gave her mom a hug. She could tell Catherine had already started cleaning. The woman could not be stopped. No mess, real or imagined, was safe when Catherine was around.

"You got me for a week, Kiddo. Now, why don't you and Jane go to bed for a bit? James and I have plans at the toy store, don't we, James?" She smiled at her grandson.

"Sure do, Gran. I'm getting a big brother gift today." Nate looked at the time. He was concerned shopping would take too long.

"I have work to do today, Bud. I can't go shopping with you," Nate said.

"Dad, you aren't invited. It's just Gran and me." Margaret and her mother laughed.

Nate chuckled. "Well, alright then. You two go shopping so Mom and Janey can sleep." Not needing any more encouragement, James grabbed Gran's hand and went out the door. Margaret was so happy to be back home in her own bed and snuggled with her sweet baby. Within minutes, Margaret fell asleep with Janey on her chest. Janey's face was tilted towards her mother's soft snores as if listening to a lullaby. Nate worked quietly at his desk with the lights low. At one point, he spun in his desk chair and watched them sleeping. *You did it, Margaret. You endured through the pain and fear again and again as if it were no sacrifice. Now you are sleeping with a smile on your face. You're stronger than me.*

THIRTY

JEFF WAS BECOMING SURE of two things. First, he had grown fond of tea. Second, he had also grown quite fond of Chelsea. Jeff found himself thinking of her often and wondering what she was doing. Last week, he had made an appointment for a haircut at the salon where Chelsea worked. Really, he just needed to find a way to be around her. Jeff had been getting his haircuts from the same old furry eared barber, José, for years. Sitting in the posh salon was a very different experience. There were high shine polished floors. Everything was chrome, glass, or mirrored. Thick upholstered chairs in the waiting area. It was very modern and trendy. Nothing like José's. José had a much better magazine selection. Jeff was pretty sure he wouldn't find a Craftsman Catalog in this place. He picked up one of the glossy magazines. It was full of celebrity gossip. Which celebrities were losing weight, breaking up, or going bankrupt.

"Morning, Jeff."

Jeff held a tea out for Chelsea.

"Thank you." She gave Jeff a hug.

"It's White Monkey Paw Tea. It has a sweet, smooth… something." Jeff didn't have a clue. "I picked it because it said monkey paw."

Chelsea laughed. He was funny. She had really come to like having Jeff around. "So, what are we doing today? Highlights? Extensions?"

"I was thinking more of a trim," Jeff answered.

She sat him in her chair, caped him, and got to work. When Chelsea finished, she swiveled the chair to face the mirror.

"What do you think?" Chelsea handed him a mirror so Jeff could check out the back.

Jeff felt bad for José. The old man had lost a customer. "Wow. It looks great." Jeff moved his head to the right and left to see it from all angles. "Are you doing anything after work? Do you want to get out of here and grab some food?"

"Thanks, I can't though. I'm leading a yoga class in an hour." Chelsea did want to spend more time with Jeff. "How about coming to the class? We can eat after, if it's okay with you."

"I can try tonight. I have a side job later but maybe I can move it." In his mind the side job was already cancelled. "Is your class the same time every night?"

"I'm there Monday and Thursday nights. One of these nights you have to give it a try."

"I will see what I can do," said Jeff.

Chelsea was excited Jeff was willing to give yoga a shot. "I have an extra mat you can use."

"Thanks. What time is the class? Should I be early?"

"The class is at six. I'll throw a mat down for you to hold your spot. All the good ones go quick. Most people set up in the same spot for every class and get cranky when some newbie takes *their* space. So much peace and love," Chelsea said with a laugh.

"Where are the good spots?" Jeff wanted the inside information. He needed to be in the yoga *know*.

"The spots near me. They have the best view of me… or, you know, the yoga poses." Chelsea was fumbling a bit. She could feel herself redden.

"Well then, you'll have to save me your best spot. I need to have a good view of… the poses."

"I will be sure to. See you soon." She kissed his cheek and walked away.

Both of them spent the rest of the day smiling.

Chelsea had to admit that she was growing to have real feelings for Jeff. There was a sweetness in Jeff's blue eyes. Very different from the dark night eyes Nate looked at her with. This may have started out as a way to get closer to Nate, or even just to get under his skin, but now she wasn't sure what it was. This gave her a control over Nate that she had never had in their relationship. He was the one with another life and all she could do was take anything he'd give her. Now, no matter how agitated Nate got with her and Jeff, there was nothing he could do. With one text she could ruin his day.

Besides, she could date Jeff. Why not? She deserved the same thing Nate's wife got. Chelsea had made friends with Margaret to keep an eye on Nate. She figured that if the good Margaret could rope Nate, Chelsea would have no problem scoring Jeff. She giggled to herself while she was washing her next client's hair.

Margaret was so in love with Janey she didn't notice the passing of her birthday or much else. Then she realized it had been almost two months since Janey had been born and she could not stay sedentary anymore. She had convinced Marie to go to Chelsea's yoga class.

grace

"Glad you could make it," Chelsea greeted them both. "You go easy, Margaret. This is your first time back on your mat." Chelsea was dressed in purple yoga pants thin enough to see through and a black half shirt. "I have three of my friends tonight. This is gonna be a fun class." Chelsea walked to the front of the hardwood floor. She first put her own mat down, followed by another in an open space in the front row.

Margaret looked down at herself, frustrated with the soft and doughy belly she still had post-Jane. "Gotta start somewhere," she whispered to her biscuit body. In a simple seated pose, Margaret began breathing slowly in and out of her nose.

"Huh, I wonder who her other friend is," Marie said, aloud, as she stretched her muscular body. "Probably some other bendy amazonian." Marie got down in a Hindi squat and closed her eyes. When she opened them, Jeff was weaving around the other mats on the floor.

Margaret tapped Marie on the arm. "Look, it's Jeff. Oh, yay, I hoped they had hit it off."

"Yeah, I see him." Marie's face grew a mischievous smile.

"Jefffffah," Marie loudly whispered. Jeff turned to see Margaret and Marie with asshole grins on their faces.

He stepped over and around mats. Margaret and Marie were at the end of the yoga mat maze. "Hey, Maggs. Hey, Marie. You girls here for some yoga?"

"No," Marie said while pointing at their mats. "We are farming." She pointed at Jeff. "What are YOU doing, Jeff? I didn't know you were interested in—" She shot an exaggerated stare at Chelsea. "—yoga."

"Uh, yeah, figured I would take a shot at it. So, good to see you two. I better get to my mat." Jeff turned.

"Yes. You shoot your shot, good sir." Marie pointed to his mat. "Make sure you pay attention."

Then, Margaret added, "Wouldn't want you to pull a muscle."

Jeff let out a nervous laugh and clumsily stepped over the other mats. Chelsea walked to the light switch and dimmed the lights. Before stepping on her mat, she hit play. Sitar music filled the room.

"Okay, class, let us begin." Chelsea spoke just above a whisper. "Please step to the front of your mat. Feet together. Spread your toes and reach your feet to all four corners of the earth. Hands together in front of your heart."

An hour later they were at the end of the class and everyone was on their backs, hands at their sides with closed eyes. This was called corpse pose, and it was killing Marie. Relaxing was not her gig. She could only get so calm for so long and Chelsea was pushing it. Finally, they closed the practice and Marie got back to normal speed.

Margaret and Marie were rolling up their mats when Chelsea glided their way. "Jeff and I are going to grab some food at the diner." She pointed over her shoulder in Jeff's direction. "You ladies want to join us?"

"Oh, thanks for asking." Margaret looked at her watch. "Jane is a bit of a badger. She's probably already giving Nate Hell. I'm on boob lockdown."

"Yes, William is on call tonight anyway. I should definitely get home." Marie had no desire to watch love bloom. She was going home to hit the treadmill.

THIRTY-ONE

THE ICE CLINKED IN the glass while Chelsea stirred her unsweetened tea with her straw. Jeff sucked down his coke and pushed his glass toward the edge. They perused the menus. A waitress stopped in front of them, placed a fresh coke on the table and asked, "Do you want to order? Or do you need another minute?"

"I'm ready. I'll have a grilled cheese with American and tomato. Oh, can I have gravy for the fries?" Chelsea took down half of her iced tea. "And another tea— when you get a chance. Thank you." Chelsea closed the ten page menu and handed it back to the waitress.

"What about you, Hun?" the waitress asked Jeff.

"A cheeseburger and fries. American cheese, medium. Thank you." Jeff passed back his menu.

"Alright then. It'll be out in a few. If you need anything, wave me down." The waitress sashayed into the kitchen to put in their order.

"So, what did you think of class tonight?" Chelsea sipped her tea.

"I really like it, but damn, I had no idea how bad my balance was. My first attempt at eagle pose— I was the epitome of grace." A clumsy Jeff made for an entertaining practice for everyone else. Especially for Margaret and Marie.

"You'll get there." Chelsea paused and looked at Jeff. It was as if she was taking the temperature. "So, this polite conversation we're always engaging in. I'm all set with politeness. Can we have a real talk?"

Jeff watched her mouth form the words she was saying. Her full lips had a bit of a smile while she talked. He barely managed to hear the actual words. "Sure. What about?" Jeff tried to sound casual. He failed.

"About you and me. Or am I alone in this?" Chelsea knew she was not. Every move, sigh, and smile was just right. She'd gone after this kind of prey before— it was going to be easy. Easier than his brother had been, Chelsea knew for sure. But, was it what she even wanted anymore? Chelsea's growing feelings for Jeff had her doubting her original goal of provoking a response from Nate, so he would make a move. Front and center is where she would be with a guy like Jeff.

"No, you are not alone at all. I think you're great." *Great*? Was this really the best Jeff could do? "I really like spending time with you. You inspire me to try new things."

"New things like my homemade tea concoctions?" Chelsea had a feeling Jeff did not really like tea. He was a malleable one and she enjoyed how easy he was to enamour.

"Yes, your tea is good stuff. Had I not gotten to know you, I may not have learned what steeped dandelions taste like." Jeff laughed. "I am more of a coffee guy. The kind with so much caffeine, it makes my kidneys vibrate."

"You are a good sport about trying new things."

The waitress was back with their order. She dropped off their food and a new bottle of ketchup. "Do either of you two need anything else?"

"I think we're all set, thank you." Jeff needed the waitress to be on her way so he could keep talking to Chelsea. With a nod, the waitress moved on to her other tables. Jeff looked at Chelsea thinking she was so damned pretty. Her blonde hair was in a messy but adorable pile on her head. Sunny wisps of hair lay on her neck. He imagined nibbling on her exposed neck. "So, you were talking about trying new things."

"Yes, I was. Jeff, do you like me?" A direct woman. Chelsea dipped a fry in gravy.

"Yes, I like you. Wait, is this where you tell me you like me *as a friend*?"

"Just friends? Have I given that impression?" Maybe Chelsea would have to come out and say it. "Jeff, I like you a lot." She watched his face light up when he heard her words. He was the cutest and, damn it all, she really did like him.

"Well, I like you too." There, he said it. Jeff's fear of bursting into flames from embarrassment did not happen. For a bit, neither one spoke. They focused on their fries. Two more drinks were put on their table as their waitress breezed by. Neither one could eat. The mutual feelings had filled their stomachs with butterflies.

"I'm not so hungry. I'm getting my grilled cheese to go. Hope you don't mind."

"You know, I was thinking the same thing. I can eat this burger for breakfast." Jeff saw their waitress and asked for the check and boxes. They each packed their food up. Jeff went to the counter and paid the bill. Then, Jeff walked Chelsea to her car.

"Thanks for dinner. Even though we didn't eat it."

Jeff's stomach was fluttering. "You're welcome." He stepped close to Chelsea, leaned in most of the way, and stopped inches from her mouth. It felt like he was hanging out there for a year. Chelsea met him the rest of the way. They kissed.

When they parted, Chelsea looked into Jeff's eyes. "Damn," she whispered. She felt herself falling. Jeff swore Chelsea heard his heart pounding. They kissed again— a long kiss full of intention. Both bags of food were dropped to the ground. They groped at each other and made out in the diner parking lot. Jeff's hand slid over Chelsea's chest. She pushed her body closer to Jeff and pressed up against him. Her hands pulled at his shirt. She gave herself over to his kiss. Jeff kissed and nibbled at her neck and the small bites sent shivers to Chelsea's lap.

"Whoa, okay. We need to reign it in." They stopped. Chelsea knew her weaknesses. Jeff's kiss was quickly becoming one of them.

"Yeah, you're right. One more kiss though." Jeff didn't have to lean in this time. Chelsea met his mouth with her own. Her tongue weaved around Jeff's. She was getting wet. Her hand went to Jeff's pants and she felt him bulge and swell with her touch. Again, Chelsea had to break the trance the kissing had gotten her in.

"You, sir, are trouble. Damn." Chelsea was tap dancing on a line she was not sure she should cross. She got into her car. Nate glimmered in her mind and she huffed as she clicked her seatbelt. Jeff knocked on the window and smiled. He was holding up a bag. She lowered the window and asked, "Did I forget something?"

"Yes." Jeff gave Chelsea her bag of leftovers. He leaned in and kissed her slow with his hand warm on her cheek. The passion in Jeff's kiss and the heat of his mouth made Chelsea fall over her imaginary line.

"We should go, Jeff." Chelsea was red faced and smiling. "Follow me." She started her car. Chelsea looked at Jeff. "Have you changed your mind?"

"Are you kidding me?" Jeff practically skipped to his truck with a cheesy grin on his face and a raging hard on in his pants. He followed her back to her place and pulled in next to her. He put the truck in park and jumped out at the same time.

They chased each other to her front door. While Chelsea fished through her keys, Jeff stood behind her with his hands on her waist. The front door opened and Jeff and Chelsea fell into her place, kissing hard and feeling each other. Taking his hand, Chelsea led Jeff to her bedroom. "Have you ever heard of edging, Jeff?"

"No, but whatever it is, I'm game." Jeff was open to whatever resulted with him inside Chelsea.

"I'll show you." Chelsea put her hand down his pants and wrapped her hand around him. Jeff was already hard. "This is a nice start." Chelsea liked the feel of him thick in her hand. "Drop your pants." Jeff of course, did what she wanted. Chelsea slowly got to her knees. Maintaining eye contact. Then, she put him in her mouth.

Jeff inhaled and almost forgot to keep breathing. Her tongue was velvet and the heat of her mouth was extreme. Chelsea began sucking and licking him.

"Oh. My. God." Jeff's head fell back. Chelsea kept sucking him. She used her hand to jerk him off while she blew him. Chelsea could feel how stiff he was in her mouth. Using her other hand, Chelsea stroked Jeff's taint. It was unexpected. Jeff sucked in his breath. "Ohhh—" Between the sucking and stroking, Jeff's knees started to feel weak.

"Let me know when you're close." Chelsea went back to it.

He groaned. "This feels good." Jeff was already there. "I'm getting close." Jeff closed his eyes, letting himself feel Chelsea's mouth slide up and down him. Then, nothing. Jeff opened his eyes. Chelsea was still on her knees in front of him. "Why did you stop? Is something wrong?"

"Not at all. This is edging. I get you almost there, then we stop for a bit." Chelsea used this kind of sex to establish both her power and find weaknesses.

"How long is a bit?" Jeff was beside himself.

"Don't worry, I will let you finish. Be patient." Chelsea stood up. She kissed Jeff on the neck. She whispered, "I'm going to give you the most intense orgasm."

"Kissing me is not helping." He smiled.

"Maybe this will help." Chelsea undressed in front of him. Her body was amazing. The yoga was not just all talk.

Jeff cupped her tits and started kissing them. He kissed down her stomach until he was the one on his knees. Chelsea backed up and sat on the edge of the bed. She laid back, her legs spread. Chelsea opened herself up and moaned. "Put your tongue in me."

Jeff crawled over to Chelsea. He put his hands on the back of her thighs, holding her legs up. He played with her clit then plunged his tongue into her. She tasted fantastic.

"Ohhhhh, Jeff." Chelsea wrapped her legs around Jeff's head and pulled him in. His tongue was deep. "Mmmmmm, yes. Don't you stop until I say."

Jeff moaned his understanding. Her body responded to every touch. She curved and arched and pushed herself into his face. Eating her was getting him worked up. Jeff devoured her.

Chelsea could feel the heat inside her building with every lick. "Ohhhhh, Jeff. Ohhhhh, yes, yes." Chelsea pulled herself away from Jeff. It was time for her to take a minute. Chelsea patted the mattress and Jeff climbed in. "Lay back for me." Jeff eased himself onto his back.

Chelsea put herself in between Jeff's legs and went down on him again. Her wet mouth and woven together fingers worked him over. Jeff closed his eyes. He concentrated on controlling himself. Chelsea's mouth made it impossible. Soon, the build up became a dire need. Taking Chelsea by the nape of her neck, he moved her off of him. This edging was tortuous. He almost let himself finish. Smiling, Chelsea ran her fingers up the inside of Jeff's thighs. She wanted him to wait, but only for a minute. It was Chelsea who could no longer wait. She straddled him backwards, sitting down on him. Jeff could feel inside of her and it was almost unreal how good she felt. Up and down Chelsea rode him.

Every stroke brought Jeff closer. Jeff put his hands on her hips and started bringing her down on him faster and harder.

"Ooooooh, Jeff. Yes. Yes. Yes. Go. Go." Jeff and Chelsea fucked full force. "Ooooooh, Jeff, now, now." Jeff flipped Chelsea on her back and plowed into her. He went hard and deep. Chelsea wrapped her legs around him, pulling him close. Her nails dug into his back.

"Breathe," Chelsea purred in his ear. "You can finish now."

Jeff's orgasm was fierce. His insides were a furnace then all of the heat gathered force and he nearly combusted from the feeling.

The look in Jeff's eyes as they rolled back and the pulsing she felt as he finished inside her pushed Chelsea past her breaking point. She yelled as she climaxed. She bit Jeff's shoulder. They collapsed into each other, sweaty and exhausted.

Jeff kissed Chelsea. "You are something else." He drank half of the glass of water on the nightstand and handed the rest to Chelsea. She finished it. "That was amazing. I don't think I have ever come so hard in my life." Jeff kissed Chelsea. "You are something else."

"Me?" Chelsea was flushed. "I gotta hand it to you, Jeff. You eat pussy like the hungriest man alive. For a while there, I was literally speaking in hieroglyphics. Jeez."

Jeff cracked up.

The two of them cuddled under the covers, talking and laughing until the sun came up. After dozing a bit in the early morning, Jeff kissed a sleeping Chelsea. He found paper and a pen on her bedside table and wrote a quick note:

> *Chelsea,*
> *I had a spectacular night. Call me when you wake up. I would like to see you again. -Jeff.*

He put the note next to the lamp on the end table and tiptoed out.

THIRTY-TWO

NATE SAT AT HIS desk working claim after claim on his computer. Margaret was using the magic of both kids napping to clean up around the apartment— beating back the piles, finding the bottom of the kitchen sink hiding under dishes, putting fresh sheets on the bed.

"Let me help you." Nate went around to the other side of the bed to help fit the sheet. In no time, the bed only needed pillows. Nate put them in cases and tossed them to Margaret who positioned them on the bed. He watched her bending and stretching. "Thanks for the assist, Babe."

"You're welcome. However..." Nate took hold of a corner of the comforter and yanked. The blanket and pillows slid down and spilled off, undoing all the bedding and all their work.

"Nate. Really? Is this what we're doing?" Margaret was exasperated. She had little free time as it was, and spent all of it cleaning. "What the hell did you do that for?"

"So we can get in." A grin spread across Nate's face. Margaret smiled. "Alone time is a rarity with two kids. We need to jump on it, so to speak."

"I like the way you think, Nate." Margaret moved close to kiss Nate.

Nate had impatiently waited eight weeks. "I smell lemon fresh and I am a wreck." Nate took the tie out of Margaret's hair, freeing it to spill down her back. She raised her arms as the cotton tee was lifted over her head.

"You are absolutely beautiful," Nate said while his fingers lightly followed the curve of Margaret. It was one of those increasingly rare moments when he saw how lovely his wife was. Nate backed Margaret up and had her lie down on the bed. He hooked the waistband of her leggings and pulled them off. Naked, Margaret got on her knees and went to the edge of the bed. She slipped Nate's shirt over his head as Nate unzipped his pants.

"I've missed you," Nate said between biting and kissing her neck.

"I have missed you too," Margaret sighed as they slid down into the covers, wrapped around each other's bodies. Kissing, tasting, biting. Nate had his leg in between Margaret's thighs, feeling the heat as she moaned and gyrated. She moaned, broke free of their knot, and went to all fours, lowering her face closer to the mattress as her legs slid open wider. Nate got to his knees. Again, he lightly ran his fingers over her skin. He watched her back arch. He placed a hand on the tattoo on the small of her back and pushed down on her. His other hand held onto her hip. Nate's thrust pushed him in all the way and Margaret gasped. She was so tight. It felt so good.

"You are fun to fuck," Nate whispered in her ear as he bent over her. He fucked her with hard, deliberate strokes. With each one he gave Margaret as much as she could handle.

She let out a short, low moan every time Nate pushed to the base. The silkenness of her swollen wet lips gripped him every time he pulled out.

Nate had to taste her. He kept her on her hands and knees as he pulled out and ate her. He took slow, long licks, tasting her deep inside with his tongue. He pulled himself away and pushed his fingers into her. He slid up alongside her, fingering her with one hand and squeezing her nipples with the other. He flipped Margaret to her back and shoved his fingers back into her. Nate took her nipple in his mouth, biting and sucking.

Margaret was hot and more turned on than she could ever remember being. She felt almost drunk. "Nate, this feels— mmmm." She raised her head and took Nate into her mouth. She sucked him hungrily while he buried his hand deeper.

"Come for me." Nate started rubbing her clit with his thumb. Two fingers inside her. In and out. He whispered in her ear, "I love this pussy. Come for me. I can feel you squeezing." Margaret was so close. Nate kept fingering and licking her. "Mmmmm" He moaned in her ear. "Give it to me." Nate fingered her hard and fast. Harder and faster. He curled his finger, hitting her G spot every damned time.

Margaret's orgasm was ferocious. She yelled and bucked, until she lay quivering with labored breathing.

Nate whispered, "I'm not done." Nate climbed on top of her, pushed himself in, and let out a deep grunt. In and out, Nate filled Margaret again and again as he fucked her without mercy. The first orgasm made way for another, even more intense one that brought her to the edge and let her go and the feeling was delicious.

"Nate..." She moaned. "Yes."

Nate could feel her squeezing around him. Her whole body felt the intensity of it all. Nate put his hand to her mouth, covering it to keep her quiet. Inside, Margaret was warm and wet. Now that Margaret was finished, Nate went at his wife with one goal in mind.

He was sweating and grunting like a beast and Margaret loved it. When the third orgasm claimed her, Nate could not hold back any more. He came inside Margaret. "Fuuuuck," he said through clenched teeth.

They took a minute to relish it.

"We needed that," Nate finally said.

"You ain't kidding." Margaret felt sleepy. It was a work day and Nate still had a lot of work to do. Margaret was feeling quite content, and the children were still sleeping. So, she curled up and fell asleep for almost an hour before her world woke her up.

THIRTY-THREE

MARGARET SPENT ANOTHER SATURDAY morning running errands. Janey was not happy about going to the store. To be fair, Janey was not amused by much. Since Nate was home, he and James got guy time while Margaret listened to Janey cry the whole way to the store. Then throughout every aisle, Jane continued to let her dissatisfaction be known. Margaret's arms were the only place Janey wanted to be, so she had to take Jane out of the carrier and hold her. Margaret had forgotten her front carrier in the car and instead held Janey with one hand and poorly steered the cart with the other. The end aisle display of Organic O's never had a chance. The cart took the corner too wide, clipping the metal shelf. Cereal boxes rained down on the aisle and the ruckus it made was loud. Other shoppers looked at sweaty, disheveled Margaret holding a baby. Jane was distracted by the scene and momentarily not hateful. A nearby employee saw the breakfast cereal avalanche and hustled right over to clean up the boxes.

"Ma'am, are you alright? I'll get this taken care of." The young man started picking up the boxes.

"Yes, I'm fine. This is so embarrassing. I took out your whole display." Margaret laughed a little. Jane was happy and gurgling as if she wasn't just being a little asshole baby two aisles ago. Margaret used her free hand to help clean up.

"Ma'am, it's very nice of you to help, but please don't worry about this," he said as he rebuilt the pyramid of cereal boxes.

"Thank you. I really am sorry." Margaret nuzzled her little honey badger baby. She managed the rest of the shopping without clearing any more shelves and even made it through checkout without disaster. Now, all the groceries were in the back of the truck. Margaret strapped Jane back into her carrier. She said a silent prayer then opened the truck door. As soon as the click of her car seat sounded, Jane went right back to asshole baby. Jane hated the car seat and was red-faced and pissed the whole ride home. Margaret did breathing exercises while Jane screamed her discontent. When the duo finally arrived home and Margaret turned into the parking spot, she side-swiped Nate's car. "Oh shit!" She could not believe she had done something so mindless."Oh, mother fuck. Like I need this. Fanfuckingtastic." She was anxious from the hellacious store trip. Jane had dragged her to the edge. Margaret drew a deep breath, held it momentarily, and let it out slow and audibly. This day had already sucked the biggest suck and now this.

"Hey guys! We're back from the store," Margaret called into the apartment. She put down the couple of bags she had brought in while holding Jane. "Can you help me with the bags?"

Nate and James heard Margaret's call. James had asked his mom for a new box of chocolate chip waffles and was eager to discover which bag held them. Nate was doing some weekend overtime and a break sounded perfect, even if it was to unload groceries. Lola came with them. She needed to sniff the grocery bags.

"Hey there. Sure. Let me put my headset down." Nate was right back and ready to unload. James was ready to help excavate his waffles and juice bags.

Margaret took a deep breath. "Okay, before we go out there, I need to tell you something." Jane was falling asleep in Margaret's arms, looking precious and perfect. She was not taking any responsibility for the shitastic time she had put her mother through. Stinking adorable, asshole baby.

"What is it? Don't tell me there was no string cheese at the store. Damn it!" Nate shook his fists with mock rage.

"Please don't be pissed," Margaret began.

"Oh, no. What did you do?" Nate got his serious face on.

"I was turning to park next to you, like I always do." Margaret stalled.

"Yeah, and what?" Nate had a tight look on his face.

"I side swiped your car. Nate, I am so sorry. Like, so very sorry. I'm going on no sleep. This little badger was not having it at the store. She cried the whole time. We knocked over shelves at the store. She cried in the car on the way home. I guess I was distracted. I am so sorry, Nate. So. Sorry."

James's eyes bugged. His hands were on the top of his head. "OOOOH, Mama, you are in trouble!"

"Alright. Alright. Take it easy. Let's see what we're dealing with." Nate and Margaret went to assess the situation.

James followed close behind them. He had to see what damage his mom had done. When he did, he was sure to let Margaret know what he thought. "Wow,

Mama! What a long mark! It looks really bad. Daddy, are you mad at Mama?"

Margaret rolled her eyes, but she had to admit, James was right. The chrome from the truck bumper dented the whole side. One long, scrapey, paint-removing dent the whole length of his car.

"Well, you did a good job on it," Nate said. He ran his hand over the damage. "This is fixable, and you and Jane are home now. It will be alright." Nate hugged Margaret, knowing this was just another thing he would have to fix. At least Nate worked in insurance and could get this taken care of quickly. "Why don't you go lay down and rest. James and I will unload. Jane can supervise."

"Oh my God, Nate. Thank you." Margaret was exhausted from the shake up at the store and at home. She was already headed down the hall when she said, "Sounds wonderful." Minutes later, she was curled up under the covers, snoring. Nate found the BabyBjörn and strapped Janey in. In no time at all, the groceries were put away. Jane fell asleep in the carrier. Nate worked with her sleeping on him. James went back to his legos. Margaret slept.

Margaret woke slowly and rolled over. Her sheet creased face was buried in her pillow. She sat up and rubbed the sleep out of her eyes. With blurry vision, Margaret squinted at her phone. 11:17 lit up the screen. A whole day was gone. Slept away. Her boobs were huge and milk had gone through her shirt. The dire pull to nurse got her moving. First she needed a fresh shirt.

"Nate? James?" she called out. "Guys?" Lola came in with her little brown tail wagging. "Hey, little La." Margaret scooped up the tiny dog and went to find Nate and James. Her head still felt dizzy from sleep. She felt off. " Hey, there you guys are." A fort had been built in the living room. It looked like every blanket and sheet had been donated to the project. It was quite the little tented city. The blankets stretched from the television all the way across the living room to the couches. Snack bag clips connected the sheets. James's head popped out between his Ninja turtle sheets.

"Look what we made! Mama, come in. You have to. We even have snacks!"

"Snacks? I'm in." Margaret parted the sheets. Inside, it was dim with a pile of pillows in the middle. There were bags of chips and fruit snacks on one side, a box of juice bags on the other. Nate had Jane in his arms while he watched *Lego Star Wars* and she drank a bottle. Nate looked up and saw Margaret.

"Hey. How was your sleep?" Nate scooted over to make room for his wife on pillow hill. He was relieved she was awake, if not to be helpful then to at least break up the relentless kid noises he had endured. James, with his constant questions, combined with Janey"s constant crankiness had done a thorough job of testing Nate's patience.

"It was alright, I guess. I feel weird though. Kind of dizzy." Margaret touched the side of her face. She had felt numb the day before, but tried to pass it off until she noticed the left side slacked a bit in the mirror. It was now over twenty-four hours of feeling something was amiss. Margaret's chest was tight with fear of what was happening and that she was powerless to stop it.

"Nate, I need to call the doctor in the morning." The two looked at each other and Nate nodded his head, acknowledging what they both dreaded. They wove their fingers together and enjoyed TV tenting with the kids until they all went to bed.

Jane crowed earlier than a rooster. Margaret opened her eyes to find her vision was doubled. She closed and rubbed her eyes. When she opened them her vision remained doubled. When Margaret covered one eye, she could see fine. When she tried looking out of both together, it was a disaster. "Nate, honey, are you awake?" A sleepy-eyed Jane was all cozied up and content with her mama. Margaret stroked her soft cheek and nursed. She didn't trust herself to walk with the baby. Nate would have to change the little lady. Margaret spoke softly. "Nate, I'm sorry to wake you."

"Hey, morning." Nate gave his body a long, deliberate stretch. "What's up? What do you need?" he asked as he scratched his chest.

"I can't see correctly, Nate. My eyes aren't focusing and everything doubles when I try to use both eyes. The dizziness makes me feel like I'm going to fall." Nate sat right up and gave Janey good morning kisses until he placed her in Margaret's arms. When Jane was done eating, Nate scooped up his baby girl and went to freshen her up. Margaret's equilibrium was horribly off, making the room feel dangerously tilted. When she tried to put her head on her pillow, Margaret felt as if she'd suddenly flipped upside down. The vomit came up quickly. Margaret fell sideways, leaning out of the bed, and threw up bile.

Nate and a freshly diapered Jane came back in to find Margaret on her stomach, her head hanging off of the bed, dry heaving. "Margaret! Jesus Christ. Okay, baby Jane, you chill here for a bit." Nate put Janey in the co-sleeper. He flew over the bed to Margaret and slid the green bucket out from under the bed and held her hair. "I love you, Margaret," was all he could say. Nate prayed this wouldn't be as bad as he feared it was.

Margaret's stomach called a truce, so Nate took advantage and helped her sit up slowly. Attempting it too fast would have her spinning and puking again. He wiped her face and smoothed her loosened ponytail. "I'll call Dr. Edmond." Nate kissed her forehead. "There will be someone on call for emergencies." Nate scrolled to the doctor's contact number and hit send and waited for someone to answer.

"The whole left side of my face feels numb." Margaret took a few cautious sips of water from the cup on her side table. Some dribbled down her chin. What managed to get in her mouth tasted and felt strange going down. Water should do none of those things. It was official. Margaret was afraid. All she could do was breathe and look calm, two seemingly gargantuan goals to accomplish.

"Hello. You have reached Empire Medical. We are now closed. If this is an emergency, dial..." He hung up. Nate searched his contacts until he found the doctor's private number. After three rings, Dr. Edmond picked up. Nate put the call on speaker.

"Hello, Doctor Edmond. This is Nate Hall. Listen, Margaret is having another flare-up. It seems worse than before. What should we do?"

"How is she right now?"

"Scared. The last few days, her symptoms have gotten worse. She was misjudging distances but we didn't realize how bad it was until after she sideswiped my parked car."

"What exactly is happening? I need to know all of her symptoms. It will help me figure out which area of her brain is being affected."

"Her equilibrium is a mess," Nate began. "When she lays down, she feels upside down and her vision is doubled. The left side of her face is numb and even water tastes weird."

"She needs to get steroids to treat the acute symptoms. Do you want to bring her to the hospital for infusions?"

Nate looked at Margaret. She had heard what the doctor suggested but didn't respond to his question.

"Or, would you feel better with a nurse coming to your house? The nurse can set it up and teach Nate how."

"Yes, please let me stay home. I don't want to leave the kids." Margaret needed to take care of her babies, which meant she needed to be home. Dr. Edmond and Nate made arrangements for delivery of meds and an appointment with a visiting nurse.

"Dr. Edmond needs you to have an MRI to gauge the location and severity of this new lesion activity. They will want to use contrast dye to better see your inflammation. Dr. Edmund said, contrast dye does not affect your breast milk." Magaret didn't give a flying fruit fig what Dr. Edmund said, she would do no such thing. Since Janey was born, Margaret pumped after she nursed. Nate would imitate the mechanical whine and jokingly call her, "Bessie".

"Nate, I am not going to nurse Jane with steroids in me. See? You didn't think I needed to pump after every time I nursed. Now we have twenty bags of boob juice ready to go. What's my Name? Bessie, is right." She laughed and winked. They needed a moment of humor before the inevitable storm.

"You're a good girl, Bessie. Good girl."

THIRTY-FOUR

LATER IN THE DAY, the doorbell rang on the Hall's apartment door. Nate quickly answered.

"Hi, I'm Ally." An icy blue eyed nurse was wearing dark purple scrubs and a matching bandana on her head. She walked in with questions. "Did the delivery make it? The doctor was adamant about getting it started as soon as possible."

"Hello. I'm Nate Hall and my wife's name is Margaret. She's inside. Yes, the meds and materials are here. You're going to show me how to do this?" Nate was feeling overwhelmed, but he had to and would do this.

"Oh, yes, Mr. Hall. When I'm done, you will be almost as good as me. Just kidding. No, you won't, but let's get to it anyway." She clapped him on the shoulder. Nate couldn't help himself and laughed. She followed Nate to the bedroom.

Margaret was in bed, propped up by pillows. She felt suffocatingly hot and freezing cold all at once and it was getting worse by the minute. Even though she was a sweaty, nauseated mess, she sat with the breast pump whirring on and on. She filled as many bags as she could before the steroids would force her to stop. She heard someone come into the house, turned off the pump, and sealed the bags. After about a minute, Nate walked in with a young nurse whose scrubs were the color of grapes. "Hello, Margaret, I'm Ally. I will be helping Nate with your IV." Margaret could barely open her eyes. She felt dizzy, like she had been on a roller coaster with no end. "We will put in a PICC line. It will stay in from the first of three days of infusion." Margaret nodded. "I will be setting you up today. Then, your handsome husband here is going to take over. You can handle this, right, Mr. Hall?" Nate nodded. He watched Margaret struggle to respond. Talking was difficult when the left side of her face was not fully cooperating, so instead, she nodded her understanding. Nate paid careful attention to Ally and asked questions to be sure he had the process down. Soon, Margaret was hooked up and receiving an infusion of steroids to fight the inflammation and hopefully get some relief.

When the run of steroids finished, Marie drove her friend to the imaging center. It had been a long time since Margaret's MS had gotten this kind of bad. Margaret was spiraling and doing worse than before the steroids, which for some reason, Margaret did not respond to. Instead, her pain level went straight to the fiery depths— scorchings pain and a whore of a headache, all thrown on top of her other symptoms. It had been days since Margaret had been fully awake or aware. A radiologist assistant came to the waiting room for Margaret. "Hello, I'm Robert. I will be performing your MRI. How are you doing today? Can you walk?" Margaret stared at him, his words took a moment to register. After a delay she slowly stood up on her shaky legs, swaying a bit, but she kept her arms out to balance. Marie was instantly annoyed with this jackass.

"Robert, does she look jaunty to you?" Robert glanced at Marie, then back at Margaret. The radiologist seemed satisfied with Margaret's shakey show of balance and waved for her to follow. She shuffled behind him with her hand on the wall for balance. Marie dropped back into her seat and aggressively turned the pages of a very dated Town and Country.

In the MRI room, Robert set Margaret up and explained the MRI of the head and C spine. Margaret was not doing well. She was starting to feel the spinsso, she held onto the edge of the machine.

"Okay, get on up. I'll help you lay down." Robert assisted Margaret onto the scan table.

"I don't think I can do this." Margaret spoke in staccato. She was feeling woozy. "When I lay down, I feel like I'm hanging by my feet and it isn't good."

"Well, you do the best you can. If you need to get out, press this button." Robert handed her the panic button. "Let me cover your eyes with a towel. It may help."

It didn't help. Also, Robert the radiologist had forgotten to give Margaret ear plugs. The banging and clacking noises were deafening. Margaret's spiral was circling downward fast. She started clicking the emergency button, signaling for help. Robert quickly came and slid Margaret out of the machine. Robert had barely gotten the halo off her head when Margaret rolled to her side and puked. She felt like she was going to pass out. She was frightened and it was getting worse. The room around her was fading away and she was falling. On her way down the rabbit hole, she heard Robert calling for assistance followed by a flurry of more voices. All around her, medical hands poked, prodded, and shined lights in her eyes. Soon after, Margaret was poured into a wheelchair and wheeled out to Marie.

"She was pulled out of the MRI machine and vomited before we could get any results and we will not try again today. We did check her vitals and she is safe to go home." Robert chose not to mention that he had forgotten to give Margaret earbuds. "Will you be driving her home?"

"Sweet Jesus. Is she okay? What the fuck, Robert?" Marie said his name as if they were familiar. Marie held Margaret's face and looked her in the eyes. "This was too much for you. I was right to be worried." Marie had never seen her friend like this and it scared her enough that she forgot to continue being a bitch to the tech. "Should I take her to the hospital?"

"No." Margaret struggled to form the word. "No."

"No? You're a mess. We need to get you—"

"Home. Please bring me home. I need to be home." Margaret got the words out, then closed her eyes and kept spinning into the abyss, praying for the elusive bottom.

Marie moved Robert out of her way and took over. She wheeled Margaret out to her car while the tech followed behind. Marie held Margaret steady while she and Robert gently sat Margaret in the passenger seat of her car. Going around to the driver's side, Marie ducked down and slid in. Marie cried with worry and love for her sleeping friend.

Marie called Nate's cell when she pulled into the driveway so he could meet them outside. His wife's eyes barely registered that it was Nate who had picked her up. He shut the car door with his foot. "Marie, thank you for getting her home safe. I've got her now. It'll be alright."

A usually bold Marie was wordless. She nodded slowly, wiped her tears on the back of her hand, and got back in her car.

Nate carried Margaret into the apartment and right to their room. Nate heard James walk into their room to see his mama. "Mama?" The little boy was frightened. "Dad, is Mama okay?" He was holding Steve by his flaps with Weebs wrapped around him like a fleece stole. "Daddy, I'm scared." The tears in his eyes tumbled down his sweet little face. He knew it wasn't Margaret's fault that James was so scared, but she was the reason. A little more resentment climbed on to his growing pile.

"James." His voice had edges and he needed to be calm. He took a deep breath and said, "Mom is very tired. We are going to take care of us, while she sleeps. What do you say to a stroll with me and Janey?" James perked up.

"Yes, I want to go. Can I ride my bike?"

"Sure you can, Pal. Let's get Janey and head out." He strapped Jane in her jogging stroller and helmeted James so he could cruise on his little red Huffy. The three traipsed all over the complex, finding interesting rocks and pretty flowers to bring home to Margaret, who was medicated and deep down the rabbit hole. Her body and brain took over and checked Margaret out in order for her to heal. While she was checked out, Nate had to carry work, home, and the kids. Like an onion, his resentment had layers.

James was the very best helper and Jane was almost pleasant. All in all, the kids were great. However, Nate had to head up two virtual meetings and during one of them, he had to give Jane a bottle while trying to discuss new accounts. By the next meeting, the integrity of her diaper had been pushed too far. While trying not to dry heave, he gave her a diaper change with the speed of a NASCAR pit crew. By the end of the day, Nate was white knuckle grabbing his hair. Mercifully, bedtime arrived and the freshly scrubbed kids were dressed for bed. Nate was ready to tap out, but he couldn't quite yet. Jane was snug in Nate's arms, drinking her bottle. He yawned hard enough for his eyes to water. The day felt absent of an end and it was just one day in this mess. Nate looked over at Margaret and felt hopeless. He began to quietly cry. His anger and resentment weighed on him. He had sacrificed so much for his wife. Work, the quality of their lifestyle, his freetime. His optimism about their future. Any time some new experience or occasion happened, MS was always the first priority. Whether or not she was too hot, too cold. What if she was too dizzy? There were days she was too fatigued or in too much pain that left Nate on his own. Too many days. All of the restrictions and the constant consideration of Margaret's illness made Nate doubtful she could be a real partner whom he could lean on. Right now, Nate was torn between loving her because of what she used to be and angry over what she was like now. He struggled with a sense of obligation to stay while trying to choke down the disappointment of knowing this would be his life forever.

THIRTY-FIVE

DOCTOR PHASIK EXAMINED Margaret's eyes. The official name for her double vision was Binocular Diplopia. Dr. Phasik used a slit lamp with a light to examine her cornea, iris, and lens. Then, the doctor used an instrument called an opthalmoscope. After the doctor put it on her head, she again examined the interior structure of Margaret's eyes. At the end of the exam, the doctor asked some questions about home.

"How have you been managing? Do you have someone home with you?"

"I've been doing okay. My husband bought me an eyepatch from the pharmacy. Every couple hours I switch it so I can give each eye a break. How much longer will this last?"

"This started about a week ago? What other symptoms are you having?"

"Along with double vision, I lost my sense of taste. My equilibrium is a mess. I can't lay down because it feels like I'm hanging by my feet. The left side of my face is numb. I'm nauseous with a constant headache."

"With Multiple Sclerosis, there are no firm guidelines for how long a flare-up might last. Give this a few weeks and your vision should start to improve. In the meantime, we will keep monitoring your progress. If you have any questions or concerns, call my office. In case of emergency, if not myself, one of my colleagues is always on call. Do you have someone to get you to the hospital?"

"Yes. My husband works from home, so he's with me almost all the time." Margaret was grateful for Nate being home. James was only five and Jane was still so itty bitty. It was scary to take care of them when Margaret couldn't see. Switching the eye patch between eyes did help. It enabled her to navigate through the house, but it meant Margaret could only use half of her vision at a time. Depending on what side the eye patch was on, a person could get within inches of Margaret before she was able to see them. A primitive fear of being vulnerable filled her. She didn't feel able to protect herself, and even scarier, she could not protect James or Jane.

While Nate waited for Margaret, he returned work emails from his phone. Nate had been focused on a surprise he had planned for himself and Margaret. He hoped she would love it despite the timing. It was already in motion when Margaret relapsed. Since there was no way to predict how far a flare up went, or how long it would take to heal, Nate figured it was best to keep it moving. The time was here and he couldn't wait any longer. Margaret came out to the waiting room with her hands full of papers and plans for another appointment two weeks later. They went to their car and sat her in the passenger seat. Once he was in the driver's seat and they were buckled, he shifted the car in drive and took a right out of the parking lot.

"Aren't we supposed to go left?" she asked.

"Yes, Magellan. I want to bring you somewhere to show you something. Don't worry, I've got you." He reached over for his wife's hand and she wove her fingers into his. She raised their married fingers and kissed Nate on the back of his hand.

"I love you, Nate. I'm sorry I'm a mess right now. You have been so good with all of this."

"I love you, too." Nate turned their embracing hands to kiss to the back of Margaret's hand. Ten minutes later, they turned right. When Nate got a few houses down, he pulled over. "Do you remember this house?" One of Margaret's favorite things to do was to comb home sales websites while she took mental notes of the features she liked in the houses, marking the ones she loved for "someday". Of all of the houses she showed Nate online, this was his favorite. This white split level ranch was at the top of Margaret's list for some time. It didn't have a lot of property, which Margaret did not mind.

"I do remember this one. The kitchen has great light and it has a sunroom off the back."

"There's an extra room for an office," Nate continued. "You like this house and location though, right? By the way, there's room for a pool too. James and Janey would love it." Nate knew Margaret would be happy with whatever house he chose, however it was a huge thing to do without telling his wife.

"This one is in my fingers crossed file. Someday, I would love a house just like this for the kids." Margaret smiled. The front porch had a ceiling fan lazily moving the summer air.

"We already do." Nate said, quietly.

Margaret stopped and asked, "What did you say?" Margaret was not sure she understood.

"We have this house. Our house. This is our house." Nate looked at Margaret. He hoped this had not been a huge mistake. Gestures like this play well in movies, but this was real life and husbands don't typically surprise wives with a house.

Margaret turned and stared a moment. "Nate." Her fingers pressed the car window. Releasing the door, Margaret carefully stepped out and took the house in. Nate gave Margaret his elbow and the two made their way up the green lawn. Margaret held the banister as she and Nate took the steps up to the front porch. Standing outside the front door, Margaret began to cry. Nate thought he had messed up making a decision of this size alone. His thoughts were cut off by Margaret.

"Nate, I can't believe you did this. I love you, love you, love you, Nate. We live here? This is our house? Ours?" She pulled off the eye patch to take it in. Her eyes were shiny with tears and excitement. Margeret let out a yell, "Woohooo!" She was smiling with her whole body.

"It is ours. We can move in whenever you're ready. We're in the same school district. James only needs to change the bus he rides. So, when you are feeling better, we will start packing up."

"Well, we are going to need to stop and get box-es." She put her eye patch on but Margaret's mind had already started different mental lists. She had said so many prayers asking for her own home. The uncertain-ty of her health made having a home more important. She whispered her prayer for a safe and happy home every day.

"Don't you want to wait until you feel better? You're still wearing your eyepatch. We have all the time in the world— there is no need to rush." Nate didn't want Margaret to feel pressured. Margaret's dream of having a house for the kids was coming true. Now, no matter what happened, they would always have a home.

"Nate, I feel better than better. I feel fantastic." She pointed at her eyepatch. "This thing? One eye, whatever." I can fill boxes with one eye. Let's pack and get moving." The two drove home with smiles on their faces and future plans in mind.

With the willing and not so willing help of family and friends, the whole apartment was packed within a week. They were ready to move in by August— James could start the new school year on his new bus. Margaret taped up the last box and put it in the back of the Tahoe. With barely a look back, she hopped into their truck and Nate drove them home.

THIRTY-SIX

GETTING THE HOUSE SQUARED away was quite the undertaking. Nate still had to work his full forty. He did not want to take too many days off. This left one-eyed Margaret to unpack nearly on her own. Baby Jane spent a lot of time in her carrier. It kept Jane happy and a visually impaired Margaret less anxious. No matter what side she wore the eyepatch, she could see Janey. James ran from one end of the house to the other. There was no longer a need to be quiet for neighbors and he took full advantage of that. Margaret's cell rang. She pulled it out of the front carrier and connected the call.

"Hey, Mama, I'm calling to check in on you. How are those eyes today?" Marie had been calling several times a day for updates on Margaret.

"Same. Still wearing my rotating eyepatch. Like I can be bothered with timing eye patch shifts. Still using this POS cane the doctor suggested. Tell me something: If I can't walk correctly with two legs, how is throwing basically a third leg in the mix a good idea? For the sake of all fucks. Of course I'm tired all the damned time. Oh, and food still tastes like ass," Margaret said into her phone as she unpacked another box of kitchenware.

Marie couldn't help but laugh at her cranky friend. Even when she didn't feel well, Margaret was entertaining.

Chelsea clicked on her directional to get off of the Northway. She and Nate had agreed to meet at the Algonquin Restaurant. It was a bit of a drive to exit twenty-two, but there was less of a chance of them running into anyone they knew. Jeff's boat was at the nearby dock and Nate had use of it whenever he wanted. Jeff was at work, so Nate knew the boat would be available today. He was inside the restaurant already. She found him at a small table, looking out at the lake. She stopped a moment to take him in before he saw her. He looked handsome, as usual, in a pair of shorts and a white polo. As she was taking in his strong jaw and tanned calves, Nate turned and noticed her walking his way. Nate stood up and pulled out Chelsea's chair.

"Hi, Nate." Chelsea sat down and smoothed her blue dress. A server materialized to take their drink order. "Can I have a Tito's and tonic with extra lime? Thank you."

"Make it two and make mine tall. Like really tall." Nate put his empty glass on the tablecloth. With a nod, the server was off to fill their order. "Hello, Chelsea. How have you been doing?"

"I've been good." No, Chelsea was doing better than good. He had said they needed to talk, but Chelsea had other plans. Even if Nate had other ideas, Chelsea was going to have him inside her. Not because she loved him, but to see if she still could. She was confident. While Nate talked, all Chelsea could do was watch his mouth move. When Nate's hand rested on the table, she slid her fingers towards his. "Did you go on the boat already?"

"No, not yet. I spent the morning cleaning her up. Jeff is good about me using it so long as I don't sink it." His muscled arms and handsome face were tan from being outside.

"You and your brother— sharing a ride." She smiled. "A boat, of course. You guys are pretty close." Chelsea knew her words were starting trouble. Nate stared darkly back at her. "What else have you been up to? Anything new?" She held onto her glass with her free hand.

"Keeping busy with work and the house." Because of Chelsea's preoccupation with Nate's mouth, she took her drink down too fast. She slid her empty glass to the corner of the table. Within seconds, the server placed down a fresh vodka tonic. Chelsea took another healthy sip from the straw.

"Keeping busy is important. How's Magaret and her eye patch?" She gestured toward her eye. "Has she become accustomed to being spoken to like a pirate?" She giggled at her own joke.

"Margaret's doing fine. It's nice of you to ask after my wife." Nate was getting heated. For whatever the reason, they made a sport out of provoking each other. Why did he suggest this? In his anger, he decided to tell Chelsea just how great things were. "Yeah, it's going to be a sweet little spot. Margaret told me how when she was a kid she would ride down the streets with the big houses with all the windows lit up. People doing their everyday moving in and out of view in the big bay window. Margaret has always wished to live in a house like this and now she does. No eyepatch is going to keep her from working on the house. It's all unpacked and it has only been a week."

Chelsea smiled at his smug face. She loved letting him think that he was the one in control. "I know, Nate, I've been in your house. Margaret, you know, your wife, asked me to help pick out a paint color. I've always liked blues." Chelsea winked at Nate. "Like the color of my dress." She slid her hand up her tan thigh and played with the hem of her powder blue dress. The verbal sparring and the glimpse of caramel legs was frazzling Nate's edges. Nate watched Chelsea's hand caress her skin. She offered more than a peek and her dress was short enough that Nate could see her sheer matching blue panties. He tried to occupy himself with the view of the lush green mountain backdrop of the lake. The sun reflected little diamonds of light that danced on the surface. Nate's eyes saw the lake, but in his mind he only saw Chelsea. She sucked down the rest of her drink and when the waitress came back, she agreed to another. So did Nate.

"I've been thinking about you and me and all of this," Nate admitted while looking into his drink. Chelsea felt very satisfied with her ability to mind fuck him.

"Nate, I've had you on my mind as well." Do you miss us?" The question seemingly woke Nate from the trance Chelsea had him in.

"You are an insane person. There is no "us". First, you made friends with my wife. Then, you showed up at my house. It was Christmas for shit's sake! For the last few months you've been creeping around my family pretending to like Jeff. I'm married to Margaret. Jeff is my brother. Do you think you can just slide in with Jeff and no big deal? Fuck, Chelsea." Nate ran his fingers through his dark hair. This broad was truly out of her mind. Chelsea's expression went from dark and seductive to death glare sincerity.

"It's exactly what I think. Why shouldn't I? What? Are you going to tell your brother about us? Hell no you won't. Besides, who says I'm pretending with Jeff? He's cute. You look so much like one another. Except Jeff has those blue eyes. He's also younger and not married." Chelsea softened her voice. "Who says we have to stop? It's perfect now. I'm friends with the family." With a smile, she said, "Now, we can be around each other without looking suspicious. Think of all the fun we could have." She leaned across the table and whispered, "I know you still think about fucking me, Nate. I think about it all the time. Taking me over the kitchen counter of your sweet little house? Or maybe the shower?" Their mouths were only inches apart. Nate's better judgement did not offer any reply. Her hand was on his knee. He grew harder as her hand traveled up his thigh. Leaning forward, Chelsea softly kissed Nate's mouth. She licked his lips with her tongue. "I bet you're thinking about it right now."

Nate pulled his head back. "Let's go out on the lake. This day is too perfect to not be on the water." Nate put down his empty glass.

Chelsea smiled and emptied her glass too. Nate left a few twenty dollar bills on the table and stood up. He held his hand out to Chelsea. Hand in hand, they walked down the wooden dock. One at a time, the pair boarded Jeff's boat. Nate turned the ignition and backed the boat away from the dock. Nate cruised out to a quiet bend of the lake. He parked the boat and took off his shirt. He dove in and was treading water, waiting for Chelsea to jump in.

"Nope. Not going to happen. I'm not a fan of fish water." She went to the cooler and popped it open. The three drinks she already had took a vote: All were in favor of another. She poured herself a Tito's and lemonade in a red plastic cup. Nate climbed the ladder at the back of the boat. While he toweled off, Chelsea gave him a sip of her drink. The two sat listening to the water lap against the boat and felt the summer sun on their skin.

Chelsea was feeling herself and the warmth of the day. She dropped her head back and closed her eyes. Chelsea loved the sun on her face. A shadow darkened her closed eyelids. She opened her eyes to see Nate standing in front of her. She knew she had gotten to him. Chelsea stood up without a word as she held his gaze. Their mouths were a breath apart. In an instant, they were kissing and frantically stripping off one another's clothes. They could not get naked fast enough. As Chelsea's top came off, Nate grabbed her and licked her nipple, slipping it into his mouth. Chelsea moaned. She did not stop him. She was proud of herself for catching her prey. Her hands were all over him. She dropped to her knees and took Nate in her mouth. She loved how he felt when he slid over her tongue.

"Damn it. You feel too good." Nate grew bigger inside her mouth. The way Chelsea worked him with her tongue had him dizzy. "My turn." Nate pulled himself out of her mouth. He pushed Chelsea down into her seat, pinned her legs open, and stuffed his tongue in her. He kissed her pussy. Full and wet with no holding back. Her moans rolled across the lake. "Ooooooh." Chelsea was becoming undone. Her lips were full. She was close. "Ohhhhh please, I'm going to come." Nate started to finger her, slowly at first. She was so warm. Going faster and faster, he fingered her with two fingers and rubbed her clit with his tongue. "Faster. Harder… faster!" Nate let her have it. He ate her and kissed her clit at the same time.

Chelsea could no longer control herself. She came in the most feral way. She held Nate's head between her knees. She was sweating and yelling out Nate's name. "Enough. I can't take any more."

"Yes you can." Nate spread her legs. "We aren't done until I say we are." Nate separated her lips and dove right in. He grunted as he pushed all the way inside. Chelsea was hot and wet. Nate pulled out almost the whole way. Then started fucking her just a little bit. It was the best kind of torture. She surrendered her body to him. Her legs fell further open. Whatever he wanted, she would give him. She would even let him think he was the one in control.His strokes became longer. "You look fantastic." Nate held Chelsea's tits while he fucked her. "Mmmmmm, you feel even better." Nate grunted with every stroke.

"Let me stand," she said. Getting to her feet, Ches-lsea smiled a long slow grin. She turned around and grabbed the side of the boat with one hand. "Fuck me, Nate. Fuck me now. Nate immediately bent Chelsea over and stuffed three fingers in her. He moved his fingers slowly over her g spot. Chelsea whimpered.

"Tell me what you want." Nate demanded. "Say it for me."

"Please fuck me. Please." Chelsea was open and wanting. Nate stood behind her. He licked his fingers and slapped Chelsea on her ass. The sudden sound and sting made Chelsea cry out. Nate thrust himself into her. He kept at her with steady full strokes. Chelsea moaned and held on. Nate was bringing her closer to the edge. When Nate felt Chelsea start to flex on him, he pulled out and started eating her and fingering her again. Chelsea's orgasm could be heard across the lake.

"Yes, that's it. Come for me." Nate slowed down and stopped fingering Chelsea. He sat down on one of the back seats. Chelsea climbed on top. Slowly, she slid down on Nate's lap. At first, she rode him slowly. It got harder and faster. Nate sat up and bit Chelsea's nipple. Shivers rolled l through her body. She rode him harder and faster. Harder and faster. Harder and faster. Nate's hips rose in perfect rhythm to meet Chelsea's. No longer able to hold back, Nate exploded. Chelsea's whole body flexed as she rode her orgasm out. Afterwards, there was no feeling of lying languid in the heat they created. Instead, it was tense and every minute felt obligatory. Lying together lost in their own thoughts. Nate made the decision this had to be his last time with Chelsea. Chelsea made the decision to get Jeff.

THIRTY-SEVEN

MARGARET SAT ON THE exam table and Nate sat in the chair, while they waited for Dr. Edmond. There was a soft knock on the door as it opened. Today, he had a *Phantom of the Opera* themed bow tie on.

"Hello, Margaret. How have you been doing? Has your vision improved?"

"I'm doing much better. It's been a month. My vision is still off. When I wake up in the morning, it's better than it was. As the day goes on, it gets blurry again. My sense of taste is getting better, too."

"This is all good news. We do need to discuss a treatment plan. Have you given any thought to the Tysabri infusions?"

Margaret had read all the information she had been given. "I have, but I'm really leery of trying a new medication. When I tried Copaxone, it did not go well. My hair fell out. And not just a little here and there either. The hair all over my body was falling out. When I tried Tecfidera, my guts felt kicked in within two hours of taking it. I was puking all the damn time."

"Yes. I understand you had negative experiences with other medications. Tysabri is light-years better than Copaxone and Tecfidera. Margaret, it is time to get ahead of your illness while you can. If you don't, you are looking at an inpatient living facility in your future."

In a facility?! The idea of being without Nate, James, and Janey made Margaret's chest tight. "I'm nursing Jane. Can I have a little more time with her before I start a new medication? I nursed James for a year."

"I don't think you should wait a year, Margaret. You're going to be in between flare ups. It's the best time to start." Dr. Edmond admired Margaret's will and discipline. But her willfulness frustrated him.

"Can I wait until after Jane's baptism?" Margaret was doing her best to stall for more time.

"Alright. After the baptism, you will get your first infusion, yes?

"Yes. I will."

"Okay. Thank you, Margaret. You are making the right choice. I'll have my assistant come in and she'll get you started. Have a wonderful baptism. See you soon." Dr. Edmond left and his assistant came in. She offered a quick handshake and introduction.

"Hello, my name is Sheila. "Please fill this paperwork out for Tysabri. We will submit the prescription to your insurance. Biogen is the company that manufactures Tysabri. They have copay assistance if you need it." The tidy little woman handed the paperwork to Nate. He would be the one filling them out. "You will have a two hour monitoring period after your first infusion. We are prepared for allergic reactions or any other immediate assistance you may need. We're better outfitted than the hospital. If you have any questions or concerns, please call me."

"Thank you. We have to read through all of this first." Nate held up the stack of literature and forms. "We will call you to set all this up." Sheila walked them out.

"Have a good day."

Nate and Margaret sat in the truck. The radio played low. "Nate." Margaret squeezed Nate's hand to get his attention. "Nate, I'm not trying to be dramatic. I am so sorry. The days go by. Bit by bit, I'm losing myself. I'm either tired or sick. Always. Now we're up to infusions. What happens when the infusions stop working? When, my body stops working? I'm really scared, Nate."

"Margaret, I love you. You haven't lost a thing. You are the toughest girl I know. We'll do this because we do. One day at a time." Nate was scared too. But as usual, his fear was his own problem not Margaret's. He held Margaret's hand the whole drive home.

THIRTY-EIGHT

NATE AND WILLIAM WERE putting a pretty nice dent in a pile of super hot wings. They had already drained their first pitcher of Blue Moon. William wiped his saucy fingers clean and raised his hand, motioning to the waitress.

"Can you grab us another pitcher of Blue Moon? Thanks." The waitress picked up the empty beer pitcher.

"Fresh iced glasses? Maybe more napkins?" She pointed to the corner of William's mouth.

William smiled and wiped his face. "Yes, I guess so."

Nate finished another wing. "Can you grab another glass? Our third is on his way." Nate read the text on his phone. Jeff was on his way. The beers were cold and Nate was glad he went out.

"How are you and Margaret doing? Is there anything Marie and I can do to help? We're good for taking the kids overnight any time." William and Marie had already talked about babysitting to give the Hall's some much needed time off.

"That's a good idea. Margaret and I could use a little down time. I'll talk to Margaret and come up with a day. Thanks, William." Nate saw Jeff looking for the table. Nate gave a holler and gestured for Jeff to come over.

"Hey, guys. Oooh wings. Nice." Jeff pulled out a stool at the high top table. The waitress came back with another pitcher and three frozen mugs. "Perfect timing." Jeff poured three beers and dealt them out. "So, what are we watching?" He scanned the row of flat screens.

"There's a Red Sox game on." William pointed at the fourth screen.

"Baby brother here is a Yankees fan," Nate volunteered.

"I am a Yankee fan and a fan of any team playing the Sox." Jeff smiled at his Sox fan brother and moved his chair to get a better view of the TV. The waitress came back with another fresh pitcher. The guys poured themselves another round. Nate couldn't keep his mouth shut. He had to know.

"So, anything new with Chelsea? The yoga chick Margaret set you up with?" Nate cast his eyes to the television screens, feigning the most casual interest.

"I am happy to report that she is a Yankees fan," Jeff said with a smile.

"Oh, yeah? What else is she a fan of? How's it going?" Nate was feeling masochistic. Why not torture himself with visions of Chelsea and his brother?

"Ah, bro. No details. Things are moving along nicely. How's that for an answer?" Jeff smiled and watched the game, beer in hand.

"Glad to hear it." Nate was seething with anger and jealousy. How could Chelsea do something like this to him? Yes, he knew the last time should be just that. Still, she was supposed to be his— not Jeff's. His ego had hoped Chelsea would ease up with Jeff after the boat. Alas, she was all in.

"Go, go, go... YES!" William yelled as the Sox scored another home run. "Nate, did you see that?" William clapped him on the shoulder, breaking Nate out of his thoughts. "Holy shit, what a good play. Yes." William topped off their glasses and held up the pitcher. "We are gonna need another."

It was after midnight when William got home. He pulled into his driveway and Wes was waiting in the bay window. The dog ran back and forth in the window, barking his ever-loving head off. "Ah, Jeez." William hit the garage door opener. He parked and hit the button again, closing the door.

William went into the kitchen from the garage. Wes was hopping and running circles of excitement around his feet. "Alright, alright." William picked up the excited dog and opened the fridge. "What have we got? Hmmm." The dog sniffed and wiggled. He went to the vegetable crisper and pulled it open. "Here it is." He took a cold beer out of the drawer, put Wes down, then popped his beer. He shut the fridge door with his foot and stood in the quiet kitchen drinking his beer. He listened to the familiar sounds of the house and to his own thoughts.

Marie was standing in the doorway, watching him. He was a tall, imposing man. Broad shouldered and strong. She always felt dainty in his arms. He knew her better than anyone ever would. Marie truly loved William.

"William."

He turned and saw her. Her hair was loose and her skin tanned from a summer outside. She was wearing a tiny orange tank top, her nipples shown through. A pair of sheer black, low cut underwear. William could see the shape of her through the thin material.

"Come here, Beautiful."

Without a word, Marie walked to him. She put her head on his chest and her hands on his hips.

"Look at me." His fingers on her chin, he tilted her face up to his. "Do you know how much I love you?"

"Yes," Marie said, the word barely audible.

"Are you sure?" William whispered in her ear, running his fingers over her nipples through her tank top.

"Yes," she said a little louder.

William put his hand on her lower jaw and kissed her mouth. He slipped his tongue in his wife's mouth and, turning her head, he whispered in her ear. "I'm going to fuck you like I hate you." William pulled his wife to him with one hand and ripped her underwear off with the other.

He licked his fingers and dove his wet fingers deep in Marie. "Yes" He moaned. "Your pussy feels so good." William ran his fingers up and down the soft, warm, wet inside of Marie.

"Oh, William." Her head fell back as she went up and down on her toes. She grabbed William's wrist with both hands.

"That's right. Ride it. Get it."

Marie clutched William's hand and pushed it deeper into herself. After she fell into her first orgasm, William picked up his petite wife. Marie wrapped her athletic legs around him and he carried her across the kitchen, getting his neck bit and licked. Once spread on their kitchen table, Marie pinned her own legs back for William to slide into her. "Oohhhhhhh." Marie bit her bottom lip, savoring how hot and hard William was. At first, he took her slowly. Inch by inch, knowing the agonizing ecstasy. Marie's legs started to quiver, the tremors before the quake. She loved him slamming into her.

He was close. He grunted and let out a rough groan, finishing inside his wife.

grace

Marie lay on the table, her body still pulsing and short of breath. "Mmmmm, William. You get me so good." She straightened her tank top. William tossed her black panties over and Marie hopped off of the table and shimmied them up her legs. She walked to the fridge to root around for something to drink. "Nice," she said out loud when she happened upon the last two beers in the crisper. Marie took a long, satisfying swig. She walked over and handed the other beer to William. The two tapped the necks of the bottles together in a toast.

THIRTY-NINE

MARGARET SAT ON THE floor with a cup of coffee and stared at the wall, considering the four large squares of color. "Yeah, you're right. Copen Blue is the one."

"Alright. One color has been chosen." Chelsea put her coffee on the floor, sitting cross legged next to Margaret. She was right about blue being the perfect color. "Any thoughts on accent colors?"

Janey's baptism was going to be the third week of September and the party was at the house. The list of things to do seemed to get longer every day. Painting the downstairs and steaming carpets were the two big projects needing to be done inside. The old blacktop driveway had been jack hammered out and a fresh concrete driveway was being poured the next day. "The accent color is going to be Muslin."

"Is it a fancy way of saying beige?" It looked beige to Chelsea. "Are the colors officially decided?"

Margaret's phone dinged. It was a text from Marie.

Marie: On my way. Do you need anything?

Margaret fired off a quick text back: Chelsea is here. Don't be a dickhead.

Marie sent back: I am done with my dickery.

Margaret: What about your hickory and doc? Eh? Hickory dickery dock. Get it?

Marie: My Lord, you are an asshole. I will leave your friend alone.

Marie would have to try harder to squelch voicing her doubts about the yogi.

Marie breezed through the door. "Hello, ladies," she said in a smarmy voice. "I came bearing food from Fred's. "We are making *sammiches*." All sorts of meats and cheeses came out of the bag. Yes, Margaret, I got your stuffed olives." She put the container full of giant green olives in front of Margaret.

"I love these briney bitches." Margaret plucked out an olive stuffed with garlic.

"You had better dig in, Chelsea. We'll clear this like hurdlers." Marie was already building a sandwich. "So, where are we on this To Do list? Or is it more of a To Do scroll?" she asked, shoving her fresh sandwich in her face. A little mustard squeezed out and took refuge on the corner of her mouth. Marie's tongue claimed the mustard as quickly as a frog could catch a fly.

"My list has sublists. Margaret pulled out a beat up spiral notebook and opened to the tabbed and sticky note laden pages. "Painting the living room, dining room, and kitchen are on the top of my pile. Thoughts?"

"Well, we can get the paint and curtains today." She took another bite of her lunch meat creation.

"If all three of us did the work, we could bang this mother in one day." Chelsea looked to Margaret and Marie to see how her suggestion landed.

"That uppity housewares store is in the same plaza as the paint place." Marie pushed a whole potato chip into her mouth and chomped away with a smile on her face.

"Do you mean the store responsible for every curtain and decorative twine ball in your house?" Margaret laughed.

"Absolutely. T'is the one," Marie said, crunching another mouthful of salty potato chips.

"One thing though— I am still not driving." Margaret pointed to her eyes while preying upon the olives.

"I will drive you biddies. I can grab the paint while you and Chelsea go procure curtains and twine balls. They really do add something to the too big bowl on my table." Janey's sweet squeals and laughter came through the monitor. "See, even Janey's excited about it."

FORTY

CHELSEA HEARD THE FAMILIAR hydraulic hiss and click of the hotel door. She smiled and adjusted her position on the bed. She had texted Nate earlier to come see her because there was an emergency. Within a half of an hour, he flew into the room, only to find her completely naked with her legs parted. Nate's clenched jaw and fierce look got her hot.

When Nate received the text from Chelsea, he barely offered a goodbye, let alone a reason for leaving the house. A few minutes later, Margaret was sending questioning texts and Nate was blowing through red lights, letting her go to voicemail. He drove like a lunatic to find that there was no emergent reason for him having made such a hasty exit from home. "Oh, nice. Great. Of course you're naked." He walked over to the side of the bed and took her by the wrist. "Get up. Stand. Now." Nate yanked her off the bed and got Chelsea to her feet. "Is this what you wanted? The boat was the last time. I don't have time for these games, Chelsea." He squeezed her wrist tighter. "Are you trying to piss me off?"

"Maybe I am. What are you going to do about it?" she said with a wink. Nate squeezed her wrist tighter still and pulled her to him. Their bodies pressed against each other. He could smell the perfume he had given her.

It worked. Chelsea had made a choice to get Jeff. Yet, she felt the need to poke at Nate. It worked and had gotten him here. Grudge fucking was fine with her. Provoking him was her own kind of foreplay.

"You are going to pay for this." He held the back of her head and kissed her hard, forcing his tongue in her mouth. Chelsea took his hand and slid it between her legs.

"You are so fucking wet."

She shoved her hand down his pants and stroked his already hard cock.

His head fell back at the feeling. He took her hand out of his pants, turned Chelsea around, and bent her over the bed. Nate gave her one long lick, starting at her clit.

From her position, she could see his pants hit the floor. "Mmmmm, yes," she whispered. She moaned when he pushed all of himself into her. Chelsea knew he was rage fucking her, but his anger turned her on and made her want to provoke him further. "Harder. Fuck me, Nate. Harder." He pounded into her.

"You fucking deserve it." Nate grabbed her hips and pulled Chelsea into him with each powerful thrust. He slapped her ass hard enough to leave a hot handprint. She yelped then smiled. He twisted her hair around his hand and whispered in her ear. "You love being fucked by me, don't you?" When she didn't answer, he gave her hair a pull. "Answer me, Chelsea."

"Yes I do." The brief answer earned her another smack. It stung in the most delicious way. "Yes." she hissed.

He reached around and squeezed her nipple hard while tightening his grip on her hair.

"I love being fucked by you." Chelsea pushed into his every thrust.

Nate grunted and fucked her as hard as he could. He grabbed Chelsea by the hips again and pulled her onto him, pushing himself as deep as possible to come inside her. He released her and she fell onto the bed.

Chelsea flipped over and lay on her back. Happily breathless, she patted the bed next to her, inviting Nate to stay. He sat with her for a minute, but was soon up and dressed.

"I'm not staying." Nate stared at his phone. "Work is crazy right now. We have Janey's baptism." He finally offered her a brief glance before saying, "There is so much to do. I told Margaret I wouldn't be at the gym too long."

Chelsea's eyes flashed with the hot anger she felt. She took a deep breath and exhaled. "It's alright, Nate." She got out of bed and started to dress. She was not at all happy, but kept it to herself. "I understand. There's been a lot going on at the house. Hey, you never said if you liked the blue walls. Margaret thinks she picked the color." She narrowed her eyes. "That wife of yours."

"Yes, the blue." Nate thought of all he'd done with Chelsea. What he was, up until a few minutes ago, still doing. Nate knew he was a raging dickhead, but those blue walls would remind him of it every damned day. "I see what you're doing. I get it. Listen, Margaret thinks you're her friend. As fucked up and weird as this all is, there's no reason for you to hate her."

"Oh no?" Chelsea slipped her second shoe on and made a conscious effort to unclench her jaw. "You listen. She is no damsel in distress. I've seen your Margaret in action. She is not fragile. You tell me you're afraid for Margaret if you leave because she needs you. Seems to me, you're afraid Margaret would be fine without you and it eats at you."

"Oh, yes, I'm afraid of leaving Margaret," Nate said sarcastically. "What are you talking about?"

"It's not the leaving, Nate. She doesn't need you. You know it, and it's obvious you're scared. So much so, you have force fed her the illusion you're needed for her survival. Every damn day, every single time. All because you don't want to lose the illusion of St. Nate. Without Margaret, who would you be? What could you use to rationalize all your shit?" Chelsea grabbed her purse and headed for the door. With her hand on the door knob, she turned around. Her blue eyes were bright. "When your baby brother asks me to marry him—"

"Marry him? Come on now. You can't be serious," Nate said, half laughing.

"Trust me, Nate, he will ask and when he does, I will say yes. Then, I will be his Mrs. Hall, which is lucky. It's obvious. He's the better Hall anyway. I'm sure you'd agree." With a flip of her long, blonde hair, Chelsea pulled open the hotel room door.

The next weeks peeled quickly off the calendar. Every day, some part of the house was prettied up for the party. Together, Nate and Jeff got the mowing and edging done. James volunteered to be their waterboy. He sat ready on the steps with Weebs and Steve on his lap. James stationed himself next to his big blue bucket filled with water bottles and juice bags on the front porch. Jeff and Nate had already set up a cooler of beers on the back steps. They figured it best to not have James monitor their cooler so as the men zipped through their work, they would take a water bottle from James in the front yard, drink what they could until they lapped the backyard. Then, water the Hydrangea bushes with whatever was left. Then, they would switch the water bottle for a beer bottle. They would pound it and drop the empties in the recyclable can as they came back around. The guys were hydrated and a smidge inebriated. When Nate finished with the lawn, he placed pots of bright yellow and orange mums down on the porch steps. He had spent the day watching Margaret, Chelsea, and Jeff while they all worked on the house. After the scene between him and Chelsea, Nate authentically felt horrible for what he had done. But he quickly realized he was getting caught up in how he thought he should feel rather than how he actually felt, which was fucking satisfied. He enjoyed fucking Chelsea, not just for the act itself, but because he was doing it behind both Margaret's and Jeff's backs. He was a fucked up man. He drank his cold beer and smiled.

"Wow, guys, this yard looks fan-freaking-tastic. You and Jeff did your work." Margaret joined them on the porch with baby Jane. As the recent flare up passed, her symptoms settled. Her sight returned with minimal permanent change, just in time for Jane's baptism the next day. A party at the new house was a lot to undertake considering her last few months, however, family was Margaret's motivation and inspiration. She was determined and stubborn. Margaret saw her goal and she had attained it beautifully. From the crisp blue walls down to her multiple twine balls, the house was perfectly dressed for a party. Margaret took as much care in choosing everyone's clothes, which were hanging and ready. Nate and James were going to look sharp in their suits and matching ties. Margaret's dress was a small houndstooth print with a pencil skirt. Miss Jane's outfit was the most special and Catherine was entrusted with it's delivery to Margaret weeks ago. It was the gown Margaret had worn when she had been baptized almost forty years ago. Grandma Clementina had created and sewn the gown by hand from the most delicate fabrics and lace. Clementina had even hand-sewn tiny, antique, lace-trimmed shoes to match.

Sitting with her family and thinking of all the good she had in her life, Margaret was overcome with love. "Tomorrow is going to be a blessed and beautiful day to celebrate you, baby Jane." A misty-eyed Margaret kissed her daughter's head. She looked up to see Marie's car pulled into the driveway. Marie got out of her car and surveyed her friends.

"Hello, group. What are we looking at?"

"We're admiring the splendid yard manicuring done by Nate and Jeff." They all turned an admiring eye to the lawn.

After only a moment, Marie said, "Well that's enough of that. What else ya got?"

Margaret smacked Marie's arm with excitement. "Want to come in and see Janey's gown? We got it sparkling white. Wait until you check out the tiny pearls on her shoes. It's so precious, it hurts."

"Yes! Of course I want to see our girl's gown. She will look perfect and I get to dress her tomorrow. Move it. Let's go see." Marie held a hand out for Margaret. Hand in hand, the two grown ladies and one little lady went into the house.

On the way to the bedroom, Marie had an opportunity to take in the finished house and all the work they had done. "Wow, Margaret, the house is perfection. It's like a whole new house. Are you jazzed for Janey's big day tomorrow?"

"You know me, both excited and twisting with my pre-event weirdness."

"Yes, you are a mess of anxiety on the inside while smiling like a Stepford on the outside." Margaret shrugged her shoulders and nodded in agreement.

"My mom will be here early tomorrow morning." Margaret sat Janey in the middle of the bed. As Janey reached out for her giraffe, she lost her sit position and happily rolled around the middle of Margaret's bed. Her giraffe squeaked as she gummed it. "What about you, Godmama? Are you excited for tomorrow?"

Looking at the gown of her very best friend's daughter, Marie was overcome with love. "Yes, Margaret, I am very excited. Oh, Janey, you are the prettiest little baby and I am the luckiest Godmama ever." She turned to Margaret. "I love your guts, my friend. Forever and always."

"I love your guts, too. Thank you for all your help these last few months."

Marie picked up Janey and hugged her baby tight. "I love your little baby guts, too, Janey. Tomorrow, all eyes are on us, kid." Marie gave Janey a baby-sized fist bump.

FORTY-ONE

JAMES LOVED THE *tap tap tapping* sound of his hard bottomed dress shoes on the kitchen tile. Of course, his Ninja Turtle underwear was the only thing needed to complete his look. Margaret's mom was showing him how to shuffle step. "Mom, are you trying to kill me? Why are you not telling this kid to get dressed?"

"I am Grandma, not bad cop. If the kid wants to dance around in his skivvies, dancing he shall do. Take it away kid!" James danced a jig. He spun around at the end of Gran's hand. Catherine was a lot of fun as a grandma. Margaret enjoyed her almost as much as the kids.

"Thanks, Mom." Margaret turned and sang out, "Nate! Please get some clothes for this kid." A few beats later, Nate came downstairs for James.

"On it. Let us men go get handsome." Nate threw James over his shoulder and started up the stairs with James laughing and squirming.

"I'm already handsome, Dad!" James squealed. Catherine gave a small laugh and shook her head. There was a knock on the door immediately followed by the entrance of Greyson, Marie, and William.

"Wow, Greyson, you look super handsome today," Margaret began. "Nate and James are upstairs. Go 'head up. Mom, can you go up and make sure they're getting themselves together?"

"Sure thing." Catherine made sure to grab her coffee and book. Margaret couldn't remember a time when her mother didn't have her traveling companions.

"I think I'll go too. Those two boys together can be a lot to tame," William said, already heading for the stairs. The ladies went to the laundry room to finish ironing Margaret's dress.

Margaret slipped the dress on and gave herself one more check in the hall mirror. The dress wrapped around her slender frame flawlessly. "Countless downward dogs were done to fit me into this. Zip me." Marie zipped the dress. The two women stood before the mirror. In their reflection, they saw the youthful girls they once were, each wide-eyed and smiling. While simultaneously, they saw the grown women each had become. Both of them felt the depth of the bond they shared.

Jeff and Chelsea parked on the street in front of the house. When Jeff took Chelsea's hand as she stepped out of the car, his heart pounded. "You look absolutely breathtaking. I am a lucky guy." Jeff loved to see her in green. The teal wrap dress made her eyes shine even brighter.

"Thank you. And I am digging those rose colored glasses you're always wearing. They make me look magical." Chelsea enjoyed Jeff. His compliments were sincere and full of feeling.

"Rose colored?" Jeff asked. They had been seeing each other for a while, but today was their first official outing as a couple. "Nope. Totally clear. Now, are you ready to go in and do this family thing with me?"

"I am so ready to do this family thing with you." Chelsea held Jeff's hand tighter. Nate and William were talking downstairs when the couple walked in. Nate's eyes immediately filled with the sight of their held hands. It agitated him to see it, yet he smiled knowing the price he would surely have her pay for it.

"Jeff, hey man." Nate gave Jeff a hug. "Hello to you too, Chelsea." Nate hugged her as well. He used the brief hug to inhale her perfume. "The ladies just went upstairs to dress Janey."

"Hello, Chelsea." William smiled then gave a nod to Jeff. "Hello, Jeff."

"Hi, guys, thanks for letting me know. I'll head upstairs." Before ascending the stairs, she placed a kiss on Jeff's lips. "Miss me," she said softly for only him to hear.

Once Chelsea was out of earshot, Nate said, "Well done, Little Brother. She is beautiful."

Jeff's face was all grin.

Nate could see Jeff was smitten. Although it was best to leave Chelsea and Jeff to it, his ego constantly nagged at him. He couldn't believe how gullible his little brother was. "Ohhhh, so you *like* like her? Is this perhaps turning into something?"

"I do *like* like her. She's smart, kind, and yes, she is stunning. Just being around her makes me feel great. Chelsea is definitely something."

Upstairs, Chelsea joined right in with the gaggle of women fawning over Janey. She wore a white bow in her chestnut hair. Her little pink fingers peeked out of the puffy lace sleeves. As the Godmother, Marie dressed Jane for her baptism. The gown was white gossamer linen with delicate lace and cultured pearls. Each pearl had been hand sewn by Margaret's grandmother all those years ago. Marie slid the satin slippers onto Janey's tiny feet and tied the white satin ribbons. "Sweet Jane, you look just like your mama." Marie gathered Jane and her gown and held her up to Catherine.

"Alright, ladies. Let's get downstairs and out the door." Catherine took her grandbaby Jane into her arms. "You, my sweet girl, are a perfect little angel." Catherine was a tough woman in many ways. Three marriages in and a widow twice over helped to shape her armor. However, being a grandma had softened her, which Catherine still refused to admit was possible. "Time to go, boys. Get your keisters downstairs." She shooed James and Greyson down the stairs. Their fancy dress shoes clicked on every step. The ladies were at the back of the staircase parade. Once everyone convened downstairs, they all left for church.

The sky was a cloudless cornflower blue. Crisp fire colored leaves rustled and danced in the wind. It really was quite a beautiful fall day for Jane. Inside St. Edward's, the sun shone through the stained glass and bathed the floors and walls in a kaleidoscope of colors. The pews filled up with the families of the babies being baptized. Nate held Janey on his lap while she sucked on her pacifier and, thank the Lord, kept quiet. James sat next to Margaret, playing with Steve. Margaret leaned over and whispered to her husband, "I have something for you. Hold out your hand." When he did, Margaret tied a red silk thread bracelet on Nate's wrist. "You are my heart, Nate. No matter where life takes us, I love you. I love us." She put her head on Nate's shoulder.

"I love us too, Margaret." He kissed the top of her head. Nate knew he had a good woman in Margaret. He felt her gratitude and devotion to him and their family.

The service was beautiful. Jane performed her own miracle and stayed quiet. The priest gathered the families of babies around the Baptismal Font. When it was time for Jane to be baptized, Marie and Jeff held Jane. First, the priest poured some holy water on her head. When he used oil to make the sign of the cross on Jane's forehead, she gave a sweet giggle and squealed— this truly was a blessed day.

After the service, the families were invited to take photos. Catherine was sure to be first in line for pictures with Father Timothy. She waved everyone over and spoke with an authoritative tone. Even Father was listening for instruction.

"Alright, put some muscle in your hustle. I want pictures of my granddaughter." Everyone stepped quickly to Father Timothy and Catherine. The priest was quite a patient man. Catherine wanted as many Holy pictures as her camera would hold. "Marie and Jeff, we need pictures of the Godparents." Marie and Jeff stood next to each other with Jane for the picture. Afterwards, Jeff walked over to Chelsea with Janey in his arms. He handed the baby to Chelsea and the two of them fawned over Jane together. Lost in the moment, Chelsea imagined a lot of what ifs. She locked eyes with Nate. She gave him a wink. Nate's chest gave a hitch.

"Nate."

He did not hear his name because he was caught in Chelsea's eyes.

"Nate." Margaret tapped him on his shoulder. "Can you get Janey from Chelsea and put her in the car? We have to get home before everyone gets there." His wife's voice brought him back to reality.

"No problem. I'll meet you at the car." Margaret gave him a kiss on the cheek and walked towards the car, holding James's hand while Steve dangled from his other.

The party at home was lighthearted and cheerful. Family and friends filled the house to celebrate Jane and visit with one another. In order for the grown-ups to do that, it was important to get the kids occupied. Margaret was prepared. Each kid got a gift bag full of treats to play with as they arrived. Little ones covered in stickers ran all over, either blowing bubbles or drawing with chalk on the new driveway or stuffing their little faces with candies and emptying pixie sticks into their mouths.

The grown-ups congregated in the dining room by the sumptuous buffet. There were cheeses and olives, marinated beef, and pasta dishes. Nate designated himself bartender and he made a damn good drink. He had a blender of Margaritas spinning and Sangria in glass pitchers. Lemons, limes, and orange slices were at the ready to straddle the rim of the glasses. Their favorite bakery had made the most delicious cake. Margaret looked around at the party guests laughing, eating, and telling tales. It was wonderful to see everyone enjoying themselves. There was still food when the party was ending, so as the guests left, Margaret gave them a plate of food and cake to take home.

Nate put his arms around his wife and said, "You did a fantastic job, Margaret. The house, the food, everything." Nate kissed Margaret. "Just relax on the couch and we'll get the rest." With all of them working, the house was back in shape in no time. Marie dropped down next to Margaret on the couch.

"How are you feeling, my friend? This day has been long for you." Marie wanted to check on Margaret.

"I am so tired." She rubbed the left side of her face. The pain had always gotten worse as the day went on. "I want to sleep for days. When the hell are you getting out of here?" Margaret smiled. "Hey, can I ask you a question?"

"Sure, whatcha got?"

"Today, he's been great. But have you noticed lately that Nate's been moody and distracted all the time? I'm not sure what his problem is, but—" They heard footsteps approaching and their conversation died. Chelsea walked into the living room to say her goodbyes to Margaret and Marie. The ladies exchanged a look. Margaret hoped she hadn't been heard talking about Nate.

"Hey there, ladies. Margaret, you throw quite the shindig. We had a really fun time."

"Thank you for all the help with the house. I'm glad you had a good time. Truthfully, though? I'm happy it's done. The lead up gets overwhelming. Now I can breathe."

"Jeff and I are heading out, but I wanted to give you a hug and say goodbye. "Come on, Marie, bring it in." Chelsea pulled Marie in for a hug. Then she turned to Margaret.

"Hug away." Margaret hugged Chelsea. Nate walked into the room.

"Margaret, where are the kids' tow— whoa." Nate's insides were ash seeing these two women hug. He quietly stepped backward up the stairs to the kids.

Margaret looked at Marie, silently telling her that this was the behavior she was talking about.

"This was a terrific party, Maggs. You did an outstanding job." Her brother-in-law said as he walked in, eating another cookie.

"Thanks, Jeff. I had these two biddies to help me." Margaret laughed. "Seriously, thank you so much for all your help. I couldn't haven't gotten this done without you guys. Is Nate around here somewhere?"

"Nate is upstairs with James and Janey," Chelsea informed her. "I think he may be at a steep disadvantage. James had a whole lot of pixie sticks."

"Uh oh. I had better get up there. I can't abandon him with a sugar rush spin out. Have a great night. Thanks again for, well, all of it."

FORTY-TWO

Jeff drove with one hand on the wheel and held Chelsea's hand in his other. Even though it was not a long drive, she'd begun to doze in the passenger seat. The passing street lights illuminated her face, long lashes casting a shadow on her cheek. Jeff was enamoured by Chelsea. She was right, Jeff thought she was magic. From the first time they had gotten together, Jeff and Chelsea stayed together most nights. *This is what love feels like.* Jeff held Chelsea's hand tighter as he drove them home.

Chelsea woke up when the engine turned off. She yawned and stretched. "Woo. Looks like I took a little nap." Chelsea leaned in and gave Jeff a kiss. Her arms loosely draped over his shoulders. "This was a fantastic day with you." Chelsea stretched and sighed. Then she said, "Well, I'm up now. Race you to the bedroom."

Jeff smiled at her. "Are you serious?" His hand hovered over his door handle.

"On your mark... getsetgo!" Chelsea hopped out of the car and jogged towards the front door.

"Oh, you're serious." Jeff hightailed it out of the driver's side. He caught up to her at the door. He grabbed her by the waist. "Gotcha!" She let out a playful squeal. He spun her around and threw her over his shoulder. He unlocked the front door and pushed it open with his foot. Jeff fireman carried her to the bedroom. Chelsea laughed and yelled in mock protest. He kicked off his shoes, still holding Chelsea hostage.

"Put me down! Jeff! You are going to get it!" Jeff kissed Chelsea up her body as he placed her on the ground. The last kiss was deep and brought out a moan from deep inside Chelsea's body. "Jeff." Chelsea's head tipped back, offering up her neck to Jeff.

"I need your loveliness in my bed," Jeff whispered in Chelsea's ear between kisses. Taking Jeff's hand, Chelsea walked him over to the bed. She brought his hand to the bow on her wrap dress.

"Pull," Chelsea whispered into Jeff's ear, following it with a playful bite. When Jeff tugged on the bow, Chelsea's dress opened up, unveiling her strong yoga body. He slid the dress from her shoulders and let it fall to the floor. He unsnapped her cream lace bra and used one finger to hook and tug off her matching panties to join the bra and green dress on the floor. The blue in Chelsea's eyes was deeper and brighter. A sensual smile rested on her lips. Slowly, she unbuttoned Jeff's shirt, kissing his neck and chest as she went down. Jeff unbuckled his belt and unzipped his black dress pants and dropped them down his legs. Stepping out of his pants pile, Jeff pressed himself against Chelsea's warm, naked body.

"You have the softest skin I've ever felt," Jeff said as he ran his fingers lightly down Chelsea's back to her waist. They sank onto the bed, knotting themselves together. They kissed and licked one another's lips. Keeping Chelsea's body wrapped around his, Jeff found his way inside her, first with his fingers. The feel of how wet she was made Jeff bulge and stiffen. Chelsea's body moved in a wave. She rode the ecstasy. Met Jeff's rhythm. "Mmm, Jeff, you feel so good. Go faster."

"I want to live inside you." He put his mouth on her warm pussy and kissed her. Slow and soft. It was an extraordinary agony. His tongue tickled her clit then slid inside her. He would never tire of the taste of her. Taking her completely in his mouth, he buried his face in her.

"Mmmmmm, Jeff. Oh my---!"

Jeff smiled to himself. He did not stop. His tongue started at her clit and slowly slid farther down, past her pussy. Jeff pushed his tongue into her. In and out. Over and over. She let out a violent moan. Chelsea broke free of Jeff's grip. Smiling, she flipped over onto her hands and knees and backed herself into Jeff's mouth. His tongue drove deeper in her still. "Oooooooooh, don't stop."

"I won't." Jeff brought his fingers a little lower.

"Oh, Jeff. I am so close. Go... go." Chelsea begged for more. She rocked back and forth, pushing Jeff's fingers in further. Jeff kept fingering her ass as he got right up behind her. As he slid his fingers into her, he entered Chelsea and heard her breath catch. Jeff fucked her and fingering her ass at the same time.

"Mmmm, you feel perfect." Jeff was rigid. He was enveloped by the hot wet silk. He grunted with each thrust. Jeff could not wait any more. "I'm getting close." Jeff grabbed her hips and pulled Chelsea onto him. He thrust into Chelsea harder and faster.

Chelsea started to tighten around Jeff and the tension built until it could only burst. She let out an animalistic growl as she came. It was more than Jeff could take. He pulled Chelsea to him and groaned as he came inside her.

grace

Afterwards, the pair lay together in bed, sharing a bottle of water. Jeff's head was on Chelsea's lap while she lazily ran her fingers through Jeff's hair, sending chills down his neck. "Jeez, woman. That was some good stuff."

"Yeah it was. Mmmmm," Chelsea said as she relished the moment. There they were, the two of them, warm with happiness and chock full of feelings. Jeff spooned up behind Chelsea, brushing her golden honey hair away from her face. He breathed in the smell of her skin. "I could sleep like this every night."

"What did you just say?" Chelsea knew what he had said, yet she needed to hear him say it again.

"I'm serious, Chels. You should live with me. We are together most every night." Jeff coiled around her, bringing her tighter to him.

"Jeff, we spend a lot of time together, but we've only been seeing each other for five minutes. Living with someone is not something to do for funzies."

"Chelsea, this is not just for funzies. Five minutes? Is that it? I have to say, it's been five mind blowing minutes, by the way." Jeff was a goner. He wanted to be the one to make her happy. "Chelsea, look at me." She turned under the covers. They shared a pillow— face-to-face. Her mane of hair was unruly and sexy. Her smile was able to bring him to his knees. "Chelsea, you are the most incredible woman I have ever met. Please live with me. I love you."

"Jeff, I love you too." Chelsea's voice was soft. "Yes, I will live with you." Jeff and Chelsea kissed deeply. Chelsea laid her head on Jeff's chest and smiled. Things were moving right along. Jeff was hers and it felt wonderful.

FORTY-THREE

CHELSEA WAS GIGGLING AS she sent the screen shot. She knew how infuriated Nate would be and it got her wet. In less than a minute, her phone rang. "Helloooo." The sing-song way she answered the phone was met with yelling.

"You are fucking moving in with him?" Nate barked into the phone. He was indeed pissed.

"Nate, you sound angry," Chelsea said in a playful way. She was happy the screenshot of her change of address to Jeff's had just the right effect.

"Angry? I'll show you angry." Nate was practically snarling.

"419," was all she said and she disconnected the call.

"Get over here now." The hotel door clicked closed. Only in her panties, Chelsea slid off of the bed and began crawling toward Nate. Leisurely and languid she moved until she was at Nate's feet. Up on her knees, she unbuckled and unzipped Nate's pants. Chelsea wrapped her mouth around Nate's cock. Her hot, wet mouth worked him until he felt like he might rip. He grabbed the sides of her head and pulled her into him, fucking her mouth. He felt her gag a bit when he pushed in all the way. "Too bad." She took all of it. Nate held her head down and spilled into her mouth. She swallowed when he came.

"Mmmm," Chelsea said as she wiped her mouth. "Are you done with me?"

"What do you think?" Nate pulled her up to her feet. He pulled her lace panties down to her ankles. "Step out of these and open your legs." He kicked her legs apart. It was Nate's turn on his knees. Just barely touching her with his tongue, Nate licked and kissed her. Chelsea moaned when Nate's warm mouth enveloped her. He stroked his fingers lightly up and down her lips and became hard again. Using two fingers, Nate began working Chelsea up. Then, he wrapped his left hand around his right wrist, using both hands to finger her harder. Under the ecstasy was pain and the pain made Chelsea smile.

"Ooooooh, Nate. Go harder. I need it." Chelsea had her hands on Nate. He fingered her harder and harder. "YES. Fuck. I'm coming. She roared. Her orgasm brought her to the ground.

"Now I'm done with you." He kissed her and she could taste herself. After getting himself together, he grabbed his phone and keys. "I'll text you later." With that, he left. Some women may not have liked his hurried exit, but Chelsea didn't mind.

"All in all, not bad," Chelsea said out loud to herself. She picked up her panties. She had succeeded in winning over the sweet, softhearted little brother, but she was even more satisfied by turning Nate into the angry, grudge fucking, mean man Chelsea knew had always been there.

FORTY-FOUR

MARGARET SAT ON THE back steps and watched her boy play. She had picked James up early from school for no other reason than she missed him. Margaret was confident her son would still graduate first grade, despite her rebellion. James was throwing a tiny yellow tennis ball for Lola. Fast as her tiny legs would go, Lola ripped through the fallen leaves after her prize. Her little dog trot was full of pride every time she came back with the ball. Jane was napping in her pack n' play on the back porch. It was a beautiful October afternoon. Warm for autumn.

"Get it, Lola! Get the ball!" James spurred Lola on. He ran after her and tossed crunchy leaves in the air. Lola bit at the air, trying to catch them. Margaret's cell rang Marie's familiar tune.

"Hey, lady, what are you up to?" Margaret asked while she smiled at James and Lola playing in the leaves.

"Did I ever tell you how fantastic you are? You really have been such a friend to me." Margaret smelled a favor coming.

"Yeah, huh? There is no need for this silly dance. What do you need me to do?"

"Will you watch Greyson for me? There is a fitness expo down at the Empire Plaza. They opened a gym at the plaza. I want to show off ANVIL." In the last two years, her fitness business, ANVIL, had really taken hold. Starting out by only training Margaret, her client list had grown quite a bit. Marie worked hard to get ANVIL where it was and she could see a real future in it. Going to this expo could up her client list and her business knowledge.

"Yes, I will watch your goblin." Margaret giggled.

"He has been a goblin lately." Marie agreed, then corrected herself. "He is a good goblin though. Barely snarly."

"Sounds fantastic, I can't wait. Hey, you should talk to Chelsea. She's going to be there doing yoga demonstrations or some such. Maybe you two could head down together." Lola trotted over with the ball and dropped it in Margaret's lap. "Yuck." The ball was soaked with dog slobber. Margaret threw the ball for little Lola to chase. James ran after the dog, hoping to get there first. Behind her, she heard rustling and turned around to see a smiley Jane. "Well, good afternoon, Lady Jane." Her hair fuzzed up from a nap, making her an even bigger slice of cutie pie. Margaret picked up Jane and smooched her chubby baby face. "Mama loves you. Looks like you brushed your hair with firecrackers." Margaret ran her fingers through Jane's baby hair, working to get it to lay flat.

Jeff came up behind Chelsea in the kitchen. She was only wearing her panties and Jeff's Yankee t-shirt. "I love you in my clothes." He nuzzled her neck.

"Be careful, I have boiling water here." Chelsea poured hot water over the tea bags in the mugs. "Speaking of clothes, have you seen my Yankees World Series t-shirt? I haven't seen it for a while. I was hoping to come across it during the move."

"No I haven't, but you have a lot of clothes. I'm sure we'll find it eventually," he said. Chelsea had been officially moved in for a week. Jeff's house, which had become their house, was covered in boxes with every room in a state of flux. She handed Jeff his mug of tea.

"I'm sorry, my love. It looks like I've done a dive bomb on your place and made the house such a mess."

Jeff looked at Chelsea. Her nipples were lightly grazing the inside of his shirt. Noticing what had caught his attention, she looked back at him coyly through her curtain of blonde bangs.

"It's our place now, Chels. It's a home because you're in it. All of these boxes will get sorted out and you know what? We will find your shirt." He kissed her slowly. "Let's go back to the bedroom. I'm positive there's a box in there to go through." Jeff took her by the hand and they went back to bed.

FORTY-FIVE

Margaret watched Nate work and wondered what was going on with him. These days, her husband's erratic moods filled their house. His brow was in a savage crease and his teeth were practically grinding from his constant clenched jaw. Whenever she tried to talk to him, it was as if she was interrupting. Not wanting to give in to his crankiness, Margaret walked over and stood behind Nate's chair. She put her arms over the back of the chair and hugged Nate, grateful to feel him relax at her touch. He tilted his head back and he smiled and she kissed his furrowed brow. Margaret pulled his chair away from his desk and spun Nate around to face her. Holding his gaze, she climbed onto his lap. She threaded her legs through the arms and down the side of his chair. Taking his face in her hands, Margaret kissed him long and deep. She could feel Nate responding, which made her want him more. Margaret undid his belt and zipper to get at him. Nate hastily pushed them down to his knees. Margaret hooked a finger around the crotch of her panties and pulled them aside. First, just the head went in. She let out a delicious hiss. Opening her up slowly, Nate felt her wet warmth all around him.

He pulled Margaret down onto his lap, all the way inside, and she rolled her hips forward and back, rocking them both. "Mmmmmm," Margaret moaned. She began to rise up and down and Nate matched her rhythm. Margaret grunted every time Nate filled her. Grabbing onto the back of the chair, Margaret rode Nate faster and faster, her whole body in the rhythm they'd created. Nate felt himself getting close, unable to keep it at bay. Holding Margaret tight, he roared as he came. Margaret stayed wrapped around him until he stopped moving and laid his head against her. "Now, get back to work," she said as she climbed off of his lap with a smile on her face. Nate was disheveled, but there was no longer a furrowed brow on his face.

It was past midnight when Nate logged off of his work computer. He headed downstairs to find Margaret asleep on the couch with Janey cuddled up on her chest and James sleeping with his head on her leg. Both kids were completely unaffected by her bestial snoring. He smiled, brushed her hair from her face, then went to the recliner and slid his hand in the side pocket. Cigarette pack in hand, he went outside.

Nate fished the joint out of the pack. Lighting it, Nate sat down in the deck chair to marinate on things for a bit. He thought of how Margaret adored him and the kids. Her life was making their lives happy. He knew how smart, funny, and sweet his wife was. It was just the hellacious mess of her disability that he had come to resent, and therefore resent Margaret. Her medications and co-pays seemed to only become more expensive and burdensome. Nate's missed days of work for her sickness had definitely upheaved his plans. He knew he would be further along at work if he'd been able to consistently put in the time. There should have been more money in savings, but there wasn't because it was difficult to have any extra when it all went to Margaret's ever increasing needs. How could she be so damn optimistic about the same life he was being crushed by? Nate couldn't leave Margaret. Walking out on his disabled wife and small kids? No way. He would look like the ultimate asshole. Her goodness itself made him choke up then get angry. Of course Margaret was good. It was easy to be happy and full of goodness when she didn't have to work. All Margaret had to do was swipe a card and sign her name. Nate was the one who shouldered it. Her MS gave her a perpetual hall pass for anything she deemed too much for her to do. Nate's other shoulder took care of those things. With such a heavy load on his shoulders, Nate deserved something for himself. Chelsea was his something.

When Chelsea put her mouth to his, she breathed a darker need into Nate. A need not based in goodness, but one based in pain. Erotic, heartpounding, soul-bending, needful pain. Every time he and Chelsea fucked, Nate tumbled further and deeper away from his family. Yet, he could not— would not— stop. The adrenaline, the anger, the raw way they fucked. She was his to have and Nate was truly the bad guy. A slow smile crept across his face thinking of the tawdry twists of his time with Chelsea. The orange glow of the joint had gotten too close to Nate's fingertips "Ah— dammit." He pinched it until it was out and dropped it. Then, rubbed is burned fingers.

FORTY-SIX

JANEY WAS ON THE floor squealing at the hippo on her playmate. The hippo grinned as drool landed in his googly-eyed face. James was mesmerized by Curious George on PBS. Nate came out of his office and into the living room.

"Today is the expo down in Albany." He tried to sound casual. He sat down on the floor next to Janey, making his signature silly face.

"Yes, I know. Marie is dropping Greyson and Wes off. I agreed to watch him for the day because William is working at the hospital until tonight."

"Well, Jeff hit me up and asked if I would help set up the equipment. Knowing him, he's probably afraid of falling in the reflective pool." They both laughed. "Do you mind if I go down there to help?"

"Of course not. I don't mind. You are a good man. How did I land such a great husband?" She leaned over and kissed Nate.

"Luck, I guess." Nate smiled. "I'm going to let Jeff know I'm in." Nate popped up to his feet and went back to his office.

Once he shut the door, he tapped a message to Jeff.

Nate: Hey little brother. Do you want a hand with setting up for the expo?

Jeff: There's not much to set up but sure, come on down. Hey, maybe we can stop somewhere after we set up. I want to run something by you.

Nate: K. see you in a bit.

With the three of them working, yoga mats and blocks were quickly set up in tidy rows. Using the extra minutes, Chelsea and the guys strolled around the reflecting pools. "Hey, I've got to use the bathroom," Jeff said. "I'll be right back. Then Nate and I will head out." Jeff jogged to the stairs down to the concourse. Nate and Chelsea were finally alone.

"It sure was nice of you to come help your brother today." Chelsea stepped close to Nate.

"I needed to see you." Nate's lips were dangerously close to her mouth. "I need to kiss you." Nate placed his lips on Chelsea's mouth, his tongue attempted to open hers. Chelsea pushed him back, feigning offense.

"Wow, look who's bold. What if someone were to see?" Chelsea's eyes narrowed as she smiled. Nate wrapped his arms around her and looked into her azure eyes. Chelsea softly licked Nate's lips.

Jeff was almost to the bathroom when he spied Marie leaving the ladies' bathroom. She was decked out in personalized fitness gear. "ANVIL" was printed across the chest of her tight black tank top. "Eh? Eh?" she said with a goofy grin while pointing to her shirt.

"Well, hey! You got yourself one snazzy shirt there. Any extras?"

Marie reached into the big black shopping bag she

was carrying. "Here you go," she pulled out a black AN-VIL shirt and tossed it to Jeff.

"Chelsea and Nate are upstairs if you want to give them shirts too," Jeff said as he held the shirt to his cheek, raising his eyebrows. "Oooh, soft. I can feel the quality. Is this organic cotton? Fancy." Marie laughed at Jeff as she bound up the stairs, taking them two at a time.

Marie hit the top of the stairs and looked around for Nate and Chelsea. There was a couple speaking very closely and kissing. Marie didn't want to interrupt their moment, so she hung back. It was only when the two broke away from their kiss that Marie saw it was Nate and Chelsea. Her breath caught in her throat. Seeing what played out in front of her seemed unreal. Chelsea caught sight of Marie staring and, for the briefest of moments, they held eye contact. *Did she just wink at me?* Nate had his back to Marie— he never saw her. Marie quickly turned and headed back down the stairs. She blew past Jeff on the way back down, mumbling some excuse about not wanting to be late.

Chelsea strapped a battery pack to herself and checked the mic for the last time. "Check 1, 2, 3. Check." Satisfied with her set up and excited to get going, she walked up to the guys. Chelsea gave Nate a short hug. "Thank you for helping today." She quickly let go and turned to Jeff and kissed him, wrapping her arms around his neck, making sure the kiss was nice and long. When they finally finished their kiss, Nate almost cracked his molars as he stood there vibrating with jealousy. There was nothing more he could do.

"Alright, my love. I will let you go zen the masses. Nate and I are going to get something to eat and wait.

grace

Call me when you're done and I'll come snatch you up."
Nate saw Jeff had the dreamy smile of a man who was in
love. He could feel the crescents of his nails digging into
his palms. With a wave, the guys hit the sidewalk in the
direction of the pub.

FORTY-SEVEN

Marie did her best to stay present for the whole day. She took groups on tours through the new work-out facility at the plaza and gave demonstrations on the equipment. She even talked a few of the newcomers into jumping on the equipment and taking it for a spin themselves. She also made sure to hand out her card and set up appointments for personal training for new clients. For hours, she spoke with people and answered countless questions for members. Even with the metal clack of weights hitting each other and the thunderous sound of footfalls on the row of treadmills, Marie could not stop the almost imperceptible murmur in her ear. It was her own voice going over and over how she would tell Margaret. She tumbled the words around in her head, hoping to wear off their sharp edges.

High Street Pub was close enough for the guys to walk to. It was a chilly fall afternoon. The sky was a shade of blue only found in autumn. Jeff opened the heavy wood door to the pub. Daylight did its best to break through the red curtains on the windows, but the light only retreated and was replaced with the shadows of the dark bar. There was a stained glass turtle in the window. It glowed softly with the light from the day outside. The brothers sat at the bar and already knew what they would be ordering. The wings were legendary and they both planned on assaulting a pile of them. The red haired bartender sashayed over. "What can I get you two?" The V of her top made it impossible for them not to notice her freckles went down into her cleavage.

"Hello, Pretty. What is your name?" Nate was always flirting on some level. It was as if he couldn't help himself— or didn't want to.

"I'm Astrid." She smiled at Nate and she slid two coasters onto the shellacked bar. She pulled a couple of menus out from underneath the bar and put them in front of the boys. "Today is two dollar domestic pints. Are you guys keeping it a liquid lunch or do you want to order food?"

"Two pints of Bud and we need forty wings. Make them hot." Nate was still tight from having to watch Chelsea and Jeff kiss. Nate could feel the jealousy swirl in his stomach. It didn't matter if he had a wife. It didn't matter that his brother Jeff was with Chelsea. Nate still wanted her for himself. In his mind, Chelsea was his.

"Thanks for helping out today." After taking a long first drink, Jeff put down his glass.

"No problem, Little Bro." Nate jokingly rustled Jeff's hair.

"Will you cut the shit," Jeff said with a smile. "I hated it when I was a kid and I hate it now."

"What? Do you hate this too?" Nate gave Jeff's hair another rustle and a biff to the back of his head. Both of them were laughing when the bartender returned with the pile of molten lava wings.

"Be careful. These SOBs are hot. Here's a pile of napkins and some wet wipes so you can have at it. Do you want another round to go with these?" She pointed at their glasses.

"Yes, we definitely do." Nate said as he put down his empty pint glass. He turned in his stool and looked at Jeff. "So, you told me you wanted to run something by me. What's going on?" Jeff grabbed a napkin to wipe his spicy fingers. He reached into the big pocket on his cargo pants. A tiny black velvet box was in his hand. Without saying a word, Jeff placed the box on the bar in front of Nate.

"Open it." Jeff's face was bright with excitement. Nate spied the small box knowing damn well what it was. Yet, a sliver of him hoped to be wrong. When he cracked the small box open all the way, he could see the diamond ring perched in the middle of the box. Even in the mellow light of the bar, the ring sparkled. Jeff kept it simple by choosing a solitaire setting in yellow gold. The brilliant two carat round diamond was stunning.

"Whoa, and damn, Jeff. It is quite a ring you have there." Nate straightened up on his bar stool and picked up the open box. With his stomach twisting, Nate plucked the ring from the box, seemingly to give it a thorough looking over. "I'm sure I won't be the only one to say you're moving too fast. So, I won't bother saying it."

"Well, you did bother saying. I would appreciate it if you didn't say anymore. Believe me, I know it's fast. Chelsea is 'The One' and I would be the luckiest idiot if she said yes."

"You are an idiot. You got one part correct." Nate put the ring down on the bar in exchange for his beer and emptied his pint glass. "Didn't she just move in?

234

grace

You're all caught up in the newness. How well can you really know her? She could be into some nutty shit. People are strange. Seriously, have you guys even had a proper fight yet?"

"For me to know if I should marry her, we have to fight with each other? Yeah okay, makes sense. I don't know how Margaret stays married to you if fighting is your yardstick. Whatever her past is doesn't matter to me. When I'm with her, I feel like my best self. The rest we'll figure out as we go." Jeff shook his head at his older brother. "Calm your parts, I'm not asking her today. I still haven't quite figured out how—"

"Figured out what? How crazy this is?"

"No, you dick." Jeff laughed. "I haven't figured out how I'm going to propose. Chelsea deserves better than breathtaking." Jeff was lost in thoughts of Chelsea already wearing the ring to notice the shift in his brother's mood. Nate knew if Chelsea could be a wife, she would do it in a breath. Which would mean for the rest of Nate's life, he would have to deal with her being within reach. Nate knew he and Chelsea would not be a couple. He could not reconcile losing out. His thoughts of her trying to refuse him brought a smile to his face. He would still take her if he wanted. Bend her over and fuck her in the bathroom at some bullshit birthday party. She wouldn't stop him. Couldn't stop him. Chelsea had this ability to make him furious and hard at the same time.

"Hey, Astrid," Nate said, getting the attention of the bartender. "We need some shots of Tequila. My little brother is going to ask a girl to marry his silly ass." The bartender popped two shot glasses onto the bar. Nate said, "Shots for everyone at the bar." She set up the two handfuls of people at the bar with shots. Nate stood up.

"Congratulations to my little brother, Jeff." Nate raised his glass with the other patrons in a toast to Jeff. Everyone downed their shot and clapped for Jeff. Nate ordered another round. Then, another. In a short time, Nate drank enough to be less than light on his feet. Seeing the engagement ring that was meant for Chelsea made him a mess. "You know what, Jeffy?"

"I can't believe you just called me Jeffy. You haven't called me Jeffy since we were kids. First it's the hair and now Jeffy. Are you getting nostalgic on me?" He chuckled.

"Well, do you?" Nate said, swaying a bit.

"Do I what?" Jeff asked. His brother was definitely loaded.

"Do you know I love you, Jeff?" Nate said, pulling Jeff into an awkward hug. Jeff laughed at his drunk-off-his-ass brother.

"I love you too, Nate. If you want to be my best man, fine. No need for you to make it weird." Looking at his watch, Jeff realized they needed to head back to the Empire Plaza. "It's time to head back. Chelsea will be between groups and I want to see how it is going."

"Indeed, Petie! That sounds like a great idea. Yes, let's go see how it is going for Chelsea." Nate slid off of his stool, out of the dark bar and into the sunshine on a brisk fall day.

FORTY-EIGHT

THE WALK BACK TO the plaza was normally a ten min-ute casual walk. With a drunk and clumsy Nate, the walk took almost half an hour. He was tripping over himself while he walked. Weaving a bit, Jeff held his brother's arm to keep him from bumping into passersby. "Jesus, Nate, how many shots did you have?"

"I had my shots and some of yours so—" Nate squint-ed his eyes and counted on his fingers. "I had—" He wrote in the air. "Carry the one." Jeff looked at his watch. He didn't want to miss Chelsea. "What was I saying?" Nate snickered. Jeff shook his head and the two kept walking.

The guys reached the plaza and found Chelsea on the marble steps drinking tea and facing the late after-noon sun. She let her hair out of its bun and let it be lifted by the cool breeze. Jeff stopped when he caught sight of her. Bathed in the golden light of the day, Chel-sea took his breath away. It took all he had to not run to her, drop to his knee, and propose on the spot. Nate giggled at himself and pulled Jeff out of his daydream. "You better reign it in, you drunken ass. Fix yourself for shit's sake." Nate put a fresh tuck in his t-shirt and straightened himself up.

"Hey, what about you? Come're. I'll fix your hair." He tried to get his hands on Jeff's head. Jeff laughed at his very drunk brother, swatting his hand away.

"Knock it off, ass. Let's go and, Nate, don't say anything about the ring. Got it?" Nate put a finger to his own lips and over Jeff's. Immediately, Jeff pulled away. "Ew, gha. Will you cut the shit?" Jeff did not want Nate's damp, drunk finger on his face.

Chelsea saw Jeff and Nate making their way up the stairs. Jeff was supporting Nate up the stairs. She hid behind her dark glasses and pretended not to see them. It wasn't until they were only a few steps away that Chelsea took off her aviators and smiled. "What have you two been up to in the last couple hours?" By the looks and smell of Nate, it was obvious the guy was ripped.

"We went to the pub around the way. Nate got a bit ahead of himself—"

Nate cut him off. "I was offering my congratulations." Nate stretched out the word and he tried to wink. Instead, he was doing it with both eyes which appeared like aggressive blinking. Jeff returned Nate's earlier biff by skipping his hand off of Nate's head. "Ow, jeez." Nate rubbed the back of his head. Jeff had to take his brother home before he opened his drunk flap. The prospect of dragging him across the plaza was ridiculous.

"Chels, I need to get my car and get him home. He may have overdone it at the bar."

Chelsea giggled. "May have? Oh, I think it's more than 'may have.'" She looked at Nate, who was smiling at her with squinty eyes. "Yeah, I will babysit him while you get the car. I do have another demonstration, though, so can you make it quick?"

grace

Jeff was already heading down the stairs. "I'll be back in two minutes." When Jeff was out of hearing distance, Chelsea turned to take in this mess named Nate. The smiley goofy Nate was gone. In his place, a nasty drunk with a mean mouth. Nate looked her up and down. He knew who and what Chelsea was. Nate leveled his eyes at her, his drunken mouth puckered, preparing to spit cruelty.

"What the fuck is your deal? Are you trying to smash my whole family to fucking bits? What did you think banging my brother was going to do?" Chelsea watched him as he tried to look sober. It made her laugh. She shook her head back and forth which only added to his agitation.

"You're such a cagey bitch," he spat.

Chelsea gave a disappointed sigh, "Who's the one cheating on his disabled wife for, oh, I don't know, the hundredth time? And now you're fucking your brother's girlfriend. Yeah, Nate, you're a real stand-up guy. This all goes down, yeah, I lost a boyfriend. But you, Nate, you will lose everything. You have this sense of entitlement for being with your broken wife, like you're some big strong man." Nate was hot with anger.

"My wife is not fucking broken. Don't say it again."

"Your wife..." Chelsea stepped closer to Nate and whispered in his ear, "is not the broken one. You're the broken one, Nate." She looked at him, her cold blue eyes dared him to say something. Instead, Nate grabbed her left wrist and yanked her close again. There was tequila on his breath as he spoke an inch from her face.

"My little brother has it in his head to marry you. He told me how breathtaking you are. Jeff clearly doesn't know you're just a filthy, fucked up girl. Face it though— you are no man's wife. There are the girls you marry, like Margaret. She is beautiful, smart, and of course, loyal.

Then, there are girls like you. They're the type a man can bend and, even better, break. The ones who do what they're told because they know that's all they're good for." Nate whispered in her ear, "All you could be is a fuck." He licked Chelsea's ear.

The condemnation was pushing Chelsea's anger. "Nate, the smart, beautiful wife you cheat on and keep small is not the disabled one in your relationship. Now I see— you are. I could not give less of a shit about what you think. You know what it is? You are a coward. You always want adoration and loyalty with no responsibility. You were never brave enough or man enough to be a good husband. If you were, we would never have happened. Your brother truly loves me. He is brave enough and man enough, everyday. He sees me and loves me for it."

"By the time I finish talking with Jeff, he won't want you." Before Nate could react, Chelsea swung. The punch landed square in Nate's unexpecting face. Blood gushed from his nose. His hands immediately covered his face. Fresh blood dripped down his hands and onto the stone stairs. "What the fu—"

"You had that one coming. You should keep your mouth shut because I've been keeping notes. If you try to ruin this for me, you will go down with me." The punch sobered him. With his hands covering his face, Nate sounded muffled.

"What the fuck!?" He pulled his hands away. Blood dripped out of his nose. "You are crazy. I never should have wasted my time messing with you." Chelsea turned and Jeff was at the bottom of the stairs with a look of confusion.

Chelsea cried out, "Jeff!"

Jeff reached the bottom step and his eyes widened when he saw Nate. "Whoa, whoa. Oh no!" Nate's dripping blood made the stairs slippery and being drunk, he lost his footing. Nate fell face first down the stone stairs. Although only a millisecond, Chelsea and Nate made eye contact as he fell past her. When Chelsea reached out her hand, she could only catch the very edge of Nate's shirt. It was not nearly enough to keep Nate from falling. The material slipped through her fingers and then Jeff heard the wet crunch of his brother's face hitting the marble steps. Nate let out a cry of pain. Then, Nate stopped making any sound. He fell down a few more steps. He slammed the back of his head before finally coming to a stop. He was a bloody mess. Jeff's mouth hung open in disbelief. In the hot second of seeing his brother, time froze and it seemed to last forever. Suddenly, real time quickly screamed back in and Jeff unfroze and really saw Nate.

"Nate, Nate!" Jeff ran to his brother, whose broken body was sprawled out on the stairs. Nate's face was decimated— a bloody mess with a repulsive gash on the side of his head. Thick darkening blood was pooling underneath him. "Nate?" Jeff felt for a pulse. A weak pulse barely beat out. "Oh. My. God. We're going to get help." Jeff's heart was hammering in his chest and his hands were too slick with Nate's blood to dial his own phone. "Help! I need help!" Chelsea stood like a statue staring down at Nate. Jeff pulled off his shirt and applied pressure to the gory wound on the side of Nate's head. A woman walking by saw the three of them and the macabre mess. Quickly, she pulled out her phone and called 911.

"There is a badly hurt man on the stairs at the Empire Plaza. Wow, the blood. Please hurry." In minutes, two police cars and an ambulance blocked off the road and the EMTs rushed to Nate. They pulled Jeff away so they could assess the damage. A mass of people started to gather too closely, so an officer drove back the herd of onlookers. Everything was awash in red, white, and blue beacon lights from the police and ambulance. The police officer in charge took Jeff aside to speak to him while the EMTs did their work.

"Did you see what happened?" he asked Jeff.

"Yes, officer, I saw him fall. He's my brother." Jeff told the officer what had happened. When he got to the part where Nate fell, Jeff's throat locked up and for a moment, his words were paralyzed in his mouth. "He went down so fast I couldn't get to him." When he was done, the officer shook his head back and forth.

"I'm going to have to take you both in. Something like this, there'll be questions you both need to answer." The officer called a female officer over for Chelsea. The officers walked both Jeff and Chelsea to separate cruisers. As Jeff was being put in the back, he heard the EMT: "No pulse, no response to light. We gotta go! Go!" Nate was strapped to the stretcher and put in the ambulance. The ambulance screamed down the downtown Albany street towards the hospital with sirens and lights filling the air.

FORTY-NINE

"Boys, if you're hungry, give me a holler," Margaret yelled upstairs. She waited and only heard the TV murmuring. When Margaret walked back into the kitchen, James popped out of the pantry.

"Boo!" Margaret jumped with surprise. "Did I scare you very much?" His big brown eyes blinked at her.

"You sure did. I almost pooped my pants." James cracked up. Potty words were comedy gold to him. Margaret picked James up. "I love you so much. I need to squeeze your guts." James started to laugh and squirm.

"No, not the squeeze!"

"Oh, yes. The squeeeeeeze." Margaret hugged him tight and kissed his face. "Now, go get Greyson. We need to vote on dinner."

"Can we have macaroni and cheese? It's Greyson's favorite."

"Sure, Bud. Macaroni and cheese coming up. Go find Greyson and we'll make it together." James ran upstairs to find his friend.

Margaret managed to keep the boys occupied with games and snacks. Jane swatted at the dangling toys on her playmat. After dinner, Iit was Margaret's turn to seek in the game of hide and seek.

Even though Marie had finished up at the expo and was able to leave, she did not yet want to pick up Greyson. It would mean going to Margaret's. Marie couldn't imagine telling Margaret her lecherous husband was making out with his brother's girlfriend, Margaret's friend. "Whore," Marie said, aloud. How could she be the bearer of this disgusting news? Yet, if Margaret was going to find out her husband was a cheating shit, her best friend should be the one to tell her. Marie wiped her eyes and took a big breath before she pulled a U-turn and headed in the direction of her best friend.

Both Jeff and Chelsea were separately questioned about the accident. The woman who had called 9-1-1 was also questioned. Her name was Leah Beam. She made sure to tell the police that she saw the whole thing. Miss Beam often spent her afternoons at the reflecting pools in the plaza. It was where she took her breaks. During her routine stroll, she heard someone yell. Now, Miss Beam was no gossip, but also not a woman to pass up drama. Miss Beam said, "I saw the woman was facing down the steps. Then the guy a few steps up from her slipped on the stairs and fell. It was a horrible thing to see so much blood. It was as if it happened in slow motion. The guy literally bounced down the steps. She made a bouncing motion with her finger in the air, then shuddered. "The other guy yelled and ran to the stairs. He crouched over the guy and then started yelling for help. That's when he saw me and told me to call."

"Thank you for coming down and telling us what you saw. It is unfortunate, however we're glad you were there. Your answers help us see the whole picture."

"Is that it? Can I go? Not for nothing, but I need a drink or three."

"Yes, Miss Beam. If we have any other questions, we will contact you." Officer Sheehy shook her hand then walked her out of the station.

Jeff sat at the table in one of the interrogation rooms. He was hoping Chelsea was doing alright. He did not know why she punched Nate or why she was crying when he saw her on the stairs. Whatever it was, it had been pushed aside when Nate fell. The police had given him a dark blue t-shirt to wear. Jeff went over what had happened with the police. They asked them the same questions ten different ways. The story did not change. Nate and Chelsea had been talking. When Chelsea turned to walk down the stairs, Nate slipped and fell. The sight and smack of Nate's head on the stairs would be on repeat in Jeff's mind forever. Officer Sheehy sat on the opposite side of the table.

"We had another witness who backs up your story."

"Thank God. Are we finally done?" Jeff's head went down on the table. Jeff had left out the wallop Chelsea delivered to Nate's face before he fell. He knew, without really knowing why, that he was protecting Chelsea.

"Yes, we are finished for now. Listen. Go home. Rest. It has been one hell of a day for you, no?" Officer Sheehy stood up.

"Yes, sir, it really has been. Is my girlfriend still here? They separated us and I have no idea where she is."

"She has also been freed to go. I believe she is waiting for you out front." Jeff had to ask about Nate. "Is my brother going to be okay?"

Officer Sheehy knew the details, but it was not his place to tell him. "If you want to go check on your brother, he was taken to Albany Med. Do you have anything else?"

"No. I have nothing else." Jeff slowly stood as well. Officer Sheehy opened the door for Jeff.

"Good. Then we're done here."

Jeff found Chelsea at the front of the precinct sitting in a metal chair, her knees to her chest with her arms wrapped around her legs. She closed her eyes and rested her head on her knees. "Hey." Chelsea lifted her face to the sweetest sight. Jeff was standing there, exhausted and dishevelled. "What the hell happened on those stairs between you two?" Chelsea had been beyond scared that Jeff had told the police. When the officer questioning her finished and let her go, she realized he hadn't. She wasn't absolutely sure Nate would not tell the police. Him falling down the stairs changed the dynamic and he might have been too angry to keep quiet.

"Right now the important thing is Nate. You need to call Margaret and get to the hospital. I can get myself home."

"Chelsea, I don't feel good leaving you here." She could feel Jeff was vibrating with worry for his brother.

"Jeff, I can totally take care of myself. Do not worry about me. I'm fine, my love. I promise. You need to go to your brother." Chelsea stood up to embrace Jeff. She kissed his forehead ever so sweetly. "I love you and I will be at home waiting for you." After another kiss, Jeff waved goodbye to Chelsea as she walked out of the station with a pounding heart. What had she done? Did anyone see her hit Nate? The witness from the plaza didn't mention anything. And Chelsea sure as hell left the punch out of her story. She told the cops she and Nate were waiting for Jeff. When Jeff called her name, she started down the stairs. Having also heard Jeff, Nate followed her. That was when he fell. Chelsea explained how she tried to reach for him but couldn't stop his fall. Her tearful tale ended with her head in her hands crying. By all accounts, a fantastic show. However, Chelsea was nauseous with fear of being found out. The fall out from this could be catastrophic. Still, no one had mentioned anything and maybe Nate wouldn't remember— his head did take some serious hits. Chelsea grimaced at the memory of Nate's head hitting the stairs. Yet underneath the fear was the prospect of getting away with it. Nate would hobble home, back to the wife, and Chelsea would have Jeff. Her lips slowly curled into a smile.

After finishing at the station, Jeff used his phone to call Margaret. It only rang once and Margaret answered, excited to hear about their day.

"Hey there, Jeff. How did it go at the plaza? Where are you two?"

"I'm outside the police station," he said in a choked whisper.

"Police station? What the hell did you two boys get up to today?" Margaret asked. "Do you need me to bring bail money?"

"It's just me, Margaret. Are you near James? Can you go somewhere he can't hear you talking?"

Margaret got goosebumps. She walked into the kitchen to peek around for James and Greyson. The boys must have gone back to James's bedroom to play. "You're scaring me. Jesus, Jeff, what happened? Okay, I'm alone. Now tell me what the hell is going on."

"Margaret, something happened to Nate." Margaret's chest tightened. "He's um... "

Hearing the tremor in her brother-in-law's voice, Margaret got loud. "What do you mean, Jeff?" Tears started to fill her eyes. "Jeff, you tell me right damn now.. What happened to Nate. Where is he?"

"Maggs, I'm so sorry." Jeff could not speak. His mouth was dry and his throat burned. Margaret listened to her brother-in-law's breathing on the phone. When he finally spoke, his voice was barely audible and raspy. "Nate is really bad, Maggs. He's at Albany Med. I'm on my way there now." Jeff's words knocked the wind out of her. She stood motionless. A moment went by then Margaret hit the red dot on her phone, ended the call, and dialed Marie. After three rings Marie picked up.

"Hey, sorry I'm running late getting back. It was a long day at the expo. I'm just an exit away."

"You need to make it here faster. I have to go to the hospital. There was an accident and Nate is at Albany Med. Can you stay and watch the kids for me?"

"Oh my God, of course. What happened? Do you know anything?"

"No, Jeff called and all he would tell me was that Nate is really bad. Please hurry, Marie. I am really freaked out."

"I'm almost there. Get your stuff together so you can run out as I come in." Marie ended the call and dropped her phone in the passenger seat. She wondered if Jeff saw what Marie saw today between Chelsea and Nate and dealt with him. "Holy shit." Marie said out loud and stomped the gas.

Margaret ended the call and, with a shaky hand, put her phone down. Suddenly, one of the lower cabinets burst open and James lept out. "Gotcha, Mama! I seeked you!" He hugged her legs.

With tears in her eyes, Margaret agreed. "You sure did, my bud." She picked up her son and squeezed him to her chest.

"Mama, you're squishing my guts again." He laughed as Margaret rasberried his neck. She breathed in her little boy and focused on remaining standing.

FIFTY

TEN MINUTES LATER, MARGARET saw headlights in her driveway. She was at the ready with her coat and purse. Janey was already in bed and the boys were watching TV, singing along with the show. Margaret opened the door as Marie stepped onto the porch. "Jeff is on his way to the hospital to see Nate. He hasn't called me back."

"You get going and call me when you find out what is going on. I love you." Marie hugged her friend. Then, she went into the house to be with the kids.

Before Marie went back inside, she pasted a smile on her face. She didn't want the kids to see her looking worried. She wanted them occupied and out of ear shot if someone called with news of Nate. "How about I set you up in the big bed upstairs? You can watch your show all snuggled up. I'll even set you guys up with juice and animal crackers."

"Yes! Let's go, Greyson. Mama and Dad's bed is the best. They have a hundred million pillows and it has a controller so you can take it for a ride!"

"Wow. I wanna ride the big bed!" Marie gave the boys juice bags and the whole box of animal crackers, hoping it would keep them busy. The boys pounded back up the stairs. Lola and Wes followed right behind them.

Jeff tore into the hospital parking lot, left his car at the entrance, and ran in. He gave the nurse his name and said whom he was looking for. The nurse typed some information into her computer, then told him she would get the doctor. A few minutes later, the doctor who had taken care of Nate came out to speak with Jeff.

"Sir, I am Dr. Ryan." The doctor shook Jeff's hand. He put his other hand on Jeff's shoulder. "You're Nate Hall's brother?"

"Yes. I'm Jeff, Nate Hall's brother. I came right from the station as soon as I could. Is he okay? Where is he? Can I see him?" Dr. Ryan suggested they go sit. "No, I don't need to sit. I need to go check on Nate."

"Mr. Hall. I am so sorry to have to tell you this. Your brother fell down marble stairs. The damage to his face and c spine were very severe."

Jeff's stomach curdled. "Doc."

"Mr. Hall. Your brother passed away on the way to the hospital."

Jeff's breath left him and the sounds of the hospital faded away. He fell to his knees and shook with tears. "No, no, no. He fell down the steps." Dr. Ryan helped a sobbing Jeff stand and walked him over to a corner of chairs. He gave Jeff a moment to take in the tragic reality of Nate being dead. "I wasn't fast enough," he muttered. "I need to see Nate. Where is my brother?"

"I will bring you to him in a moment, Mr. Hall. As

I said, your brother's injuries were severe. You need to know this before you see him."

"It's fine. I'll be fine. Bring me to my brother."

Margaret broke every traffic law on her way to the hospital. Her fear was firing up her symptoms. Her gait was off and her breathing had changed. Dysarthria affected her ability to speak. She was going to need to find Jeff to explain everything. She came around the corner of the endless hospital hallway to find Jeff sitting in a chair with his head in his hands. Looking at him, Margaret was worried Nate had gotten hurt worse than she thought. She prayed he would not need surgery. Her poor Nate.

"Jeff." Margaret said softly and with a higher pitch. Her breath was getting harder to catch. As she put her hand on his shoulder, he looked up at her with tears in his eyes. With her breathy and broken voice, Margaret got her questions out. "What is going on? What did the doctors say about his injuries? Will he come back and update us?" Jeff said nothing but shook his head slowly back and forth. Margaret was confused. "What no? The doctor isn't coming back soon?" Jeff's head kept shaking back and forth.

"He's gone, Maggs. Nate died. He fell and...when he did, the base of his skull and temple...." Jeff could not finish. Another wave of tears traveled down his face.

Margaret's wordless mouth filled with her scream. She screamed from the most inner part of her heart and soul. A broken cry weighted in such despair. She fell to the hospital floor, sobbing.

The doctor who worked on Nate came running. He had heard this sound hundreds of times. Tonight, this woman's heart breaking wail was the saddest and almost unbearable sound he had ever heard.

Jeff got himself together enough to make the call to Marie. The news was a punch to the gut. Jeff let her know he and Margaret were on their way home where Marie was on the couch petting Lola and Wes, waiting for them. Feeling the heaviness in the air, the dogs greeted Margaret and Jeff gently, without barking or jumping. Marie wrapped her arms tightly around her best friend. She felt Margaret surrender and both of them cried while Marie held her. "Shhhh. Shhhh." When Margaret's tears abated, Marie brought her upstairs and helped her into the shower. The shower water mixed with the hot tears running down Margaret's face. Her legs felt so weak and were no longer able to keep her standing. Margaret slid down to the floor of shower. Her arms wrapped around her knees and her head pressed against the tile.

"My brother is dead. He was my best friend," Jeff said when Marie questioned him about what had happened. "I saw him, Marie. It was horrible." Jeff shivered thinking of his brother's broken face.

"Can you tell me what happened?" Marie needed to put together the sequence of events.

"Thing is, I am not sure what happened." Nate and I went to the bar to eat and have a few beers. Then shots. Nate did a lot of shots. We got to the plaza to find Chelsea."

The mention of Chelsea made Marie bristle. She had never liked the vibe coming from that woman and now she knew why. However, Marie kept what she had seen to herself. "Uh huh? Keep going."

"Because Nate was pretty ripped and I didn't want to drag his drunk ass, I left him with Chelsea while I ran to my car. When I got back to the stairs, Nate had Chelsea by the wrist and they were talking close. Then, I see her blast him in the face. I was too far away to hear what it was about. Chelsea turned and saw me. When she started down the stairs, Nate started to follow her, but he slipped. Chelsea reached out to get him, but he must have had enough momentum. Before I knew it, Nate was tumbling down the steps. I heard his head hit the stairs, Marie. He fell forward, broke his arms. His face, his neck..." Jeff breathed in deeply and exhaled. The vision of Nate's crushed and bruised face would never leave him.

"My God, Jeff. I am so very sorry." Marie listened for the shower to make sure Margaret wasn't out yet. "Margaret is going to be dealing with a herculine-sized shitstorm. Jeff, please leave out what you saw with Nate and Chelsea. Start from when he fell down the stairs."

"You know, I didn't tell the police about it either. I said I saw him fall, nothing before it.. I don't know why but something told me not to. Do you think I should have? I'm sure Chelsea will clear up what was going on."

"Doubt that very fucking much," Marie said under her breath.

"Huh?"

Jeff was completely unaware. Naive idiot. Marie wanted to keep him unaware. She would deal with Chelsea. "I said, 'Don't tell Margaret too fucking much. And no, leave it as is. It will be worse if you go back to the cops. Then God knows what fresh hell. We have to be considerate of not only what she is going through, but how it affects her body. I'm afraid a full-blown flare up right now would be more than she could take. Promise me you won't mention the punch or Nate with Chelsea."

"No, I won't say anything to her." Marie let out a sigh of relief. Jeff was worried for his mother and father. "Besides, I have to call my parents and let them know. How am I supposed to tell them Nate died?" Jeff sat on the couch, exhausted, with his head resting in his hands. He had been trying desperately to arrange the words in his mind, only for them to play hide and seek in his mouth. Marie was too concerned with Margaret to worry much for Jeff. Margaret, fresh from the shower and in her robe, came into the living room and sat on the couch, next to Jeff.

"Marie, if you want to stay here with Greyson, I can make up the fold out in Nate's office. He won't care—" She heard the words as they came out of her mouth. Margaret dropped her head and took a deep breath. Marie quickly filled the silence.

"Yes, I will stay. It will be great for Greyson to wake up and see me. I will take them to the diner for pancakes." Marie wanted to stay because she would not let her best friend go through this devastation alone. "I'm going to snag a pair of your sweats too." Marie padded up the stairs, mentally going over what she had seen and what she was being told.

FIFTY-ONE

As devastated as she was, Margret could not let Jeff go through the pain of telling his parents alone. She was Nate's wife. This was her responsibility too.

"I'm right here." Margaret placed a loving hand on Jeff's shoulder, try to help keep him together. Jeff's and Nate's mother, Evelyn, picked up on the second ring.

"Hello. Hall residence," she chirped in a happy tone.

"Hi, Mom. Is Dad with you?" Evelyn knew her son did not sound right.

"Jeff, honey. What's wrong? You don't sound good." Evelyn called for her husband. "Roman! Jeff is on the phone and he wants to talk to you." She got back on the phone. "Your father is slow as all get out. Give him a minute." Jeff was shaking. Everything was collapsing in on him. Margaret held Jeff's hand, sending what strength she had to him.

"Hello, son. What's the good word?" Roman was all ears.

"Dad, can you put me on speaker? I have something you and Mom need to hear." Jeff breathed slow and deep to keep from passing out and concentrated on what he needed to say.

"Sure, son. Is it good news? Getting married?" Roman clicked the speaker button on the phone.

"No, Dad. I'm not getting married. Mom, are you there?" Jeff needed them both to hear it. He could not handle saying it twice.

"Yes, honey, I'm here." Evelyn was fiddling around in the kitchen.

"Dad, Mom. The reason I'm calling…" Jeff took another deep breath. "It's Nate."

"What's it Jeff?" Evelyn called out over the water she was filling the teapot with.

"For Pete's sake, Evey! Turn the water off. I can't hear the boy."

"As if you could hear anyway," Evelyn yelled. She put the pot on the stove.

"Well, I heard that." Roman gave his wife a matter-of-fact smile. On the other end Margaret took the phone from Jeff and put it on speaker.

"Hey, you two. You should both sit down." Chairs scraped across the kitchen floor. With a huff and a groan of arthritis, his parents sat down.

"Alright. You sound serious." Evey smoothed her housecoat. "We're sitting. Now, will you please tell us what is going on?" Roman and Evelyn instinctively reached out and held hands.

"We love you both so very much. It breaks me to be the one to tell you this." Margaret paused and took a deep breath. "It's about Nate. There has been a terrible accident." There was pin drop silence. Jeff's shoulders shook. He cried quietly into his hands and leaned on his sister-in-law. Margaret kissed the top of his head while she rocked him. Evelyn gasped and cried out. Roman said nothing. Through tears, Margaret told them what the doctor had said. "He fell down the marble stairs at the Plaza. He slipped and fell all wrong. He was alive in the ambulance. The injuries to his head and neck were too severe. He passed away on the way to the hospital." Each word Margaret spoke tasted like an old copper penny in her mouth, dirty and metallic.

"My baby! Oh, Nate. Roman, my boy." Evelyn slid off of her plastic covered kitchen chair to the floor. He could do nothing to stop her tears. Slowly he got on the tile floor next to his crying wife. He would sit with her right there as long as she needed. Roman eased her head onto his shoulder, took the phone off of the speaker and got back on, sounding all business.

"Take me off the speaker thing. We have to talk." Margaret took her father-in-law off the speaker. Margaret leaned Jeff back on the couch. She took off his shoes and put his feet up. Lastly, she covered him with his brother's favorite blanket. Margaret and Roman needed to see to the details of Nate's death.

Some time later, after Margaret and Roman finished their phone call, she found Jeff quiet and staring. Destroyed by the day, he felt numb and useless. "Maggs, thank you for talking to Dad. Here Nate is your husband and I'm the one who can't hold it together."

"When, after I hung up the phone and before I came in here, I was in the bathroom dry heaving and crying into a towel afraid the kids would hear. The fact is for me, I'm going to have to handle this. Those two kids upstairs need me even more now. Losing it is a luxury I don't have. You, on the other hand, must be so depleted. You need to get home to Chelsea and take a hot shower. Then get to bed. I'm going to try to lay down." Jeff hugged his sister-in-law. He kept his promise and did not bring up Chelsea and Nate being on the stairs. On the porch, Jeff turned around.

"I love you, Maggs. I'll check on you in the morning."

"I love you, too." When he left, Margaret locked the door. Once it was shut, she turned to go upstairs. First, she checked on sleeping Jane, whose long eyelashes brushed her cheeks while she slept. Bunny could barely be seen from his spot wedged under sweet Jane. James and Greyson were asleep in James's room. The two loyal little dogs were coiled at their feet. Marie had fallen asleep with her phone. Margaret gently put it on the side table and quietly closed the door. Margaret stopped in the hallway. Leaning on the wall, she inhaled deeply. She needed more time than the hallway reprieve could possibly give her.

FIFTY-TWO

EVEN THOUGH NATE HAD previously made arrangements for his passing, there were still decisions to be made. After viewing his dead son's damaged face, Roman did not want an open casket. The mortician was confident she could reconstruct his face. Although it would be difficult, Margaret thought an open casket would ultimately be best. She wanted to give everyone time to say their "goodbyes". Through their grief, Roman and Evelyn were sure to be there for Margaret. Evelyn held her husband's hand through the painful phone calls to family and friends. No matter how many times as Roman had to break the news, it never got easier. He would fall into tears every time. Every person they told had a moment of disbelief followed by tears. An unexpected tragedy taking a young man from his wife and children. Margaret called James's school to tell them Nate had died. Well meaning school parents called the house for the kids. Their invites for birthday parties and playdates went unaccepted. James waffled between crying for Nate and then asking to play a few minutes later. It was as if he would forget then remember again. Each time he remembered, he would wail for his father all over. His child mind was not able to fully understand the permanence of his father's absence.

Nate would be viewed for one day. The next day, there would be a service at the church. From there, Nate would be going to the crematorium. Margaret choked on her tears going through Nate's closet. She decided on his dark gray suit and blue button up shirt. Nate had never been one for ties, however, Margaret found his favorite Red Sox t-shirt. The mortician would put it on under his suit. This small gesture, one only she would know about, was Margaret's goodbye to her husband. Sitting down on their bed, hugging the t-shirt, breathing in the scent of him, Margaret, in her agony and tears yelled, "Damn it, Nate. FUCK!" She cried into her husband's clothes. Marie was in the room in a flash.

"Shhhh." Marie stroked her hair, brushing strands away from the tears. Marie had decided to stay with Margaret and the kids for a while. Margaret was her very best girl. Throughout their years of friendship, their loyalty to each other never wavered. Margaret had always kept Marie safe. This time, Marie would keep Margaret safe, even from the horrible truth about her dead, bag of dicks husband.

There was no question of whether or not Marie had seen Nate and Chelsea kiss. Marie saw them with her own eyes. For fuck's sake, Chelsea smiled right at her like a fucking pyscho! Why, though? What could possibly justify something so disgusting and cruel? Marie hated keeping things from Margaret, especially something like this. Her questions for Chelsea would have to wait.

FIFTY-THREE

Nate being dead made things a lot easier for Chelsea. If there were a part of her that was going to feel bad about simply watching Nate die, it hadn't shown up yet. When she and Jeff talked about what he saw going on between Chelsea and Nate, her version of the story would be the only one. With tears in her eyes, she explained what Jeff had seen. "He was drunk and slurring a bit when we were on the stairs. He told me he was going to make sure you didn't marry a stuck up bitch like me. He went to grab my arm and something just came over me. I punched him then turned to get away from him. When I saw you at the bottom of the stairs I started down to get to you and Nate followed. Oh my God, Jeff, it was horrible. I tried to grab him, but I couldn't. Then Nate just—" Chelsea's tears and imploring eyes did their work on Jeff.

"I don't understand. What the hell would make Nate come out with such bullshit? Then to go after you? I'm so—" Jeff felt poker hot anger, but that was quickly dissolved. His anger at his dead brother was washed away by the waves of sadness crashing over him.

"I think I know. Oh my God, I feel terrible for not telling you this sooner. I should have told you when it happened." Chelsea took another deep breath as if she were preparing to confess something huge. "It was the night I met you at the Christmas party at Margaret and Nate's." Jeff listened to Chelsea tell him of his brother making a pass at her in the hallway. "He got real close to me and touched my face. I was confused and uncomfortable. Then, he ran his hand down me, grazing my chest. He shocked me and I tried to step back but Nate was so fast. He had me by the wrist and pulled me in close. I could feel his breath on my face." Chelsea paused for a minute to collect her thoughts about the rest of the encounter. "He whispered to me how I looked like I would be fun to fuck. I was so afraid. Here I was in a new friend's house for the first time and her husband does... does this. I didn't know what to do. I yanked my hand away and fled to the kitchen. I've made a point of not being alone with him since." Chelsea rested her head on Jeff's shoulder. "I didn't know I would be meeting the man of my dreams the same night. When we fell for each other, I was afraid if I told you what happened, you would blame me."

Jeff gathered her in for a hug while his mind tried to process what he was hearing about his brother. It was hard to hear his brother was the kind of guy Chelsea was describing. Yet, he couldn't imagine anyone would lie about something so terrible. He tilted Chelsea's face upward and looked at her.

"Sweetie, you did nothing wrong. I am so sorry you had to go through that and carry the weight of it all this time. I love you and nothing could change the way I feel for you." With everyone being in a terrible state, Jeff wanted to wait for a better time and a much more romantic way to propose, but something told him it was time. "Stay here. I will be right back." He kissed Chelsea on her forehead and zipped down the hallway. Chelsea stopped crying, wiped the tears from her face, and smoothed her hair.

Jeff walked back into the living room and stood before Chelsea. With a smile, he got down on one knee and opened the box. "Chelsea, you are the most beautiful, loving, kind person I have ever known." This was the moment Chelsea had dreamed of. Her heart was pounding, but she tried to remain calm. "Will you, Chelsea, save me from my boring self and be my wife?"

She burst, "Oh my God, Jeff! Yes, yes, yes!" Jeff stood up and Chelsea threw herself into his arms. "I love you, Jeff, and I can't wait to be yours." Chelsea could not take her eyes off of the two carat sparkler as it caught the light and reflected it a million times. It was absolutely astonishing. "Jeff, this ring is ridiculous!" She moved her hand to see the fire from all angles.

"Good, I am so glad. I had to plow a lot of snow. It was worth it, because I am ridiculously in love with you, so you should have a ring to match." Jeff and Chelsea looked into each other's eyes and kissed.

"Jeff, I love you. With the way everything is right now, maybe we should wait until a little time passes. I want to be respectful of the family." She turned her eyes back to her ring, hypnotised by its brilliance.

"Chelsea, I couldn't have waited another minute, but of course you are thinking of others. It's one of the millions of reasons I love you. How about for now, we keep the engagement between us? We can announce it when things settle down a bit. Chelsea, I do understand this is not perfect timing, but with all the sadness around us, we need to have something wonderful to look forward

grace

to. You've made my dreams come true— even the ones I didn't have the courage to recognize. I can't wait until you are Mrs. Hall." Jeff leaned down and kissed his fiancé as she got on her tiptoes to kiss Jeff. They were both so content that the timing of the proposal did not matter. In the sweet, protective, rose colored bubble of love, they could not hear anything on the outside.

FIFTY-FOUR

MARGARET FELT OUT OF her own body in the days following Nate's death. Aside from Nate's life insurance and the fresh mortgage on the house, a mountain of things still needed attention. The incessant phone calls frayed Margaret's already tenuous hold. When would there be time to sort through details? Before Nate had died, they were always so wrapped up in Margaret and her health. This chronic condition kidnapped her confidence, leaving Margaret mistrustful of her own abilities. Her life had evolved into Nate deciding their day-to-day and doling out the finances. It's not as if Margaret received an allowance from him— she had her own card to use whenever the need arose, but she was used to being part of a team. Nate's lead position with his company allowed him to work full-time from home, only traveling for work when he absolutely had to. Their dry erase board was covered in a constant flurry of times to take medications and appointments to see some doctor or other. Margaret felt terrible more often these days, which added more to all Nate was already responsible for. Never wanting her to worry, he had taken on most things. He had always told her he had it all under control and there was nothing for her to worry about. Now with him gone, it was all she could do.

Despite the hollow state of her insides and lack of confidence, she handled everything. It was all on her now. From the succession of phone calls and financial decisions to be made to the caterer for gathering at home after the services. Margaret got up every morning ready to mom. Even with her heart broken and her body on the edge of falling, she came through.

The night of the wake, the Hall family took their places next to Nate's coffin. Each steeled themselves in their own way for the hours they would be immersed in the sadness and pain of losing Nate. James and Janey were being watched in the sitting room across the hall. With everyone coming to the services, there was no one around to watch the kids at home. As much as Margaret didn't want it this way, James and Janey had to come. James losing his father was tragic enough. Having to look at him in a coffin for hours was beyond bearing for a boy his age. Marie set up James with his tablet and toys in the corner of the over furnished funeral home sitting room. She made sure he had his headphones too. This way he would be out of sight and unable to hear those coming to view Nate. "So, you are all set up. Look, I brought snacks." Marie handed James a cheese stick from the stocked Darth Vader lunch box. "If you need anything, Uncle William and I are here for you." Marie kissed James on his head. Janey was snuggled up against Marie, having fallen asleep in her front carrier. Marie gave her tailored navy dress a tug, trying to smooth it around the straps of the carrier.

"Hello, Marie." Chelsea stood in the doorway wearing a charcoal colored skirt with a dove gray sweater.

Her blonde hair was in a neat twist at the base of her neck. Marie's hackles went up and her eyes narrowed.

"Hello, Chelsea. How have you been? I've been wanting to talk to you." Suddenly, Jeff materialized next to Chelsea.

"Hey, Chels." He kissed her. "Marie." Jeff leaned in and gave a kiss to Marie on the cheek. "You've been amazing, Marie. Thank you for everything."

"Margaret is my very best friend and I love her and her babies. There isn't anything I would not do for her," Marie said. Her eyes shot venom at Chelsea, whose poker face revealed nothing. Marie had to remove herself, because the proximity between her fist and Chelsea's face was dangerous. "I'm going to get back to the kids and keep them occupied." She checked the time on the diamond face of her black Chanel watch. "The wake is almost over and then I'm taking Margaret and the kids home."

Chelsea put her hand on Marie's arm. "Is there anything I can do, Marie? What Margaret is going through..." she trailed off. Marie pulled her arm from Chelsea's touch.

"We're all set." Marie spoke in a very clipped tone. "If I need anything from you, Chelsea, I know where to find you." Marie turned and walked back to James with Janey. Jeff and Chelsea went back into the funeral home's viewing room.

Mourners signed the memorial book and took some time to look at the photo collage of Nate. There was one of Nate and Jeff from when Nate got his first car. Jeff smiled remembering the excitement of riding in the car with his big brother. One of his best memories was going to the drive-in with Nate and his friends. The only room Nate had left for Jeff was the trunk. Happy to be asked at all, Jeff hopped in the trunk, with the snacks and the stolen beers from various parents' homes, to be bounced around in the dark dank while the stolen beers bounced around too. When the car was at the gate to pay for the movie, there was a bang and what sounded like a struggle. Nate smiled at the cute freckle-faced ticket attendant as if unaware of any noise and paid the admission. Once parked with the speaker hooked onto the window, Nate finally decided to extricate his little brother from the trunk. Nate opened the trunk and took a good look at little Jeffy, soaked with beer and with an angry red bump blossoming on his forehead. "Jeez, little brother, what happened to you? Did you fight the spare tire?" Jeff rolled his eyes and tossed the empty Genesee can, hitting Nate in the chest and hitting the ground with a hollow thump.

"It's hot as all get out in here, so I figured I'd have a beer. Since you felt the need to go over every bump on the road. Which, by the way, well played asshole." Nate had smiled with pride then chuckled. "Yeah, laugh, you dickhead. I opened the beer and it sprayed every fucking where. Without thinking, I went to sit up and bashed my head on the trunk door." He rubbed the red spot, wincing at how tender it was.

"Yeah, it looks like it will bruise up nicely." Nate got close up. "Hey, guys, come look at Jeffy's lump." Soon the trunk was surrounded by Nate and his friends peering into the trunk at a beer soaked and bruised Jeff. They carefully opened a beer and cheered, "Jeff, Jeff, Jeff," and vowed to never let him live it down.

Jeff stared at the picture and rubbed his forehead with teary eyes and a smile on his face. Margaret appeared next to him, having left the receiving line for a reprieve from all the emotions. Jeff gave her a sad smile and pointed to the picture. "Ah, yes, Nate's first car. He loved this picture of the two of you. You guys went everywhere in that ride. Hey, remember the Genesee beer explosion?" Margaret asked.

"Actually, I was just thinking about it and how damn hard I hit my bean in the trunk. I swear I got concussed." He rubbed the ghost of the bruise. Margaret let out a small laugh remembering the joy on Nate's face every time he told the story.

"You must have been concussed. It is the only thing to explain this right here." She looked him up and down. They both smiled and wrapped an arm around each other's waists as they perused the memories on the picture board.

After getting James and Janey cleaned up and ready for bed, Catherine had her grandbabies into bed for a sleepover with her in Nate's office, now the spare room. James hopped into bed with his gram and got cozy under the down comforter. Next to the fold out bed, Margaret slowly rocked back and forth in the glider, nursing Janey until she was milk drunk. Her long dark lashes fluttered then closed as she slipped off to sleep in her mother's arms. Gently, Margaret lay the baby down in the travel crib, peeling herself off in tiny increments or else risk waking up the badger. James was up to his eyeballs in cartoons and giggling. The last week had been so excruciating, she was grateful for any lift in her boy's mood. "Mom," Margaret said. Catherine looked over her grandson's head at her daughter.

grace

"You need to get yourself situated with a shower— a long one. Then get yourself into one of those pairs of pajama bottoms you're always wearing. Why do you never buy the top?" Catherine commented more to herself, "Always with the half pajamas. What is that?" Then she went back to Margaret. "So, after the pajamas you get your keister to bed. It's been a long day and you still have tomorrow to get through. We need to move furniture to make more room for people. The caterer will be setting up while we're at the service. Also, the flowers..." she trailed off, seeing the sad, far away look in her daughter's eyes. "You know what? We'll deal with tomorrow, tomorrow. You get going so we can watch our cartoons." Catherine kissed James on his head, turning her attention to the television.

"I love you, Mom." Margaret kissed her mother's offered cheek, then James on his. "I'm off to take a shower. If you need anything, don't ask me." Margaret smiled weakly then, went to her bathroom.

First she slid the dimmer switch on the bathroom wall, lowering the lights, then hit play on her phone. Soothing music drifted over the sound of the water. Soon, her reflection disappeared in the steam on the bathroom mirror. Dropping her dark clothes in a pile on the floor, she opened the fogged glass door and stepped inside. Standing under the shower head, the spray thundered down on her skin. Rivulets of gloriously hot water journeyed down her sadness soaked body, washing away the ache of the day. Yet, it was impossible for the water to be hotter than the ache of her heart. "One more day. You can do this," she said to the tile wall. Margaret had told herself this everyday now. The spray from the shower mingled with her endless tears. When

271

all the hot water was spent, she stepped out. Every step was razor painful. She knew after her shower she would go to bed alone. Getting into bed without Nate again, Margaret felt smaller and the mattress seemed to have grown wider. She spent the night on the edge of sleep, unable to finally fall. When her phone alerted her to the morning, she had already been fully awake. The hollow feeling had become her new companion.

FIFTY-FIVE

CATHERINE LEANED AGAINST THE kitchen counter and watched the kids while she drank her coffee. "Morning, Ma. How did you sleep with James there?" Margaret said, shuffling toward the counter to grab some coffee. Margaret's scant amount of sleep showed. Catherine handed Margaret her favorite mug to warm her perpetually cold hands.

"Who? Mr. Ants in the Pants? My favorite part was when his little Jimmy leg caught me in the back." James giggled. Catherine clutched her back. James giggled hard enough to make bubbles in his chocolate milk.

"Grandma, it's a James leg. My name is not Jimmy." He laughed. Margaret snorted in her coffee cup.

"Oh, very nice to see you laughing. You kicked your grandma in the kidney and you laugh? Nice kid." Janey gurgled in her bouncer and squealed as the animals overhead blinked to music. Margaret stood behind James's chair and bent down to kiss the crown of his head.

"James, don't assault your grandma. It's not nice," Margaret said, kissing him again.

'Well hello, Lady Jane." Margaret smiled, putting down her coffee mug to free her hands for Jane. "Good morning." Jane rested her head on her mother's chest, nuzzling and looking for breakfast. There wasn't too much time left for this connection because infusions would begin soon. "Jane and I are going to take our breakfast on the couch." Jane on one hip and coffee in hand, Margaret and Jane went into the living room. James followed behind with his cup of chocolate milk.

"I want to take breakfast, too." James smiled around his crazy straw. Catherine raised her coffee mug to him.

"Sure, buddy, come with us." All too soon the day would fill with more tears and sadness. Why not, if only for a little while, keep the day waiting? They all got comfy on the couch with their favorite morning beverages and Disney Junior.

Outside Nate's funeral service, the sky, the warm sun, and the fire-colored leaves that swirled down from the disrobing trees went unappreciated. The pieces of her obliterated heart spiraling down and were swept away with the leaves into the crisp autumn air. The priest's words were for someone else, someone else's husband, right? Another wave of nausea and spirit-crumbling grief came for Margaret. Catching fresh tears, she became very aware of everyone looking at her. The priest must have concluded his "The glory of God in the Kingdom of Heaven" spiel. The ferocious heartbreak roaring in her ears rendered her deaf to all else.

Margaret carefully stood and smoothed the skirt of her matte black widow dress. Marie offered Margaret her cane, but she gave a subtle back and forth of her head, so Marie tucked the cane between her and William then laid her head on her husband's strong shoulder with a sigh. William found his wife's hand with his own and lifted it to kiss. Jeff and Catherine watched, standing off to the side to give Margaret support if she needed it. Trying to keep her breathing even, she limped over to the bronze steel casket. Looking down at Nate, he appeared to be simply sleeping. In a moment of irrational grief she hoped he was. She pressed her hand to her heart then placed it on Nate's arm, leaving the red silk thread bracelet inside. "In a million lifetimes, I am yours." Her chest squeezed. It was the last time she would get to say this to the love of her life. Sobbing into her fist of tissues; Margaret's knees felt weak and she began to sway. She clutched the fittings of the coffin to steady herself. Catherine and Jeff moved quickly. Flanked by her stoic mother and brother-in-law Jeff, she made her way back to her seat. After the service, the funeral home would bring Nate's body to the crematory. Here her husband and father of her sweet babies would be burned to gray ash.

Six-year-old James tucked himself into his mother's side as she wrapped her arm around her son and kissed his dark-haired head. In her car seat, Janey was mesmerized by the subtle color changing light trimming the interior of the stretch limo. Jeff sat next to Margaret, giving her shoulder a squeeze. He was in awe of how she handled this bone breaking grief. He dropped his head into his hands, rubbing the heels into his eyes hoping to rid himself of the spinning feeling. Yet, closing his eyes opened a gate in his mind to play Nate's last moments over and over on a loop. He was never fast enough to catch him. Marie and Margaret held hands across the leather seat. Their over twenty-year friendship ran deep, surpassing words years ago. Nate and Jeff's mother, Evelyn, wept while Roman protectively held his wife. Margaret's mother, Catherine, sat near the window, her experienced hand sliding over her green glass Rosary. Her thin lips cleared Hail Marys by the tens.

Roman was the first to exit, brushing away the driver's hand as if the driver had offered him his middle finger. He turned and extended his hand to the next person to exit. One by one the family had filed out, leaving Margaret alone in the limo. Thoughts of Nate's unexpected death assaulted Margaret's love, faith, and stability. It was an irrevocable change of direction in her life she had to learn to navigate through. Ceaselessly wary of thieves disguised as time and circumstance, Margaret knew she could not hide forever in the safety of the soundproof limo. First, she unzipped her black purse, fished around for her pills, and shook a dose from the orange bottle. Then, she tossed the pills into her mouth and washed them down with a soda from the limo bar. It would be almost an hour before the pills quelled the pain. Margaret needed to leash this pain sooner. With a goal in mind, she slid to the end of the seat and reached to open the car door. It opened to the driver standing guard. "Mrs. Hall." He offered his open hand. Placing both her feet outside the car, she took the driver's offer and got out. Slowly, she walked up the driveway, mindful of her worsening limp.

The house was bursting with family, friends, and acquaintances all looking to earn points and hopefully stave off their own clock-out time. The sadness thickened the air to an almost suffocating level. Margaret stepped in the front door of their home and saw Nate's parents standing off to the side. Evelyn's face was pressed into Roman's navy lapel. The sofa and loveseat were pushed to the edge of the room. Every cushion hosted someone. Nate's worn brown recliner was moved to the furthest corner of the room. Margaret fell heavily into it and closed her aching eyes. She opened them instantly to a distant aunt thundering her way over with Jane gumming on her own pudgy fist. "I think she wants her mother." The near stranger handed Janey off and frantically searched through her ginormous purse for hand sanitizer.

"Oh, alright. Hello, Drooly Andrews." Margaret wiped the drool from Jane's chin just as James jumped up and huddled up in his mother's lap. Margaret burrowed deep into the chair with her babies and did what she hadn't been able to do in days: breathe. When she breathed in, the scent of Nate was still alive in the leather chair. She could smell his clean, citrusy cologne. The men's Nivea soap he got every year in his Christmas stocking. His Nateness. Her head relaxed back against the chair. The pain took another vicious bite of Margaret's neck. She reached into the side pocket on the recliner where Nate kept the remote, magazines, and his favorite candy that he tried unsuccessfully to hide. Making her way past the regulars, her hand found the pack of Nate's Marb reds she was also not supposed to know about. She pulled it out and found what she was looking for. James was cozy in his dad's chair. Jane would be fine in the pack and play next to James. She desperately needed to get some air. She put Janey in her travel crib and tucked James in deeper, then her eyes traveled the room and rested on Chelsea who was sitting in an armchair with Jeff, who stood nearby holding her hand. Janey batted at the toys dangling in front of her and James snuggled into a little red, white, and blue cocoon.

Planting a kiss on both of his cheeks, James smiled and put his hands where her kisses landed. "Now, you two stay put." She peered down at Jane. "I'm talking to you." Margaret covered Janey with kisses from her bunny. Jane giggled and gathered her fuzzy bunny in for a sloppy, drooly smooch. James smiled up at his mom and said, "Don't worry, Mama. I'll keep her safe." Margaret's eyes filled with more tears. They spilled onto James's head as she gave him a smooch.

Chelsea saw Margaret scanning the room and prayed she wasn't looking for her. Every time Margaret was near, Chelsea could hear her own heartbeat screaming in her head. She was constantly worrying about Margaret finding out about not only the punch, but all that came before it. "Oh God," Chelsea whispered. There was eye contact. Margaret was headed her way.

"Hello, you two. I need a hand with something outside, come with me." She grabbed Chelsea's hand and motioned to Jeff to follow her outside. Their exit was not simply done, considering her limp, the terrain of awkward hugs, and the constant sympathetic shoulder squeezes. After making it through the emotional obstacle course, the three made it to the back sliding door. Chelsea could feel her scalp begin to sweat as the two followed Margaret out the back door to the deck. Margaret finally felt far enough away from the house. "This is happening." Chelsea heard the words and readied herself for the blow.

She relaxed when Margaret pulled out a pack of smokes and slipped out a joint and lit it with a lighter that looked like an owl with a very stern look on its beaked face. Margaret would bet the very reason Nate had picked this lighter was because of the asshole expression on the square bird's face. "Whatever, square bird." Margaret inhaled deeply and the orange end of the joint glowed. She slowly let out the hit and watched the smoke weave into the brisk air above her. She held the joint out to Chelsea. With a nod, Chelsea took it and put it to her lips, taking a deep drag. She passed the joint to Jeff. He took a good pull and handed it back to Margaret.

"Well, it looks like you've been practicing," Margaret said, taking the joint. "Jeff used to be such a Dudley Do-Right." She had to tell on him. "He finally smoked with Nate when he was twenty-two years old and this poor little guy was a complete pair of panties."

"She called you panties," Chelsea said, throwing her head back. "Panties," she snickered again.

"Jeff got wicked paranoid. He was THAT guy."

"I'm one of those people who doesn't get affected the same way," Jeff said. He tried to downplay it. "I was fine." A pot cloud coughed out of Margaret's mouth in her laughter, which was punctuated by more coughing. Finally, she tamed her cough while still smiling and pointing at Jeff.

"Yes, Jeff, you are right. Not everyone handles weed the same way. This guy was staring back and forth all shifty-eyed for over an hour. All while he crammed chips pawful by the salty pawful into his giant food hole." Chelsea fell into snorty laughter, pointing at Jeff who laughed along with her. Those were some of the deliriously good times. Smoking memories of Nate brought a wistful expression to Margaret's face. Immediately after came the sadness, vanquishing her minuscule moment of happiness. Taken up and away with the lacey smoke, Chelsea saw the transition of Margaret's mood darken her face.

"How are you doing with all of this?" she asked. Margaret had been buried under a mountain of sorrow since Nate's death and her feelings weren't something she had the tools to properly dig through right now.

"You know those precious first seconds when a person first wakes up? Those perfectly content moments before the person actually wakes up and remembers all the shit? Before reality falls and pulverizes everything?" Chelsea nodded but said nothing. Jeff put his arm around Margaret's shoulder as she spoke. "I live for those few seconds every day. My day is gone after that." Margaret's eyes filled. Chelsea brought her in for a hug, soothing her with whispered words of comfort. On the inside, Chelsea's gut churned with guilt of all she had done. Not enough to confess— that would be crazy. She kept on hugging Margaret and feeling her cry. After breaking their embrace, the three quietly passed the joint around, each in their own heads. Behind them, the back slider opened and whooshed shut. Marie's heels clicked as she walked up to the three of them and broke up the moment.

"Hey, ladies. Yes, Jeff, including you. It's a lot in there, no?" Marie stepped into the circle and took the passing joint. "How are your stems, my friend?" She took a colossal hit, hoping to soften the edges of her anger at seeing Chelsea near Margaret. Marie's hands itched to beat her ass every single time she saw her.

"These legs are holding up alright. My fancy purse rattles more than maracas because of my pills," Margaret said as she swiped the joint from Marie's long, manicured pincer nails. "My infusion is a few days from now. Marie, I'm sure you're super jazzed to be taking care of my goblins for me."

grace

"So super jazzed." Marie laughed as she choked on her hit. Margaret had made the appointment before the accident. She had pushed it off as long as she could. Being scared of an infusion was infinitesimal compared to her fear of being without Nate. So, Margaret kept the appointment and would handle whatever came of it. "If you want me to come with you, I will drop those kids on William and we are out."

"No, I'm fine on my own." Margaret smiled. You're taking care of James and Janey. I should only be gone a few hours." Margaret had managed her daily symptoms and battled through the flare ups. In Margaret's mind, to sign on to monthly infusions for the disease progression was weakness. Another defeat. Indisputable proof of her losing battle. Margaret lived with a depleting body and mind. Her eyes had more tears prepared to jump. However, tears wouldn't change anything. Crying would only create more pain and she had no time for it. "We need to get back in there." Margaret took another hit off the joint, careful not to let the roach burn her fingertips. After depositing the roach back in with the cigarettes, Margaret took Marie's hand, followed by Chelsea and Jeff, and walked back into the house. More uncomfortable hugs and shoulder squeezes came along with murmured clichés about death and loss. Listening to it was becoming too much and, frankly, pissed Margaret off. Catherine took her post at the end of the sofa, working her Rosary. She must have gone thirty laps since the car ride. Margaret's very Catholic mother took her faith seriously. Her whole life, Margaret had been taught God was omnipotent. God had a plan for everyone, including her being a widow. The thought actually made Margaret laugh to herself. *What's my next move, Big Guy?*

It took forever and a week before all the mourners left. Her mother had gotten the kids ready for bed while William and Marie whipped the house back into shape. Margaret peeked in on Jane, warm and cozy in feety pajamas sleeping soundly with Bunny pinned under her. She found James involved in civil unrest between his army guys and dinosaurs, and sat beside him. "Are you excited about spending time over at Aunt Marie's and Uncle William's in a few days?"

"Oh, yeah. I want to show Greyson my new fossil kit. I bet there are real dinosaur bones in it." His eyes squinted with question, pondering the treasures he would chip out. To see her boy's sad expression dissolve, if only for a moment, was a precious gift.

"I got a kit for him too, Bud. Now the two of you can go on a dino adventure together."

"You did? Thanks." The corners of his mouth slouched back down. The momentary uplift evaporated.

"You're welcome." James pulled back his shark sheets and wiggled under the covers. When Margaret sat down on the side of the bed, James climbed into his mom's lap, coiling his arms around her and squeezing her tight to his little self. Margaret hugged him and gave him a kiss on his forehead. "I love you."

"I love you too, Mama. Do you miss Daddy? I miss Daddy so much my whole heart hurts all the time." James buried his head in his mother's neck as she hugged him. She could feel his hot tears rolling down her skin and the hiccups in his little chest. Her own tears burned down her face.

"I know missing Daddy hurts the worst, Bud." Margaret held James and rocked him. What else could she say? Every day since the accident seemed to speed past, yet the passing of each day was agonizing slow motion. Margaret took a deep breath and gave James a deeper squeeze, reveling in the love she felt in his hug. "The sun rises in the East and sets in the West," she whispered in his ear.

"The hours in between, we do our best," James finished. Margaret kissed his wet cheek and got him under the covers. James put his hand on his mother's cheek and wiped her tears. "I love you, Mama. We'll be okay."

Checking in on her mother, she stopped by the spare room that was once Nate's office to find Catherine all situated. On the side table was her enamel medication case, cell phone, and the latest novel she was speed reading. A reflection of a MASH rerun she was watching on the television showed in her reading glasses. Catherine looked away from the scene unfolding on TV to her daughter and simply opened her arms. No one would claim Catherine to be the soft or affectionate type. Yet, this gesture was monumental and desperately needed. Margaret's hiccupped sobs were soothed by Catherine swaying herself and Margaret back and forth.

Through her staccato breath, Margaret said, "Mom, I'm... I'm destroyed. I.. can't... do.. this." She shook with grief and her face buried in the curve of her mother's neck.

"Of course you can do this. You already are and you will do more. Just not now. And not all at once, Sweetie. It's time for you to rest. I have to leave for home tomorrow, however, I can be back next week if you need me." She brought her daughter to arms length. "Margaret, please accept help. If not for you, then for James and Jane." She kissed her mother's weathered cheek.

"Thank you for being here, Mom. I love you." Catherine nodded, then the window of tenderness took it's leave. Catherine went back to paying attention to the television. "I know you have a thing for Alan Alda, Ma. Don't let Hawkeye keep you up too late." Catherine rolled her eyes and made a shooing motion.

"Get out of here. You're interrupting my show." She smiled at her daughter over her dollar store reader glasses.

Margaret went on her way in search of her friends. She adored them and would be forever grateful for Marie and William. They had given all they could to hold Margaret up. Marie kept an eye on her best friend at all times, ready with love and understanding. The days of mourning Nate were especially difficult for Margaret. Marie and William formed a protective barrier around her, intercepting well-intended mourners. William was sure to go over all the details of Nate's employment and personal insurance. He also helped Margaret get a better handle on her future finances and doctor appointments.

She came upon the couple having a hushed conversation. Margaret couldn't interpret the hiss of words going back and forth. With no desire to interrupt, she hung back from the doorway. William stacked plates in the dishwasher just to have Marie reconfigure them. "Marie, I don't know if it'll be any good to tell her." He held up a plate. "I mean, Nate's gone. What will it change?" He dropped the plate into place. "It would only hurt her and the rest of their fami—" His wife's head was shaking back and forth before he finished his sentence.

"No. Just, no. No way am I going to watch my friend cry endlessly over St. Nate." She took the same plate back out. "For what?" She shoved the accosted plate down into place. "I'm sick of everyone thinking Nate had to sacrifice so much for her as if she was a burden to bear." Marie was getting aggressive with the silverware. She stabbed spoons and forks into the side tray. "Taking care of his disabled wife? My ass. No matter what, she shows up. Always has. Don't you think she deserves to know the truth?"

Margaret loved people. In big ways and in the small details of their lives. It was part of why Marie adored her so much and it was also what drove Marie crazy. Margaret was there when someone needed her. She always tried to do more because she felt bad about her illness. Margaret's guilt made her too forgiving of others, especially Nate. Margaret had been worried because Nate seemed so distant and all Margaret did was blame herself. To realize how Nate had taken Margaret for granted both disgusted and infuriated Marie.

"Besides, it's not as if the tramp has admitted to knowing that I know. And she knows I do."

"Yes, I know." William wasn't signing on to tell Margaret.

"She's a cow."

"A cow or not, now is definitely not the time." He squirted lemon soap into the dispenser. Marie used her foot to flip the dishwasher up and then pushed it closed, locking it like an exclamation point. Margaret's dead husband was a liar and a cheat. To make matters worse, Marie had known and said nothing.

"So, you expect me to watch Margaret be nice to— You must be crazy. I want to—" Marie's chest was boiling. She was now gunning for the cabinets, shutting them with ferocity as she put things away.

"Shhh. Be quiet. What if she hears us?" Just then, Margaret stepped into the kitchen, putting a halt on the conversation.

"What are you two all sharp whispery about?" Marie smiled at Margaret.

"Just our run of the mill list of nags. Nothing at all," William offered. "Her list gets longer by the day."

Marie threw the dish towel at him. "I'm adding to it right now." Marie hugged her friend while exchanging a worried look with William. She squeezed tighter as if her embrace could keep Margaret together.

"About your infusion. Are you absolutely super sure you don't want me to drive you?"

"No thanks, Marie. I'm positive I can do this. It's an hour infusion with a two hour waiting period so I can be monitored for any reaction. After the first one, the waiting period is only an hour."

"What if you have a reaction?" Marie was worried about Margaret. Tysabri was a powerful medicine with serious, sometimes dangerous side effects.

"The infusion room is specially equipped for such things. I'm in better hands there than I would be at the hospital. At least, that's what they told me. I gotta tell you, it's not the procedure bothering me. It's what it all means. How fast I must be deteriorating. For some time I was able to find a way to put the MS in the back of my mind. Now, my body finds ways to remind me every day." The three were quiet. Each marinated in their own pain. William broke the quiet.

"Well, Marie, I think it's time for us to head out. If you need anything, please call. I will be here in ten minutes," William said as he came in for a hug. Margaret held out her arms for his bear-sized squeeze. "Thank you for all your help today. I will see you both probably entirely too much for the foreseeable future." Margaret walked them to the front door. After she had locked the door behind them, she went through the house locking anything and everything possible. Lights were left on at all hours since Nate had died. She could not abide any more darkness.

Margaret sat upright in bed, unable to find real sleep since the accident, even though she was weary to her bones. Every night without Nate, the bed grew colder. Margaret would wake the same way every morning. All of her muscles taught with clothes soaked in sweat, shivering in a tight ball with her back against the headboard. Here she was again, watching television, hoping for a housewife to watch. At the end, the sheer exhaustion would overtake her insomnia, freeing her to half-sleep by five in the morning. Margaret worried non-stop for James and Janey. It was paramount she be there for them. Yes, it was healthy for them to see her go through this, but she would not allow sadness or disability to affect her momming. It was her job to be there for James and Janey. With Nate gone, now more than ever, the kids needed to feel safe and protected.

FIFTY-SIX

When Margaret pulled into Marie's driveway to drop James and Janey, Wes was barking with the same vigor as if it were a break in. As soon as the car was in park, James burst out of the back passenger door and ran. Margaret unhooked Jane's carrier then followed James to the door. Using her free hand, she was just about to twist the knob when the door opened.

"James!" Greyson pulled his buddy in the door. Wes was beside himself with dog glee, jumping all around the boys and barking. James handed Greyson his fossil kit.

"Whoa, this is flipping cool. Let's go." The boys tramped up the stairs with Wes taking up the rear. Jane babbled to her dangling owl that hung from the handle. William walked up with an extra coffee in his hand. "Time for one coffee before you head out?" Margaret happily handed the Jane-filled carrier to William in exchange for the dark roast coffee.

"Yes, thank you." Marie was at the kitchen counter when William and Margaret walked in. Marie gave Margaret a hug.

"You ladies go ahead and chat. Sweet baby Jane and I will be in the living room." William took Jane and left.

The two women sipped coffee and let the quiet breathe for a bit. Marie asked, "Are you nervous? I've done some reading on Tysabri. PML is an untreatable brain infection. It can be fatal. How are you not nervous?"

"Yes, it can be fatal. But, it's very rare." I tested negative for JC virus which is very good. I'll be getting blood work every three months. Everything is going to be just fine. Listen, I'm getting these infusions every month. So you might want to stop scaring the crap out of me and get used to it. I'm really trying here." Margaret knew she needed to just get in her car and go. She needed to stop thinking about it. Marie felt awful for firing her up and, on this rare occasion, decided to stop talking.

Margaret hugged James. "Give me a hug and kiss. I love you and I will be back in a flash. Please be a good boy and help with Janey." She kissed Janey who was in William's arms. The group waved goodbye from the door as she put her car in gear and drove away.

Margaret walked into the infusion room. Recliners lined the light blue walls. A nurses' station was at one end. Drawers holding various medical supplies were along the back wall. IV poles and machines formed a daunting perimeter. There were a few people in the recliners. Snacks and drinks were on the collapsible table tops attached to each recliner. "Hi, I'm Margaret Hall. I'm here for my eight a.m. appointment." A pretty nurse was sitting at the desk at the end of the room.

"Hello. My name is Sandy. I'm your infusion nurse. How are you feeling today? Do you have symptoms you want to report? Any new symptoms?"

"No new symptoms. I am a bit glitchy from stress. We recently had a loss in the family."

Sandy nodded her head. "Yes. We are so sorry to hear about your husband. Go ahead and take a seat. I will be right over. We'll get you all set up." Margaret took a recliner in the corner. There was a whip of a woman in the recliner next to Margaret's. She had fallen asleep during her infusion. Margaret wondered if the woman was also on Tysabri. Sandy came over and hung Margaret's IV bag on the pole and set out the fixings to hook her up. First, she put a pillow on Margaret's lap so she would have a place to rest her arm. Then, Sandy tied off Margaret's arm before her expert hands moved quickly and painlessly. Before Margaret could wince about the needle, it was already in. Sandy removed the tourniquet and applied a saline lock. After injecting 5 ml of saline to make sure the fluid moved freely. Lastly, she stabilized the needle with a transparent film dressing. Finally, Margaret was hooked up and the fluids were slowly making their way through Margaret's blood stream. Sandy looked up to see Margaret crying. "Did I hurt you?"

"No, not at all. I'm feeling a little overwhelmed. We could never have expected this to happen to our family. I'm barely standing as it is. Now I have this to deal with." Margaret nodded towards her IV. "When I was first diagnosed, I had such fight. Special diet, exercise, supplements— I even had my chakras aligned. MS was not going to get me. Now, here I am. It's hard to accept being this far in and needing medication. Now, my arms are half numb most days. Sometimes it feels like there isn't much fight left in me.

"You made the right decision to start treatment. MS is very unpredictable. It is also treatable. Tysabri is good stuff. It's a very clean drug. Side effects are minimal. If something should happen today, we are totally prepared. This is what I do and you will be amazed at how much better you feel. Stick with me. I promise to take care of you. And after one look at you, I can tell you have a lot of fight left."

Margaret watched the drip of the medication and the clock tick. There was nothing to do but sit with her thoughts. Thoughts she could not get a firm hold of long enough to sort things out. Her body ached for Nate. The last few months he was so distracted. He was moody and short with both her and James. Afraid of his reasons, she didn't ask. She was not ready to hear his reason.

An hour later, Sandy unhooked Margaret from her IV. Now, Margaret was going to be monitored for two hopefully uneventful hours. Margaret rested her head again and closed her eyes. She opened her eyes to Sandy.

"Hello, Sleeping Beauty. It's two hours. See? You made it. By the way, you snore loudly." Sandy smiled. Margaret laughed and stretched. "Let's make your next appointment. Four weeks from now? Is Thursday good for you?" Margaret blinked her eyes and stretched.

"Yes, I'm pretty much available whenever. Thank you for today. You made me feel like I can do this." Margaret got her purse and headed out the door. "See you next month."

Margaret was tired after her infusion. She drove home with the windows open and Annie Lennox singing. As soon as she parked in her driveway she called Marie. After two rings, Marie picked up. "Hey, how did it go? Are you home? Do you need anything?"

"Whoa, easy does it eager beaver. There is a nurse, Sandy. She's great and she made it easy. I am really tired though. Is there any way you can keep James and Janey a bit? I need to sleep."

"Oh, yeah, of course. You're tired and need some sleep. No problems at all, Mama." The two hung up. Margaret yawned, got out of her car, and went inside. Lola was dancing on her hind legs and licking Margaret's fingers. After coaxing the dog back in the house with treats, Margaret football carried little brown Lola up the stairs to bed. Margaret toed off her shoes, yanked off her pants, then shimmied under the blankets. Lola squeezed behind Margaret's knees. Her last thought before falling down the rabbit hole was, *Marie is taking care of the kids... I want juice... Where is my juice?* Deeper into the blankets, Margaret fell asleep.

William came in from the yard. He set the boys up at the outside table with their fossil kits. They were each armed with tiny plastic excavating tools and brushes.

"The boys will be busy for a while. Those kits will keep them digging until dinner. We should be able to talk without them hearing us."

"Jane is napping in the guestroom." Marie tilted her head in the direction of the baby monitor. "Margaret thinks of everything." William followed her to the table and sat across from his wife.

"I agree we have to make some kind of plan, Marie." As she was about to reply, William held up a hand. "Other than going 'Braveheart on the hag,' as you put it.

"Do you have any idea of how to go forward from here? Because, William, I truly do not know what to do." Marie felt terrible for holding this and not bringing it to Margaret.

"Like I said, maybe we don't even have to tell Margaret. Let her keep Nate the way she saw him. We can't change what has already happened. As I see it, Nate won't be hurt at all, but this will hurt Margaret, her kids, and Nate's whole family." Marie knew that what William was saying was the more peaceful approach.

"You're right, William. We can't change the past. Oh, and what about going forward? With her on Jeff's ass, it seems she plans on being around. At some point, I am going to have to take this broad out back."

"Understood. How about talking first? If only to not involve police or paramedics?" William raised his eyebrows. Marie hated his common sense.

"Yeah, I'm thinking the same thing." Marie's eyes conveyed her murderous thoughts.

"For Margaret." William was concerned for how strong Margaret would need to be to withstand another brutal blow.

"For Margaret." Begrudgingly, Marie agreed.

"You are a delicate flower— dainty like dynamite." William kissed his feisty wife.

"You shut it," she said, leaning into his kiss.

Margaret woke to find her bedroom had grown dark. The time on her phone read 5:15 p.m. Margaret had slept for hours. Sitting up, she smoothed her hair and stretched. Listening to the house, the quiet told her the kids were still at Marie's. Little chubby Lola was curled up on Nate's pillow, her little tail happily thumping now that her person was finally awake. Margaret swung her legs out of bed, gave her toes a test wiggle, then stood up. "Man, I'm thirsty. I need juice," she said out loud then went down the stairs.

When Marie and the kids came through the door, the hush was broken. Lola was beside herself with dog glee, jumping all around and barking her salutations. Margaret put down her juice and took a sleepy Jane from Marie to cuddle while James hugged Margaret's leg. "We missed you, Mama. Are you all better now?"

"I am doing great. Did you have fun at Aunt Marie's? What kind of shenanigans did you get yourselves into today?" James regaled his mother with his account of the day's events. As he went through the details, they made their way to the kitchen. Margaret set the boys up with juice pouches and peanut butter cookies. "You boys sit and eat while I put Janey to bed." James and Greyson spun lazily on the stools, sucking down their juice. Marie walked upstairs with Margaret to put Jane down.

Margaret brought Jane's bedroom door within an inch of closing before turning for one more peek at Janey's fluttering lashes as she quickly fell into dreams. Bunny smiled from her closed fist clenched tight against her chest. "Night, Beans," Margaret whispered.

"She really is the sweetest thing," Marie whispered. They tiptoed downstairs so Margaret and Marie could hear about the adventures of the pint-sized paleontologists.

That night, after Margaret locked up the house on her way to her room, she checked on the kids one more time.

First, she went to James's room to find him sleeping like a starfish, blankets kicked to the foot of his bed.

Smiling, she pulled his covers up and kissed his cheek. When Margaret looked in on Janey, she was still snoozing peacefully with Bunny clutched in her fist. It was another blow to her heart to know perfect sweet Janey would not remember her father. Turning to face her lonely bedroom, she again made the mile long walk to another night of sweaty, solitary half sleep. "One infusion down," she whispered to herself.

FIFTY-SEVEN

CHELSEA'S HEART WAS BEATING fine. Maybe a smidge fast, but she always got nervous at the doctor's. The nurse assistant took out the thermometer and slowly ran the tip over Chelsea's forehead. The thermometer beeped. "98.6," she said, then tapped the results into the computer. If she had no fever, why had she been feeling nauseous and so damn tired? Once finished with all the preliminary notes, the nurse assistant said, "The doctor will be with you in a minute." Taking advantage of these few quiet moments, she lay down on the exam table with her hands in the pocket of her hoodie and closed her eyes. A few minutes later, there was a polite knock on the door, then her doctor came in. A tall woman wearing glasses and a crisp white coat over camel-colored slacks and a dark blue sweater. "I see here you haven't been feeling so great. Tired all the time, nausea?" Her head shook in agreement with the chart. Chelsea sat up.

"Yes, I have been super tired. Food smells gross to me. I'm sure some boogery virus from the gym hitched a ride on me."

Her doctor smiled. "I've looked at the results of your blood work."

Already tired, Chelsea's body slumped down further. "As if I haven't had enough already. What is it? What antibiotics will I have to take to cure this?"

"There are a few options."

Fear was beginning to creep in. "What are my options? What the hell do I have?" Not at all enjoying the suspense the doctor had her in, Chelsea braced herself for the news.

"You are pregnant." The doctor smiled again, then said, "Is this something you were working on? Or, is this news a bit of a surprise?" The doctor continued, "I'm looking at your shocked face so I am going with surprise." Chelsea's mouth hung open.

"Oh my God. Oh my God." Chelsea was completely dumbfounded. *Jeff, we are having a baby.* All she could do was cry. She would definitely be getting married. However, doing math in her head, Chelsea's chest tightened. "How far along am I?"

"According to your hCG levels, you are about seven weeks." Backtracking in her mind, seven weeks was early September. That had been her last few days with Nate. Her period not coming had been dismissed as stress from the accident and losing him. It had not occurred to her that she could be pregnant. Yet, here she was. Good and pregnant with a baby Hall. She just wasn't sure which one. Wiping her tears away, Chelsea hopped off the exam table. "How are you with this news? Do you want to go over your options?"

"No other options are necessary. I am having a baby. This is the best news." Chelsea had already decided to tell Jeff their happy news in hopes of getting her engagement ring on her finger for everyone to see, especially hate-filled Marie. Now, Chelsea was pregnant and engaged to Jeff. What point would there be in diming her out? There was no proof other than what Marie thinks she saw at the plaza. Nate certainly wasn't going to blab.

"This is terrific. I will send in a prescription for prenatal vitamins and also set an appointment for an ultrasound so we can get a good look in there. Bring Dad along so he can meet his baby." Chelsea's face was a big happy smile. Finally things were working for her. She beamed with pride at the thought of being a mom and wife. "I am going to head out while you get redressed and my medical assistant will give you pamphlets and a list of dos and don'ts. Congratulations, Chelsea."

The leaves crunched under her leather boots as she walked back to her car. Checking her missed calls, Chelsea saw her mother had called earlier. With a finger hovering over the send button, she contemplated sharing the good news. Years of conditioning told her not to waste her time. Instead, she tapped Jeff's picture to call him. Jeff picked up and she could hear the smile in his voice. "Hey there, Beautiful. How did your appointment go?"

"Thankfully, I do not have any virus. Actually, the doctor is very happy with my health." Chelsea wondered if he could hear the smile in her voice too.

"You sound like you're smiling." Of course he could tell.

"I might be smiling." She gave him nothing.

"Well, are you going to tell me why or do I have to guess?" Jeff was curious but couldn't put the pieces together on his own.

"When you come home tonight I will tell you all about it. I love you." Chelsea ended the call, got in the car, and turned up the music to sing along.

FIFTY-EIGHT

Halloween was marred by pouring rain and bitter cold, which meant Trick-or-Treating was not going to happen this year. Janey, a ladybug for her first Halloween, was content using her nub of a tooth on her bug antennae. James, dressed as a pouty Voltron, sighed wherever he went. Giving out candy to the bigger kids braving the rain was not Voltron's idea of fun. Sure to make himself heard, he stomped his way into the kitchen. He held out his blue jack o' lantern candy bucket.

"Mama, how am I supposed to get candy if I don't trick-or-treat?"

Margaret had already figured out a way around this. "There are tricks and treats hidden all over the house. Whatever you find, you keep."

"OKAY!" Off Voltron went in search of candy. Margaret heard his excited "woohoo" when he found his first treat. Janey was still working her antennae when the doorbell rang.

"I got this one, bud," she called out as she headed to the door, pausing to grab the candy bowl. Lola was already off the couch and barking up a frenzy as Margaret opened the door. Instead of damp ghouls, witches, and zombies, it was William and Greyson. Lola finished alerting everyone then hopped back on the couch and curled up in her spot.

"Hi, Aunt Margaret. We came with candy for James." He extended his Spiderman-gloved hand. He had a bucket full of candies and tiny toys. Margaret got down on one knee and looked into the bucket.

"Wow, I bet James is going to love it. Oooo, Smarties. Can I have these?" Greyson smiled.

"Sure." Then, Greyson whispered in her ear, "Mom and Dad eat my candy all the time. Don't tell them I know."

"Cross my heart." Margaret crossed her heart with her finger. "Let me go back into the kitchen— we need more candy for the hunt." She padded back to the kitchen for more fun-sized chocolate when Chelsea seemingly came out of nowhere, startling an unsuspecting William.

He both jumped and yelled out. "Jesus!" flew out of his mouth.

"Hey, William, are you a ghost hunter for Halloween? You look like you've certainly seen one." Chelsea giggled. Janey's antennae fascination ended when Chelsea picked her up. Now, Janey was intrigued by Chelsea's sequin cat ears and sleek whiskers. William stopped himself short of taking Chelsea to task right then.

"No, but you surprised me for sure." He regained his calm. "I apologize. I didn't notice your car outside." Greyson came tearing around the corner looking for his friend. Chelsea pointed up the stairs.

"He just went that way." Greyson excitedly took the stairs to join in the hunt, leaving Chelsea and William alone. "I left my car on the road to free up the driveway for trick-or-treaters. I'm here to help out Margaret for a while. I'm surprised Marie isn't over here with you to check on Margaret." There was an almost unnoticeable sourness to her comment. Almost as in, William indeed picked up on it.

"Marie had planned to be here tonight after her last client. However, it went late. I'm happy to fill in. Her business is building quickly. Mostly, word of mouth from her clients after they see the results. She's built herself quite a reputation. You know how it goes, people love to talk and word gets around." William let his comment do its work. Chelsea leveled her eyes on William.

"I absolutely agree with you. I remember when I first started at the gym and the stories I was told about Marie." She made a *yikes* face. "To see her now with such positive results and that kind of reputation after such an interesting past is a show of her hard work and dedication. You must be very proud of your wife, William." Chelsea kept right on cooing and laughing along with Janey in her arms, but from the corner of her eye, she watched her comment do its work as William's face grew even paler than usual.

Marie and he had done their best to leave Marie's past behind. It had become easier to do the more time had gone by, but years of heavy drug use and borderline sex addiction are hard to keep buried, no matter how deep. Apparently, Chelsea liked to dig. Just then, there was a knock on the door and the boys came thumping back down the stairs to open it to a fresh gaggle of trick-or-treaters.

"Trick-or-treat!" The group of pint-sized ghosts, ghouls, and such hollered with their bags open for candy.

FIFTY-NINE

PERFECTLY BROWNED CHEESE LATCHED to the edges of the still warm pan of baked ravioli. Chicken cutlets lounged on a serving platter. Long, cream colored candles dripped their melted heads down the side of the holders. All the other lights were low and soft music played. Jeff truly adored Chelsea. Looking at the perfectly set table with his favorite food, it was easy to see why. "How was your day at work?" Chelsea purred as she wrapped her arms around his waist from behind. She rested her head on his back, feeling the terrain of muscles through his t-shirt. "Halloween with the kids at Margaret's was fun. She always comes up with epic Mom ideas. We had a treasure hunt and crafts— this fun game with donuts on string. I hope one day I'm half as good a mom." Jeff turned and tipped Chelsea's chin up to look in her eyes.

"I have no doubt. Look at how you take care of me. Now, I am a big baby."

Chelsea gave him a playful swipe. "Do you really think I would be a good mom, Jeff?" Her eyes held his as she waited for his answer. Yes, they were engaged, but Chelsea needed to hear him say the words.

"I think you would be an amazing mother. I can absolutely see you with a couple little Halls in one of those double stroller dealies."

Chelsea was unable to wait another second. "Jeff, I'm pregnant." Three words scared away any words Jeff may have been about to speak. "Jeff, did you hear me?" Jeff stared at her unblinking. "Oh no, are you mad?" Her insides went cold, fearing the worst was about to unfold. She was not losing another baby in hopes of a man's happiness with her.

"Mad? Am I mad?" Jeff asked looking in her hopeful blue eyes. "Oh God, Chels, no I am not mad. This was the thing you had to tell me?" His face immediately pinked up with a ridiculously gooney grin on his face. "This is fantastic news. I mean, I think it's fantastic. Do you think it's fantastic?"

"What? Yes, absolutely, this is going to be so fantastic." They began kissing and forgot about dinner. Jeff and Chelsea kept kissing until they fell onto the bed, bumping heads and laughing. Jeff suddenly straightened his arms, creating space between them, and looked down at Chelsea.

"Wow, you are nothing short of magic."

"Show me," she said, pulling him in for more.

"No cuddling and sweetness for this girl, huh?" He eased himself down her body. His hand slipped down her pants and felt her silky wet warmth as his fingers slid over her lips. Taking his hand from her pants, Chelsea watched Jeff lick her off of his fingers. He got up and stood next to the bed, then grabbed her ankles and pulled her right to the edge of the mattress. Smiling at her, he pointed to the ceiling and immediately Chelsea's legs shot straight up. "Nicely done. Now—"Jeff got a hold of her leggings and in one, smooth upward move, Chelsea was bottomless. Jeff's thick fingers traced her skin from thigh to calf. Then, wrapping his hands around her ankles, he spread her legs wide and opened her lips. Jeff dropped to his knees and allowed the tip of his tongue to just barely glide over her.

"Ohhhhhh." Taking Jeff's head in her hands, Chelsea tilted herself up, bringing her pussy to his mouth for Jeff to enter again and again with his tongue. "Yes, yes, oh my— ohhh..." She trailed off when he pulled back, alternating between lapping at her clit and long slow licks followed by sucking on her lips.

"You taste so sweet." Jeff licked her clit and his two fingers pushed inside and began slowly coaxing her climax.

"Oooooh, Jeff, more," Chelsea whimpered. Jeff followed his instructions. "Uhhh,yes, Jeff." He loved the sound of Chelsea getting off. The sound of her moan with every push of his hand. "Why are you not in me?" She sounded desperate for Jeff. "Flip me over and fuck me." Jeff looked at Chelsea, wiped his face, and stood up. He grabbed Chelsea's hand and stood her up. She raised her arms overhead. First, Jeff lifted her shirt up and off of her. Then, he sucked her nipples while his fingers were inside her again. In and out and in and out his fingers over and over buried themselves into her. Soon, Chelsea was begging to be fucked again. "Fuck me, Jeff, ple—" Before she could finish, Jeff spun her around and bent her over the bed. He pushed his fingers in and slid them out to wet his dick. Without warning, he filled Chelsea. "Oh my fuck. Oh, oh, oh." Jeff fucked her hard and fast.

He grunted with every stroke. He reached underneath and held her tits as he fucked her harder and faster.

"Yes, yes, yes. Fuck me." Chelsea got what she demanded. Jeff grabbed Chelsea's shoulders from underneath and drove himself into her over and over, harder and faster. He did not stop fucking her while he came.

"Damn, woman!" This time, they did not bump heads when they collapsed on their bed. "I think you might be trying to kill me." He reached for a bottle of water that was on the end table and offered it first to Chelsea. She motioned for him to take it. In seconds, the plastic made a crinkling sound as Jeff drained the life out of it.

"Jeff." Chelsea cozied up next to him, taking his arm and laying it over her. Jeff turned on his side and pulled Chelsea into his protective embrace. "Do you think it's too soon to tell our families we're engaged?" Up until now, the two had kept it to themselves, which was nearly impossible for Chelsea to do. What girl wouldn't want to show off both the extraordinary ring and equally extraordinary man? Squeezing her closer to him, Jeff got quiet in contemplation. She worried his silence was hesitation. "It's just, with the baby and—" He silenced Chelsea's worries with a kiss.

"We've been invited to Margaret's for Thanksgiving, along with my parents, William, Marie, and the kids. You should have your mom come and have her bring your brother, Eric." Chelsea's face paled with nausea. Not because she was pregnant, but because of the familiar stomach flip of embarrassment and fear Chelsea felt every time she thought of them. Eric's perpetually simmering anger was partly responsible for his relentless bullying. Their single mother Diane's god-like reverence for her police officer son left Eric with a total lack of boundaries and a mindblowing sense of entitlement. Bill, Diane's new husband, entered into their lives optimistic and ready to have a relationship with Chelsea and Eric. As she and Bill's relationship grew, Chelsea took to calling him her "Bonus Dad" because bonus meant extra, while the term "step" seemed to diminish such a great man. Not only did Eric challenge Bill constantly, but he also orchestrated situations he knew would cause riffs between his mother and Bill. All too often, her brother gave his mother the "him or me" ultimatum. If she even appeared to side with her husband, Eric would explode with jealousy and anger, accusing his mother of betrayal. This led to a cycle of tantrums from Eric followed by begging and bribing from Diane in hopes of calming down his ever growing tirades.

After Bill passed, the co-dependant pair decided, or more accurately, Eric decided, he would move back home to help. He required his mother give up the master bedroom she had shared with Bill for almost three decades. Diane quickly whittled down her belongings to better accommodate the second, smaller bedroom. There was a bigger third room Diane and Bill had used for their home office. Diane loved the sofa in there, where she and Bill would watch movies while he worked late. When Eric moved in, however, he took over that room too for his disaster of a desk and stocked gun safe. Diane's computer and filing cabinet were wedged in the corner of the cubby-sized second bedroom. Eric assumed the couch to be his and quickly stunk it up with his dickheadedness. "Hey, Chels? Woohoo. Earth to fiancé... over." Jeff smiled.

"Oh, I'm sorry. I guess I just zoned out for a second." Chelsea quickly brushed off her concerns and focused on the present.

"Did you hear my question?" Jeff asked.

"I'm sorry, no, I didn't. What was the question?" He got out of bed, pulled on his jeans, and tossed Chelsea her purple satin robe. After she tied it closed, Jeff took her hand and got down on one knee.

"Chelsea, you are the most remarkable woman I have ever known. From the moment we met, I could see you were special. You've already said yes. No more waiting. It's time for everyone else to know that you and I are getting married. Chelsea, I love you with all my heart."

"Jeff, I adore you. Yes, I would love for everyone to see how wonderful you are and that I am yours." Jeff once again slipped the sparkler on Chelsea's slender finger. It took her breath away every time. Whenever she looked at it, a million tiny fires burst from her ring, casting a universe of stars onto the wall. This meant more to Chelsea than Jeff could possibly know. To have someone love her this much and find her deserving of astonishing beauty. Jeff swept Chelsea up in an embrace and she pressed herself up against Jeff. She wanted to be absorbed by him; have him over, under, and through her.

SIXTY

MARGARET HAD BEEN WORKING hard to get strong for herself and the kids. She was determined to be the best version of herself. James and Janey impressed Margaret with their resilience. James went back to school and despite a few moments of tears, he was in the swing of things and looking forward to Thanksgiving. Although Janey was wee, she felt the vibe in the house calming down and it showed. Soon, she was back to her sleep routine. Yoga two days a week kept Margaret flexible. She rolled out her lone mat and missed Chelsea teaching the class. After three classes went by with a sub instructor, she had to make a call to check up. Chelsea had complained of some kind of virus. Offers to bring food or pick up anything from the pharmacy were met with, "No, thank you." Margaret sat on her mat in Lotus position, closed her eyes, and steadied her breath. The tiny, lean instructor floated in with her black hair in a long braid thrown over her shoulder. Again, not Chelsea. Her stomach bug had best be vile. Actually, they had not spent any time together since Halloween. Margaret was still sad these days with spontaneous bouts of tears. Maybe she was too much of a drain and Chelsea needed a break. She was pondering this when the lights were dimmed and the music started to play. "Everyone please stand and come to the front of your mat." Margaret stood and set her intention for her practice, hoping to soothe her hurting heart.

"Tell me what she said, William," Marie said, trying to keep her anger at bay. Whatever assine crap Chelsea said to William on Halloween had obviously bothered him. No amount of harassment from Marie could pry it out.

"Marie, she didn't say anything in particular. It was more her tone. Either way, I still think telling Margaret anything is a bad idea."

"Have we met? You can't roll in here and say you saw Chelsea, she made a comment about nothing in particular, and now we are to stay out of it. So, tell me what she said to you. God dammit, William, are you protecting her too?" He abruptly pushed his chair from the table and stood up.

"Marie," he boomed. "You know better." His volume came down. "Now, I am telling you to leave it alone, so please listen to me." William turned and left the dining room. She heard his footfalls up the stairs then the door of his office shut. William knew how difficult it was for Marie to work through her addictions and she still was fighting every day. When Marie and William got serious, she confessed her weaknesses. Instead of being angry, William told her to never feel ashamed of herself. Then, he stood by her side while she got a therapist and joined a support group. For the first few years, they struggled with Marie finding her true self. Some days were still a struggle. But she persevered. Now, she was an incredible wife, mother, and friend. He would not have her years of work and growth torn down by Chelsea.

Staring into her wine glass, Marie contemplated William's demand for silence. She swirled the red around the glass and her mind was made up. Tipping her head back, she finished the pinot noir. She refilled her glass and topped off William's. With a glass in each hand, she tiptoed up the stairs, past her husband, and into the bathroom.

Marie turned the shower knob to hot. She took off her sweaty gear and released her hair from its long braid. One foot, then two, Marie stood under the hot water that steamed up the bathroom. Marie let the water spill down her, yielding to the steam and heat as she dropped her head back. The hot water carved through her long hair. The stress of the day took its time leaving while the scent of almond and vanilla filled the shower as Marie soaped her body. The delicious scent mingled with the steam. Marie's hand was on her thigh and then in between her legs. She lightly stroked herself and let out a soft moan. The shower was not enough.

Marie stepped out of the bathroom and onto the soft dove colored carpet of their bedroom to find William was indeed waiting. He was sitting in his armchair by the window with the lights low. Marie walked slowly naked and wet to William, climbed into the chair, and lay across his lap. William's fingers barely grazed her wet skin. He leaned forward and wrapped his arm around Marie, holding her tightly. With William's other hand, he parted her thighs then slid two of his fingers inside her.

"Mmmmmm," rolled out from Marie's mouth as she filled herself with William's fingers. William began slowly rubbing her with his thumb. With her ass in the air, she waited, swaying her hips slowly. The first loud

grace

smack got Marie's attention. Each crack of his hand made Marie yelp a little. "Again." *Crack. Crack.* William put a vibrator in Marie's hand. She turned it all the way to max and put the vibrator on her clit. She moaned.

Crack. Crack.

William delivered two fresh smacks to her already pink cheeks. Then, he caressed Marie's warm, tingling skin.

"Wouldn't want it to sting too much."

"Again," Marie whispered. William smiled with his blue eyes blazing.

Crack. Crack.

Marie started to gyrate in his lap. The heat of the spanking and vibration were doing her in. "I have to have you. I can't take it."

Crack. Crack.

"You can take it. I'm yours." Marie felt William's hands rubbing her rosy skin. His hand went between her legs, barely touching her lips. When William felt Marie relax, he delivered more smacks.

CRACK! CRACK!

William shoved his fingers inside her and started fingering her, switching between rubbing her and spanking her.

"Uuu— Nnn— Oooooh!" She started to buck and William's fingers pushed in deeper. "I need to fuck you." She freed herself from his hand. "Lay down right here on the floor." He dropped to the floor and pressed his back against the carpet. Marie stood above William and straddled him with a sly smile on her face. Marie lowered herself, hovering just above him. She brought her hands up and squeezed her nipples. Slowly, Marie wrapped herself around William. She slid down at an achingly slow pace. "Mmmmmmm, you feel so good inside me." She moaned then leaned forward, her face over William's. Her long hair dropped down around them both. She parted his lips with her tongue and kissed him as she slowly rode him. When William moaned in her mouth, it got Marie hotter. Marie sat up and reached for the vibrator again. The hum hit Marie almost immediately. Again, she began to buck. William grabbed her ass in his hands and pulled Marie onto him, grinding her hips into him. Marie was hot and soaking wet. The hum of the vibrator with William so deep, was perfect. Watching the rhythm and sway of her body was mesmerizing. Marie curved over William, riding and undulating. She dipped her nipple into his mouth. She offered only a quick lick then gave him the other to taste. He put his hands on her shoulders, pulled her down, and fucked her like a savage. Marie's orgasm was an explosion. William could feel her wet and velvety inside tighten. She was dripping as she rode her husband. She collapsed on top of him, breathing hard. "Oh, not quite, little lady." William put Marie on her back and shoved himself back inside her. He fucked her until he made her come again. Then, William straddled her.

"Crush me." He pinned her shoulders with his knees then leaned forward. Marie opened her mouth and he slowly slid inside. The heat of Marie's mouth and her soft, circling tongue hardened him to steel. William's eyes glowed with intensity when he began to stroke himself and Marie's open, wet mouth sucked at every thrust.

"Come for me," she hummed when he pulled himself out of her mouth. "I want it," she whimpered." He pushed himself back in. Marie arched her back and pushed him to the brink. William roared as he came. She could taste him on her lips and feel his warmth on her skin.

grace

Later, Marie cuddled on William's lap, luxuriating in the after sex. "William," she began.

"Marie," he responded.

"William, plea—"

"Yeah, I'm still not telling you." William smiled as he lifted his wine glass.

SIXTY-ONE

THANKSGIVING DIDN'T HAVE A festive feel. It was
the first big family holiday without Nate. Chelsea and
Jeff showed up early to lend Margaret a hand. Chelsea
had earned a spot and was allowed in the kitchen. Jeff
was kicked out of the kitchen because he kept putting
his thieving hands on not yet served trays of food, de-
stroying the meticulously laid cracker trails on the hors
d'oeuvre platters. Instead, he was strapped with the kids
and it wasn't a bad gig. Jane was taking her morning
nap on him in the recliner. James was underneath the
raised footrest, hiding behind the blanket hanging over
the edge. He was warned not to, as Jeff was confident
in the fact that trapping a kid in a recliner was frowned
upon. Still, his nephew had set up shop. Pillow, a juice
pouch, Weebs, and Steve. All three watched the Macy's
Thanksgiving Day parade from under uncle Jeff.

Roman and Evelyn knocked as the parade was ending. James scrambled from his post. Then did some kind
of running skip to the front door. Margaret and Chelsea came out of the kitchen, each wiping their hands
on a dish towel. "Gram! Grampa! Happy Thanksgiving!"
James declared as he opened the door. Immediately off

the rails with glee, he donned his crafty creation. A construction paper turkey hat. Gobs of glue cemented the colorful feathers to the bird. James began gobbling like a turkey whilst flapping his arms. His enthusiastic flapping made gold glitter from the tacky turkey dance in the air. "Look, I made this turkey hat in school. Gobble gobble gobble!"

"Wow. You did a fantastic job. This is the best turkey hat I have ever seen." Evelyn picked James up and covered her giggly grandson in kisses. Roman held two warm covered dishes in his hands. Margaret and Chelsea each took one of the glass dishes.

"Now that I have two free hands, Jeff, how about helping me bring in the rest of the food? Your mother felt it necessary to make enough food for twenty." Evelyn was hanging up her wool coat, shaking her head at Roman's nonsense. She kissed her husband on the cheek.

"Your father thinks it necessary to tell me what 'enough' is. There will be nine of us. Fifteen pounds of potatoes is the minimum amount to use. They need to be able to take home leftovers." Roman rolled his eyes and smiled.

"This woman." He returned the kiss to her cheek.

"Nine of us?" Jeff questioned while spreading the blanket on the floor and laying Janey on it.

"Yes, nine. Well, not including the kids."

"It will be us four and Chelsea's mother and brother," Jeff said.

Margaret took over. "No one else is coming." Marie had called a few nights ago to let Margaret know they would not be able to make it over for Thanksgiving. Instead, they were going to spend the holiday with William's family. Something sounded very off about Marie when she called. When she denied Margaret's observation, there was no strength in her to press the matter.

"This year William's family really wanted them to visit. However, don't worry. We love mashed potatoes." Margaret had a smile on her face. Chelsea stood quietly by, silently proud she had scared Marie off with her warning to William.

"It's because Mama thinks Aunt Marie is being weird," James volunteered as he gobble gobbled his way past them.

"No, it is not, James, and keep your gobbler closed. Let's sit in the living room."

After getting comfortable on the couch, James asked, "Then why did you say it to Uncle Jeff?" Apparently, James was not done sharing.

"Aunt Marie and Uncle William have been busy. I'm sure we will see them soon." Margaret needed to start checking around for James before opening her mouth so he couldn't narc her out again.

"Well, it's a shame they can't be here," Evelyn offered. "I'm sure you two girls will figure out whatever it is. You and Marie are like sisters. My two boys are so close." Evelyn realized she was talking about Nate. Roman put his hand on her shoulder. They took a silent moment to mourn their son. Jeff came over with his coat on.

"Hey, Dad, let's go grab the other dishes before they get too cold."

Roman turned to his son, "You're right, Jeff. Let's get out there before the yams freeze." He chuckled, wiping a discreet tear from his eye.

"Margaret, dear, let's go into the kitchen and see how our bird is doing. Chelsea, would you keep an eye on things out here for us?"

"Of course, Evelyn." Chelsea smiled. After bringing in six assorted side dishes, two homemade apple pies, and one pumpkin custard, the guys came back into the living room. Chelsea's heart warmed seeing Roman ready with a bottle for a freshly awake Janey. She dreamt about when it would be her and Jeff's baby. "James, you play with Jeff. Gramps and Janey look like they have got it under control already." Margaret was with Evelyn in the kitchen praying James would shut his beak and not repeat anything else he'd heard during his new favorite thing: Eavesdropping on adult conversations. She didn't need any more conversation starters from her fowl boy.

Margaret slid a pilgrim shaped oven mitt on. Opening the oven, the scent of rosemary and shallots whirled around the kitchen. Margaret hefted the bird out and set it on the counter. Evelyn was impressed.

"Margaret, I am glad you took over Thanksgiving." Margaret handed Evelyn the baster.

"Yeah? Why is that?" Margaret was preparing the glaze for the turkey.

"Because the food is fantastic and I don't have to cook it. I get to eat and enjoy myself. No work." She must have forgotten the twelve or so things she cooked at home. Evelyn grabbed the other set of oven mitts and moved the rack back into the oven and shut the door. Sitting down at the table, Evelyn spied sugar cookies in need of eating and plucked a cornucopia shaped cookie from a tray.

Margaret went about prepping for dinner. She cut stale bread into cubes. Removed thyme leaves from their stems and crushed rosemary. Stuffing was a very personal thing. "Margaret, how are you going to go about packing up Nate's things?" Margaret's hands stopped working. It was a simple question, but Margaret had no answer. When Nate died, he left everything to Margaret and the kids. There was more than enough to pay off the mortgage on the house and Margaret was now in charge of the monthly bills. Once a week, Roman and Evelyn would pick up James and Janey to give Margaret some time alone. However, she had not been able to budge anything from where Nate had left it. Nevermind packing up his things and not having them around so she could at the very least feel him close to her. She had taken to sleeping in his t-shirts on his side of the bed. Margaret used her own pillow for fear of losing the smell of Nate if she slept on his. Night after night, she would fall into a restless sleep with her fist curled around the corner of his pillow case.

"Evelyn. This is an incredibly tough day. Our first holiday Nate is not with us. What am I saying?" Margaret took Evelyn's hand. "Every single day has been God damned tough."

Evelyn squeezed her daughter-in-law's hand. "It is the worst pain a mother could feel. I keep finding myself looking out the front window hoping to see his car pull in the driveway, thinking he's coming for dinner. He used to have dinner with us once a week. Well, two times a week." Margaret found Nate and Jeff having dinner with their parents to be quite sweet. It showed his love for family, which in turn made Margaret love him all the more. "Nate was always with his brother fixing things at the house for us. Our boys took care of our yard together, always goofing off on the rider mower. Nate was good at remembering the little things like replacing light bulbs and remembering the batteries in the smoke detectors." Evelyn smiled through her tears. "One time, one of the detectors did get too low. That blasted thing was chirping like a starving baby bird and it wouldn't shut off. Roman was fit to be tied because he couldn't get it to open. There is Roman on my kitchen step stool, swinging and whacking at it. Boy, he cursed up a storm. Damned if he didn't keep swinging and whacking until he got it." Evelyn laughed. "The best part is he went ass over tea kettle at the same time. Whoop! There he was, on his back with the broom in one hand. The detector cover was under him. Like a turtle rolling side to side, trying to flip itself. Huffing and cursing, he fished it out and held it in the air, his sign of victory. It didn't stop the beeping though." Evelyn and Margaret were both laughing, imagining her seventy-two-year-old father-in-law rolling around cursing was delightful. "We called Nate and he came right over. The cover was on the kitchen table. The detector was even louder without it. Roman turned up the TV, ignoring the infernal beeping while watching his court shows. Lickety split, Nate replaced the batteries and stopped the beeping." Reminiscing about Nate made Evelyn feel better. A little reprieve for her broken heart before getting back to the matter at hand. "I will come help with Nate's things only when you're ready. Oh, and there is no need for Roman to get all involved."

"Seeing how he handled the smoke detector debacle, I agree." Evelyn couldn't help but smile. Margaret continued. "You are right, Evelyn. It is time to take care of putting his things away. First, we'll go through and see what we'd like to keep to remember Nate. After packing what we want to keep, we'll donate his clothes to those green boxes all over the place. Whatever we can't handle going through yet, there's plenty of room in the basement for. We'll tackle those boxes when I am ready."

"Margaret, you have been strong for all of us with everything. Nate was a lucky man. I hope my son knew it."

"No worries there— I was happy to remind him." Margaret gave Evelyn a smile.

SIXTY-TWO

CHELSEA CHECKED THE TIME and looked out the living room window for her brother's crimson pick-up truck. She said another silent prayer while keeping her eyes locked out the window. Just as peeled herself away and the blinds snapped straight, Chelsea split them with her fingers, eyeballing Eric's truck coming down the road. "Here we go," she muttered to herself, ringing her hands on her way to the door. Lola was a ball of barks when Eric's aggressive knock announced his arrival. "I'll get the door." If only to give them the "keep your shit together" stare, she needed to get to them first.

Chelsea opened the front door and her mother and brother stepped in. Her mother's blonde hair was pulled back in a tight chignon and she was dressed in a very conservative, dark brown twin set and a pair of twill slacks. Her brother of course came in wearing jeans, a t-shirt, and his police-issued coat. "Hey, Mom, Eric." She smiled and hugged her mother, bringing her in close. "Please keep what I have told you to yourself, Mom. This is Margaret's house and the whole family is here." Diane tutted.

"Say things? What ever could you mean?" her brother interjected. Chelsea had told her mother about Nate when they first began seeing each other. Her brother's immediate ribbing made her regret having told her mother so much. Eric's eyes narrowed.

"So, today we meet the wife?" Diane whispered anxious about the day. These comments cemented her regret for sharing anything with her mother.

"Hey, Mother, can we go? I'm sick of standing in the doorway." The holidays did nothing for Eric's attitude. He was his usual self. "I got something to do tonight so I'm not sitting here all day." Like a gift from above, Jeff walked up and put one arm around Chelsea and extended his hand to Eric. Her brother put out his hand and said, "Hey, I'm Chelsea's brother, Eric. You must be Nate." Jeff's hand momentarily stopped mid handshake. Chelsea gasped. She was glad everyone else was out of ear shot.

Jeff was momentarily thrown off balance by the mention of Nate, but was able to recover. "Uh, no, I'm Jeff. Nate is… was my brother. He recently passed away. It's good to meet you, Eric."

"My apologies. Chelsea told us about your brother." Chelsea's eyes widened in fear and embarrassment. "My condolences." Eric's misstep was the beginning of the chasm between the two men. Jeff then turned to Chelsea's mother, Diane. "It is lovely to meet you Mrs.—"

"Please, call me Diane." Diane took in the very fit and very handsome man with his strong arm around her daughter. She could see why her daughter had gone to such lengths. "Chelsea has been bragging about you for some time." She put out her hand and smiled at Jeff. He could see where Chelsea's lavender blue eyes and smile came from. He took her hand.

"You are every bit as beautiful as Chelsea has told me." Jeff offered his arm and Diane rested her hand on his forearm. Eric snorted at Jeff's attempt to win his mother over. Jeff introduced them to Roman and the kids.

Janey sat in her pack n' play and grabbed at the animals on the pad, squawking when she couldn't pick them up. His nephew was hypnotized by the television and didn't seem to notice. "Dad," Jeff said. Roman sat in the recliner, equally hypnotized. "Dad." Nothing. "Dad!" Jeff must have gone too loud on his third try. Roman got startled and his hands immediately covered his crotch.

"Jesus, Jeffy, what the hell are you yelling about? Are you trying to give me a heart attack?" Jeff chuckled at his old man.

"No, I am not trying to give you a heart attack. I am also pretty sure no one is going for your business." Jeff smiled and pointed to his dad's lap. Roman reddened.

"My grandson likes to surprise me by jumping into my lap. My 'business' as you call it, has been taking knee shots and kicks all day." Jeff winced in sympathy for his father. James had delivered quite a few kung fu kicks to Jeff, leaving him breathless with tears in his eyes.

"Well, now that I have you, this is Chelsea's mom, Diane, and her brother, Eric." Jeff turned to his future in-laws. "This is my father, Roman." Roman went to shake the woman's hand, then remembered where his hands were last and pulled it back. Diane laughed and gave a wave, also remembering where his hands had been. Eric stood there looking unamused and annoyed.

"Pardon me. Why don't you come into the kitchen and meet my wife, Evey, and my daughter-in-law, Margaret?"

"I would love to," Diane said, backing up to give him room. Roman pushed himself out of the recliner then put his hands on his aching lower back before blaming the chair.

"Damn chair is a nightmare to get out of." Bending at a glacial pace, Roman picked up his granddaughter and called James over. "This is my grandson." He ruffled the boy's hair. James smiled as he put his floppy turkey hat on.

"Happy Thanksgiving to you. I made this hat all by myself." The boy was so proud of his most fashionable bird hat.

Diane said, "You made this yourself, young man? It looks like it was made by a professional." She turned him in a slow circle so she could take it all in, oohing and ahhing over his festive fashion choice.

"Actually, I am a profess'nal with glue and glitter," James assured her. Diane giggled at the way he said professional. This boy was a real charmer.

"Now, this little lady is Jane, the prettiest baby in the whole world." Jane let out a gurgle then a drool string started on her bottom lip. Diane's face lit up at meeting this little nymph she had been hearing so much about from Chelsea.

"You have adorable grandchildren," Diane said.

"Why, yes I do." Roman beamed with pride. "To the kitchen," he announced. With the others behind him, he led the way with Chelsea as the caboose behind everyone else. She was cursing her brother in her mind for accidentally calling Jeff by his brother's name. There was more than a little of her wondering if he had said it on purpose. When she confided in her mother about the relationship with Nate, she swore her mother to secrecy. Chelsea should have known better to think Diane's loyalty ever rested with her daughter.

SIXTY-THREE

AFTER THE REST OF the introductions were made, Roman was sufficiently roasted for his cat-like reflexes when protecting his business. The hors d'oeuvres and a charcuterie platter were brought out to the dining room table. Eric took no time diving into the bottle of wine he had brought and held center court. He regaled everyone with his puffed up stories of police work. He monopolized dinner with his weaved tales of saving lives and catching perps. Margaret went upstairs with a sleeping Jane to put her to bed, relieved for the reprieve. When she returned, Eric was telling a rather gruesome story. By the gleam in his eye, she could tell he really loved being a cop.

"My finger was literally in the hole. I still can't believe I put my finger in a bullet hole to save a man's life."

"Pfffft, neither can anyone else," Chelsea whispered just loud enough for Jeff to hear. While still appearing to listen to Eric, he smiled and under the table took her hand. Instantly, Chelsea exhaled.

"So, the ambulance is still not on the scene, which means I got my finger in this perp's shoulder wound. He's crying like a bitch and in general making a scene of himself. I pull my finger out to let him, ya know, see how bad it is, and the guy starts wailing. Then, blood starts really gushing. Like, it's everywhere." Eric's hands were telling the story with him and when he got to the part of gushing blood, he knocked his wine over. As if he was aiming for her, the red wine splashed all over Chelsea's shirt. "Woah, shit!" He laughed and snorted. "Ha! Gotcha, Chelsea." The serious red splashed across her champagne colored top and soaked through to her skin. Margaret hopped up and came around to Chelsea, who looked like she was the one shot.

"Alright, we have to get you out of this and get your shirt soaking. I will be right back with something for you to wear while we beat this stain back." After a few minutes, Margaret returned from the laundry room. "Here. It's from my never-going-to-charity bag of clothes. You can put this t-shirt on while we get yours cleaned up."

"Thank you, Margaret. I'm sorry about your table-cloth getting hit in the melee." Chelsea took the shirt from Margaret. Looking down, Chelsea saw it was a Yankees t-shirt. She looked at Margaret who was smiling.

"Don't worry about the tablecloth— it's supposed to get things spilled on it. Come with me and get changed then toss me your shirt to soak."

After changing her clothes, Chelsea looked at her reflection in the bathroom mirror. The Yankees signature NY was on the short sleeve. This shirt was from the 2009 World Series when the Yankees beat the Phillies 7-3 in game six. She felt herself smiling with the great memories of the day with her stepfather. Eating hot dogs and getting a sugar high from the sweet clouds of cotton candy and sucking down sodas. When he bought her the shirt at the team store, Chelsea threw her arms around Bill and hugged him with all the love she felt for him. The happy memory morphed into a memory of her brother being a petulant whine ass complaining the whole day. On the way home from the game, he took her shirt, stabbing through the cotton with his pocket knife, tearing the material. Even though it was a small rip, it was big enough for Chelsea to mention it. Their mother believed Eric's passionate denial and admonished Chelsea for accusing her brother.

Now, years later, here she was wearing her long lost Yankees shirt with no idea of how or when it got here. There was no way Margaret could know it was Chelsea's, right? Otherwise, how could Margaret be so calm about it? On the inside, she was melting with doubt, however, Chelsea knew she had to play it cool and hope dickhead Eric didn't open his flap and sell her out. Nervous with the risk of blowing everything, she tucked in the shirt, hiding the telltale tear from Police Officer Peckerhead. Chelsea gave herself a final once over, grabbed her wine covered blouse, then left the bathroom to get back to the table. Passing the living room on her way to the dining room, Chelsea saw Jeff's sweater over the arm of the sofa. "Thank you, Universe," she whispered to herself. She pulled the sweater over her head and thought she heard her name. Chelsea stopped moving, her arms above her with her head trapped in knit cotton, unable to see. Suddenly her head popped up through the neck and she was face-to-face with Margaret.

"Good, the shirt fits and Jeff's sweater will definitely keep you warm." Margaret picked up the wine laden shirt. "I gotta tell you— it's not looking good for you." Chelsea was quick to question.

"What's not looking good for me?" Margaret looked at Chelsea for a beat too long before holding up her top.

"Your top. I'll do what I can to remove the stain, but I don't know if it will come completely clean." Margaret tssked reading the tag on the collar of the shirt as she started in the direction of the laundry room, talking over her shoulder. "Get yourself back to the table so you don't miss dessert and coffee." The mention of dessert motivated Chelsea to quicken her steps to the table. Yet, there was something in the way Margaret looked at her that made Chelsea sweat.

SIXTY-FOUR

ROMAN HELD UP THE iced lemon Bundt his wife placed on the table next to the brownies. Out of the mile long list of insanely delicious desserts Evelyn had made, the lemon Bundt was his favorite. "What? Oh, come on, Evey, not the Bundt." Being forced to share his wife's good cooking felt like a betrayal.

"Roman, I made you your own and it's at home waiting for you." She gave her husband a little bump with her hip. "Greedy."

"I'm not sorry." Roman beamed up at his wife of forever. Evelyn leaned down for the kiss waiting for her. Jeff loved seeing his still very much in love parents flirt with each other. He took Chelsea's hand and kissed it.

"Are you ready to do this?" he quietly asked.

"Yes, Jeff. I've been dreaming of this day." Jeff stood up, still holding his future bride's hand. Margaret came in with a fresh pot of coffee and started filling coffee cups.

"Hey, can you all give me your attention?" Jeff began.

Eric rolled his eyes in obvious agony of still sitting here with his crazy sister. The second bottle of wine he had brought for himself had proved necessary. His plans were to leave right after dinner to meet some of his buddies from the precinct. There was no need for him to be here and he could not give a fuck less. His mother had told him about this bullshit engagement announcement and now he had to endure it. Eric didn't even have a cunt hair of faith in his sister's marital longevity. Jeff heard Eric's sigh; the chasm between the two men grew by miles. Chelsea stood up from her seat, giving Jeff's hand a squeeze, then he continued, "I have asked Chelsea to marry me and she said yes." Jeff pulled her engagement ring out of his pants pocket and danced it onto her ring finger. She lit up like her sparkling diamond in its solitaire setting. Evey was the first to gush over the news.

"Oh, Jeff, this is wonderful" Evelyn came around the table and took Chelsea's hand. "Chelsea, you are a dear girl. Jeff is always talking to me about you with a big smile on his face. My boy is certainly taken with you and it warms my heart knowing Jeff has found such a great girl." She and Chelsea hugged, but Evelyn wasted no time asking, "Do you have plans to marry soon?"

"It had better happen before nine months from now," Eric said under his breath. Jeff was agitated by Eric's stream of bullshit. Jeff asked him to repeat what he had said. Eric was not one to be challenged. "I said..." Eric made sure to speak louder and slower. "It had better be before nine months from now. I know my sister and she got her hooks into you somehow and I would bet my badge she's knocked up." He picked up his wine glass, which had been replaced since he broke one earlier, and emptied the wine into his mouth. He set his glass down with a smug look on his face. Wow, Jeff wanted to punch him in his mouth and watch his wine-stained teeth fly.

Margaret could see by Jeff's clenched jaw and stoney stare the tension at the table needed to ease before a fight ensued. Thankfully, James was busy eating too many cookies and blowing bubbles in his milk to register what was happening around him.

"Well then." Chelsea was tired of Eric's hate and her mother's metered responses. "Eric, you will be happy to know, you are right. I am pregnant and we are deliriously happy." Chelsea smiled at Jeff.

"Ha! See, just like I suspected— you can't get anything by me." He nodded his head slowly. The copious amounts of wine had dulled the officer's already slow personality. This time, Chelsea was the one to roll her eyes.

"Oh, and for your information, we were already engaged when I found out." Evelyn's clasped hands covered her heart. A lightness came across her face. As the smile grew, she yelled to her husband, who was only a few feet away. "Roman, we are having another grandbaby!"

Roman was overjoyed for his son. "This is wonderful! Evey, can you believe this? Jeffy's having a baby." Roman's pride made him stand taller as he walked over and swept Chelsea up in a bear hug. Her feet came off of the floor and she laughed out loud.

The announcement of a baby to come had lifted the room and her brother's snark couldn't bring it down. Roman went to his son and it was Jeff's turn to be wrapped in one of his bear hugs.

"I'm so proud of you, Jeffy. You got yourself a terrific girl and a baby on the way. Seems like life has put you in the express lane." He laughed and patted his son on the shoulder. Both Evelyn and Margaret clapped and smiled and offered congratulations and help with anything the couple needed. Diane, who knew of this "surprise" already, looked on quietly with her afixed smile. She had concerns about her daughter's latest life plans.

They had been here before and what if something went wrong and the family found out? Chelsea had sworn she knew what she was doing, so Diane did her best to push the thought to the back of her mind.

"Far be it from me to break up this warm family moment, but I need to get going. So, Mother, wrap this up and let's go." Just like that, Eric halted another good time. Diane excused herself then returned in a few minutes already wearing her coat with her black purse over one arm and Eric's navy policeman's coat draped over her other. Eric took the coat from his mother without so much as a thank you and put it on.

"Duty calls? The holidays must have you working over time," Margaret said looking at his gleaming badge.

"Nah, no work for me tonight. Just a good time with friends." His tone made it obvious he was not having any kind of good time here and was itching to hit the front door. Margaret was an inch from losing her patience and was happy to free him.

"Oh, then by all means, you should get to it. Thank you for bringing Diane with you." She turned to Diane. "It was lovely to meet you and I'm sure we'll be seeing a lot more of each other with a wedding and a baby on the way." Margaret looked at Chelsea and Jeff, who were still holding hands and falling into one another's eyes. Eric was shifting his weight on his feet and checking the time on his phone. Diane knew she had pushed Eric too much by making him stay and it was time to go.

"Thank you for having us and welcoming us into your home," Diane said, embarrassed by her son's agitation. But, she knew better than to challenge him and made fast steps toward the door. After sending Chelsea's family home, armed with leftovers (including a heavy helping of potatoes), the rest of the evening went quickly. Roman and James watched Thomas the Tank Engine while the others whipped the kitchen back into shape. Margaret and Chelsea took care of the dishes while Jeff and Evelyn secured all food in either plastic containers for taking home or for the fridge. When they finished clearing away the holiday, the four of them walked back into the living room to find James sleeping on his grandpa's lap while Roman softly snored and held his grandson.

"Let me get him. I can bring him up while you guys rouse the old man." Gently lifting James and resting his sleeping head on his shoulder, Jeff made his way up the stairs, careful not to miss one step.

"Roman," Evelyn spoke softly and gently woke her dozing husband. "It's time to head home, my love. Don't worry, I can drive us." At the mention of his wife driving, Roman shook himself awake.

"Nope. You have no business driving anything other than me crazy." Roman stood up and the chorus of cracking joints sang out in preparation of the drive.

"It works every single time." Evelyn laughed then placed a kiss on his warm cheek. Roman huffed and put on his coat and fished the car keys out of his pocket. "This was some Thanksgiving, wasn't it girls?" Evelyn asked Margaret and Chelsea. "It started out quietly sad and ended with a wedding and a baby announcement." Evelyn brought Chelsea in for a warm hug. "We are so happy you are joining our family. It is plain to see how much you and Jeff love each other. If you need anything at all, do not hesitate to call us. Roman and I are just two old farts wasting time watching game shows."

"Speak for yourself, woman. I do not spend my days watching those fixed shows."

Evelyn winked. "You're right, Rome. You don't spend your days watching those shows. You spend your days napping while I watch them." Jeff came into the room laughing at his parents' back and forth. He walked up behind Chelsea and surprised her with a kiss and wrapped his arms around her middle.

"Let's all get out of here and give Margaret some peace and quiet after running the gauntlet of another family holiday." Everyone agreed and made their way out the door, stopping only to pick up the containers of food slated to go home with them. Jeff claimed a win because he made off with what was left of the lemon Bundt.

SIXTY-FIVE

UNDER THE COVERS AND on her own side of the bed, Margaret drank vodka on the rocks. She took her nightly scroll through Nate's phone, taking in the string of pictures of their life through Nate's perspective. Every time she swiped, the next picture of the kids would be sweeter than the last. One of her favorites was the one of James holding his sister for the first time in the hospital. James's smile was huge for the camera. He was chock full of pride over his promotion to big brother.

Taking a generous swig of Tito's, she opened the file she had found. A cache of photos jockeyed for position designated by date. Having poured over these pictures a million times by now, Margaret had softened. The first time she came across the pictures and saw the shirt from Nate's gym bag, she immediately ran to the bathroom with her hand covering her mouth. She kneeled in front of the toilet and was sick. A Sox fan would never have a Yankees shirt. Even when she found the shirt in his gym bag, Margaret knew but refused to acknowledge. To acknowledge it would mean she would have to do something she had no confidence she could do. She also faced tremendous guilt for being a burden to her husband. It took time for her to put this heavy piece down. Nate's affair, and whatever else he may have done, was not because of anything she had done wrong or wasn't able to be. It was because something in him rationalized his behavior. She would not carry Nate's burden. Not even one more step.

She found them during her maiden stroll through Nate's phone. The face of the woman in the first picture could not be seen— obscured by a pile of long golden hair. The lack of panties was, however, very evident. There was no golden hair to hide anything from Margaret's view in the fourth picture. She may not have seen the face, but the woman's flaxen hair was tucked behind her ear and there was a glint from an earring she could not make out. So, Margaret pinched and zoomed in on the diamond and emerald earring that dressed the woman's lobe. She had seen those earrings in Chelsea's ears when she came to their place last Christmas. Margaret remembered being jealous of them. These days, Margaret was only jealous of the connection Chelsea had obviously shared with Margaret's now dead husband. Hitting the lock button on Nate's phone, the screen went dark. She took another swallow of vodka and put the phone back in the drawer of her nightstand.

Margaret had every intention of dealing with Chelsea when she discovered the affair. To hold her accountable for the rift in Margaret and Nate's marriage. She had spent the night pacing and drinking, orchestrating her assault on Chelsea. At the end of the night, Margaret fell asleep on the couch with her drink still in her hand and Nate's open phone on the coffee table.

When the morning sun sliced through the blinds, casting stripes on Margaret's face, she woke up with an insane headache and still no words to sufficiently shame Chelsea. As she sat there with the quiet of the house and the loneliness of it all, she came to the conclusion Nate was gone now and nothing could change it. Jeff and Chelsea were truly in love. If she tore them apart because of her pain, she would be no better than Chelsea. Nate would be forever tarnished and Jeff's heart would be broken. What good would it do to scorch whatever green earth was left in her life?

It was then Margaret decided to keep Nate's phone and the truth a secret. Now, Chelsea and Jeff had a baby on the way.

SIXTY-SIX

MARGARET SAT IN ONE of the ten recliners and waited to be hooked up to her meds. She happily dove into her bakery to-go bag to pull out her precious. Eating a strawberry frosted donut was the best part of infusion day.

"How have you been feeling this month? Any sickness? Have you noticed any new symptoms?" Sandy asked as she ran the wand across her forehead.

"Nothing I can think of. For a few days after the infusion, I'm tired. Then, I have a couple of good weeks. The last few days before my next infusion, the fatigue comes back like my batteries have worn down. Then, the cycle starts again next month." Sandy quickly wrote in Margaret's chart.

"You seem right on track. How are you doing as far as your outlook? Does coming here still make you sad?" Sandy knew there were a lot of different facets to her patients. How the patients were doing on all levels was important to her.

"This donut is definitely making me less sad," Margaret said, enjoying her sticky donut. "I do miss nursing my Janey. Not in some creepy weird way. There was so much I could not help during my pregnancy, including having a natural birth. Nursing her made me feel the most female and useful. I was able to feed and nurture her. It's selfish, I'm sure."

"Not at all. It was not an easy decision to make, but you made it. It's the making of a good mom. Doing what you have to do to give your kids as much love as possible." Sandy patted Margaret on the shoulder. She paused for a moment then said, "Margaret, you are doing great. If you ever need to worry, I will let you know." Sandy winked and closed Margaret's chart.

Margaret had two hours of thinking to do. Two hours could be filled in with a lot of crazy if she let it. A soft silver haired woman next to her was dealing with neutralizing antibodies. Margaret had eavesdropped. It was an allergic reaction to Tysabri. Thinking about such a thing happening choked Margaret's breath. Having to go off of disease modifying drugs could cause an exacerbation. Some were devastating and the damage could be life changing for the patient and their families. Worse, for those fighting alone. There was always a new medication waiting in the wings for a body to try and acclimate to. Another medication with its own mile long list of serious side effects. Margaret could feel the pain of the crying woman. So, Margaret took a hold of her IV pole and took a few steps to the woman's chair.

"I'm Margaret. I happen to have the rare and beautiful gift of making moments super awkward. Feel like hugging a stranger?" Margaret's ridiculous humor got the woman's attention. The woman looked up at Margaret and wiped the tears from her eyes. The corners of her mouth relaxed out of the frown.

"My name is Sue, and you know what? I could use it, so lay it on me." Being careful of each other's IV poles and tubes, they embraced each other, instantly creating a connection and friendship. The two women shared their diagnosis stories with one another. Sue told Margaret she was old enough to not tell her age and a widow of seven years with grown children. She was on her own with the day-to-day struggle of Multiple Sclerosis. Sue had been on Tysabri successfully for three years. It seemed this medication was finally going to help, and it had improved her cognitive function. Sue was relieved to find her emotions more stable. Then, for the last two months, within two days after infusion, she would break out in giant hives with severe itching and redness. The Tysabri infusions had to be stopped so further testing could be done to find the cause. This was Sue's last infusion, then she wanted to wash out her system. Then, hold steady and hope a flare-up didn't do her in. The pain was not what scared Sue. It was having no control of the situation inside her. Falling spinning and dizzy, not knowing where the bottom was as her body and mind raced to batten down the hatches as it worked to protect her most vital self from herself. Sue would have to deal with this alone. Listening to Sue, Margaret had been humbled. Her own battle seemed diminished when she thought about how brave Sue was. Being in the presence of such a woman helped Margaret realize how strong she could be.

SIXTY-SEVEN

WINTER WAS SLOW TO leave and spring took its sweet-ass time arriving or as Margaret called this time of year, Sprinter. The seasonal purgatory before actual spring rolled in. March was cold, wet, and blustery. The ground was thick with dark mud. Giant snow mounds in parking lots melted too slowly while the crusty snow on roadsides was dirty with traffic filth. Margaret and the kids were getting used to life after Nate. Up early, she would strap her daughter into her high chair and brew coffee. As usual, Janey would busy herself making a mess with vanilla yogurt. Margaret was again on the boy's case about getting ready. "James, the bus was coming around the corner. Every single day with this. Why?"

"Mama. I can't help when I need to pee. It just happens. What do you want me to tell you?" With shrugged shoulders, James looked at Margaret as if he really wanted her suggestion. Margaret couldn't help it and snickered into her coffee mug. James giggled knowing he got his mama to smile. It was his favorite thing.

"You're right. Sometimes it sneaks up on you." Margaret took another swig of coffee as the bus pulled up and James hopped aboard. As the bus was pulling away, Margaret suddenly stopped waving and turned tail back into the house, unzipping her jeans as she went.

SIXTY-EIGHT

CHELSEA WOKE JEFF WHEN her contractions got to five minutes. "Sweetie, it's time," she said with a gentle hand on his shoulder. The dry runs, as Jeff had called them, prepared him to be up and standing in a flash.

"Okay, let's get going." Jeff moved like a dancer, graceful and steady. He got the bags in the car. When Chelsea stepped into the garage, he was waiting with his hand out. She took his hand and came down the few steps then sat in the car. He buckled Chelsea's belt for her. "How are those contractions coming?" Jeff asked, double checking the seat belt.

"Did you call Margaret and your parents?"

"Yes, I sure did. Margaret was up when I called to let her know. I told her she didn't need to come now. She told me to shut my mouth and that she was coming to the hospital anyway." He shifted the car into gear.

"Thank you. Now, babe..." Chelsea said gently.

"Yes?" Jeff asked as he stopped at a red light.

"Um, could you haul ass? This kid is coming out and will drive us the rest of the way." Jeff hit the gas when the light turned green. Chelsea tried to focus on the contractions and not Jeff's driving. She was happy to know a doctor at the hospital. Although William and Marie could not stand Chelsea, they loved Jeff, which was why William made sure to have a room ready and Chelsea's doctor paged when Jeff called.

"Hello," William said. He seemed to be in a playful mood that did not match the stress of the moment. "Big day today, Dad."

"I know it. Thanks again for getting her in quickly. Can you keep an eye out for my parents?"

"I will be on the lookout for a bear of a man and a little lady with enough cake for the whole maternity ward."

"Okay, okay. I'm going. I will keep you posted," he called over his shoulder while trotting down the hall.

Chelsea was astonished by the intensity of her contractions. The force and pain had intensified significantly. Every time Chelsea heard a new set of footsteps, she prayed they belonged to the promised anesthesiologist. Hearing another set of footsteps, she looked to the doorway. It was William in his white coat with charts under his arm. Jeff shot him a look of helplessness. William had seen the expression on many fathers during birth.

"Hey there. How are you holding up?" William asked.

"Barely." Chelsea breathed in slowly through her nose and grit her teeth. "This is ridiculous pain." She let out a long exhale from her mouth. "Please, for the love of all fucks, go find me an epidural." William must not have heard her. "GO!" Out the door William went to find the anesthesiologist, but smiled to himself when he heard her yell, "Son of A!" as she took on another contraction.

The anesthesiologist kept up with William's quick step. When they entered the hospital room, Chelsea's doctor had just finished checking her progress.

"Hello. Nice of you to make it."

The anesthesiologist shrugged his shoulders. "I was on my break." He thumbed a finger in William's direction. "This guy literally pulled the food out of my hand. I'm still chewing for Christ's sake."

Jeff whispered his thanks to God.

"Uh huh, this is great and all." Chelsea spoke in a clipped way. Beads of sweat on her forehead. "Can I get the damned epidural now? Like right the hell now? Yeah, NOW, now." Within a very short time, Chelsea got her epidural. The easing of pain with the contractions was everything. She could finally breathe, even as contractions continued. Dr. Walsh returned to do a check on her cervix. It was at complete dilation. Her contractions lasted longer. She had an overwhelming need to push. "I need to push." The next contraction was starting. Jeff helped shift Chelsea up to more of a squat position. Two nurses came in to assist if needed.

"Okay, Chelsea, this is the homestretch. Bear down and hold for ten seconds."

She tucked her chin to her chest and pushed. Gritting her teeth, growling through the contraction. When her uterus eased, Chelsea barely had time to take a full breath before another contraction began. Chelsea focused on her navel to remind herself where the pushes originated. Jeff was right beside her, sacrificing the bones in his hand to her every contraction.

"Chelsea, you are doing fantastic. Two more pushes and our baby is out," Dr. Walsh said with his front row seat. Chelsea believed him.

"Come on, my love. You're almost done." Jeff kissed her damp forehead. Exhausted as she was, Chelsea's chin dropped down as she pushed and let out a primitive yell. "Chelsea, the baby is crowning. We need to get past those shoulders. Give me your best push." The nurses were ready for the baby.

"Yes, Chelsea. Push, push, push," Dr. Walsh called out. Chelsea grit her teeth and pushed. "Okay, now stop pushing for a second." The brief rest gave her the strength she needed. "Now, give me this last one." Using the last shred of her, Chelsea pushed, getting the baby's head then one shoulder out. When the second shoulder slipped out, the baby made her official entrance. Chelsea was covered in sweat with her wet blonde hair stuck to her cheeks. Her head fell back in exhaustion as their baby let out a strong cry. The doctor proudly announced, "You have a beautiful baby girl." They brought the baby over to meet her mother. Chelsea was crying and smiling.

"Hello there, precious. I've been so excited to meet you." She looked at Jeff. "Isn't she the most perfect baby you have ever seen?" Jeff had tears in his eyes, instantly in love with his daughter and utterly in awe of Chelsea. One of the nurses called out the weight and height.

"Six pounds ten ounces. Nineteen and a quarter inches." Then, the baby was cleaned up and given a matching bracelet to her mother. The nurse brought their baby back to them. She was wearing a little pink knit hat with her dark hair peeking out. She was perfect.

"Chelsea, you did it. That was some of the craziest stuff I've ever seen. I adore you and I am so proud. You two are the most beautiful girls in the world." Jeff kissed his future wife then their newborn's head. "Do you still want to name her after your grandma?"

grace

"Yes, I do. My grandma was so special to me. She always told me I was going to have a good life." She looked at their baby. "You will have a good life too, Grace May."

SIXTY-NINE

ALTHOUGH JEFF AND CHELSEA had thought about having a big wedding celebration, Grace May coming along created in them an urgent desire to be married. The girlhood dreams of a white dress and giant church faded and were replaced by the beautiful reality. Jeff loved her truly and wanted her to be his wife. She didn't care anymore for the details. Chelsea wanted to be a wife a lot more than she ever wanted to be a bride. It was no surprise to anyone, only days after being home with Grace, the couple announced they would be married at home the coming weekend.

"By the power vested in me and the Universal Church, I now pronounce you husband and wife. You may kiss your bride." The minister waited for the newly married couple as they shared their first kiss then said, "I would like to introduce Mr. Jeff and Chelsea Hall." Jeff swept Chelsea up and smelled the flowers in her hair as they kissed. Evelyn and Roman looked on with love and happiness for them. Diane was able to be there, but fortunately, Eric could not make it to the ceremony because he was working. A wedding wish come true for Chelsea and Jeff. Standing by the window, Margaret held Grace and talked with Marie. Time did not soften the edge Marie had for Chelsea. The best Chelsea would get from Marie was icy indifference, to which Chelsea didn't care to defrost. Chelsea knew what she had done with Nate was seen as diabolical on a thousand different levels, however, considering how her life had turned out, she had no real regrets.

Margaret watched Jeff and Chelsea smile and laugh with the joy of a newly married couple.

"I don't know what you're all smiley about," Marie said. "I cannot believe you are keeping this secret for her." When Marie tried to sit down with Margaret and let her know what she had seen the day Nate had died, Margaret stopped her before she even could say three words. When Marie and William heard Margaret's intention, they were dumbfounded. How could Margaret look past such cutting betrayals and find forgiveness?

"I am holding this precious sweet girl and because I've had plenty of terrible. Too much, frankly. We will never know exactly what happened on those stairs at the plaza. I do know nothing good can come from picking over the past." Marie watched her friend smile at the newest family freshie. Margaret looked into the onyx eyes of the baby she had seen in her dreams for so many nights. She smoothed Grace's wisps of raven hair and said, "Marie, I'm not keeping this secret for Chelsea. It's for all of us. Roman, Evelyn, Jeff, the kids. It's for me, too. I will always watch over all of my husband's children. Isn't that right, Gracie?"

the end

about the author

DELANEY PARKER is a writer and author of the sexually charged emotionally raw erotic fiction, *grace.* Her life experiences as a woman, a mother and of having Multiple Sclerosis have given her a voice that is unique and refreshing. She allows her characters to be themselves with their real language, real personalities and real actions.